The Best
AMERICAN
SHORT
STORIES
1994

The Best
AMERICAN
SHORT
STORIES
1994

Selected from
U.S. and Canadian Magazines
by TOBIAS WOLFF
with KATRINA KENISON

With an Introduction by Tobias Wolff

HOUGHTON MIFFLIN COMPANY
BOSTON • NEW YORK 1994

ISSN 0067-6233
ISBN 0-395-68103-0
ISBN 0-395-68102-2 (PBK.)

Printed in the United States of America

AGM 10 9 8 7 6 5 4 3 2 1

Contents

Foreword

COMMON WISDOM has it that a short story requires less of a commitment — on the part of both its author and its readers — than a novel demands. A writer may labor for years to produce one novel; a reader settling down with that book tacitly agrees to make a certain investment of time and emotional energy as well. Novels are major undertakings for all concerned. As readers, we dive in knowing full well that we'll be pulled along for three or four or five hundred pages or more. We may stay up too late reading chapter twelve, miss the subway stop because we were too engrossed in someone else's life to pay attention to our own, close the office door and turn off the phone in order to savor a denouement undisturbed. Or we may never even make it to that final scene. The juicy page-turner begun in the hammock at the rented cottage tends to get buried under the detritus of daily life back home, never again to beckon with the same languorous attraction.

Most of us are drawn to short stories with different expectations. Need something to read in bed for ten minutes before nodding off? Pick up a short story. You can read a short story and be done with it in the time it takes soup to thicken on the stove, a baby to nurse, a mechanic to change the oil in your car, an airplane to lift off the runway. Stories fit easily into the interstices of life, enhancing its quality. A story that takes only minutes to read can alter the entire tenor of a day, refreshing the soul and realigning the heart. And, although a novel may end up gathering dust on the night table, there's always time to finish a story.

Because we tend to think of stories as pieces to be read in a sitting, devoured in one gulp, it's easy to assume that they are produced the same way — quick work by writers looking to occupy themselves between more demanding projects. But stories rarely spring fully formed onto the page. Indeed, the best stories — the indelible ones that seem to keep tugging at you long after you've finished reading them — seem to emerge from the depths of a writer's soul, refusing even to coalesce into stories until their creators have labored long and hard to achieve something just shy of perfection. A story writer can't afford to wallow around for a few pages, finding his or her way; every word must lead inexorably to the next or the whole enterprise will fail. The form allows no margin for error; a story writer must be willing to write and rewrite — even as he keeps a tenacious hold on the emotion that gave rise to the story in the first place — until the final product is thoroughly planed and honed, impervious as a gem. Even the briefest story belies the time it took to write, the time it took to get it right.

This truth is brought home by this year's collection of short stories, chosen by Tobias Wolff. If these pieces have anything in common — besides their level of accomplishment — it is perhaps the sheer effort their creators devoted to the process of bringing them to fruition. You have only to read through this volume in order to be possessed of twenty-one of the finest pieces of short fiction published in North America in 1993. But let it be acknowledged that the authors of these stories did not come by their creations quite so easily. Each year, the contributors' essays at the back of the book offer readers a glimpse of writers at work. In this year of new voices and literary discovery, the authors' comments might well be characterized by their shared dedication to that work.

Carol Anshaw reveals that she took "Hammam" through six or seven drafts before she felt comfortable with it, conceding, "I've become patient with the process, giving it its time." John Rolfe Gardiner's "The Voyage Out" took shape in a similar fashion. "To pretend to an orderly, controlled process here would only produce a second fiction," he says. "The story did not manifest itself full blown. Nor did it arrive in a straight line of discovery." Ann Cummins, recalling her own experience working in a clothing factory at age nineteen, blazed through the first draft of "Where I Work" in an hour — but then felt compelled to tinker with the story for several years before she could let it go. Tony Earley ruminated on "The Prophet from Jupiter" for years, collecting bits and pieces which he then tried to wrestle into a traditional narrative. Only through a long process of finding out what the story *wasn't* did he finally realize what it was: a work studded with so many themes and images dear to him that, upon completing it, he worried that he might not be able to write anything else. David Gates wrote the first draft of "The Mail Lady" ten years ago, had it rejected for publication, and put it away, but he never lost faith in the story's beginning and ending. Years later, he returned to it and worked out the rest.

Several of the stories grew out of painful experiences that refused to be tucked away in memory, demanding instead to be transformed into fiction. Haunted by the death of a neighbor, John Keeble wrote "The Chasm," which, he tells us, was "a long time in the making." "Indeed," he says, "several other stories, articles, and a book were written between its drafts." Chris Offutt also traveled a tortuous path with "Melungeons," a story that was transformed by the suicide of a close childhood friend. Offutt says he drastically revised his story every day for a week, finally concluding that it had become so tied to the death of his friend that he had to set it aside. According to its author, "Melungeons" survived eighteen revisions and eleven magazine rejections. "Things Left Undone" grew out of a few days Christopher Tilghman spent under the specter of a child's grave illness. The pain of those hours did not evaporate, finding its way into a story instead — but not until much later. "The story was there to be written," the author explains, "but I avoided it for several years, out of superstition and fear and a reluctance to traffic in other people's anguish."

By and large, the stories in this collection had their genesis in real life — in the lives of the authors or those close to them — and the result is a sense of immediacy and authenticity that informs every page. Rooted in experience, conceived with urgency and conviction, and then executed, over time, with painstaking deliberation, these stories mark the emergence of a new generation of American writers. In their determination to get beneath the surface of our everyday lives, to articulate and give shape to our experiences, they have produced work that reaches out to us all. The dedication to the craft of writing exhibited in these pages offers as much cause for celebration as the stories themselves.

Tobias Wolff read this year's stories with infectious enthusiasm and a seemingly insatiable appetite. In our first conversation he advised, "When in doubt about a story, just send it along — the more the better." Every writer who serves as guest editor of this series inevitably gives up a good deal of his or her own writing time to the task of reading. Toby never hinted at the sacrifice, even as he was hit with a deluge of stories at the end of the year. He may well be every writer's ideal reader — passionate, knowledgeable, willing to be surprised, and, above all, open to delight. We are grateful for his efforts.

The stories chosen for this anthology were originally published in magazines issued between January 1993 and January 1994. The qualifications for selection are: 1. original publication in nationally distributed American or Canadian periodicals; 2. publication in English by writers who are American or Canadian, or who have made the United States or Canada their home; 3. publication as short stories (novel excerpts are not knowingly considered). A list of magazines consulted for this volume appears at the back of the book. Publications that want to make sure that their fiction will be considered each year should include the series editor on their subscriptions list (Katrina Kenison, *The Best American Short Stories,* Houghton Mifflin Company, 222 Berkeley Street, Boston, Massachusetts 02116-3764).

K.K.

Introduction

IN MY FIRST year of high school I discovered that I could curry favor with older boys by writing their essays for them. I was writing up a storm then, essays on demand but mostly short stories, which I handed in for extra credit as fast as I could turn them out.

One morning a senior everyone called Windows — he wore glasses — stopped me in the hall and asked if I could give him something for his English class; they'd had a free writing assignment which his dog had eaten. He was in luck, or so it seemed. It happened that I did have a piece on hand, a story about a family of Italian trapeze artists who, to collect the insurance money on their tightfisted patriarch, empty the pool into which he dives as the finale of his act. Windows followed me to my locker and took the story and went off to write it out in his own hand.

The next week I saw him in the cafeteria and asked how he'd done with it. He told me he'd gotten an F.

An *F?*

Yeah, Windows said, and I told her, I went up to her after class and told her that was really unfair, there was no way that was an F story.

What'd she say?

She said, I know, but you didn't write that story. Jack Wolff wrote that story.

And I thought, *She knows my work!*

Well, she should have — she was my teacher too. Her ability to pick me out of a lineup may have had more to do with my trick endings than with my music, my footwork, my dramaturgy. But damn it, she had read something of mine under another name and recognized it, and the depth of pleasure this gave me was nothing less than the understanding that a story, once written, can somehow carry you with it wherever it goes, have its own life and at the same time give distinctive evidence of yours: represent you in the world. Obvious when stated, but mysterious when felt, especially the first time. Vocations are made of such moments.

If we can live on in stories, that is only because stories live on in us. Try to forget Chekhov's "Lady with Pet Dog" once you've read it, or Joyce's "The Dead." The picture of Gabriel Conroy watching his wife Gretta on the staircase above him as she listens to a tragic ballad, unconscious of him, caught up utterly in memories of a life in which he played no part, has become for me and probably for others the very emblem of that final distance which a lifetime of domestic partnership can never overcome. I wonder if there isn't an echo of this image in Raymond Carver's "Will You Please Be Quiet, Please?" when Ralph, returning from a walk on his honeymoon, sees his bride, Marian, "leaning motionless on her arms over the ironwork balustrade of their rented *casita* . . . Her hair was long and hung down in front over her shoulders, and she was looking away from him, staring at something in the distance." Something in the distance. Where else? Here, as in "The Dead," we come upon a moment in which the fundamental separateness of two people is so truly seen and expressed that it becomes indistinct from our own experience and memory.

Stories give form to what otherwise remains imperfectly known to us — hidden or denied. There's a scene toward the end of Crane's "The Open Boat" when the men have been forced out of their lifeboat into the frigid surf. They have a hard time of it — one of them drowns. As the correspondent struggles among the breakers, dragged down by the weight of his clothes, feeling his strength ebb, he happens to glance around and sees their water jar "bouncing gaily over the waves." That image, even more than Crane's evocation of the vastness of the sea, fixes in the reader an indelible knowledge of human frailty and the perfect indifference of everything else to that frailty. The word "gaily" — it strikes the heart like a fist.

I read for such moments, can't imagine life without them. And I'm happy to say that I found plenty of them in the stories you're about to read.

It wasn't easy to arrive at this selection, though I thought it would be. When I agreed to serve as this year's editor I did so believing that with a few exceptions I would know very quickly which stories I'd want to include. And this proved to be true. The problem was that I wanted to include just about everything Katrina Kenison sent me, which would have amounted to seven volumes of this size. It's the convention to say such things, but I can't avoid it. The work I received was of an extraordinarily high quality. This shouldn't have surprised me, given the number of stories Katrina Kenison read — over 2,500, from nearly 300 magazines and journals — before sending her selections on to me. Story after story went on the "definite" stack, several to the "maybe," very few to the "no." After my first tour through these stories I had a tower of manuscripts, none of which I wanted to part with.

It got ridiculous. Toward the end I had them all spread out on the living room floor, where I brooded over them, shuffled and reshuffled them, tried to see them in relation to each other. It was an exercise in despair. A good story is good on its own terms, not on the terms of another story; comparison is therefore not only odious, it's absurd. But I had agreed to make choices; I did; here they are.

I know that you will discover four or five or eight or nine stories you could live very happily without, and that you will think I'm a fool for not including the obvious masterpiece you and your friends passed around last summer. You're right. It was a mistake.

But I can say this: It was an honest mistake. I chose stories, not writers. To hold myself to this purpose I followed the custom of several former editors and had the names erased from the manuscripts before they were sent to me. This I did in the interests of objectivity, but also out of a sense of indebtedness, because I myself have benefited from the method. When Mark Helprin edited this annual in 1988, he had the names blacked out and as a consequence ended up choosing a story of mine which, as he himself said in his introduction, he would otherwise have had a very hard time persuading himself to like. We've never met, but Mr. Helprin is still vexed with me for writing a less than worshipful review of one of his books eighteen years ago. In fact he mentioned the review ("one of the stupidest reviews I have ever read") as a demonstration of the necessity of reading blind to achieve a fair result. I was instructed; I thought then that if I ever had the chance, I would try to be equally fair.

Objectivity is a mirage. Even with their names erased I couldn't help recognizing some of the writers whose work was passed on to me (Chris Offutt has to be the only writer in the country who applies himself to the subject of Melungeons), though not nearly as many as I'd feared — only five of the final group. There was also the question of gender. I had hoped that my final selections would be perfectly balanced, but when I finally learned the names of my authors, I found this hadn't happened. I chose more stories by men than women in the same proportion that last year's judge, Louise Erdrich, chose more stories by women than men. She also read blind. What can you make of this? The only answer is that with the best will in the world, neither she nor I could escape the particular receptivities that make us who we are. I won't apologize. Justice will be done in the long run, through the very wise policy of changing editors every year.

Anyway, there's nothing at all to apologize for in this offering of stories. I had assumed that once the names were made known to me I'd be smacking my forehead: *Of course!* In the event, this happened only once, when I learned that Barry Hannah had written "Nicodemus Bluff." (On second thought, it seems a forgivable miss on my part, because that story is something of a departure for him.) Except for Barry Hannah and the five I'd recognized, the work of the writers gathered here was new to me. At least half of them are fresh on the scene. In possession of such mastery at the outset of their writing lives, what won't they do in the years to come?

Look at Nancy Krusoe's "Landscape and Dream." The form itself is immediately striking, odd. The story is divided into sections — "Cows," "The Farmer," "The Kitchen" — almost like the headings of a schoolgirl's essay. And the voice has at first that same quality: "A barn is a beautiful place where cows are milked together." Like the headings, the forced simplicity of the language is soon understood to be the speaker's way of trying to control her knowledge that on her farm, the barn is not a beautiful place, but a terrible place where "The Farmer" — her father — beats his cows almost to death with a lead pipe. He is, she comes to recognize, a stranger, full of hatred not so much toward the animals themselves as toward their sex — her sex. Under the pressure of that knowledge her innocence collapses, and the language takes on weight and power. "When a man is beating a cow, a young cow, what is he thinking? Does he think how beautiful she is, struggling to stand? Does he think how she will never stand again unless he lets her, *unless he lets her?*"

Carolyn Ferrell is another writer whose work was new to me. Her "Proper Library" is one of this year's indisputable jewels, a beautifully wrought piece told by a boy named Lorrie who is trying to keep his head above water while just about everything — his gayness, his blackness, the tumult of his family life — conspires to pull him under. The voice feels deadly accurate, without condescension or false naiveté, and finally, almost without the reader's noticing it, achieves a tragic eloquence. What he most wants is to be himself, yet he understands, and we understand, as Lorrie reveals himself to us, that in his circumstances being himself will kill him, just as surely as not being himself will kill him. The story is passionately sympathetic without mawkishness, more true than anyone will want to admit.

Sherman Alexie's "This Is What It Means to Say Phoenix, Arizona," introduced me to an artist already in full bloom. Two young men, Thomas and Victor, travel to Phoenix from their reservation outside Spokane to fetch home the ashes of Victor's father, who had abandoned his family and reservation life some years earlier. They aren't friends, these two; some years back Victor gave Thomas a savage beating, out of sheer drunken cussedness. Thomas is a storyteller, and, by the reckoning of others, a criminal bore. The journey they make is brilliantly, unsentimentally evoked. No phony bonding, no forced epiphanies, just the facts of the case and their pasts and their futures closing in on them, daring them to do any better than Victor's father. The material is grave. The story is not. It is full of light and open spaces and a daft, sidelong humor, and moments of plain beauty.

One after another, these emerging writers astonished me with their talent and range and generosity. Tony Earley has found his own way of putting a story together, wrapping time around itself, mixing desire and memory so that you can hardly tell one from the other. "The Prophet from Jupiter" is a wholly singular performance. So is Laura Glen Louis's "Fur," a constantly surprising account of a wealthy widower's attachment to a girl who wants things. They are neither of them who they seem to be, nor, even more interestingly, who they believe themselves to be. The story continually renews itself in the freshness of their discoveries of each other and themselves, forcing us to lay aside all the instruments of judgment the opening scenes invite us to take up. Jonathan Wilson's "From Shanghai," set in the post-Holocaust Jewish community in London, tells of a man's compulsive collecting of the works of Hans Christian Andersen, in any language, any edition. His obsession comes up hard against a young boy's determination to hang on to his copy of the *Tales* in the face of all manner of bribery and ridicule. Hugo, the collector, seems at first grasping, preposterous, impossible, but the story redeems him from absurdity; the ending is one of the most moving I have ever read.

I could go on. Every story in this book deserves particular mention, and I would have no trouble supplying it except for the danger of exhausting your patience and taking up room that should be left to the stories themselves, writing a Borgesian introduction to a nonexistent book. A few last words.

Because I was so struck by the newer voices, which are, after all, the voices we will be hearing in time to come, I have said nothing about the veterans. This work represents them at their best, writer by writer. They continue to give evidence that the American story is in the very fullness of its powers, that no subject or manner or effect is beyond its grasp. Distinct as they are, they all use the story as a way of seeing better, bringing the hidden to light. You feel the depth of their vocation in the solidity of every sentence.

The literature that makes life possible for me and others is not a given. It has to be made, day after day, by those who are willing to take on the solitude and uncertainty of the work. Writing affords pleasure too, but mostly it's hard work. So here is cause for celebration. To the writers of all these stories, I say, Friends, it was worth it. Every day you came up empty, every false start you had to start again from, every word you had to fight for, it was worth it, it was all worth it.

TOBIAS WOLFF

The Best
AMERICAN
SHORT
STORIES
1994

SHERMAN ALEXIE

This Is What It Means to Say Phoenix, Arizona

FROM ESQUIRE

JUST AFTER Victor lost his job at the Bureau of Indian Affairs, he also found out that his father had died of a heart attack in Phoenix, Arizona. Victor hadn't seen his father in a few years, had only talked to him on the telephone once or twice, but there still was a genetic pain, which was as real and immediate as a broken bone. Victor didn't have any money. Who does have money on a reservation, except the cigarette and fireworks salespeople? His father had a savings account waiting to be claimed, but Victor needed to find a way to get from Spokane to Phoenix. Victor's mother was just as poor as he was, and the rest of his family didn't have any use at all for him. So Victor called the tribal council.

"Listen," Victor said. "My father just died. I need some money to get to Phoenix to make arrangements."

"Now, Victor," the council said, "you know we're having a difficult time financially."

"But I thought the council had special funds set aside for stuff like this."

"Now, Victor, we do have some money available for the proper return of tribal members' bodies. But I don't think we have enough to bring your father all the way back from Phoenix."

"Well," Victor said. "It ain't going to cost all that much. He had to be cremated. Things were kind of ugly. He died of a heart attack in his trailer and nobody found him for a week. It was really hot, too. You get the picture."

"Now, Victor, we're sorry for your loss and the circumstances. But we can really only afford to give you one hundred dollars."

"That's not even enough for a plane ticket."

"Well, you might consider driving down to Phoenix."

"I don't have a car. Besides, I was going to drive my father's pickup back up here."

"Now, Victor," the council said, "we're sure there is somebody who could drive you to Phoenix. Or could anybody lend you the rest of the money?"

"You know there ain't nobody around with that kind of money."

"Well, we're sorry, Victor, but that's the best we can do."

Victor accepted the tribal council's offer. What else could he do? So he signed the proper papers, picked up his check, and walked over to the Trading Post to cash it.

While Victor stood in line, he watched Thomas Builds-the-Fire standing near the magazine rack talking to himself. Like he always did. Thomas was a storyteller whom nobody wanted to listen to. That's like being a dentist in a town where everybody has false teeth.

Victor and Thomas Builds-the-Fire were the same age, had grown up and played in the dirt together. Ever since Victor could remember, it was Thomas who had always had something to say.

Once, when they were seven years old, when Victor's father still lived with the family, Thomas closed his eyes and told Victor this story: "Your father's heart is weak. He is afraid of his own family. He is afraid of you. Late at night, he sits in the dark. Watches the television until there's nothing but that white noise. Sometimes he feels like he wants to buy a motorcycle and ride away. He wants to run and hide. He doesn't want to be found."

Thomas Builds-the-Fire had known that Victor's father was going to leave, known it before anyone. Now Victor stood in the Trading Post with a one-hundred-dollar check in his hand, wondering if Thomas knew that Victor's father was dead, if he knew what was going to happen next.

Just then, Thomas looked at Victor, smiled, and walked over to him.

"Victor, I'm sorry about your father," Thomas said.

"How did you know about it?" Victor asked.

"I heard it on the wind. I heard it from the birds. I felt it in the sunlight. Also, your mother was just in here crying."

"Oh," Victor said and looked around the Trading Post. All the other Indians stared, surprised that Victor was even talking to Thomas. Nobody talked to Thomas anymore because he told the same damn stories over and over again. Victor was embarrassed, but he thought that Thomas might be able to help him. Victor felt a sudden need for tradition.

"I can lend you the money you need," Thomas said suddenly. "But you have to take me with you."

"I can't take your money," Victor said. "I mean, I haven't hardly talked to you in years. We're not really friends anymore."

"I didn't say we were friends. I said you had to take me with you."

"Let me think about it."

Victor went home with his one hundred dollars and sat at the kitchen table. He held his head in his hands and thought about Thomas Builds-the-Fire, remembered little details, tears and scars, the bicycle they shared for a summer, so many stories.

Thomas Builds-the-Fire sat on the bicycle, waiting in Victor's yard. He was ten years old and skinny. His hair was dirty because it was the Fourth of July.

"Victor," Thomas yelled. "Hurry up. We're going to miss the fireworks."

After a few minutes, Victor ran out of his family's house, vaulted over the porch railing, and landed gracefully on the sidewalk.

Thomas gave him the bike and they headed for the fireworks. It was nearly dark and the fireworks were about to start.

"You know," Thomas said, "it's strange how us Indians celebrate the Fourth of July. It ain't like it was our independence everybody was fighting for."

"You think about things too much," Victor said. "It's just supposed to be fun. Maybe Junior will be there."

"Which Junior? Everybody on this reservation is named Junior."

The fireworks were small, hardly more than a few bottle rockets and a fountain. But it was enough for two Indian boys. Years later, they would need much more.

Afterward, sitting in the dark, fighting off mosquitoes, Victor turned to Thomas Builds-the-Fire.

"Hey," Victor said. "Tell me a story."

Thomas closed his eyes and told this story: "There were these two Indian boys who wanted to be warriors. But it was too late to be warriors in the old way. All the horses were gone. So the two Indian boys stole a car and drove to the city. They parked the stolen car in the front of the police station and then hitchhiked back home to the reservation. When they got back, all their friends cheered and their parents' eyes shone with pride. 'You were very brave,' everybody said to the two Indian boys. 'Very brave.'"

"Ya-hey," Victor said. "That's a good one. I wish I could be a warrior."

"Me too," Thomas said.

Victor sat at his kitchen table. He counted his one hundred dollars again and again. He knew he needed more to make it to Phoenix and back. He knew he needed Thomas Builds-the-Fire. So he put his money in his wallet and opened the front door to find Thomas on the porch.

"Ya-hey, Victor," Thomas said. "I knew you'd call me."

Thomas walked into the living room and sat down in Victor's favorite chair.

"I've got some money saved up," Thomas said. "It's enough to get us down there, but you have to get us back."

"I've got this hundred dollars," Victor said. "And my dad had a savings account I'm going to claim."

"How much in your dad's account?"

"Enough. A few hundred."

"Sounds good. When we leaving?"

When they were fifteen and had long since stopped being friends, Victor and Thomas got into a fistfight. That is, Victor was really drunk and beat Thomas up for no reason at all. All the other Indian boys stood around and watched it happen. Junior was there and so were Lester, Seymour, and a lot of others.

The beating might have gone on until Thomas was dead if Norma Many Horses hadn't come along and stopped it.

"Hey, you boys," Norma yelled and jumped out of her car. "Leave him alone."

If it had been someone else, even another man, the Indian boys would've just ignored the warnings. But Norma was a warrior. She was powerful. She could have picked up any two of the boys and smashed their skulls together. But worse than that, she would have dragged them all over to some tepee and made them listen to some elder tell a dusty old story.

The Indian boys scattered, and Norma walked over to Thomas and picked him up.

"Hey, little man, are you O.K.?" she asked.

Thomas gave her a thumbs-up.

"Why they always picking on you?"

Thomas shook his head, closed his eyes, but no stories came to him, no words or music. He just wanted to go home, to lie in his bed and let his dreams tell the stories for him.

Thomas Builds-the-Fire and Victor sat next to each other in the airplane, coach section. A tiny white woman had the window seat. She was busy twisting her body into pretzels. She was flexible.

"I have to ask," Thomas said, and Victor closed his eyes in embarrassment.

"Don't," Victor said.

"Excuse me, miss," Thomas asked. "Are you a gymnast or something?"

"There's no something about it," she said. "I was first alternate on the 1980 Olympic team."

"Really?" Thomas asked.

"Really."

"I mean, you used to be a world-class athlete?" Thomas asked.

"My husband thinks I still am."

Thomas Builds-the-Fire smiled. She was a mental gymnast too. She pulled her leg straight up against her body so that she could've kissed her kneecap.

"I wish I could do that," Thomas said.

Victor was ready to jump out of the plane. Thomas, that crazy Indian storyteller with ratty old braids and broken teeth, was flirting with a beautiful Olympic gymnast. Nobody back home on the reservation would ever believe it.

"Well," the gymnast said. "It's easy. Try it."

Thomas grabbed at his leg and tried to pull it up into the same position as the gymnast's. He couldn't even come close, which made Victor and the gymnast laugh.

"Hey," she asked. "You two are Indian, right?"

"Full-blood," Victor said.

"Not me," Thomas said. "I'm half magician on my mother's side and half clown on my father's."

They all laughed.

"What are your names?" she asked.

"Victor and Thomas."

"Mine is Cathy. Pleased to meet you all."

The three of them talked for the duration of the flight. Cathy the gymnast complained about the government, how they screwed the 1980 Olympic team by boycotting the games.

"Sounds like you all got a lot in common with Indians," Thomas said.

Nobody laughed.

After the plane landed in Phoenix and they had all found their way to the terminal, Cathy the gymnast smiled and waved goodbye.

"She was really nice," Thomas said.

"Yeah, but everybody talks to everybody on airplanes," Victor said.

"You always used to tell me I think too much," Thomas said. "Now it sounds like you do."

"Maybe I caught it from you."

"Yeah."

Thomas and Victor rode in a taxi to the trailer where Victor's father had died.

"Listen," Victor said as they stopped in front of the trailer. "I never told you I was sorry for beating you up that time."

"Oh, it was nothing. We were just kids and you were drunk."

"Yeah, but I'm still sorry."

"That's all right."

Victor paid for the taxi, and the two of them stood in the hot Phoenix summer. They could smell the trailer.

"This ain't going to be nice," Victor said. "You don't have to go in."

"You're going to need help."

Victor walked to the front door and opened it. The stink rolled out and made them both gag. Victor's father had lain in that trailer for a week in hundred-degree temperatures before anyone had found him. And the only reason anyone found him was the smell. They needed dental records to identify him. That's exactly what the coroner said. They needed dental records.

"Oh, man," Victor said. "I don't know if I can do this."

"Well, then don't."

"But there might be something valuable in there."

"I thought his money was in the bank."

"It is. I was talking about pictures and letters and stuff like that."

"Oh," Thomas said as he held his breath and followed Victor into the trailer.

When Victor was twelve, he stepped into an underground wasps' nest. His foot was caught in the hole and no matter how hard he struggled, Victor couldn't pull free. He might have died there, stung a thousand times, if Thomas Builds-the-Fire had not come by.

"Run," Thomas yelled and pulled Victor's foot from the hole. They ran then, hard as they ever had, faster than Billy Mills, faster than Jim Thorpe, faster than the wasps could fly.

Victor and Thomas ran until they couldn't breathe, ran until it was cold and dark outside, ran until they were lost and it took hours to find their way home. All the way back, Victor counted his stings.

"Seven," Victor said. "My lucky number."

Victor didn't find much to keep in the trailer. Only a photo album and a stereo. Everything else had that smell stuck in it or was useless anyway. "I guess this is all," Victor said. "It ain't much."

"Better than nothing," Thomas said.

"Yeah, and I do have the pickup."

"Yeah," Thomas said. "It's in good shape."

"Dad was good about that stuff."

"Yeah, I remember your dad."

"Really?" Victor asked. "What do you remember?"

Thomas Builds-the-Fire closed his eyes and told this story: "I remember when I had this dream that told me to go to Spokane, to stand by the falls in the middle of the city and wait for a sign. I knew I had to go there but I didn't have a car. Didn't have a license. I was only thirteen. So I walked all the way, took me all day, and I finally made it to the falls. I stood there for an hour waiting. Then your dad came walking up. 'What the hell are you doing here?' he asked me. I said, 'Waiting for a vision.' Then your father said, 'All you're going to get here is mugged.' So he drove me over to Denny's, bought me dinner, and then drove me home to the reservation. For a long time, I was mad because I thought my dreams had lied to me. But they hadn't. Your dad was my vision.

Take care of each other is what my dreams were saying. *Take care of each other.*"

Victor was quiet for a long time. He searched his mind for memories of his father, found the good ones, found a few bad ones, added it all up, and smiled.

"My father never told me about finding you in Spokane," Victor said.

"He said he wouldn't tell anybody. Didn't want me to get in trouble. But he said I had to watch out for you as part of the deal."

"Really?"

"Really. Your father said you would need the help. He was right."

"That's why you came down here with me, isn't it?" Victor asked.

"I came because of your father."

Victor and Thomas climbed into the pickup, drove over to the bank, and claimed the three hundred dollars in the savings account.

Thomas Builds-the-Fire could fly.

Once, he jumped off the roof of the tribal school and flapped his arms like a crazy eagle. And he flew. For a second he hovered, suspended above all the other Indian boys, who were too smart or too scared to jump too.

"He's flying," Junior yelled, and Seymour was busy looking for the trick wires or mirrors. But it was real. As real as the dirt when Thomas lost altitude and crashed to the ground.

He broke his arm in two places.

"He broke his wing, he broke his wing, he broke his wing," all the Indian boys chanted as they ran off, flapping their wings, wishing they could fly too. They hated Thomas for his courage, his brief moment as a bird. Everybody has dreams about flying. Thomas flew.

One of his dreams came true for just a second, just enough to make it real.

Victor's father, his ashes, fit in one wooden box with enough left over to fill a cardboard box.

"He always was a big man," Thomas said.

Victor carried part of his father out to the pickup, and Thomas carried the rest. They set him down carefully behind the seats, put a cowboy hat on the wooden box and a Dodgers cap on the cardboard box. That was the way it was supposed to be.

"Ready to head back home?" Victor asked.

"It's going to be a long drive."

"Yeah, take a couple days, maybe."

"We can take turns," Thomas said.

"O.K.," Victor said, but they didn't take turns. Victor drove for sixteen hours straight north, made it halfway up Nevada toward home before he finally pulled over.

"Hey, Thomas," Victor said. "You got to drive for a while."

"O.K."

Thomas Builds-the-Fire slid behind the wheel and started off down the road. All through Nevada, Thomas and Victor had been amazed at the lack of animal life, at the absence of water, of movement.

"Where is everything?" Victor had asked more than once.

Now, when Thomas was finally driving, they saw the first animal, maybe the only animal in Nevada. It was a long-eared jackrabbit.

"Look," Victor yelled. "It's alive."

Thomas and Victor were busy congratulating themselves on their discovery when the jackrabbit darted out into the road and under the wheels of the pickup.

"Stop the goddamn car," Victor yelled, and Thomas did stop and backed the pickup to the dead jackrabbit.

"Oh, man, he's dead," Victor said as he looked at the squashed animal.

"Really dead."

"The only thing alive in this whole state and we just killed it."

"I don't know," Thomas said. "I think it was suicide."

Victor looked around the desert, sniffed the air, felt the emptiness and loneliness, and nodded his head.

"Yeah," Victor said. "It had to be suicide."

"I can't believe this," Thomas said. "You drive for a thousand miles and there ain't even any bugs smashed on the windshield. I drive for ten seconds and kill the only living thing in Nevada."

"Yeah," Victor said. "Maybe I should drive."

"Maybe you should."

Thomas Builds-the-Fire walked through the corridors of the tribal school by himself. Nobody wanted to be anywhere near him because of all those stories. Story after story.

Thomas closed his eyes and this story came to him: "We are all given one thing by which our lives are measured, one determination. Mine are the stories that can change or not change the world. It doesn't matter which, as long as I continue to tell the stories. My father, he died on Okinawa in World War II, died fighting for this country, which had tried to kill him for years. My mother, she died giving birth to me, died while I was still inside her. She pushed me out into the world with her last breath. I have no brothers or sisters. I have only my stories, which came to me before I even had the words to speak. I learned a thousand stories before I took my first thousand steps. They are all I have. It's all I can do."

Thomas Builds-the-Fire told his stories to all those who would stop and listen. He kept telling them long after people had stopped listening.

Victor and Thomas made it back to the reservation just as the sun was rising. It was the beginning of a new day on earth, but the same old shit on the reservation.

"Good morning," Thomas said.

"Good morning."

The tribe was waking up, ready for work, eating breakfast, reading the newspaper, just like everybody else does. Willene LeBret was out in her garden, wearing a bathrobe. She waved when Thomas and Victor drove by.

"Crazy Indians made it," she said to herself and went back to her roses.

Victor stopped the pickup in front of Thomas Builds-the-Fire's HUD house. They both yawned, stretched a little, shook dust from their bodies.

"I'm tired," Victor said.

"Of everything," Thomas added.

They both searched for words to end the journey. Victor needed to thank Thomas for his help and for the money, and to make the promise to pay it all back.

"Don't worry about the money," Thomas said. "It don't make any difference anyhow."

"Probably not, enit?"

"Nope."

Victor knew that Thomas would remain the crazy storyteller who talked to dogs and cars, who listened to the wind and pine trees. Victor knew that he couldn't really be friends with Thomas, even after all that had happened. It was cruel but it was real. As real as the ash, as Victor's father, sitting behind the seats.

"I know how it is," Thomas said. "I know you ain't going to treat me any better than you did before. I know your friends would give you too much shit about it."

Victor was ashamed of himself. Whatever happened to the tribal ties, the sense of community? The only real thing he shared with anybody was a bottle and broken dreams. He owed Thomas something, anything.

"Listen," Victor said and handed Thomas the cardboard box that contained half of his father. "I want you to have this."

Thomas took the ashes and smiled, closed his eyes, and told this story: "I'm going to travel to Spokane Falls one last time and toss these ashes into the water. And your father will rise like a salmon, leap over the bridge, over me, and find his way home. It will be beautiful. His teeth will shine like silver, like a rainbow. He will rise, Victor, he will rise."

Victor smiled.

"I was planning on doing the same thing with my half," Victor said. "But I didn't imagine my father looking anything like a salmon. I thought it'd be like cleaning the attic or something. Like letting things go after they've stopped having any use."

"Nothing stops, cousin," Thomas said. "Nothing stops."

Thomas Builds-the-Fire got out of the pickup and walked up his driveway. Victor started the pickup and began the drive home.

"Wait," Thomas yelled suddenly from his porch. "I just got to ask one favor."

Victor stopped the pickup, leaned out the window, and shouted back.

"What do you want?" he asked.

"Just one time when I'm telling a story somewhere, why don't you stop and listen?" Thomas asked.

"Just once?"

"Just once."

Victor waved his arms to let Thomas know that the deal was good. It was a fair trade. That's all Thomas had ever wanted from his whole life. So Victor drove his father's pickup toward home while Thomas went into his house, closed the door behind him, and heard a new story come to him in the silence afterward.

CAROL ANSHAW

Hammam

FROM STORY

CARMEN PRETENDS TO read, although she is distracted by the thin, abrading fumes and the light scuttling of the polish bottle across the tray table next to her, and by the tentative brush strokes with which Heather is painting her nails a high-gloss black — her splayed fingers bringing to mind a row of chorus-line dancers, their feet slipped into patent tap shoes.

Heather doesn't acknowledge Carmen's interest. She is masterly at making it seem not as though she is ignoring Carmen, rather that she simply isn't in the frame. To avoid any possible engagement, she has worn her Walkman through the five-plus hours they've been on this flight.

On the other side of Heather is her father, whom Carmen has been dating for the past few months. Rob is at the moment bent over an open folder of paperwork. His calculator runs out of solar juice, and as he shifts in his seat and reaches up to rejuvenate it with the light from the reading bulb, he looks over at Carmen and winks. As though they are linked in a conspiracy of fun.

Heather is seventeen and taking time off from school because of an ailment Rob is vague about. Since she is so very thin, and because there's a therapist involved, Carmen thinks it's probably an eating disorder. She suspects Heather is along with them on this short business-pleasure trip at the therapist's recommendation.

So far Heather seems to hate Carmen, but not, apparently, because Carmen is her father's new girlfriend. His old girlfriend, Angie, is only two years older than Heather. Which by all emotional logic should have been extremely hard to take. But apparently they are great friends, take ceramics classes together.

For her part, Carmen can't seem to get a generation's distance on Heather, who, with her studied hipness and basically black wardrobe, works a kind of voodoo, thaws out a Carmen long since left behind, frozen in late adolescence. Heather lures this Carmen out naked and shivering, dripping into a blue puddle of un-sureness. Heather is a stand-in for all the terrible, expertly snob-bish girls in Carmen's high school. For the quiet, seemingly affable roommate who, after the first semester of Carmen's freshman year in college, asked to be moved to another room. Heather brings out stuff in Carmen that is so far back, so layered over, that she's astonished, really, to find it still exists, that it's still possible to rile it all up.

A few hours later, in their hotel room in Paris, Carmen and Rob are alone together for the first time on this trip. She wants to call home, check on her son, who is staying with her sister for these days she will be gone. But it is four in the morning in Chicago.

Rob spins around with his arms in the air, like Zorba. "Fabuloso, eh?" he says. "And I spell that F-A-B-U-L-E-A-U-S-E-A-U. They really know how to do old here, when not to mess with it. We have to test the mattress, though." With this, he falls dead backward from the ankles, like a magician's accomplice. His body bounces only slightly. "Ah. Hard as a china plate. We won't be stooped over with motel backaches. Come on, neck with me." He looks at his watch. "Just for two and a half minutes. I have to leave soon. So this is a low-commitment assignation."

He changes into his business clothes — soft black pants and black silk shirt and shoes that are like slippers. Rob's business is that of smoothing things out. He is a troubleshooter for MarcAntony, a global chain of hair salons. He's based in Chicago but travels about half the time to various franchises, checking on product sales and staffing problems along the corporate connect-a-dots. Everything has to be handled delicately, he says. It's a business of delicacy. He says this like a gangster.

Carmen met Rob in a *Ulysses* class at the Newberry Library. This is exactly the way she imagined meeting someone, only Rob isn't the someone. The kind of person she was sure she'd meet in a *Ulysses* class at the Newberry is Jeremy Irons. Rob is the opposite. Smooth, but a little too smooth, and not in the right way. He wears cashmere V-necks, but with no shirt underneath. He favors vacation spots that have casinos.

But, after four years of trolling the dating shallows, Carmen feels lucky to have come up with someone who's even possible. At least he's near her own age (forty-four to her forty). Several of her friends are now dating men twenty years older than they are. Which, at their age, means these are not older guys but truly *old* guys, with ear hair and white belts and the solid paunches Carmen's sister calls "front butt." Rob still has a hungry look about him, a bit of future left. He still holds the possibility of a few surprises.

He's not perfect. She can see this, even now in this beginning when he should probably still be at least seeming perfect. He has been involved with too many women before her. There are too many different names populating his anecdotes, and once he let slip that he has had to change his phone number four times in the past few years, since he got out of his marriage.

Of course, she's not offering perfection in return. She has her tics, her crotchets — she'd be the first to admit. She's too already-formed for some men, too proper for others. A little too demanding, she supposes, although she likes to think of this as rigor. Her nature runs pretty much counter to her name, with its implications of passion and temper. It's as though her parents had been expecting someone else entirely.

Her Jungian therapist asks her what she thinks this relationship is about, and Carmen lies at eighty dollars an hour and says she doesn't know. But of course, it's about sex. She has tried to be aroused by the sort of men who turn up along her path. Other curators at the museum. Conservators and gallery owners. But these are mostly shallow breathers, careful livers of life. They have good insurance policies, are adequately tax sheltered. They order decaffeinated coffee with their egg-white omelets. Carmen wants someone on top of her who's a carnivore, someone with a little too much body hair, someone who has come out of a jungle and still smells of it.

She realizes this makes her slightly ridiculous, being drawn to

some personally watered-down version of rough trade, that a lot
of her attraction to Rob is about how his attraction to her makes
her see herself. Which is to say, in a black slip. And this seems more
important than being able to bring him easily to gallery openings,
where Rob will quite often point his index finger gun-fashion at
some piece of art and say, "*Like* it."

Before he leaves, he asks Carmen if she will go along with Heather
for the afternoon.

"Don't make it look as though we've talked, as though you're
chaperoning. Just . . . if you could pretend to be interested. Whatever it is."

Carmen laughs. "Oh, why do I have the feeling it's going to be
that tour of the sewers?"

Heather longs to escape into the Paris promised by her guidebook — *The Hip Pocket Guide to Paris,* with the emphasis on "hip."
It doesn't even mention the Eiffel Tower (Carmen looked) and
remarks on the Louvre only to say that it has an uncrowded post
office branch in the basement.

Heather is interested in exploring the margins of the city, and
this guidebook is ready to take her there. On the plane, Carmen
noticed her circling an entry on anachronistic matinee dance
halls, the ones sent up in Bertolucci's *Last Tango in Paris.* Heather
is deeply into film, particularly old foreign films, particularly those
that offer critical reevaluations of the culture, indictments of "civilization." She seems to have the pretensions not just of youth but
of a youth that happened twenty years ago.

"She's really an O.K. kid," Rob says on his way out the door.
Carmen doesn't imagine he believes this, but she recognizes it has
to be said. Just as she has to say yes to taking on Heather for the
afternoon, even though the Xanax she took after dinner on the
plane didn't kick in until the last hour of the flight, leaving her
now both exhausted and doped up. Even though she has a business lunch she'll now have to hurry through; a gallery owner who
has a semi-important collage she may be interested in buying for
the museum.

She and Heather arrange to meet at three.

"What about if we find each other in the Luxembourg Garden?"
Carmen suggests. "By the boat pond."

"I don't know if I'll be able to find it," Heather says.

"Oh, I'm sure you will."

Carmen arrives late, but not terribly. Scanning the midafternoon crowd around the boat pond, she spots Heather reading her guidebook, putting a filter on all immediate experience with her Walkman. She is sitting in a metal park chair, one booted foot propped on the other. Although the day is warm, particularly here in the park, in the steeply angled afternoon sun, Heather is wearing a black leather jacket that's scuffed to brown in places and torn away altogether at one shoulder.

She knows from Rob that Heather spends a great deal of her weekend time dressing and making up and disheveling her hair for nights spent with the black-leather-and-silver-stud kids who mill around the parking lot of the Dunkin' Donuts at Clark and Belmont. Whenever she used to drive past this regular weekend scene, Carmen assumed they were all on their way somewhere, waiting for someone to show up or something to begin, but Rob says no, often Heather just hangs out all night in the parking lot, then takes a bus home.

It could be she's not been looked after enough. She doesn't talk about friends, or a boyfriend (but then she wouldn't, of course, not to Carmen). Heather's mother, according to Rob, is deeply troubled. There are drugs involved.

"Prescription stuff. You know. Sometimes you can find doctors who are really pushers. They're into curing boredom, restlessness. Mona's in advertising. Everyone in advertising is bored and restless."

Carmen sits down on the chair next to Heather, and when she still doesn't look up, Carmen announces her presence by tapping her rolled up *Pariscope* against the ripped knee of Heather's jeans.

To which Heather responds by jumping with a shout of "No!" She drops her book, rips the plugs from her ears, and goes into a martial-artistic position, a half crouch, her hands circling smoothly through the air in front of her. Only then does she realize — or rather only then does she pretend to first realize — that it's Carmen, and not a madman.

She then places a hand over her heart, as if to subdue the wildness of its beating. Carmen now sees she is just going to keep making it impossible.

"Look . . . Carmen . . ." she says, pushing at the air with the heels of her hands, the gesture usually reserved for talking lunatics down off ledges. "Just, let's say . . . don't ever touch me like that again."

Quite a few of the people around them — loungers and readers and mothers of the small children pushing toy sailboats across the pond of the fountain — have stopped and are watching this showdown.

"I'm sorry, Heather," Carmen says, trying to bring this stupid situation down from its hysterical heights, while not really giving Heather anything. To this end, she holds her voice as far off from sincerity as possible. "I didn't mean to frighten you."

"Yeah, well," Heather says.

"Have you found us something to see?" She nods at the book dangling from Heather's hand.

"Oh," Heather says. For a suspended moment, Carmen thinks this might be all she's going to say. But then she begins again, with seemingly great effort. "Yeah, well . . . there's this hammam. It's like a steam bath."

"Oh, yes. My sister went to one once. When we were touring Morocco together. We were in college. I didn't have the nerve myself. It sounded too exotic. But then I was very different from you at your age."

"Right," Heather says, as though Carmen has pulled up a potbelly stove and a rocking chair and a piece of whittling and has begun telling Heather about each of the big snows since the turn of the century. "So do you want to go, or what?"

It now occurs to Carmen that Rob has not only asked her to look after Heather, he has also asked Heather to pay some attention to Carmen. Which would explain why everything Heather says sounds novocained.

"Sure," Carmen says to this limp invitation, even though it is probably the worst idea Heather could have picked out of all the terrible ideas in her guidebook. The actual reason Carmen hadn't gone into the hammam in Morocco with her sister Alice all those years ago is that she has always been extremely modest. Of course, maybe this hammam will be an updated, Westernized version, someplace where everyone keeps a towel around herself.

On the Métro, though, she borrows the guide from Heather and reads, with a heavy heart, that this place is highly recommended

(of course) for its cultural authenticity. "A bit of the ancient me-
dina in the heart of Paris, with mysterious rituals of ablution," she
reads, translating this into "everybody will be stark naked."

The hammam turns out to be part of a larger building, white-
walled as it would be in its indigenous desert setting. Once through
its portals, they are in an interior garden where many people,
mainly men but some women, all in Arab dress — veils on the
women, and on the men wool robes and pointed leather shoes of
the most lurid yellow — sit drinking glasses of mint tea and talking
in what gathers up into a pleasant hubbub. Through another
archway is a tea room where men sit huddled over cigarettes or
are eating from low tables a variety of vividly colored pastries, as
well as ones that look to be sealed, like souvenirs, in honey.

"Here it is," Heather says.

On a large wooden door to their left a cardboard sign hangs at
a tilt: AUJOURD'HUI — LES FEMMES.

"What luck," Carmen says as Heather pushes against the door
and holds it open behind her with just the tips of her black
fingernails.

In three steps and an instant, they have gone back a dozen
centuries. They are in a room that is ancient and cavernous,
detailed with Moorish arches and tiled floors, the walls narrative
with worn mosaics. Her first, curatorial impulse is to lift these walls
free and bring them to her museum, restore them and bring them
under the proper lights, show them to their best effect. Immediately, she is embarrassed for being so acquisitively programmed.

To their immediate left is a high counter.

"*C'est votre première fois?*" asks the red-haired woman behind it.
She towers over them, like a nun in a dream.

"Oh," Carmen says. "*Oui.*" It is most definitely their first time.
And with that, she has run out of hammam vocabulary and puts
up the palms of her hands in defeat and supplication. The counter
woman takes pity and exchanges their shoulder bags for a single
claim check and two towels.

"*Là-bas,*" she says, pointing with a hand whose fingers bear at
least twenty rings. "*Déshabillez-vous là, et ensuite entrez-y.*"

Carmen nods and stares around the room. In the center is a
small stone fountain lapped by water. There are brushes, like

shoeshine brushes but not quite, on the low, surrounding wall, and sandals, all of a uniform wooden type.

Around the sides of the room are raised platforms covered with padded gym mats on which women are sitting or lying. Hardly anyone is wearing much more than underwear; most are naked. They are also of all ages, from young teenage girls with their mothers to extremely aged women. Most appear to be Arabic. The rest are French, Carmen guesses, although two have such an assertively blond look she thinks they might be Scandinavian tourists. They are also of an amazing variety of sizes, from cigarette-thin women to women who, naked, look like giant soft-serve sculptures, their bodies great graduated, overlapping fountains of flesh.

Some of these women are sleeping, fetally positioned and lovely in their easy nakedness, there being nothing threatening in the situation. Most, though, are awake and socializing in an unfocused way that Carmen — her own friendships maintained through brisk lunches or evenings centered on one or another cultural event — has never encountered.

Along with the socializing there's a lot of languorous grooming, the way cats lick each other, the way monkeys pick through each other's fur for nits. The women here are rubbing each other's limbs with oils, or combing each other's hair, or applying henna. Many of them, Carmen now notices, have hair of the same muddy red color. For the first few moments she is taken out of herself, her fears left behind. They come back in a rush only when she realizes this isn't a PBS special, but rather a ritual in which she is almost immediately going to be expected to participate.

"We don't have to do this," Heather says in a low voice next to her, perhaps the first words of kindness she has ever spoken to Carmen.

"No. Let's go on." Carmen nods toward the open archway at the far end of the room, from which steam is rolling out like a low-lying fog.

"Like the entrance to hell," Heather says. "You know. In cartoons."

As they are standing there, an attendant, a wiry woman, scurries in from the bar with a tray full of jiggling, clinking glasses of mint tea. These are quickly bought up by customers from among those lounging and grooming and gossiping, often smoking cigarettes under clouds of heavy, loitering smoke. She comes up to Heather and Carmen and motions with quick rushing flutters of her hands for them to take two adjacent mats from which she clears the towels of the previous occupants. She points at the pegs lining the wall.

"I think we hang our stuff there," Carmen says.

Heather nods and hops up onto the raised platform. Carmen follows, stepping onto the squooshy empty mats next to an ancient woman who has also just arrived. She is wearing long robes, her face covered by the traditional veil, but she also has with her an Adidas gym bag.

None of Carmen's old locker-room routines of disrobing will work here. There is no dark corner, no locker door to slip behind. Worse, they are on a platform, nearly a stage. She feels abandoned by her clothing as she steps out of her skirt, unbuttons her blouse, unhooks her bra, hangs them on a pair of side-by-side pegs in the wall. She is profoundly chilled, even though, only moments earlier, the room seemed too warm, too close with the sighing breath of all these women. Who — Carmen suddenly realizes — have now become quiet, as though their collective breath is being held. She is suddenly awake in the middle of her worst nightmare. They are turned, looking at her. She instinctively crosses her arms in front of her breasts and feels a flush of humiliation spreading through her.

It is only when she is able to look up again that she sees it's not her they're fascinated by, but Heather, who has emerged from her leather and denim and gender-generic underwear. Her ribs bow out below her tiny flattened breasts, her arms look snappable as bird wings, her collarbones jut like stones at the base of her neck. The flesh that stretches over this frame is the watery blue-white of skim milk.

Heather, snapping her underpants off a toe, looks up and catches the stares of the assembled. She doesn't seem offended, or put off. Carmen sees it is possible she may find their interest flattering. She has, after all, gone to a great deal of trouble to become this emaciated.

In a rush of pure impulse, Carmen wants to fold her up in her arms, wants to stand Heather's toes on her own and dance her around this ancient room like her father did with her in their basement rec room, the way she does now with her son Nicky when he's having an especially rainy day.

But of course, she can't.

"Ready?" Heather says, challenging Carmen with her nakedness.

Carmen looks away, at nothing, and nods.

She sees that some women are emerging from the steam bath in their underpants, and so she leaves hers on. She keeps her arms crossed over her breasts and follows her Vergil into the depths.

Which begin with a bank of showers surrounding two tables with padded, cloth-covered tops on which lie women undergoing what must certainly be the NETTOYAGE À PEAU—55 FR advertised on a paper sign taped to the wall.

"What is it?" Heather asks.

"'Cleansing of the skin' is how it translates," Carmen says, and they stand watching the women on the tables being ministered to by hulking masseuses, who look to be sanding them down with rough wet cloths. Carmen can't tell whether this process would feel heavenly or torturous.

Beyond this is another large cavern with raised, tiled cubicles lining the walls. Within these, women in pairs and threes are taking amateur turns at rubbing each other down, and pouring water over each other from the sawed-off plastic soda bottles that litter the floors. There is water everywhere, from the fountains and the hoses snaking around on the tiles, and standing water in the many depressions worn through the ages both in the floor and in the sitting platforms.

With Heather leading the way, Carmen follows, so close to Heather's back she has to fight down the urge to reach out and feel the sharp blades of her shoulders. She seems so insubstantial and vaporous, and with the steam rolling up and around her, it almost seems an outstretched hand would merely pass through her.

They move slowly over the slick floors, through a third chamber and into a fourth, the heat growing progressively more oppressive, the steam clouding ever thicker, until finally Carmen can barely see anyone else, and only a misty specter of Heather, which relaxes her a bit in her modesty.

"Want me to dye your hair?" Heather asks, the first time Carmen can remember her just fooling around.

"How can anyone stay in here long enough to do *anything?*"

"Kind of challenging, though, in a weird way," Heather says, holding on to Carmen's arm briefly, for support.

They totter over and sit down in a shallow lake on the edge of an empty tiled alcove. "Let's see how long we can stand it," Heather suggests, and disappears behind the drape of vapor that closes around her as she reclines.

Carmen moves to the back of the niche and collects water from the small fountain carved into the wall, pressing her face into it, then spilling the water down the front of her body, over one then another shoulder. For the next few moments, she loses Heather's terrible troubles and her own. For a few moments in the depths of this place, so far inside it's almost impossible to think of an outside; in here, for a few moments she becomes someone she feels only vaguely acquainted with.

When she tries, she has great difficulty standing up. She waits a moment for the confidence of balance to return, then reaches through the mist to find Heather, and finally makes contact with a shoulder that is an immodesty of bone.

"Are you O.K.?" she asks.

"It *is* kind of intense," Heather admits.

"Let's go back," Carmen says, taking Heather's hand, the two of them moving with the smallest, most tentative of steps. Carmen is still a little woozy when she enters the previous room, but at least she is freed from the weighted air of the deepest chambers. They progress slowly until they reenter the first, mildest steam cavern, where they stop and sit for a while and watch two women large as sumo wrestlers, in black thong underwear, one scrubbing the other in a slow, trancey way, cooling the cloth under a running tap, wringing it out, then scrubbing some more.

"This place is a trip," Heather says, and Carmen can see she is trying to cut the experience down to size, trim it into a tidy story to tell some night, to someone else in black, in the Dunkin' Donuts lot.

"Let's cool off," Carmen suggests, and they stand again, much steadier now, and retreat into the showers, which only run cold and are stunning.

"Ahhhh," Carmen says.

Heather moves in next to her, under the same flow of brilliant liquid ice. Carmen feels her presence through the water and opens her eyes into Heather's vacant, wash-blue stare. She sees that Heather is putting herself through a private set of locks, raising herself out of this unalterably shared experience into the pale Paris afternoon they are about to reenter, once again separate. But she won't be able to get there. They can no longer retreat into their previous positions, simply because they have been here together. Carmen sees that everything up until this afternoon has been prelude between them, overture, that now is the exact starting point, the place where she and Heather will begin.

The three of them go for dinner to a restaurant Rob knows, in the Marais. Filled with people, mostly of an oldish-young stripe, ordering cigarettes that are then brought to their tables on silver trays, the pack opened, the matchbook folded back, everything in a state of readiness, as though smoking were an urgently necessary element, an integral part of the hilarity, along with the many bottles of champagne brought up the circular steps from the basement, their popping corks punctuating the laughter and conversations. The decor so informal, the food so simple, yet lovely. An atmosphere so effortlessly achieved it's shocking, and oddly thrilling, when the bill arrives, always in the hundreds and hundreds of francs.

Rob orders a bottle of red wine, something excellent he has written in a thin leather notebook he keeps in an inside breast pocket. Rob didn't go to college. He went to cosmetology academy and, in the years since, has risen to a social level he's had to cram for.

For dinner, he orders the steak frite. Heather, who is vegetarian, orders the vichyssoise and a spinach terrine. Carmen orders quail. They arrive the traditional way, two very dead birds with their heads bowed.

"Oh gross, how can you possibly?" Heather says, actually throwing the back of her hand across her eyes, a bad actress in a silent movie.

"You make me wish they were ortolans," Carmen says, trying to remember where she knows about ortolans from. Proust? *Larousse Gastronomique*? "People used to eat them under their damask napkins. They covered their heads and the plate. To intensify the delicate aroma."

She means to be witty, to defuse Heather's horror.

"Really," Heather says, "I'm going to be sick if I have to watch her" — here she stops and turns away from her father, toward Carmen, granting her the concession of direct address — "watch *you* eat them."

"Maybe we should send them back," Rob says, grazing Heather's cheek with his knuckles. He asks her, "Would that be better?" He's careful with his daughter, as though they've just gotten to know each other, as though she might be fragile in ways as yet unrevealed to him. The same way he is with Carmen, whom he asks, "Would that be okay? Would you let me order you something else, something less connected with its live version?"

He is acting as though the problem at the table is a small one, merely another matter to be smoothed out. He is pretending not to be taking too seriously what Carmen has now seen; he's still enjoying the beginning of their romance while she is now much farther down the road of their cluttered lives.

This was not what she had in mind. She'd been looking for something neat, and now it's clear that everything about this will be a mess. She doesn't even know if she loves Rob, or even likes him enough to take this on; until now she hasn't had to ask herself the question. And now, of course, it's beside the point.

He persists in relentless cheer until the shoals of the evening have been steered clear of, and the rest of the meal takes on a light, peppy rhythm. Carmen orders the sole. Rob, in a gesture just shy of a toast, lifts his glass and rolls the red wine so that it coats the inside, leaving a trace of itself behind as it washes up the other side.

"I know I should feel exhausted by now, considering in Chicago, it's" — he shoots a wrist out of his shirt cuff and tries to calculate off his watch — "one o'clock in the afternoon. Considering I haven't slept in . . . thirty-one hours," he says. "But I'm not. I feel hyperalive. It's Paris. That's what this town does to you."

Carmen and Heather sit by, not looking at each other, but strongly in each other's presence, and pretend to listen while Rob overpaints their troubles with a fantasy in which they are simply three sophisticated people enjoying one another's splendid company in the City of Light, in a Brassaï photograph.

Carmen's sole arrives; Heather picks at her terrine, taking a few bites, then pushing pieces under a shell of radicchio. As soon as the waiter has cleared their plates away and is setting out small cups for espresso, she excuses herself from the table.

"Let's be corny tonight," Rob says to Carmen as Heather passes behind him. "Let's go up to Montmartre and have our portraits done by terrible artists. Go to a cancan show."

Carmen nods, watching Heather over his shoulder as she goes down the tight winding staircase into the basement, where the champagne and the toilettes are. With each circle she makes in her descent, there is less and less of her, until she is gone.

ROBERT OLEN BUTLER

Salem

FROM THE MISSISSIPPI REVIEW

I HAVE ALWAYS been obedient to these true leaders of my country, even for their sake curling myself against a banyan root and holding my head and quaking like a child, letting my manhood go as we all did sooner or later beneath the bellow of fire from the B-52s. I said yes to my leaders and I went into the jungle and gave them even my manhood, but I sit now with a twenty-four-year-old pack of Salem cigarettes before me and a small photo trimmed unevenly with scissors and I whisper softly no. I whisper and I raise my eyes at once, to see if anyone has heard. No one has. I am alone. I look through my window and there is a deep-rutted road, bright now with sunlight, leading into the jungle and we are at peace in Vietnam, hard stuck with the same blunt plows and surly water buffaloes but it is our own poverty now, one country, and I turn my face from the closing of trees a hundred meters down the path. I know too much of myself from there, and I look at the objects before me on the table.

He was alone and I don't know why, this particular American, and I killed him with a grenade I'd made from a Coca-Cola can. Some powder, a hemp fuse and a blasting cap, some scraps of iron and this soda can that I stole from the trash of the village: I was in a tree and I killed him. I could have shot him but I had made this thing and I saw him in the clearing, coming in slow but noisy, and he was very nervous, he was separated and lost and I had plenty of time and I lobbed the can and it landed softly at his feet and he looked down and stared at it as if it was a gift from his American gods, as if he was thinking to pick up this Coca-Cola and drink and refresh himself.

I had killed many men by that time and would kill many more before I came out of the jungle. This one was no different. There was a sharp pop and he went down and there was, in this case, as there often was, a sound that followed, a sound that we would all make sooner or later in such a circumstance as that. But the sound from this particular American did not last long. He was soon gone and I waited to see if there would be more Americans. But I was right about him. I'd known he was separated from his comrades from just the way he'd picked up one foot and put it ahead of the other, the way he'd moved his face to look around the clearing, saying to himself, Oh no, no one is here either. Not that I imagined these words going through his head when I first saw him — it is only this morning that I've gone that far. At the time, I just looked at him and knew he was lost and after the grenade I'd made with my own hands had killed him, I waited, from the caution that I'd learned, but I knew already that I'd been right about him. And I was. No one appeared.

And then I came down from the tree and moved to this dead body and I could see the wounds but they did not affect me. I'd seen many wounds by then and though I thought often of the betrayal of my manhood beneath the bombs of the B-52s, I could still be in the midst of blood and broken bodies and not lose my nerve. I went to this dead body and there were many jagged places and there was much blood and I dug into each of the pockets of the pants, the shirt, and I hoped for documents, for something to take back to my leaders, and all that I found was a pack of Salem cigarettes.

I do not remember if the irony of this struck me at the time. I was a young man and ardent and at turns full of fury and of shame and these are not the conditions for irony. But we all knew, even at that time, that one of the favorite pleasures of the dear father of Vietnam, Ho Chi Minh, was to smoke a Salem cigarette. A captain in our popular forces had a personal note from Father Ho that thanked him for capturing and sending north a case of Salem cigarettes. This was all common knowledge. But I, too, liked American cigarettes, encouraged in this by the example of our leader, and I think that when I took this pack of Salem from the body, I was thinking only of myself.

Like now. I am, it seems, a selfish man. Ho Chi Minh died that same year and we all went through six more years of fighting before our country was united and I owe my obedience to those who have brought us through to our great victory, but they have asked something now that makes me sit and hesitate and wait and think in ways that surprise me, after all this time, after all that I have been through with my country. The word has come down to everyone that we are to find any objects that belong to dead American soldiers and bring them forth so that the American government can name its remaining unnamed dead and then our two countries can become friends. It's like my wife's old beliefs and her mother's. These two women live in my home and they love me and they care for me but they do not change what they deeply believe, in spite of what I've been through for them, and they would understand this in their Buddhist way. It is as if we had all died and now we were being reborn in strange new bodies, destined to atone in this particular new incarnation for the errors of our past. The young V.C. and U.S. soldier reborn as middle-aged friends doing business together, creating soda cans and cigarettes.

Is it this that makes me hesitate to obey? I only have to ask the question to know that it is not. In the clearing, I put the pack of Salem cigarettes in my pocket and then I slipped back into the jungle and I smoked one cigarette later in the afternoon, shaking it out of the pack with my mind elsewhere as I sat beside a stream, a little ways apart from my own comrades. I did not wish to share these cigarettes with them and when I lit one and drew the smoke into my body, there was that familiar letting go from a desire both created and fulfilled by this thing I did, and I looked down the stream away from the others and in a few hundred meters the jungle closed in, black in the twilight, and I blew the smoke out and my nostrils flared from an odd coolness. I had never before smoked this favorite cigarette of Ho Chi Minh and for a moment I thought this soft chill in my head was somehow a sign of him. Such a thought — the vague mysticism of it — came easily to me and I never questioned it, though I think Ho himself would have been disappointed in me because of it. This was not the impulse of a mature Communist, and much later, when I learned that there was a thing called menthol in some American cigarettes, I remembered my thoughts by the stream and I felt ashamed.

But at the time I let this notion linger, that the spirit of Ho was inside me, and I took the pack of cigarettes out of my pocket and now I looked at it more carefully: the blue-tinted green bands of color at the top and bottom, the American words, long and meaningless to my eyes except for the large *Salem* in a central band of white — this name I'd known to recognize. And there was a clear cellophane wrapper around the pack, which I ruffled a little with my thumb and almost stripped off, but I stopped myself. This was protection from the dampness. Then I turned the pack over and there was a leaping inside me as if a twig had just snapped in the jungle nearby. A face smiled up at me from my hand, a woman's face, and I stopped my breath so that she would not hear me. I suppose that this reflex ran on even into my hands where I was ready to draw my weapon and kill her.

And she is before me now. The pack of Salem is in the center of the oak table that I made with my own hands, breaking down a French cabinet from an old provincial office building to make a surface of my own. The cigarette pack lies in the center of this table and the photo looks up from behind the cellophane, just where he put it, the man from the clearing. I have never taken the photo out of its place and I have never smoked another cigarette from the pack and these are things that I knew right away to do, even before my hands calmed and the beating of my heart slowed again beside the stream, and I did not ask myself why, I just knew to look once more at the woman — she had an almond-shaped face and colorless hair and a vast smile with many teeth — and then to put the cigarette pack into my deepest pocket with the amber Buddha pendant my wife had slipped into my hand when I went away from her.

I expect her soon, my wife. I look through my window and down the path and she and her mother will come walking from out of the closing of the trees and she will be bearing water and her sudden appearance there along this jungle path will make my hands go soft and I am wrong to say that the hair of this woman in the picture has no color, there are times of the day when the sunlight falls with this color on our village and her hair has no color only against the jungle shadow of my wife's hair.

I wish I had the reflexes of the days when I was a freedom fighter. Instantly I could decide to kill or to run or to curl down and quake or to rob a dead man's pockets or I could even make such a strange and complicated decision as to put this pack of cigarettes into my

pocket with the secret resolve — secret even from myself — to preserve it for decades. Now I sit and sit and I can decide nothing.
Something tells me that my leaders will betray all that they have
ever believed in and fought for, that they will make us into Japanese. But even shaping that thought, I do not have a reflex, my
hands do not go hard, they just lie without moving on the table
top before the smile of an American woman, and perhaps what
began beneath the bombs of the B-52s is now complete. Perhaps
I am no longer a man.

Still, I will not act in haste about this. That is the way of a
twenty-year-old boy. I am no longer a boy, either. And even the boy
knew to put this thing away and not to touch it. Why? I bend near
and I wait and I watch as if I am hidden in a tree and watching
the face of the jungle across a clearing. The photo has three sharp,
even edges, top and bottom and down the left side, but the right
side is very slightly crooked, angling in as it comes down through
a pale blue sky and a dark field and past the woman's shoulder
and then it seems as if this angle will touch her at the elbow, cut
into her, and the edge veers off, conscious of this, leaving the arm
intact. I speak of the edge as if it created itself. It is of course the
man who made the cut, who was careful not to lose even the
thinnest slice of the image of this woman he clearly loved. He
trimmed the photo to fit in the cellophane around a pack of
cigarettes and I understand things with a rush: he placed her there
so that every time his unit stopped and sat sweating and afraid by
a jungle stream and he took out his cigarettes to smoke, she would
be there to smile at him.

Is this not a surprising thing? A sentimental gesture like that
from an American soldier who has come across an ocean to do the
imperialist work of his country? Perhaps that is why I kept the pack
of cigarettes. I am baffled by such an act from this man. Even my
wife has such ways. We still have an ancestor shrine in our house.
A little altar table with an incense holder and an alcohol pot and
a teakwood tabernacle that has been in her family for many years
and there is a table of names there, written on rice paper, with the
names of four generations, and she believes that the souls of the
dead need the prayers of the living or they will never rest and I
tell her that this is not clear thinking in a world that has thrown
off the tyrannies of the past, but she turns her face away and I

know that I hurt her. This altar and the prayers for the dead do not even fit her Buddhism, they are from the Confucianism of the Chinese who oppressed us for centuries. But she does not hear me. It is something that lives apart from any religion or any politics. It is something that comes from our weakness, our fearful hopes for a life beyond the one that we can see and touch, and it is this that allows governments to oppress the poor and create the very evils I helped fight against.

But as I look more closely at these objects and think more clearly, I realize I should not have been surprised at the sentimentality of this American soldier. I am confused in my thinking. His wife was alive. This was the picture of a living person, not a dead ancestor. And whatever excess of sentiment there was in his wanting to see his wife in the jungle each time he stopped to smoke a cigarette, his government had bred such a thing in him — it was their power over him — and I look beyond this smiling woman and there is a sward of blue-green nearby but then the land goes dark and I bend nearer, straining to see, and the darkness becomes earth turned for planting, plowed into even furrows, and I know his family is a family of farmers, his wife smiles at him and her hair is the color of the sunlight that falls on farmers in the early haze of morning and he must have taken as much pleasure from that color as I take from the long drape of night shadow that my wife combs down for me and the earth must smell strong and sweet, turned like that to grow whatever it is that Americans eat, wheat I think instead of rice, corn perhaps. I am short of breath now and I place my hand on this cigarette pack, covering the woman's face, and I think the right thing to do is to give these objects over to my government. I have no need for them. And thinking this, I know that I am trying to lie to myself, and I withdraw my hand but I do not look at the face of the wife of the man I killed. I sit back instead and look out my window and I wait.

Perhaps I am waiting for my wife: her approach down the jungle path will make it necessary to put these things away and not consider them again and then I will have no choice but to take them in to the authorities in Da Nang when I go, as I do four times a year to report on the continued education of my village. If my wife were to appear right now, even as a pale blue cloud-shadow passes over the path and a dragonfly hovers in the window, if she were to appear in this moment, it would be done, for I have never spoken to my wife about what happened in those years in the jungle and she is a good wife and has never asked me and I would not tempt her by letting her see these objects. But she does not appear. Not in the moment of the blue shadow and the dragonfly and not in the moment afterward as the sunlight returns and the dragonfly rises and hesitates and then dashes away. And I know I am not waiting for my wife, after all. It is something else.

I look again at the face of this woman. The body of her husband was never found. I left him in the clearing and he was far from his comrades and he was far from my thoughts, even after I put his cigarettes in a place to keep them safe. Perhaps she has his name written on a shrine in her home and she lights incense to him and she prays for his spirit. She is the wife of a farmer. Perhaps there is some belief that she has that is like the belief of my own wife. But she does not know if her husband is dead or he is not dead. It is difficult to pray in such a circumstance.

And am I myself sentimental now, like the American soldier? I am not. I have earned the right to these thoughts. For instance, there is already something I know of that is inside the cigarette pack. I understood it in a certain way even by the stream. I think on it now and I understand even more. When I shook the cigarette into my hand from the pack, the first one out was small, half smoked, ragged at the end where he had brushed the burnt ash away to save the half cigarette, and I sensed then and I realize clearly now that this man was a poor man, like me. He could not finish his cigarette, but he did not throw it away. He saved it. There were many half-smoked cigarettes scattered in the jungles of Vietnam by Americans — it was one of the signs of them. American soldiers always had as many cigarettes as they wanted. But this man had the habit of wasting nothing. And I can understand this about him and I can sit and think on it and I can hesitate to give these signs of him away to my government without thinking myself sentimental. After all, this was a man I killed. No thought I have about him, no attachment, however odd, is sentimental if I have killed him. It is earned.

Objects can be very important. We have our flag, red for the revolution, a yellow star for the wholeness of our nation. We have the face of the father of our country, Ho Chi Minh, his kindly beard, his steady eyes. And he himself smoked these cigarettes. I turn the pack of Salem over and there is something to understand here. The two bands of color, top and bottom, are color like I sometimes have seen on the South China Sea when the air is still and the water is calm. And the sea is parted here and held within is a band of pure white and this word *Salem*, and now at last I can see clearly — how thin the line is between ignorance and wisdom — I understand all at once that there is a secret space in the word, not *Salem* but *sa* and *lem*, Vietnamese words, the one meaning to fall and the other to blur, and this is the moment that comes to all of us and this is the moment that I brought to the man who that very morning looked into the face of his wife and smoked and then had to move on and he carefully brushed the burning ash away to save half his cigarette because this farm of his was not a rich farm, he was a poor man who loved his wife and was sent far away by his government, and I was sent by my own government to sit in a tree and watch him move beneath me, frightened, and I brought him to that moment of falling and blurring.

And I turn the pack of cigarettes over again and I take it into my hand and I gently pull open the cellophane and draw the picture out and she smiles at me now, waiting for some word. I turn the photo over and the back is blank. There is no name here, no words at all. I have nothing but a pack of cigarettes and this nameless face, and I think that they will be of no use anyway, I think that I am a fool of a very mysterious sort either way — to consider saving these things or to consider giving them up — and then I stop thinking altogether and I let my hands move on their own, even as they did on that morning in the clearing, and I shake out the half cigarette into my hand and I put it to my lips and I strike a match and I lift it to the end that he has prepared and I light the cigarette and I draw the smoke inside me. It chills me. I do not believe in ghosts. But I know at once that his wife will go to a place and she will look through many pictures and she will at last see her own face and then she will know what she must know. But I will keep the cigarettes. I will smoke another someday, when I know it is time.

LAN SAMANTHA CHANG

Pipa's Story

FROM THE ATLANTIC MONTHLY

My mother worked in charms. She could brew a drink to brighten eyes or warm the womb. She knew of a douche that would likely bring a male child, and a potion to chase away unborn children. Except in emergencies, she gathered her own herbs and animal parts. I was not allowed to help.

The villagers said she had learned her craft from a Miao tribeswoman. A group of Miao — strangers from the west — had stayed in our village for a few months shortly after my father's death. My mother had mixed potions to forget, wandering in the woods to learn where mushrooms grew. My earliest memories are of watching the smoke from her kettle: white smoke, blue, gray, and black smoke.

When I was a child, she seemed all-powerful, and although time passed and I grew tall, she continued to loom over me until I thought I would disappear if I could not get away from her shadow. When I was nineteen, I decided to leave the village. For four days I watched my mother stir a mixture over the stove kettle. On the fourth evening I gathered the courage to tell her.

"I will go to Shanghai and work for a family there," I said to her back. "I'll send you an envelope filled with money at New Year."

My mother added a bowl of ice that hissed and crackled against whatever was in the pot. Then she turned to look into me. I forced myself to look back into her black eyes.

"Sit down," she told me, gesturing to the wooden chair by the window.

I sat and watched her strain the cooling potion into a wooden

bowl. Then she unbraided my hair and combed it, dipping the
comb into the potion. It was a warm evening in early spring. The
half-moon gave us light.

"What is the potion?" I said.

"It is a mixture to make you ready for departure."

I lost a breath. My mother tugged and pulled at me, braiding
my hair into a four-stranded plait.

"There are herbs here that will protect you against bodily harm
from illness, loss of energy, and unclear thinking. There are also
herbs that will fix your memory, your past. You will never forget
me here, no matter how far away you go."

She wrapped the end of my braid around and around with red
thread. "You want to leave," she said. "You have my permission if
you make one promise to me."

"I promise," I said. Anything if she would let me go.

She looked out the window to make sure that no one was
standing by. "Come here," she said. I followed her to a corner of
the room, where it was dark.

Three steps from the corner my mother knelt down and began
digging into the dirt with a spoon. She unearthed a small box,
muddy but with dull tin showing in patches. We walked to the
window, where we could see. My mother opened the box, took
something out, and handed it to me. It was a lump, smaller than
the palm of my hand, wrapped in rough cotton.

"Open it," she said.

I unfolded the cloth. Inside glowed a pinkish stone, a craggy
piece of our mountain.

"Lao Fu will take you to Shanghai," my mother said. "Find work
with a family named Wen. They have a large household and
probably many servants. You're still rough, straight from the country, and they may not want to hire you, but I'm sure you can
persuade them. Don't tell them that you're from this village, and
don't tell them my name."

"Why not?" I said.

"That doesn't concern you. If you don't like working for the
Wens, you may leave and go wherever you like, but before you
leave, you must do one thing for me."

"What is it?"

"Find the heart of the house," she said. "It's a huge, modern place. I'm sure. Wen will have become involved with Western business, and he will have a large Western house. You'll have to spend some time searching. Let the house seep around you; listen for its rhythm. Before three months are up, find the center and hide this stone there."

"What are you talking about?" I said rudely. "I never learned anything about houses. You never told me. How would I know?"

My mother didn't scold me but squatted on the floor and looked into the beam of pale moonlight.

"Tell me," she said, "where the heart of our own house is."

I thought for a minute. Then I pointed to the middle of the floor.

"No," she said. "The physical center is not what I mean."

I sighed. Our house — a hut, really — was quite small, and as far as I could tell had no other center. We had a table, our beds, some rickety chairs. The corner shelf held storybooks, *Dream of the Red Chamber* and *Outlaws of the Marsh,* that my mother had been teaching me to read for years. Our house had no male presence, because my father had died before I was born. My mother earned our living. I thought about my mother, her long gray braid hanging down her back, hunched before the stove kettle full of glowing coals.

"The fire," I said. "The stove is the heart of our house."

My mother nodded. "Good," she said.

At her praise I felt cold and heavy. "What is this about?"

She shook her head. "It's better if you don't know," she said. "It began before you were born. Your deed will be the end of it." She stood up and walked to the window again. "It's something that happened long ago."

I left with the stone sewn into my pocket. I rode in a cart with Lao Fu, my mother's old friend, who was bringing ginseng to sell around the city. The precious roots grew wild on the mountains. I watched Lao Fu's thick, arthritic hands on the reins, carelessly guiding his spotted horse. Now and then he flicked a tattered whip. In those days the trip to Shanghai took weeks. Lao Fu didn't usually make such long trips. He was taking me as a favor to my mother, who often rubbed an ointment into his knuckles. We didn't speak for hours, by which time the most familiar mountains had grown pale blue in the distance and we were surrounded by shapes I had seen before only from far away. Then Lao Fu turned an eye to me.

"You're a *nenggan* girl, Pipa," he said in his rusty, wheezing voice. "A capable, dutiful girl. Traveling hundreds of miles in order to help your mother."

He smiled kindly, exposing four brown teeth. I glared at the stains on his gray beard and wished that someone else were driving me, someone I had never met. Even in this remote region the lines of the surrounding hills seemed to shape my mother's face. The stone in my pocket, my secret, weighed so heavily I could hardly sit upright. I wanted to rip it out of my smock and fling it into the next river. She would never know.

But when we reached Shanghai, I felt so terrified by my first view of the great port that I held on to the stone like a talisman. I sat close to Lao Fu, dreading our approach to the Wen house, where he would leave me. The city seemed to whirl past. The wide streets were cluttered with travelers — in carts like ours, but also in rickshaws and automobiles. I had never seen either before, nor had I seen the kind of people, foreigners, who rode in them.

In those days foreigners were everywhere: stiff soldiers in uniforms from England and America, businessmen from Russia, hurrying in and out of large, square, Western buildings. I sat paralyzed, blocking my ears against the roaring, honking automobiles. I turned away from the rickshawmen, their faces drawn, their feet slap-slapping against the pavement. We stopped at an intersection. I saw a man with yellow eyes lurch toward our cart. Lao Fu twitched his whip in that direction. "Opium," he said. "Don't look."

On another corner I spotted a powerfully built Chinese man dressed in Western clothes, his short, glossy hair oiled back from his forehead. He was talking to three foreigners, standing as straight as any of them. For a moment he seemed to stare at our cart, at Lao Fu adjusting a strap on the harness. Then he looked away.

As we went on, the shops and businesses gave way to houses: tall brick boxes set back from the road, with no round doorways or Chinese gardens. Shining black automobiles veered around us. One of them nearly struck the horse. I turned to Lao Fu in alarm, but he merely shook his head and guided our cart closer to the side of the road.

"Lao Fu, where are we?"

"Close."

After one more street he turned to our right. The horse clip-clopped around a long bend, and suddenly we were twenty yards from an entrance to an immense house built of brick and wood. I spotted a woman watching us from a window. Lao Fu stopped the cart.

"Here you are, Pipa. That door is the servants' entrance." I stared at my lap. "*Xialai.* Get down. I'll take your bundle."

I climbed from the cart, my legs stiff, my left hand clutching the stone in my pocket. Lao Fu came around the back of the cart holding my blue cotton bundle.

"Go in," he said. I wrinkled my mouth to hold back tears. "You will be all right," he said. "I'll be in the surrounding towns for a few months. I'll come visit you."

We faced each other and bobbed our heads. Lao Fu climbed back onto his cart and picked up the reins in his gnarled hands. He nodded again before turning away.

I stood watching his cart go back around the bend. I realized that I had said goodbye to the last of the village, and to my mother. After years of avoiding her sight, I had gone to a place where she could not see me. Suddenly I was filled with an emotion so terrible that I turned and vomited at the side of the road.

A very pretty girl stood at the servants' door, waiting. She wore black pants and a clean white blouse. From the way her hair was done, I guessed that she had been the one looking out the window.

"Are you all right?" she asked in a low, pleasant voice. Close up, I stood a head taller than she.

"Yes," I said. I clutched my bundle. "I want to work here."

Her eyes darted over my rough cotton clothes. "Come in," she said. "Clean up inside. You should bathe, and change. Then I'll introduce you to the housekeeper."

I walked inside the great house and smelled the warm, rich odor of food and spices. We stood in a square room lined with wood. A door to my right opened into a hallway. I could see at the end a room where a number of people were chopping vegetables.

"Come here quickly," whispered the girl, darting toward another doorway. She led me to a very white, shining room with a long

white basin on four feet. I had never seen a bathtub before, and
I stopped to stare. The girl, who said her name was Meisi, turned
two silver fixtures at one end of the tub, and out of them poured
steaming water. She held a huge towel in front of me so that I
wouldn't be embarrassed while she stayed in the room.

I took off my dirty traveling clothes and stepped into the tub.
The warm water rushed around my body, erasing the village dirt.
I unbraided my hair, and my mother's spells were washed away in
a swirl of steam. I felt myself changing, like a tadpole, and I looked
at my hands and limbs as if they were new.

Behind her towel Meisi chattered away.

"Of course they'll hire you; the family just moved into this new
residence, and they need servants. They hired me only three
months ago. I'll have you fixed up so that no one will think twice."

"Why did you come to work here?" I said.

"I'm from Beijing. My mother died giving birth to me, and my
father was in the Kuomintang army. He died last year in the
fighting. I am an orphan. I had to find work. This is a good place.
The master is rich and good-looking. Supervision is not very strict."

After a minute I said, "Fighting? What fighting?"

"You really are from far away! There's been terrible fighting, not
in Shanghai, but maybe soon!" Her voice dropped, and I had to
lean close to the towel in order to hear.

"I don't know anything about these events," I said. "Our village
is so remote, even the Japanese ignored it."

When I was finished, she found a pair of black trousers and a
white shirt that were both a little too small for me. "We'll get some
others after you've started," she said. "I'll steal them from the
closet."

"Thank you for helping me," I said.

Meisi smiled. "This is nothing," she answered. "There is plenty
here; why not share it? And besides, you look like a nice person."
She picked up my old blue cotton smock. "Do you want this saved?"

I thought of the stone sewed into the pocket. "No," I said.

The Wens lived on one of the most stylish new streets in Shanghai.
For weeks I marveled at their house; I had never even dreamed of
anything like it. The rooms were broad and tall, with glossy, patterned wooden floors built by English carpenters and covered with

flowered Persian carpets. English curtains draped down by long windows, blood-red velvet curtains with gold-colored tasseled cords. Everything in that house was new, from the mysterious electric lights to the great wooden tubs in the kitchen, filled with live clams in salt water in case one of the family should have a craving for them.

The housekeeper, Lu Taitai, was an immense older woman whose face lay as still as a mud bog. When she was very angry, she would slowly lift one fat finger into the air. I lived in terror of her. I was the newest of thirty servants, so unskilled that at first I worked in the servants' quarters, which, as Meisi pointed out, had to be kept clean along with the rest of the house. Meisi's swift hands and pretty face had earned her a job on the third floor, where the family lived. I imagined that the upstairs must be a magical place.

"Can you show me the upper floors?" I asked her once, as we ate dinner at one end of the long servants' table.

She looked right and left before answering. "We have to watch out for Lu Taitai," she said. "And it's harder to get away with things upstairs. The women have sharp eyes. If I have a chance, I'll take you."

"What women?" I said. "The servant women?"

Meisi put down her chopsticks. "Pipa," she said, "the master has four wives." She smiled. "Stop blushing, and keep eating."

I looked at the table. We ate what the Wens left. The night before, they had feasted on duck done ten ways, and there was a pile of crackling duck skins, which I had discovered I particularly liked. There were also jelled duck eggs, pigeon eggs in sauce, shrimps with chicken and peas, and chicken and scallops with ginger, scallops in sauce, salted prawns, spicy prawns, late oysters, early asparagus, several other vegetable dishes, and a great fish that lay on its side, barely touched. I thought that if a man was wealthy enough to serve four dishes for each member of the family, then perhaps four wives was to be expected.

A few weeks later Lu Taitai was suddenly called away to her home province.

"Good," Meisi said. By flirting with the second housekeeper, she arranged for me to bring tea to the master upstairs in his library, during a meeting with some of his Western associates.

"If it weren't for you, I would be lost," I said when I thanked her. "I've been here for a month and I've never seen him."

"Well," she said, "he's very good-looking. I can see why the women fall for him: rich, handsome, and powerful! Of course, he seldom looks at people like you and me — we can only watch. But if that's what you want, my dear friend Pipa, you shall have it." And she made me practice several times with the bamboo tea tray.

On the day of the meeting we waited to hear the men's heavy shoes start up the staircase. "Go up now," Meisi said. She fixed some of the coarse hair that constantly escaped from my pinned-up braids. The cook's assistant stared with grim disapproval while I balanced the tray.

For the first time I climbed the polished staircase.

The second floor was quiet. The carpet melted under my feet. Meisi had instructed me: "Turn left at the top, go down two doors, and you've reached the library." The heavy, unfamiliar tray hindered my progress; delicate teacups slid on their bits of lace. I reached the library door, braced the way as securely as possible against my hip, and knocked.

"Come in," said a resonant male voice.

I looked at the big china knob. How could I possibly turn it? I moved to brace my feet and felt the smooth wooden tray slide against my blouse.

Suddenly the door opened and a man stood over me, holding a book in one hand. For a moment I forgot my manners and stared at him. I had seen him before: the arrogant man whom I had noticed while riding with Lao Fu on my first day in Shanghai. Now he stood and looked at my face, my blouse, my hands holding the tray. I felt as if a piece of burning ash had been put down my back. I gasped; the tray tilted in my hands. The house with its soft rugs fought against me, making me lose my balance. Hot tea spilled on the master's arm and over the book he carried.

"*Duibuqi*," I gasped, hastily putting down the ruined tray. I grabbed an embroidered linen napkin and reached to dry his arm.

"I'm fine," he said. "Dry this." He handed me the book, and even in my horror it occurred to me that this man must have strength not to so much as flinch at the boiling water. I waited for him to scold me, or even strike me, but he did not move.

"*Duibuqi*," I repeated, and indeed at that moment I did not think

I could ever look him in the face again. I wiped the pages. "*Xiang-gang Falu*," I read aloud. Why was he studying Hong Kong laws?

"You can read," he said.

"My mother taught me," I blurted out.

"Then you'll still be of some use to us," he said. "It's obvious you're not a good maid. Come in."

I tiptoed into the room. Opposite me stood three crowded bookshelves. The foreigners sat at the end, before the fireplace.

"You're tall," Wen said. "You can read. Find the books I want and bring them over. Find me the volume about transportation on the Yangtze and the Grand Canal."

I turned toward the shelves, my hands sweating. Wen went back to the fireplace.

"If you want factual proof, I'll give it to you," I heard him say to the foreigners. "But I guarantee, they'll wait. They've won too many battles too quickly. They need to regroup. It will be months before they reach Shanghai, maybe a year. You needn't worry."

Someone coughed. "Oh, certainly, certainly." This man spoke Chinese with difficulty. "It's just that we have received some — reports from farther north. Of course," he continued, searching for the words, "we're not worried about them. The Kuomintang troops have regrouped themselves to defend our side of the Yangtze . . . We are just — making sure that we understand the situation."

"Those who flee are fools," Wen said. "I tell you, it's not time to leave yet. They would never touch a foreigner. Remember, the longer you stay, the more you'll make."

"And you as well," one of the men said.

"You can believe me." Wen's voice grew hard. "I know what Mao will do. I'm one of them. I was born a peasant, you know."

In the bottom right corner of the shelf I spotted a blue volume on waterways, which I pulled and brought to Wen. I watched for a minute as he studied the book, the firelight flickering on his face, and I could sense his force, his intelligence and cunning.

"Ha!" he said, pointing to a paragraph of characters. "You see, I was correct." He showed the book to one of the Western gentlemen, who squinted, nervously stroking his blond beard.

"What does it say, Stanton?" one of them asked.

"Ah, yes! Mr. Wen is correct," Stanton said. I wondered if he could read characters well enough to know what he was talking about.

"Now," Wen said, "about those collections. I'll have the first half to you by Monday next week." He turned to me. "You can go now," he said. "I'll call you the next time there is a meeting."

As I left the library, I saw the tea tray sitting in the hallway. I bent down to pick it up.

"What are you doing?" said a musical, imperious voice.

I straightened. I had not heard her walk across the carpet. She was tiny, beautiful, with large eyes and a curved lower lip like an orange slice. She wore a *qipao* of shimmering sea-green silk.

"I came with the tea," I tried to explain. "I was helping in the library."

"*Helping*," she said. Her eyes flickered up and down my body.

"Getting books."

Her lower lip swelled with dissatisfaction. She walked past me to the library door. "Are they still inside?"

I nodded.

She lifted her chin. "Hmph!" she said. "Get back downstairs."

I picked up the tray and hurried away, cold tea splashing on the carpet.

Downstairs Meisi waited for me.

"I was worried!" she cried. But when I explained what had happened, she smiled and patted my arm. "Now you've earned your job in the house. No more rag-pushing for you!" Her eyes sparkled.

"Your mother will want to know how you are doing," Lao Fu said.

I didn't answer. Lao Fu guided his horse past two arguing street peddlers. He had returned to the city and come by to take me on a ride. I felt ashamed that the others would see me with him, with his patched clothes and shabby cart. But it was a beautiful day in May. The fresh warm air reminded me how seldom I had a chance to go outside, now that I was working at the Wen house.

"Before we left, she asked me to check on you," Lao Fu said, "and to ask you if you kept your promise."

"Why is everything so crowded?" I said, changing the subject. Even on the quieter streets we could not drive in a straight line.

"In the past few months more and more people north of us have fled the Red Army, seeking safety."

"Where is the army now?"

"Since the end of the year it has been waiting north of the Yangtze River."

I remembered the conversation in the library. "What will happen when it moves south again?"

Lao Fu looked at me, and I saw his cloudy cataracts. "Things will change."

"How will they change?"

"Ah," he said. "Who knows? These days I demand silver in payment. The Kuomintang is crumbling. Why won't you answer your mother's question?"

"I don't have time to think about her anymore," I said.

Lao Fu ignored me. "Look over there," he said. "A decent noodle house, and not too busy. Let's have lunch."

After we had taken care of the cart and horse, we stood for a minute outside the noodle shop, watching the people on the street. A thin man carrying a large wicker basket shuffled close to us. "*Zhuan qian, zhuan qian,*" he repeated under his breath. Lao Fu nodded and handed him a piece of silver. The man opened his basket and counted out sixteen bundles of paper money. They nodded at each other, and we entered the dark, noisy noodle shop.

"You see?" Lao Fu said as we sat down at a corner table. "By the time we leave, that coin will be worth sixteen and a half bundles of paper money."

I felt as if he were saying this to make a point against me. Stubbornly I folded my hands in my lap.

"What will happen when the Communist army reaches this city?" Lao Fu lit his long, large pipe. "They'll go after people like your master, rich people who flourished under the Kuomintang by working with foreign capitalists. There's a word for your master, Pipa. He's an *ermaozi*, a comprador."

"He's a peasant," I said. "He's a former peasant who used his wits to make a fortune for himself, to move away from his village."

"Ha," Lao Fu said. He fitted the pipe between his four stubby teeth. "You're a young girl, Pipa. You're young, and the world is a strange place."

I scowled and took a sip of the tea that a greasy-haired, smudge-faced woman had flung on the table.

"What difference do his origins make to you?" I said. "You're here with a message from my mother. You don't know Master Wen or anything about him."

"But I do know him," Lao Fu said. "I used to know him well."

I stared at my wavering saucer of tea.

"When he was a young man in the village, we used to call him Xiao Niou, Little Bull. He was once a friend of your father's."

There was a terrible pounding in my ears. Lao Fu's rusty voice sounded like a shout. I waited for him to stop, but he continued. "Some people forget their histories, but they don't realize that others remember," he said. "Not everyone forgets the wrongs they've suffered."

He raised the saucer to his mouth. His loud slurp brought me back to my senses.

"What do you mean?" I forced out the words.

"Ah. Well, this is an old story. Something that happened before you were born. It is, shall I say, a village secret."

"There aren't any secrets in the village."

"Well, it's possible. There were only four of us who knew. One died, one has forgotten, and two of us have chosen not to tell. That is, until now."

At that moment the woman brought us two broad, steaming bowls of noodle soup. Lao Fu nodded. "Good. Eat."

I took a spoonful of soup, waiting. The food and even the serving utensils were so much coarser than what I had grown used to.

Lao Fu began. "Your father and mother were the two village orphans. No one arranged their marriage. When they wed, it was a love match."

He took a mouthful of noodles and went on. My father, he said, was gentle and kind. He had spent years learning to read in his spare time; he sat and daydreamed over his tea. My mother was clever, forceful. She never rested. And she had an astounding talent that everyone in the village knew about. If an object was lost, my mother could almost always find it. On the mountains she understood the natural order and discovered more ginseng roots than anyone else. It was she who suggested that she and my father supplement their income by collecting ginseng roots. Xiao Niou and Lao Fu agreed to help them.

"There was one problem," Lao Fu said. "Perhaps because she was so sure of herself, your mother underestimated Xiao Niou. He was a ruthless, ambitious boy who wanted to be the best at everything. And the more he saw of your mother, the more he wanted her as well. He desired her. He wanted to stop her constant thinking and doing; he wanted her to think and do only for him.

"Your mother was not beautiful, but she had so much vitality that she was impossible to ignore. She knew that Xiao Niou wanted her, but she thought she could control him. This goaded Xiao Niou until he couldn't bear it."

One cloudy fall day the four of them had gone to gather ginseng. For part of the day they worked together. All morning Xiao Niou watched my mother out of the corner of his eye. After lunch my mother suggested that they split up and search on different parts of the mountain. And Xiao Niou suggested that he and my father go off together.

That afternoon the fog grew so thick that my mother and Lao Fu, working close together, could hardly see each other. It was very quiet. The path became almost impossible to find; trees and stones looked like people and animals. If not for my mother, Lao Fu said, they might not have found the pathway down the mountain, back to the village.

When they reached the village, my mother waited for Xiao Niou and my father to return. She built a fire, cooked dinner. But the other two did not come back. She began to worry. Finally, after the gray fog had turned dark, Xiao Niou stopped by our hut.

"Where's Dangbei?" he asked.

"What do you mean?" my mother said. "I thought he was with you."

"He left early," Xiao Niou told her. "He decided to go back to the village."

All that night my mother waited, but my father did not come home.

The next day my mother went out on the mountain, in the fog, searching for him. She looked and looked, but she could not find him. Finally some men from the village had to force her to stay inside — she was pregnant, after all. Then winter set in.

"All winter your mother mourned," Lao Fu said. "She would speak only to me and Xiao Niou. Xiao Niou asked her to marry him, but she refused to discuss anything until your father's body was discovered. That spring, right before you were born, the villagers found him at the bottom of a ravine, lying on a bed of pinkish quartz. After the birth your mother insisted on going up on the mountain and to the spot where they had found his body."

"Now here is the secret," Lao Fu said. "Your mother told only me. After seeing the site where your father's body was discovered, she felt certain that he had not gotten there on his own. If the two of them had gone to dig ginseng in the place Xiao Niou had described, your father would not have died where his body was found."

"How did she know?" I said. "On foggy days in our mountains, a person could wander anywhere."

"I asked her. 'I know Dangbei,' she said. 'He would never have gotten lost there,' she said. And I believed her. She knew the mountains. I felt foolish and angry. So much had been going on right under my nose, and I had not understood."

He looked at me. I ignored him, studying my soup. "I was younger in those days, and I hated being wrong about things," he said.

"That summer Xiao Niou again asked her to marry him. She accused him of killing Dangbei, and Xiao Niou left the village. He disappeared for years, and when we heard about him next, he had taken the name of Wen."

After this my mother had begun to brood before the stove, to speak to Miao travelers and learn their arts. She was unable to forget what had been lost.

"Now," Lao Fu said when the story was finished and our bowls were empty, "when I return to the village, your mother will ask me if you have kept your promise to her."

I looked at him. He leaned toward me; a noodle hung from his beard. I felt my eyes grow hot with confusion and anger. I felt as if my inner world had been turned inside out. He had cast her shadow over me again, and I could not forgive him.

"Leave me alone!" I said. "You tell my mother that I will not keep my promise to her. None of this has anything to do with me. I'm far away, and she can't reach me. She can't make me do what I don't want to do. Besides, it's impossible now."

Lao Fu's wrinkled lids lowered. He nodded. "You do what you must do. I'll be in the city another week —"

"Don't visit me anymore," I said.

Back at the Wens' house the servants were getting ready for an important business dinner. I looked for Meisi. I wanted to talk to her, but the second housekeeper gave me a pile of rags and some scented oil, and set me to work on the yards of rich wood paneling in the sitting room and dining room.

As I wiped and polished, certain thoughts traced themselves over and over in my mind. The scented oil filled my nostrils, reminding me of my mother's potions. I remembered her sorting out bundles of herbs on the wooden table in our hut, her frown deepening in the firelight. She had loved my father, whom I had never met. For years I had secretly believed that the purpose of her herbs, her potions, and her utterances was not to help others but to keep me near her. But now it seemed that even my flight from her fit into some incomprehensible design. I began to see that Lao Fu was right. I was young; the world was a mystery.

I finished the woodwork and walked into the hall. And for the first time I noticed something odd about the Wens' house. I saw the great house, with its women and servants, as testimony to the unquenchable desire of its master, desire that destroyed all obstacles and then discarded them. The house seemed raw and unexplained, as if it were hiding its origin. The rooms were big and empty: too clean, too new, too cold. I looked down the hall at the dozen servants cleaning and sweeping as if there were more than dirt to get rid of.

As I entered the dining room, one of the rags dropped out of my hands and fell to the wooden floor with a small thud. I knelt down to pick it up, but then I stopped, crouching, and stared at the rough blue cotton fabric.

Snatching the rag, I sprang up and ran toward the staircase. I had to find Meisi, my friend, and tell her what had happened. I needed to hear what she would say. I had to see her. I pounded up the stairs, past the second floor, and up to the family quarters.

The upstairs was lit by the fading light from a few windows. I had never been up so high before, but I remembered the stories from the servants' table: the four wives each in a suite of rooms, and at one end the master's room, near a separate staircase to the outside door, so that he could get away. The doors were closed. Sweet scents of soap and perfume filled the air. They must all be getting ready for dinner. I would never find Meisi.

I heard a doorknob turn, and then another door open and shut. I saw two doors at the north end, and one was ajar. I hurried toward it and ran straight into Meisi coming out. When I saw her face, I forgot to think for a moment.

"What's wrong?" I cried.

Meisi buried her face in her hands. "Oh!" she sobbed. "It's terrible — I have to get away from here! I can't work here anymore."

"What happened?" I said. She clutched herself around the waist and ran down the hall. I followed her down the two flights of stairs, rushing past a few surprised-looking servants. "Meisi," I begged, "let me help you!"

She ran into the room we shared with some other servants.

"Please let me help you," I said. "You're always so kind to me."

"Do you have a clean shirt?" she whimpered, her arms still crossed. "Mine are in the wash."

"It'll be too big," I said. But I handed her one. She reached for it, and I saw the huge rip in the one that she had on. She took off her torn shirt. I saw four blue bruises, in the shape of fingerprints, on her arm. More bruises and scratches were on her chest.

Then I knew what I had to do. I found a pair of scissors and cut the stone from the rag I still held in my hand. I went back up the stairs, past the second floor and the library, up to the third floor. The door to the master's room was still ajar. The shades were closed, but I made out a huge square shape in the semi-darkness. I walked to the great canopied bed, and I hid the stone inside it.

When I came back downstairs, Meisi and her things were gone.

Late that night I was asked to work in the library. My eyes smarting with weariness, I searched the tall bookcases in the flickering light from the fireplace.

"You're making a mistake," I heard him say. "They won't harm you or your business. You'd be better off staying in China and keeping what you have. There's no telling what will happen if you run off and leave everything."

The men by the fire said nothing.

"They would never touch you," he said.

After a minute one of the foreigners spoke. "What will happen to you, Wen? Where are you burying your money? How much of it have you sent abroad?"

"I told you," Wen said confidently. "How could they betray one of their own kind? They won't get me."

Finally I found the book he wanted, and he dismissed me for the evening. The room was utterly silent as I left.

I went downstairs, put on my nightclothes, and lay in bed.

When I shut my eyes, I found that I had grown as light as a straw. I floated high on the wind over the Wens' great house and back to where I had come from. I soared over the rich green Yangtze Delta, with its fishermen and rice paddies, following the broad river as it narrowed into rushing rapids, and then continuing westward toward the mountains of my village. Evening fell; the stars wheeled over my head. When I landed, the air smelled of thawed earth and sweet plum blossoms. I walked quietly down the dark road, past the well, and to the corner where my mother's hut stood, slightly sagging.

I looked through the window. Her face was deeply grooved, bloodless with concentration. She had unbraided her long gray hair. She sat cross-legged in the firelight in front of a group of small paper figures. Her voice rattled into the air, making an incantation. She swayed, muttering low deep sounds under her breath, an endless curse word. I looked at the firepot; coals glowed through the slits in its iron sides. I watched through the window until my vision faded into smoke.

Sometime after midnight I was awakened by the sound of gunfire. It was May 12, and the Communist army had reached the outskirts of Shanghai.

Considering the events that have since taken place in China and the world, my own story is small and not very interesting. But it is mine. Like ginseng roots, our buried pasts have different shapes. I never saw my mother again. After Lao Fu rescued me from the Wens' house, I fled to Taiwan. A year later I met up with a man from our village who told me what had happened there: the Communists had reached the village a few months after the fall of Shanghai, and they had executed my mother as a witch.

In Taiwan, I worked at a library. Now I shelve books in the Chinese collection at an American university. I have a husband and two children who both attended college. We own our small house. I don't keep the house too clean, and I tried not to frighten my daughters the way my mother frightened me. But there are things I can't forget, and things my family knows they should never do. They do not light fires in the fireplace, not even if I won't be home for hours. Because the smell of smoke, the faintest trace, reminds me of my mother.

I see her brooding over her past and I remember that it's not wise to look back too long and deep at what has gone. It is not wise to think of Shanghai, the broad houses now shabby and sectioned off for twenty families. Or to dwell too long on my friend Meisi and her kindness. Or to remember the fire that the Communists started when they reached our section of the city.

The flames leaped through the house, feeding themselves along the expensive wood paneling, ruffling the curtains, exploding the leaded-glass windows. I stood outside with the other servants and watched the sparks and ashes fly up into the night. We looked on as four soldiers led our master out onto the lawn. The soldiers wore red stars on their caps. They struck the back of his knees to make him kneel to them. He knelt with his head held high and with anger burning in his face. One of them raised a long machete, twirling the knife so that the blunt side came down on the back of his neck to make him fall forward. For a moment we were silent; only flames moved. Then the soldier raised his arm again, and the sharp blade sliced all our lives in two.

ANN CUMMINS

Where I Work

FROM ROOM OF ONE'S OWN

IT'S PIECEWORK that brings in the money. You get four bucks an hour or ten cents a pocket. The old-timers can sew two pockets a minute and make eighteen an hour. They're a whiz. Most get between ten and fifteen. Me, I get four, today maybe five. I'm on my way. You don't worry if you're no good at first. You catch on. You're guaranteed the four bucks no matter if you can't get one pocket on in an hour. This is my third day.

Sam Hunt with the measuring tape comes to my machine and measures the straightness of my stitching. He wears the tan vest, tan creased pants, brown polished shoes, white shirt. He has a perfectly formed nose, neither upturning nor downturning, and when he stands in front of my machine, I can smell a mysterious cologne coming from him. When he comes this close, I can see that the white shirt does not stick to any part of his skin, because he does not sweat.

But the fat women from Galveston sweat like pigs. Turn up the air conditioning! they'll yell. Today at lunch, I sat with the fat women from Galveston, Texas. You can hear them all over the lunchroom talking about the Texas heat, complaining about this rain. They say, My bones never ached like this in Texas. In Galveston, the fat women plopped their rumps on the beach and watched the hurricanes come in. I have never seen a hurricane. When I sit with the Texans, they tell me all about it.

And they say, How's your love life, darling? These women mull things over.

It is my duty to make them laugh. This is a social skill my brother,

Michael, taught me. Make them laugh, he said, and you won't get fired.

Make them laugh or compliment them. Don't tell lies. Don't say things like, "I'd like to tear her little twat out"; if you have to say something like this, say it approximately, not exactly, or you'll scare people. He told me I scare people, and that's one reason why I can't hold a job, and because I tell lies. If you have to tell lies, tell little ones, he says. Try not to talk out loud when you're not talking to anybody.

At lunch yesterday, when they asked me about my lover, I said, He has a waterbed on his roof.

A waterbed on his roof? they said. In this rain?

Some laughed, some didn't. It's difficult to say what will make the women around here laugh.

But I admire their industry. They hardly make mistakes. Sam Hunt docks you a pocket for every mistake, and these add up.

Sam Hunt drives a scooter to work, a very little one. I have seen him from the bus window. He drives on the edge of the road, on the white line, and the Sandy Street bus could squash him like a penny. Then who would see to the time cards? It takes a certain kind of man. Serious. Not a drinker, I'd say. Nice fitting suit, gleaming face.

My brother says my face is better than what you usually see. I would marry my brother in an instant, though he's sinister and disrespectful.

My brother drives a taxi and knows the timing of the streetlights by heart. He drives two-fingered with his foot both on and off the gas pedal, never speeding up, never slowing down, through the city neighborhoods. Some nights I sit on the passenger's side, and the customers sit in the back. My brother's taxi smells like fire. Cinder and ash. In the ashtrays, fat men have stuffed cigars.

I wouldn't mind a fat man. A fat man would be somebody you could wrap yourself around and never meet yourself coming or going. If I married a fat man, I'd draw stars on his back every night. I'd say, How many points does this star have? Now pay attention, termite, I'd say. How many points does this star have?

In his taxi, my brother totes around the downtown whores. Some have the names of the months. June, July, and August. Ask them how much they make a night. Depends on how fast your brother drives, they say. Hurry up, baby, time's money, they like to say. And they spend it in Washington Park, just junkies in Washington Park.

Washington Park smells like garbage, those houses around there. In the Washington Park housing project, don't go up to a black woman's door. They don't want you. Don't go up to the men on the steps. Keep your hands at your sides. Walk fast or run. Don't look in the windows of a car slowing down. Walk slow if there're dogs or they'll chase you. Keep your hand on your purse. If somebody approaches you, if he gets within ten feet, say, "I am fully proficient in the use of semi-automatic weapons."

My brother bought me a gun when I moved out on my own, because a woman living alone in this city should be able to defend herself. You go for the knees. We put cardboard circles on a fence post in the country. I can hit them the majority of the time. If you go for the heart or head and murder a person, you could be held liable by the dead man's family, even if he broke into your apartment. This is the justice system in our country, my brother says, and he's right. The justice system in this country treats us like a bunch of stinking fish.

There. A perfect pocket. This is a keeper, so that's one. These are my practice days. They give you a couple of practice days to start out, and after the third day or so, you begin to develop a system. Like one thing is not to stop when you're coming to a corner — not to slow down or speed up, and keep your hands going with your foot on the pedal and just turn the corner without thinking. If you ruin one, put it in your purse — if it's really bad.

Next week, we're moving to a new line. Sam Hunt said when he oriented me that we're moving out of the blue and into the white. We'll have enough blue by the end of the week. How's your eyes? he says. The white stitches on the white material can blind you, so remember to blink often.

There's something wrong with my eyes. I can't cry. I'm just a happy idiot, my brother says, but I say there's something wrong with my eyes. They are deteriorating in my head. I have that condition — you read about it — where the eyes dry out unnaturally. I don't cry.

All of the women at this table wear glasses. And smoke. The lunchroom's like a chimney. And they say, How's your love life, darling?

The reason I'm not married yet is because I haven't found the right man. I don't know who he is, but I'll know him when I see him, and he'll look like something, and he won't whore around. Which, I'd shoot him, any man who whored around on me. Like that man in the laundry room. He was married, because I saw the ring. And he says, How thin are your wrists? Look at how thin your wrists are. See, he says, I can put my fingers around you and not touch any part, a married man said this.

A lot of the good ones are married. He had green eyes and a friendly manner, and he asked me which was my apartment. He lives right above me — him and his wife. Says, come up and watch TV sometime. I may just do that. I would like to see their home and their furnishings.

I will ask him to help me move furniture in. When I get my first check I'm going to buy a lamp, a nice brass one, and when I save enough I'm going to buy a brass bed, too, and one of those checkerboard coffee tables, the kind with different colors of wood in squares, and some rugs, throw rugs, and ask them to dinner, the man and his wife, which, you could never ask anybody to dinner at Michael's house because nobody ever does the dishes, and there's nothing in that house but Bob Marley posters and dirt and screaming fits.

My brother has paid my rent for the last time. If he's got to have such a screaming fit about it.

Outside the window in my new apartment on the east side is a mystery tree. We don't know what it is. I've asked around but nobody knows. On a muggy night, if you don't turn the light on, you can see animals in the tree. Opossum. Eight, nine, ten of them, gliding along the mystery tree and the tree's branches all in a panic. Black like tar, the branches gleam in the moonlight, all the little opossum claws scratching where you can't see or hear. Shall I open the window? my brother said when he came over. Want some pets? Hold on to your hair. They could get into your hair. He says they're rats, but I have seen them up close. On this, he's wrong. He says this because he's jealous.

Who pays your rent? he says. He says, Who the fuck pays your rent?

My brother has paid my rent for the last time if it's such a big deal.

"My brother had a fire in his taxi."

"What?"

"My brother drives a taxi and somebody started a fire in the back seat."

"Ain't that something." She's the nice one. She says, Sit with us, honey, and tells me about the Texas hurricanes. She's someone you can talk to. "Did he have insurance?"

"What's the difference between a tornado and a hurricane?" The woman has bitten her fingernails to the quick. You can see it from here.

"A tornado? You know, I never considered it. Hey, Lynn. What's the difference between a hurricane and a tornado?"

"One's by sea, one's by land."

"One thing I do know. They can both come up on you in a minute."

"Same with a fire. My brother had a fire in his taxi."

"Ain't that something."

"Somebody left a cigar or cigarette burning in the back. It went, just like that."

"Anybody hurt?"

"They're made of straw. That's why the seats can go just like that."

Then you're walking.

So let him walk. See how that feels.

In the Projects a man came up to me. He says, Woman? Woman? He says, Where can I find a pepper grinder? He says for fish, that he was cooking fish and he wanted some fresh ground pepper, and then started laughing and laughed his fool head off.

In the Projects, a person can get shot and nobody's going to look for you. In the Projects, someone has busted out every streetlight, and there's glass in the street, and children playing in it. In the Projects, you can walk down one street, up another, a street without lights so you don't see the dirty yellow walls all alike, street after street, with dogs that'll chase you and black women who don't want you, and it smells like garbage in the Projects. Those people are filthy.

I don't care if it is cheaper there. He says, You don't have to worry. I'm not going to let anything happen to you. Don't make me cry, Michael. Joyce, I'm not going to let anything happen to you, he says. I told him I'd cry, but there's something wrong with my eyes.

Damn! Now that thread's broken. Where's Sam Hunt? Where's that weasel? Run the flag. Got a problem, he says. Pull this little string. I'll see your flag and respond. They can't be having girls run up and down the aisles looking for the weasel. That way if anything's missing or disturbed anyplace in the vicinity, we'll blame it on Betsy Ross's ghost, he says to me, and has equipped every sewing machine in the place with a little flag. If you have to go to the bathroom, raise the flag, take your purse, don't put it on the floor in the stall, because the weasel is not responsible for stolen or lost property.

Somebody should burn that man up.

There are instances where fires occur by spontaneous combustion, and instances where water will not put a fire out. There are oil slicks on the ocean. In dreams, too — there are people burning on the ocean or in impossible places, instances where burning oil floats on water and your clothes are on fire, and your hair is on fire, and in the water the fire goes inward. If it's dirty with oil and muck. Sometimes there's no way to put the fire out.

In such a dream, go into a well. Make it from rocks. The bottom of the well is very smooth, and the rocks are cool. Close your eyes. Put your cheek against a rock. If you're dizzy, reach your arm out. Touch the other side. Twirl in a circle. Put yourself in a blue well, and keep your eyes closed. Turn around and around until the fire stops.

"Joyce? What is it?"

"My thread broke."

"Your thread broke? Do you remember how I showed you to reload your thread? Did you try that? Here. Show me. Remember? Here now, you hook it around this wire first. Remember. Okay, good. That's right. Yes. Down the pole, into the needle. You pull that back or it's going to know when you begin to sew. Good. Very good. See? That wasn't so hard. Was it?

"How you doing? You getting along okay? You getting to know people?"

"Yes."

"Let's see what you've done today. No, now you're holding your

material too tightly. That's what'll give you the tangled stitches.
Remember how I told you to roll it under the foot — just like it's
a rolling pin and you're making pie crusts. Remember? You
bake, Joyce? Just roll it under the foot with a nice, steady movement."

"Yes, I bake."

"No, now this one's not going to work. See, you've got the X in
the corner. You can't overshoot the pattern or you'll have a little
X. See? And here's another one.

"Joyce, where are the rest of them? I counted sixty pockets out
for you this morning. Now I count — let's see — where're the rest
of them?"

"That's all you gave me."

"No. This morning I counted out sixty, and now there are —
they can't just disappear. Let's see. Forty-eight . . .

"This your third day? You're not picking this up, are you? Maybe
we should transfer you to pant legs. There aren't as many angles.
Come and talk with me when your shift's over."

"I can't. I'll miss my bus."

"Catch the next bus. Come and talk to me. We'll take a look at
your file. See what we can do."

I can do this.

This is a cinch. Go forward and backward to lock in the stitch.
Be careful not to overshoot the pattern — be careful not to overshoot the pattern because that's when the X occurs. You can't rip
it out because the buying customer will see where the ripping
occurred. Now that's ruined. Put it in your purse.

Here's the rest of them. These are ruined. I forgot about these
in my purse.

Forgetting is not lying. I'll say, I didn't lie. I forgot, and that's
the truth.

What's she smiling at? What's so funny about that pocket? That's
a hilarious pocket. These women will laugh behind your back.
They listen in on every conversation and then they laugh behind
your back. Well, fuck them.

I can do this. So let them laugh. You go forward and backward.
Every system has its routine. In a house when you live alone, you
check the rock by the front door when you come home to see if
it's been moved in your absence. If it's been moved, someone has

gone into your house. This is just real funny. I'd like to squash her pea brain. Now that's ruined.

Check the rock and you check for broken windows before you unlock the door, and you keep your gun in the drawer by your bed. I'm going to tell him to give me another chance. This wasn't so good today, but tomorrow's a different story. My brain's ruined for this day. That's a sad thing how a woman will just laugh in your face like that. They think they're so hot.

You keep your gun in the drawer by your bed. If, at three in the morning, some person breaks in your house, you take the phone off the hook, dial O. You don't have time to dial 911. You've got your gun and you're kneeling in bed or on the floor, and you say, I'm fully proficient in the use of semi-automatic weapons. I live at One One-Three Four East Holly. You're saying this to the operator who will call the cops.

Say, "I am proficient in the use of semi-automatic weapons —"
"What?"
"What are you looking at?"
"What did you say?"
"I didn't say anything."
"Yes, you did."
"What are you looking at?"
"Hey, don't worry about it. Don't sweat it. Sam's okay. Gets a bee in his lugudimous maximus every now and again, but he's O.K."
"They're going to fire me from this job."
"Nah, they ain't going to fire you."
"He's going to look at my file."
"Listen —"
"They look at your file, and then they look at you."
"You've got to —"
"Don't look at me."
"Now, honey —"
"Don't look at me! Don't look at my face."
Don't look anywhere.

They open your files and then they fire you. Everything is ruined now. So who cares.

These are ruined. I ruined these. Meaning to or not doesn't count. Did you or didn't you? Did you or didn't you? he'll say. He'll call me on the phone. Did you or did you not? Michael will say. I'll say —

When Michael calls —

I'll say, I didn't get to these yet. These were misplaced, I'll say. I'll say, I forgot about these in my purse.

This place is filthy. Somebody ought to clean this place up.

You just do your work. You just pay attention.

I'll leave my coat in the locker. I'll sneak out the back way, and I'll leave my coat in the locker.

I'll say, These are my practice days, Mr. Hunt. I can do this.

I'll sneak out the back way.

I'll catch the Sandy Street bus. If I miss the Sandy Street, I'll catch the Burnside. I won't look at the bums sleeping there. When I walk across the bridge, across the Burnside Bridge — if they ask me for money, I'll look straight ahead.

When Michael calls to ask me how it went — If my brother calls —

I'll say, Not too bad. That's what I'll say.

He'll say, Way to go, Joyce. That's money in the bank.

For dinner, I'll make mashed potatoes or I'll make rice. I'll sit at the table by the kitchen window. I'll watch the sun go down.

I will set my alarm for six so I can catch the Sandy Street bus at seven, because the Burnside bus will get me here too late. Sam Hunt sees to the time cards. Don't be late or you're docked pockets, and these add up.

I will set the alarm for six and I'll go to bed at ten. If I wake up in the night — if a dream or nightmare wakes me. I must not wake up in the night. A working girl needs her sleep.

ALICE ELLIOTT DARK

In the Gloaming

FROM THE NEW YORKER

HER SON WANTED to talk again, suddenly. During the days, he still brooded, scowling at the swimming pool from the vantage point of his wheelchair, where he sat covered with blankets despite the summer heat. In the evenings, though, Laird became more like his old self — his *old* old self, really. He became sweeter, the way he'd been as a child, before he began to cloak himself with layers of irony and clever remarks. He spoke with an openness that astonished her. No one she knew talked that way — no man, at least. After he was asleep, Janet would run through the conversations in her mind, and realize what it was she wished she had said. She knew she was generally considered sincere, but that had more to do with her being a good listener than with how she expressed herself. She found it hard work to keep up with him, but it was the work she had pined for all her life.

A month earlier, after a particularly long and grueling visit with a friend who'd come up on the train from New York, Laird had declared a new policy: no visitors, no telephone calls. She didn't blame him. People who hadn't seen him for a while were often shocked to tears by his appearance, and, rather than having them cheer him up, he felt obliged to comfort them. She'd overheard bits of some of those conversations. The final one was no worse than the others, but he was fed up. He had said more than once that he wasn't cut out to be the brave one, the one who would inspire everybody to walk away from a visit with him feeling uplifted, shaking their heads in wonder. He had liked being the most handsome and missed it very much; he was not a good victim.

When he had had enough he went into a self-imposed retreat, complete with a wall of silence and other ascetic practices that kept him busy for several weeks.

Then he softened. Not only did he want to talk again; he wanted to talk to *her.*

It began the night they ate outside on the terrace for the first time all summer. Afterward, Martin — Laird's father — got up to make a telephone call, but Janet stayed in her wicker chair, resting before clearing the table. It was one of those moments when she felt nostalgic for cigarettes. On nights like this, when the air was completely still, she used to blow her famous smoke rings for the children, dutifully obeying their commands to blow one through another or three in a row, or to make big, ropy circles that expanded as they floated up to the heavens. She did exactly what they wanted, for as long as they wanted, sometimes going through a quarter of a pack before they allowed her to stop. Incredibly, neither Anne nor Laird became smokers. Just the opposite; they nagged at her to quit, and were pleased when she finally did. She wished they had been just a little bit sorry; it was a part of their childhood coming to an end, after all.

Out of habit, she took note of the first lightning bug, the first star. The lawn darkened, and the flowers that had sulked in the heat all day suddenly released their perfumes. She laid her head back on the rim of the chair and closed her eyes. Soon she was following Laird's breathing, and found herself picking up the vital rhythms, breathing along. It was so peaceful, being near him like this. How many mothers spend so much time with their thirty-three-year-old sons? she thought. She had as much of him now as she had had when he was an infant; more, in a way, because she had the memory of the intervening years as well, to round out her thoughts about him. When they sat quietly together she felt as close to him as she ever had. It was still him in there, inside the failing shell. *She still enjoyed him.*

"The gloaming," he said, suddenly.

She nodded dreamily, automatically, then sat up. She turned to him. "What?" Although she had heard.

"I remember when I was little you took me over to the picture window and told me that in Scotland this time of day was called the 'gloaming.'"

Her skin tingled. She cleared her throat, quietly, taking care not to make too much of an event of his talking again. "You thought I said 'gloomy.'"

He gave a smile, then looked at her searchingly. "I always thought it hurt you somehow that the day was over, but you said it was a beautiful time because for a few moments the purple light made the whole world look like the Scottish Highlands on a summer night."

"Yes. As if all the earth were covered with heather."

"I'm sorry I never saw Scotland," he said.

"You're a Scottish lad nonetheless," she said. "At least on my side." She remembered offering to take him to Scotland once, but Laird hadn't been interested. By then, he was in college and already sure of his own destinations, which had diverged so thoroughly from hers. "I'm amazed you remember that conversation. You couldn't have been more than seven."

"I've been remembering a lot lately."

"Have you?"

"Mostly about when I was very small. I suppose it comes from having you take care of me again. Sometimes, when I wake up and see your face, I feel I can remember you looking in on me when I was in my crib. I remember your dresses."

"Oh, no!" She laughed lightly.

"You always had the loveliest expressions," he said.

She was astonished, caught off guard. Then, she had a memory, too — of her leaning over Laird's crib and suddenly having a picture of looking up at her own mother. "I know what you mean," she said.

"You do, don't you?"

He looked at her in a close, intimate way that made her self-conscious. She caught herself swinging her leg nervously, like a pendulum, and stopped.

"Mom," he said. "There are still a few things I need to do. I have to write a will, for one thing."

Her heart went flat. In his presence she had always maintained that he would get well. She wasn't sure she could discuss the other possibility.

"Thank you," he said.

"For what?"

"For not saying that there's plenty of time for that, or some similar sentiment."

"The only reason I didn't say it was to avoid the cliché, not because I don't believe it."

"You believe there is plenty of time?"

She hesitated; he noticed, and leaned forward slightly. "I believe there is time," she said.

"Even if I were healthy, it would be a good idea."

"I suppose."

"I don't want to leave it until it's too late. You wouldn't want me to suddenly leave everything to the nurses, would you?"

She laughed, pleased to hear him joking again. "All right, all right, I'll call the lawyer."

"That would be great." There was a pause. "Is this still your favorite time of day, Mom?"

"Yes, I suppose it is," she said, "although I don't think in terms of favorites anymore."

"Never mind favorites, then. What else do you like?"

"What do you mean?" she asked.

"I mean exactly that."

"I don't know. I care about all the ordinary things. You know what I like."

"Name one thing."

"I feel silly."

"Please?"

"All right. I like my patch of lilies of the valley under the trees over there. Now can we change the subject?"

"Name one more thing."

"Why?"

"I want to get to know you."

"Oh, Laird, there's nothing to know."

"I don't believe that for a minute."

"But it's true. I'm average. The only extraordinary thing about me is my children."

"All right," he said. "Then let's talk about how you feel about me."

"Do you flirt with your nurses like this when I'm not around?"

"I don't dare. They've got me where they want me." He looked at her. "You're changing the subject."

She smoothed her skirt. "I know how you feel about church, but if you need to talk I'm sure the minister would be glad to come over. Or if you would rather have a doctor . . ."

He laughed.

"What?"

"That you still call psychiatrists 'doctors.'"

She shrugged.

"I don't need a professional, Ma." He laced his hands and pulled at them as he struggled for words.

"What can I do?" she asked.

He met her gaze. "You're where I come from. I need to know about you."

That night she lay awake, trying to think of how she could help, of what, aside from her time, she had to offer. She couldn't imagine.

She was anxious the next day when he was sullen again, but the next night, and on each succeeding night, the dusk worked its spell. She set dinner on the table outside, and afterward, when Martin had vanished into the maw of his study, she and Laird began to speak. The air around them seemed to crackle with the energy they were creating in their effort to know and be known. Were other people so close, she wondered. She never had been, not to anybody. Certainly she and Martin had never really connected, not soul to soul, and with her friends, no matter how loyal and reliable, she always had a sense of what she could do that would alienate them. Of course, her friends had the option of cutting her off, and Martin could always ask for a divorce, whereas Laird was a captive audience. Parents and children were all captive audiences to each other; in view of this, it was amazing how little comprehension there was of one another's stories. Everyone stopped paying attention so early on, thinking they had figured it all out. She recognized that she was as guilty of this as anyone. She was still surprised whenever she went over to her daughter's house and saw how neat she was; in her mind, Anne was still a sloppy teenager who threw sweaters into the corner of her closet and candy wrappers under her bed. It still surprised her that Laird wasn't interested in girls. He had been, hadn't he? She remembered lying awake listening for him to come home, hoping that he was smart enough to apply what he knew about the facts of life, to take precautions.

Now she had the chance to let go of these old notions. It wasn't
that she liked everything about Laird — there was much that remained foreign to her — but she wanted to know about all of it.
As she came to her senses every morning in the moment or two
after she awoke, she found herself aching with love and gratitude,
as if he were a small, perfect creature again and she could look
forward to a day of watching him grow. Quickly, she became greedy
for their evenings. She replaced her half-facetious, half-hopeful
reading of the horoscope in the daily newspaper with a new habit
of tracking the time the sun would set, and drew satisfaction from
seeing it come earlier as the summer waned; it meant she didn't
have to wait as long. She took to sleeping late, shortening the day
even more. It was ridiculous, she knew. She was behaving like a
girl with a crush, behaving absurdly. It was a feeling she had
thought she'd never have again, and now here it was. She im-
mersed herself in it, living her life for the twilight moment when
his eyes would begin to glow, the signal that he was stirring into
consciousness. Then her real day would begin.

"Dad ran off quickly," he said one night. She had been wondering when he would mention it.

"He had a phone call to make," she said automatically.

Laird looked directly into her eyes, his expression one of gentle
reproach. He was letting her know he had caught her in the central
lie of her life, which was that she understood Martin's obsession
with his work. She averted her gaze. The truth was that she had
never understood. Why couldn't he sit with her for half an hour
after dinner, or, if not with her, why not with his dying son?

She turned sharply to look at Laird. The word "dying" had
sounded so loudly in her mind that she wondered if she had
spoken it, but he showed no reaction. She wished she hadn't even
thought it. She tried to stick to good thoughts in his presence.
When she couldn't, and he had a bad night afterward, she blamed
herself, as her efficient memory dredged up all the books and
magazine articles she had read emphasizing the effect of psycho-
logical factors on the course of the disease. She didn't entirely
believe it, but she felt compelled to give the benefit of the doubt
to every theory that might help. It couldn't do any harm to think
positively. And if it gave him a few more months . . .

"I don't think Dad can stand to be around me."

"That's not true." It was true.

"Poor Dad. He's always been a hypochondriac — we have that in common. He must hate this."

"He just wants you to get well."

"If that's what he wants, I'm afraid I'm going to disappoint him again. At least this will be the last time I let him down."

He said this merrily, with the old, familiar light darting from his eyes. She allowed herself to be amused. He had always been fond of teasing, and held no subject sacred. As the de facto authority figure in the house — Martin hadn't been home enough to be the real disciplinarian — she had often been forced to reprimand Laird, but, in truth, she shared his sense of humor. She responded to it now by leaning over to cuff him on the arm. It was an automatic response, prompted by a burst of high spirits that took no notice of the circumstances. It was a mistake. Even through the thickness of his terrycloth robe, her knuckles knocked on bone. There was nothing left of him.

"It's his loss," she said, the shock of Laird's thinness making her serious again. It was the furthest she would go in criticizing Martin. She had always felt it her duty to maintain a benign image of him for the children. He had become a character of her invention, with a whole range of postulated emotions whereby he missed them when he was away on a business trip and thought of them every few minutes when he had to work late. Some years earlier, when she was secretly seeing a doctor — a psychiatrist — she had finally admitted to herself that Martin was never going to be the lover she had dreamed of. He was an ambitious, competitive, self-absorbed man who probably should never have got married. It was such a relief to be able to face it that she wanted to share the news with her children, only to discover that they were dependent on the myth. They could hate his work, but they could not bring themselves to believe he had any choice in the matter. She had dropped the subject.

"Thank you, Ma. It's his loss in your case, too."

A throbbing began behind her eyes, angering her. The last thing she wanted to do was cry. There would be plenty of time for that. "It's not all his fault," she said when she had regained some measure of control. "I'm not very good at talking about myself. I was brought up not to."

"So was I," he said.

"Yes, I suppose you were."

"Luckily, I didn't pay any attention." He grinned.

"I hope not," she said, and meant it. "Can I get you anything?"

"A new immune system?"

She rolled her eyes, trying to disguise the way his joke had touched on her prayers. "Very funny. I was thinking more along the lines of an iced tea or an extra blanket."

"I'm fine. I'm getting tired, actually."

Her entire body went on the alert, and she searched his face anxiously for signs of deterioration. Her nerves darted and pricked whenever he wanted anything; her adrenaline rushed. The fight-or-flight response, she supposed. She had often wanted to flee, but had forced herself to stay, to fight with what few weapons she had. She responded to his needs, making sure there was a fresh, clean set of sheets ready when he was tired, food when he was hungry. It was what she could do.

"Shall I get a nurse?" She pushed her chair back from the table.

"O.K.," Laird said weakly. He stretched out his hand to her, and the incipient moonlight illuminated his skin so it shone like alabaster. His face had turned ashy. It was a sight that made her stomach drop. She ran for Maggie, and by the time they returned Laird's eyes were closed, his head lolling to one side. Automatically, Janet looked for a stirring in his chest. There it was: his shoulders expanded; he still breathed. Always, in the second before she saw movement, she became cold and clinical as she braced herself for the possibility of discovering that he was dead.

Maggie had her fingers on his wrist and was counting his pulse against the second hand on her watch, her lips moving. She laid his limp hand back on his lap. "Fast," she pronounced.

"I'm not surprised," Janet said, masking her fear with authority. "We had a long talk."

Maggie frowned. "Now I'll have to wake him up again for his meds."

"Yes, I suppose that's true. I forgot about that."

Janet wheeled him into his makeshift room downstairs and helped Maggie lift him into the rented hospital bed. Although he weighed almost nothing, it was really a job for two; his weight was dead weight. In front of Maggie, she was all brusque efficiency, except for the moment when her fingers strayed to touch Laird's pale cheek and she prayed she hadn't done any harm.

*

"Who's your favorite author?" he asked one night.

"Oh, there are so many," she said.

"Your real favorite."

She thought. "The truth is there are certain subjects I find attractive more than certain authors. I seem to read in cycles, to fulfill an emotional yearning."

"Such as?"

"Books about people who go off to live in Africa or Australia or the South Seas."

He laughed. "That's fairly self-explanatory. What else?"

"When I really hate life I enjoy books about real murders. 'True crime,' I think they're called now. They're very punishing."

"Is that what's so compelling about them? I could never figure it out. I just know that at certain times I loved the gore, even though I felt absolutely disgusted with myself for being interested in it."

"You need to think about when those times were. That will tell you a lot." She paused. "I don't like reading about sex."

"Big surprise!"

"No, no," she said. "It's not for the reason you think, or not only for that reason. You see me as a prude, I know, but remember, it's part of a mother's job to come across that way. Although perhaps I went a bit far . . ."

He shrugged amiably. "Water under the bridge. But go on about sex."

"I think it should be private. I always feel as though these writers are showing off when they describe a sex scene. They're not really trying to describe sex, but to demonstrate that they're not afraid to write about it. As if they're thumbing their noses at their mothers."

He made a moue.

Janet went on. "You don't think there's an element of that? I *do* question their motives, because I don't think sex can ever actually be portrayed — the sensations and the emotions are . . . beyond language. If you only describe the mechanics, the effect is either clinical or pornographic, and if you try to describe intimacy instead, you wind up with abstractions. The only sex you could describe fairly well is bad sex — and who wants to read about that, for God's sake, when everyone is having bad sex of their own?"

"Mother!" He was laughing helplessly, his arms hanging limply over the sides of his chair.

"I mean it. To me it's like reading about someone using the bathroom."

"Good grief!"

"Now who's the prude?"

"I never said I wasn't," he said. "Maybe we should change the subject."

She looked out across the land. The lights were on in other people's houses, giving the evening the look of early fall. The leaves were different, too, becoming droopy. The grass was dry, even with all the watering and tending from the gardener. The summer was nearly over.

"Maybe we shouldn't," she said. "I've been wondering. Was that side of life satisfying for you?"

"Ma, tell me you're not asking me about my sex life."

She took her napkin and folded it carefully, lining up the edges and running her fingers along the hems. She felt very calm, very pulled together and all of a piece, as if she'd finally got the knack of being a dignified woman. She threaded her fingers and laid her hands in her lap. "I'm asking about your love life," she said. "Did you love, and were you loved in return?"

"Yes."

"I'm glad."

"That was easy," he said.

"Oh, I've gotten very easy, in my old age."

"Does Dad know about this?" His eyes were twinkling wickedly.

"Don't be fresh," she said.

"You started it."

"Then I'm stopping it. Now."

He made a funny face, and then another, until she could no longer keep from smiling. His routine carried her back to memories of his childhood efforts to charm her: watercolors of her favorite vistas (unrecognizable without the captions), bouquets of violets self-consciously flung into her lap, chores performed without prompting. He had always gone too far, then backtracked to regain even footing. She had always allowed herself to be wooed.

Suddenly she realized: Laird had been the love of her life.

One night it rained hard. Janet decided to serve the meal in the kitchen, since Martin was out. They ate in silence; she was freed from the compulsion to keep up the steady stream of chatter that she used to affect when Laird hadn't talked at all; now she knew she could save her words for afterward. He ate nothing but comfort foods lately: mashed potatoes, vanilla ice cream, rice pudding. The days of his strict macrobiotic regime, and all the cooking classes she had taken in order to help him along with it, were past. His body was essentially a thing of the past, too; when he ate, he was feeding what was left of his mind. He seemed to want to recapture the cosseted feeling he'd had when he'd been sick as a child and she would serve him flat ginger ale, and toast soaked in cream, and play endless card games with him, using his blanket-covered legs as a table. In those days, too, there'd been a general sense of giving way to illness: then, he let himself go completely because he knew he would soon be better and active and have a million things expected of him again. Now he let himself go because he had fought long enough.

Finally, he pushed his bowl toward the middle of the table, signaling that he was finished. (His table manners had gone to pieces. Who cared?) She felt a light, jittery excitement, the same jazzy feeling she got when she was in a plane that was picking up speed on the runway. She arranged her fork and knife on the rim of her plate and pulled her chair in closer. "I had an odd dream last night," she said.

His eyes remained dull.

She waited uncertainly, thinking that perhaps she had started to talk too soon. "Would you like something else to eat?"

He shook his head. There was no will in his expression; his refusal was purely physical, a gesture coming from the satiation in his stomach. An animal walking away from its bowl, she thought.

To pass the time, she carried the dishes to the sink, gave them a good hot rinse, and put them in the dishwasher. She carried the ice cream to the counter, pulled a spoon from the drawer and scraped off a mouthful of the thick, creamy residue that stuck to the inside of the lid. She ate it without thinking, so the sudden sweetness caught her by surprise. All the while she kept track of Laird, but every time she thought she noticed signs of his readiness to talk and hurried back to the table, she found his face still blank.

She went to the window. The lawn had become a floodplain and was filled with broad pools; the branches of the evergreens sagged, and the sky was the same uniform grayish yellow it had been since morning. She saw him focus his gaze on the line where the treetops touched the heavens, and she understood. There was no lovely interlude on this rainy night, no heathered dusk. The gray landscape had taken the light out of him.

"I'm sorry," she said aloud, as if it were her fault.

He gave a tiny, helpless shrug.

She hovered for a few moments, hoping, but his face was slack, and she gave up. She felt utterly forsaken, too disappointed and agitated to sit with him and watch the rain. "It's all right," she said. "It's a good night to watch television."

She wheeled him to the den and left him with Maggie, then did not know what to do with herself. She had no contingency plan for this time. It was usually the one period of the day when she did not need the anesthesia of tennis games, bridge lessons, volunteer work, errands. She had not considered the present possibility. For some time, she hadn't given any thought to what Martin would call "the big picture." Her conversations with Laird had lulled her into inventing a parallel big picture of her own. She realized that a part of her had worked out a whole scenario: the summer evenings would blend into fall; then, gradually, the winter would arrive, heralding chats by the fire, Laird resting his feet on the pigskin ottoman in the den while she dutifully knitted her yearly Christmas sweaters for Anne's children.

She had allowed herself to imagine a future. That had been her mistake. This silent, endless evening was her punishment, a reminder of how things really were.

She did not know where to go in her own house, and ended up wandering through the rooms, propelled by a vague, hunted feeling. Several times, she turned around, expecting someone to be there, but, of course, no one ever was. She was quite alone. Eventually, she realized that she was imagining a person in order to give material properties to the source of her wounds. She was inventing a villain. There should be a villain, shouldn't there? There should be an enemy, a devil, an evil force that could be driven out. Her imagination had provided it with aspects of a corporeal presence so she could pretend, for a moment, that there was a real enemy hovering around her, someone she could have the police come and take away. But the enemy was part of Laird, and neither he nor she nor any of the doctors or experts or ministers could separate the two.

She went upstairs and took a shower. She barely paid attention to her own body anymore, and only noticed abstractly that the water was too hot, her skin turning pink. Afterward, she sat on the chaise longue in her bedroom and tried to read. She heard something; she leaned forward and cocked her head toward the sound. Was that Laird's voice? Suddenly she believed that he had begun to talk after all — she believed he was talking to Maggie. She dressed and went downstairs. He was alone in the den, alone with the television. He didn't hear or see her. She watched him take a drink from a cup, his hand shaking badly. It was a plastic cup with a straw poking through the lid, the kind used by small children while they are learning to drink. It was supposed to prevent accidents, but it couldn't stop his hands from trembling. He managed to spill the juice anyway.

Laird had always coveted the decadent pile of cashmere lap blankets she had collected over the years in the duty-free shops of the various British airports. Now he wore one around his shoulders, one over his knees. She remembered similar balmy nights when he would arrive home from soccer practice after dark, a towel slung around his neck.

"I suppose it has to be in the church," he said.

"I think it should," she said, "but it's up to you."

"I guess it's not the most timely moment to make a statement about my personal disbeliefs. But I'd like you to keep it from being too lugubrious. No lilies, for instance."

"God forbid."

"And have some decent music."

"Such as?"

"I had an idea, but now I can't remember."

He pressed his hands to his eyes. His fingers were so transparent that they looked as if he were holding them over a flashlight.

"Please buy a smashing dress, something mournful yet elegant."

"All right."

"And don't wait until the last minute."

She didn't reply.

Janet gave up on the idea of a rapprochement between Martin and Laird; she felt freer when she stopped hoping for it. Martin rarely came home for dinner anymore. Perhaps he was having an affair? It was a thought she'd never allowed herself to have before, but it didn't threaten her now. Good for him, she even decided, in her strongest, most magnanimous moments. Good for him if he's actually feeling bad and trying to do something to make himself feel better.

Anne was brave and chipper during her visits, yet when she walked back out to her car, she would wrap her arms around her ribs and shudder. "I don't know how you do it, Mom. Are you really all right?" she always asked, with genuine concern.

"Anne's become such a hopeless matron," Laird always said, with fond exasperation, when he and his mother were alone again later. Once, Janet began to tease him for finally coming to friendly terms with his sister, but she cut it short when she saw that he was blinking furiously.

They were exactly the children she had hoped to have: a companionable girl, a mischievous boy. It gave her great pleasure to see them together. She did not try to listen to their conversations but watched from a distance, usually from the kitchen as she prepared them a snack reminiscent of their childhood, like watermelon boats or lemonade. Then she would walk Anne to the car, their similar good shoes clacking across the gravel. They hugged, pressing each other's arms, and their brief embraces buoyed them up — forbearance and grace passing back and forth between them like a piece of shared clothing, designated for use by whoever needed it most. It was the kind of parting toward which she had aimed her whole life, a graceful, secure parting at the close of a peaceful afternoon. After Anne left, Janet always had a tranquil moment or two as she walked back to the house through the humid September air. Everything was so still. Occasionally there were the hums and clicks of a lawnmower or the shrieks of a band of children heading home from school. There were the insects and the birds. It was a straightforward, simple life she had chosen. She had tried never to ask for too much, and to be of use. Simplicity had been her hedge against bad luck. It had worked for so long. For a brief moment, as she stepped lightly up the single slate stair and through the door, her legs still harboring all their former vitality, she could pretend her luck was still holding.

Then she would glance out the window and there would be the heart-catching sight of Laird, who would never again drop by for a casual visit. Her chest would ache and flutter, a cave full of bats.

Perhaps she had asked for too much, after all.

"What did you want to be when you grew up?" Laird asked.

"I was expected to be a wife and mother. I accepted that. I wasn't a rebel."

"There must have been something else."

"No," she said. "Oh, I guess I had all the usual fantasies of the day, of being the next Amelia Earhart or Margaret Mead, but that was all they were — fantasies. I wasn't even close to being brave enough. Can you imagine me flying across the ocean on my own?" She laughed and looked over for his laughter, but he had fallen asleep.

A friend of Laird's had somehow got the mistaken information that Laird had died, so she and Martin received a condolence letter. There was a story about a time a few years back when the friend was with Laird on a bus in New York. They had been sitting behind two older women, waitresses who began to discuss their income taxes, trying to decide how much of their tip income to declare to sound realistic so they wouldn't attract an audit. Each woman offered up bits of folk wisdom on the subject, describing in detail her particular situation. During a lull in the conversation, Laird stood up.

"Excuse me, I couldn't help overhearing," he said, leaning over them. "May I have your names and addresses, please? I work for the IRS."

The entire bus fell silent as everyone watched to see what would happen next. Laird took a small notebook and pen from the inside pocket of his jacket. He faced his captive audience. "I'm part of a new IRS outreach program," he told the group. "For the next ten minutes I'll be taking confessions. Does anyone have anything he or she wants to tell me?"

Smiles. Soon the whole bus was talking, comparing notes — when they'd first realized he was kidding, and how scared they had been before they caught on. It was difficult to believe these were the same New Yorkers who were supposed to be so gruff and isolated.

"Laird was the most vital, funniest person I ever met," his friend wrote.

Now, in his wheelchair, he faced off against slow-moving flies, waving them away.

"The gloaming," Laird said.

Janet looked up from her knitting, startled. It was midafternoon, and the living room was filled with bright October sun. "Soon," she said.

He furrowed his brow. A little flash of confusion passed through his eyes, and she realized that for him it was already dark.

He tried to straighten his shawl, his hands shaking. She jumped up to help; then, when he pointed to the fireplace, she quickly laid the logs as she wondered what was wrong. Was he dehydrated? She thought she recalled that a dimming of vision was a sign of dehydration. She tried to remember what else she had read or heard, but even as she grasped for information, facts, her instincts kept interrupting with a deeper, more dreadful thought that vibrated through her, rattling her and making her gasp as she often did when remembering her mistakes, things she wished she hadn't said or done, wished she had the chance to do over. She knew what was wrong, and yet she kept turning away from the truth, her mind spinning in every other possible direction as she worked on the fire, only vaguely noticing how wildly she made the sparks fly as she pumped the old bellows.

Her work was mechanical — she had made hundreds of fires — and soon there was nothing left to do. She put the screen up and pushed him close, then leaned over to pull his flannel pajamas down to meet his socks, protecting his bare shins. The sun streamed in around him, making him appear trapped between bars of light. She resumed her knitting, with mechanical hands.

"The gloaming," he said again. It did sound somewhat like "gloomy," because his speech was slurred.

"When all the world is purple," she said, hearing herself sound falsely bright. She wasn't sure whether he wanted her to talk. It was some time since he had talked — not long, really, in other people's lives, perhaps two weeks — but she had gone on with their conversations, gradually expanding into the silence until she was telling him stories and he was listening. Sometimes, when his eyes closed, she trailed off and began to drift. There would be a pause that she didn't always realize she was making, but if it went on too long he would call out "Mom?" with an edge of panic in his voice, as if he were waking from a nightmare. Then she would resume, trying to create a seamless bridge between what she had been thinking and where she had left off.

"It was really your grandfather who gave me my love for the gloaming," she said. "Do you remember him talking about it?" She looked up politely, expectantly, as if Laird might offer her a conversational reply. He seemed to like hearing the sound of her voice, so she went on, her needles clicking. Afterward, she could never remember for sure at what point she had stopped talking and had floated off into a jumble of her own thoughts, afraid to move, afraid to look up, afraid to know at which exact moment she became alone. All she knew was that at a certain point the fire was in danger of dying out entirely, and when she got up to stir the embers she glanced at him in spite of herself and saw that his fingers were making knitting motions over his chest, the way people did as they were dying. She knew that if she went to get the nurse, Laird would be gone by the time she returned, so she went and stood behind him, leaning over to press her face against his, sliding her hands down his busy arms, helping him along with his fretful stitches until he finished this last piece of work.

Later, after the most pressing calls had been made and Laird's body had been taken away, Janet went up to his old room and lay down on one of the twin beds. She had changed the room into a guest room when he went off to college, replacing his things with guest room decor, thoughtful touches such as luggage racks at the foot of each bed, a writing desk stocked with paper and pens, heavy wooden hangers and shoe trees. She made an effort to remember the room as it had been when he was a little boy; she had chosen a train motif, then had to redecorate when Laird decided trains were silly. He had wanted it to look like a jungle, so she had hired an art student to paint a jungle mural on the walls. When he decided *that* was silly, he hadn't bothered her to do anything about it, but had simply marked time until he could move on.

Anne came over, offered to stay, but was relieved to be sent home to her children.

Presently, Martin came in. Janet was watching the trees turn to mere silhouettes against the darkening sky, fighting the urge to pick up a true-crime book, a debased urge. He lay down on the other bed.

"I'm sorry," he said.

"It's so wrong," she said angrily. She hadn't felt angry until that moment; she had saved it up for him. "A child shouldn't die before his parents. A young man shouldn't spend his early thirties wasting away talking to his mother. He should be out in the world. He shouldn't be thinking about me, or what I care about, or my opinions. He shouldn't have had to return my love to me — it was his to squander. Now I have it all back and I don't know what I'm supposed to do with it," she said.

She could hear Martin weeping in the darkness. He sobbed, and her anger veered away.

They were quiet for some time.

"Is there going to be a funeral?" Martin asked finally.

"Yes. We should start making the arrangements."

"I suppose he told you what he wanted."

"In general. He couldn't decide about the music."

She heard Martin roll onto his side, so that he was facing her across the narrow chasm between the beds. He was still in his office clothes. "I remember being very moved by the bagpipes at your father's funeral."

It was an awkward offering, to be sure, awkward and late, and seemed to come from someone on the periphery of her life who knew her only slightly. It didn't matter; it was perfectly right. Her heart rushed toward it.

"I think Laird would have liked that idea very much," she said.

It was the last moment of the gloaming, the last moment of the day her son died. In a breath, it would be night; the moon hovered behind the trees, already rising to claim the sky, and she told herself she might as well get on with it. She sat up and was running her toes across the bare floor, searching for her shoes, when Martin spoke again, in a tone she used to hear on those long-ago nights when he rarely got home until after the children were in bed and he relied on her to fill him in on what they'd done that day. It was the same curious, shy, deferential tone that had always made her feel as though all the frustrations and boredom and mistakes and rushes of feeling in her days as a mother did indeed add up to something of importance, and she decided that the next round of telephone calls could wait while she answered the question he asked her: "Please tell me — what else did my boy like?"

STUART DYBEK

We Didn't

FROM ANTAEUS

> We did it in front of the mirror
> And in the light. We did it in darkness,
> In water, and in the high grass.
> — *"We Did It," Yehuda Amichai*

WE DIDN'T in the light; we didn't in darkness. We didn't in the
fresh-cut summer grass or in the mounds of autumn leaves or on
the snow where moonlight threw down our shadows. We didn't in
your room on the canopy bed you slept in, the bed you'd slept in
as a child, or in the back seat of my father's rusted Rambler which
smelled of the smoked chubs and kielbasa that he delivered on
weekends from my Uncle Vincent's meat market. We didn't in your
mother's Buick Eight where a rosary twined the rearview mirror
like a beaded black snake with silver, cruciform fangs.

At the dead end of our lovers' lane — a side street of abandoned
factories — where I perfected the pinch that springs open a bra;
behind the lilac bushes in Marquette Park where you first touched
me through my jeans and your nipples, swollen against transparent
cotton, seemed the shade of lilacs; in the balcony of the now
defunct Clark Theater where I wiped popcorn salt from my palms
and slid them up your thighs and you whispered, "I feel like Doris
Day is watching us," we didn't.

How adept we were at fumbling, how perfectly mistimed our
timing, how utterly we confused energy with ecstasy.

Remember that night becalmed by heat, and the two of us, fused
by sweat, trembling as if a wind from outer space that only we could

feel was gusting across Oak Street Beach? Wound in your faded Navajo blanket, we lay soul kissing until you wept with wanting.

We'd been kissing all day — all summer — kisses tasting of different shades of lip gloss and too many Cokes. The lake had turned hot pink, rose rapture, pearl amethyst with dusk, then washed in night black with a ruff of silver foam. Beyond a momentary horizon, silent bolts of heat lightning throbbed, perhaps setting barns on fire somewhere in Indiana. The beach that had been so crowded was deserted as if there was a curfew. Only the bodies of lovers remained behind, visible in lightning flashes, scattered like the fallen on a battlefield, a few of them moaning, waiting for the gulls to pick them clean.

On my fingers your slick scent mixed with the coconut musk of the suntan lotion we'd repeatedly smeared over one another's bodies. When your bikini top fell away, my hands caught your breasts, memorizing their delicate weight, my palms cupped as if bringing water to parched lips.

Along the Gold Coast, high-rises began to glow, window added to window, against the dark. In every lighted bedroom, couples home from work were stripping off their business suits, falling to the bed, and doing it. They did it before mirrors and pressed against the glass in streaming shower stalls, they did it against walls and on the furniture in ways that required previously unimagined gymnastics which they invented on the spot. They did it in honor of man and woman, in honor of beast, in honor of God. They did it because they'd been released, because they were home free, alive, and private, because they couldn't wait any longer, couldn't wait for the appointed hour, for the right time or temperature, couldn't wait for the future, for messiahs, for peace on earth and justice for all. They did it because of the Bomb, because of pollution, because of the Four Horsemen of the Apocalypse, because extinction might be just a blink away. They did it because it was Friday night. It was Friday night and somewhere delirious music was playing — flutter-tongued flutes, muted trumpets meowing like tomcats in heat, feverish plucking and twanging, tom-toms, congas, and gongs all pounding the same pulsebeat.

I stripped your bikini bottom down the skinny rails of your legs and you tugged my swimsuit past my tan. Swimsuits at our ankles, we kicked like swimmers to free our legs, almost expecting a tide to wash over us the way the tide rushes in on Burt Lancaster and Deborah Kerr in their famous love scene on the beach in *From Here to Eternity* — a scene so famous that although neither of us had seen the movie, our bodies assumed the exact position of movie stars on the sand and you whispered to me softly, "I'm afraid of getting pregnant," and I whispered back, "Don't worry, I have protection," then, still kissing you, felt for my discarded cutoffs and the wallet in which for the last several months I had carried a Trojan as if it was a talisman. Still kissing, I tore its flattened, dried-out wrapper and it sprang through my fingers like a spring from a clock and dropped to the sand between our legs. My hands were shaking. In a panic, I groped for it, found it, tried to dust it off, tried, as Burt Lancaster never had to, to slip it on without breaking the mood, felt the grains of sand inside it, a throb of lightning, and the Great Lake behind us became, for all practical purposes, the Pacific and your skin tasted of salt and to the insistent question that my hips were asking, your body answered yes, your thighs opened like wings from my waist as we surfaced panting from a kiss that left you pleading *oh Christ yes,* a yes gasped sharply as a cry of pain so that for a moment I thought that we *were* already doing it and that somehow I had missed the instant when I entered you, entered you in the bloodless way in which a young man discards his own virginity, entered you as if passing through a gateway into the rest of my life, into a life as I wanted it to be lived *yes* but O then I realized that we were still floundering unconnected in the slick between us and there was sand in the Trojan as we slammed together still feeling for that perfect fit, still in the *Here* groping for an *Eternity* that was only a fine adjustment away, just a millimeter to the left or a fraction of an inch further south though with all the adjusting the sandy Trojan was slipping off and then it was gone but yes you kept repeating although your head was shaking no-not-quite-almost and our hearts were going like mad and you said yes Yes wait . . . Stop!

"What?" I asked, still futilely thrusting as if I hadn't quite heard you.

"Oh, God!" you gasped, pushing yourself up. "What's coming?"

"Julie, what's the matter?" I asked, confused, and then the beam of a spotlight swept over us and I glanced into its blinding eye.

All around us lights were coming, speeding across the sand.

Blinking blindness away, I rolled from your body to my knees, feeling utterly defenseless in the way that only nakedness can leave one feeling. Headlights bounded toward us, spotlights crisscrossing, blue dome lights revolving as squad cars converged. I could see other lovers, caught in the beams, fleeing bare-assed through the litter of garbage that daytime hordes had left behind and that night had deceptively concealed. You were crying, clutching the Navajo blanket to your breasts with one hand and clawing for your bikini with the other, and I was trying to calm your terror with reassuring phrases such as, "Holy shit! I don't fucking believe this!"

Swerving and fishtailing in the sand, police calls pouring from their radios, the squad cars were on us, and then they were by us while we sat struggling on our clothes.

They braked at the water's edge, and cops slammed out brandishing huge flashlights, their beams deflecting over the dark water. Beyond the darting of those beams, the far-off throbs of lightning seemed faint by comparison.

"Over there, goddamn it!" one of them hollered, and two cops sloshed out into the shallow water without even pausing to kick off their shoes, huffing aloud for breath, their leather cartridge belts creaking against their bellies.

"Grab the son of a bitch! It ain't gonna bite!" one of them yelled, then they came sloshing back to shore with a body slung between them.

It was a woman — young, naked, her body limp and bluish beneath the play of flashlight beams. They set her on the sand just past the ring of drying, washed-up alewives. Her face was almost totally concealed by her hair. Her hair was brown and tangled in a way that even wind or sleep can't tangle hair, tangled as if it had absorbed the ripples of water — thick strands, slimy-looking like dead seaweed.

"She's been in there a while, that's for sure," a cop with a beer belly said to a younger, crew-cut cop who had knelt beside the body and removed his hat as if he might be considering the kiss of life.

The crew-cut officer brushed the hair away from her face and the flashlight beams settled there. Her eyes were closed. A bruise or a birthmark stained the side of one eye. Her features appeared swollen — her lower lip protruding as if she was pouting.

An ambulance siren echoed across the sand, its revolving red light rapidly approaching.

"Might as well take their sweet-ass time," the beer-bellied cop said.

We had joined the circle of police surrounding the drowned woman almost without realizing that we had. You were back in your bikini, robed in the Navajo blanket, and I had slipped on my cutoffs, my underwear still dangling out of a back pocket.

Their flashlight beams explored her body, causing its whiteness to gleam. Her breasts were floppy; her nipples looked shriveled. Her belly appeared inflated by gallons of water. For a moment, a beam focused on her mound of pubic hair which was overlapped by the swell of her belly, and then moved almost shyly away down her legs, and the cops all glanced at us — at you, especially — above their lights, and you hugged your blanket closer as if they might confiscate it as evidence or to use as a shroud.

When the ambulance pulled up, one of the black attendants immediately put a stethoscope to the drowned woman's swollen belly and announced, "Drowned the baby, too."

Without saying anything, we turned from the group, as unconsciously as we'd joined them, and walked off across the sand, stopping only long enough at the spot where we had lain together like lovers in order to stuff the rest of our gear into a beach bag, to gather our shoes, and for me to find my wallet and kick sand over the forlorn, deflated-looking Trojan that you pretended not to notice. I was grateful for that.

Behind us, the police were snapping photos, flashbulbs throbbing like lightning flashes, and the lightning itself still distant but moving in closer, thunder rumbling audibly now, driving a lake wind before it so that gusts of sand tingled against the metal sides of the ambulance.

Squinting, we walked toward the lighted windows of the Gold Coast, while the shadows of gapers attracted by the whirling emergency lights hurried past up toward the shore.

"What happened? What's going on?" they asked us as they passed without waiting for an answer, and we didn't offer one, just continued walking silently in the dark.

It was only later that we talked about it, and once we began talking about the drowned woman it seemed we couldn't stop.

"She was pregnant," you said. "I mean I don't want to sound morbid, but I can't help thinking how the whole time we were, we almost — you know — there was this poor dead woman and her unborn child washing in and out behind us."

"It's not like we could have done anything for her even if we had known she was there."

"But what if we *had* found her? What if after we had — you know," you said, your eyes glancing away from mine and your voice tailing into a whisper, "what if after we did it, we went for a night swim and found her in the water?"

"But, Jules, we didn't," I tried to reason, though it was no more a matter of reason than anything else between us had ever been.

It began to seem as if each time we went somewhere to make out — on the back porch of your half-deaf, whiskery Italian grandmother who sat in the front of the apartment cackling before *I Love Lucy* reruns; or in your girlfriend Ginny's basement rec room when her parents were away on bowling league nights and Ginny was upstairs with her current crush, Brad; or way off in the burbs, at the Giant Twin Drive-In during the weekend they called Elvis Fest — the drowned woman was with us.

We would kiss, your mouth would open, and when your tongue flicked repeatedly after mine, I would unbutton the first button of your blouse, revealing the beauty spot at the base of your throat which matched a smaller spot I loved above a corner of your lips, and then the second button that opened on a delicate gold cross — that I had always tried to regard as merely a fashion statement — dangling above the cleft of your breasts. The third button exposed the lacy swell of your bra, and I would slide my hand over the patterned mesh, feeling for the firmness of your nipple rising to my fingertip, but you would pull slightly away, and behind your rapid breath your kiss would grow distant, and I would kiss harder trying to lure you back from wherever you had gone, and finally, holding you as if only consoling a friend, I'd ask, "What are you thinking?" although, of course, I knew.

"I don't want to think about her but I can't help it. I mean it seems like some kind of weird omen or something, you know?"

"No, I don't know," I said. "It was just a coincidence."

"Maybe if she'd been further away down the beach, but she was so close to us. A good wave could have washed her up right beside us."

"Great, then we could have had a *ménage à trois.*"

"Gross! I don't believe you just said that! Just because you said it in French doesn't make it less disgusting."

"You're driving me to it. Come on, Jules, I'm sorry," I said, "I was just making a dumb joke to get a little different perspective on things."

"What's so goddamn funny about a woman who drowned herself and her baby?"

"We don't even know for sure she did."

"Yeah, right, it was just an accident. Like she just happened to be going for a walk pregnant and naked, and she fell in."

"She could have been on a sailboat or something. Accidents happen; so do murders."

"Oh, like murder makes it less horrible? Don't think that hasn't occurred to me. Maybe the bastard who knocked her up killed her, huh?"

"How should I know? You're the one who says you don't want to talk about it and then gets obsessed with all kinds of theories and scenarios. Why are we arguing about a woman we don't even know, who doesn't have the slightest thing to do with us?"

"I *do* know about her," you said. "I dream about her."

"You dream about her?" I repeated, surprised. "Dreams you remember?"

"Sometimes they wake me up. Like I dreamed I was at my nonna's cottage in Michigan. Off her beach they've got a raft for swimming and in my dream I'm swimming out to it, but it keeps drifting further away until it's way out on the water and I'm so tired that if I don't get to it I'm going to drown. Then, I notice there's a naked person sunning on it and I start yelling, 'Help!' and she looks up, brushes her hair out of her face, and offers me a hand, but I'm too afraid to take it even though I'm drowning because it's her."

"God! Jules, that's creepy."

"I dreamed you and I were at the beach and you bring us a couple hot dogs but forget the mustard, so you have to go all the way back to the stand for it."

"Hot dogs, no mustard — a little too Freudian, isn't it?"

"Honest to God, I dreamed it. You go off for mustard and I'm wondering why you're gone so long, then a woman screams a kid has drowned and immediately the entire crowd stampedes for the water and sweeps me along with it. It's like one time when I was little and got lost at the beach, wandering in a panic through this forest of hairy legs and pouchy crotches, crying for my mother.

Anyway, I'm carried into the water by the mob and forced under, and I think, this is it, I'm going to drown, but I'm able to hold my breath longer than could ever be possible. It feels like a fly- ing dream — flying under water — and then I see this baby down there flying, too, and realize it's the kid everyone thinks has drowned, but he's no more drowned than I am. He looks like Cupid or one of those baby angels that cluster around the face of God."

"Pretty weird. What do you think it means? Something to do with drowning maybe, or panic?"

"It means the baby who drowned inside her that night was a love child — a boy — and his soul was released there to wander through the water."

"You really believe that?"

We argued about the interpretation of dreams, about whether dreams were symbolic or psychic, prophetic or just plain nonsense, until you said, "Look, you can believe what you want about your dreams, but keep your nose out of mine, O.K.?"

We argued about the drowned woman, about whether her death was a suicide or a murder, about whether her appearance that night was an omen or a coincidence, which, you argued, is what an omen is anyway: a coincidence that means something. By the end of summer, even if we were no longer arguing about the woman, we had acquired the habit of arguing about everything else. What was better: dogs or cats, rock or jazz, Cubs or Sox, tacos or egg rolls, right or left, night or day — we could argue about anything.

It no longer required arguing or necking to summon the drowned woman; everywhere we went she surfaced by her own volition: at Rocky's Italian Beef, at Lindo Mexico, at the House of Dong, our favorite Chinese restaurant, a place we still frequented because they had let us sit and talk until late over tiny cups of jasmine tea and broken fortune cookies earlier in the year, when it was winter and we had first started going together. We would always kid about going there. "Are you in the mood for Dong tonight?" I'd ask. It was a dopey joke, and you'd break up at its repeated dopiness. Back then, in winter, if one of us ordered the garlic shrimp, we would both be sure to eat them so that later our mouths tasted the same when we kissed.

Even when she wasn't mentioned, she was there with her drowned body — so dumpy next to yours — and her sad breasts with their wrinkled nipples and sour milk — so saggy beside yours which were still budding — with her swollen belly and her pubic bush colorless in the glare of electric light, with her tangled, slimy hair and her pouting, placid face — so lifeless beside yours — and her skin a pallid white, lightning-flash white, flashbulb white, a whiteness that couldn't be duplicated in daylight — how I'd come to hate that pallor, so cold beside the flush of your skin.

There wasn't a particular night when we finally broke up, just as there wasn't a particular night when we began going together, but I do remember a night in fall when I guessed that it was over. We were parked in the Rambler at the dead end of the street of factories that had been our lovers' lane, listening to a drizzle of rain and dry leaves sprinkle the hood. As always, rain revitalized the smells of the smoked fish and kielbasa in the upholstery. The radio was on too low to hear, the windshield wipers swished at intervals as if we were driving, and the windows were steamed as if we'd been making out. But we'd been arguing as usual, this time about a woman poet who had committed suicide, whose work you were reading. We were sitting, no longer talking or touching, and I remember thinking that I didn't want to argue with you anymore. I didn't want to sit like this in silence; I wanted to talk excitedly all night as we once had, I wanted to find some way that wasn't corny-sounding to tell you how much fun I'd had in your company, how much knowing you had meant to me, and how I had suddenly realized that I'd been so intent on becoming lovers that I'd overlooked how close we'd been as friends. I wanted you to know that. I wanted you to like me again.

"It's sad," I started to say, meaning that I was sorry we had reached a point of sitting silently together, but before I could continue, you challenged the statement.

"What makes you so sure it's sad?"

"What do you mean, what makes me so sure?" I asked, confused by your question, and surprised there could be anything to argue over no matter what you thought I was talking about.

You looked at me as if what was sad was that I would never understand. "For all either one of us knows," you said, "she could have been triumphant!"

*

Maybe when it really ended was that night when I felt we had just
reached the beginning, that one time on the beach in the summer
between high school and college, when our bodies rammed together so desperately that for a moment I thought we did it, and
maybe in our hearts we had, although for me, then, doing it in
one's heart didn't quite count. If it did, I supposed we'd all be
Casanovas.

I remember riding home together on the El that night, feeling
sick and defeated in a way I was embarrassed to mention. Our mute
reflections emerged like negative exposures on the dark, greasy
window of the train. Lightning branched over the city and when
the train entered the subway tunnel, the lights inside flickered as
if the power was disrupted although the train continued rocketing
beneath the Loop.

When the train emerged again we were on the South Side and
it was pouring, a deluge as if the sky had opened to drown the
innocent and guilty alike. We hurried from the El station to your
house, holding the Navajo blanket over our heads until, soaked, it
collapsed. In the dripping doorway of your apartment building,
we said goodnight. You were shivering. Your bra showed through
the thin blouse plastered to your skin. I swept the wet hair away
from your face and kissed you lightly on the lips, then you turned
and went inside. I stepped into the rain and you came back out
calling after me.

"What?" I asked, feeling a surge of gladness to be summoned
back into the doorway with you.

"Want an umbrella?"

I didn't. The downpour was letting up. It felt better to walk back
to the El feeling the rain rinse the sand out of my hair, off my legs,
until the only places where I could still feel its grit was the crotch
of my cutoffs and in each squish of my shoes. A block down the
street, I passed a pair of Jockey shorts lying in a puddle and
realized they were mine, dropped from my back pocket as we ran
to your house. I left them behind, wondering if you'd see them
and recognize them the next day.

By the time I had climbed the stairs back to the El platform, the
rain had stopped. Your scent still hadn't washed from my fingers.
The station — the entire city, it seemed — dripped and steamed.
The summer sound of crickets and nighthawks echoed from the
drenched neighborhood. Alone, I could admit how sick I felt. For

you, it was a night that would haunt your dreams. For me, it was another night when I waited, swollen and aching, for what I had secretly nicknamed the Blue Ball Express.

Literally lovesick, groaning inwardly with each lurch of the train and worried that I was damaged for good, I peered out at the passing yellow-lit stations where lonely men stood posted before giant advertisements, pictures of glamorous models defaced by graffiti — the same old scrawled insults and pleas: FUCK YOU, EAT ME. At this late hour the world seemed given over to men without women, men waiting in abject patience for something indeterminate, the way I waited for our next times. I avoided their eyes so that they wouldn't see the pity in mine, pity for them because I'd just been with you, your scent was still on my hands, and there seemed to be so much future ahead.

For me it was another night like that, and by the time I reached my stop I knew I would be feeling better, recovered enough to walk the dark street home making up poems of longing that I never wrote down. I was the D. H. Lawrence of not doing it, the voice of all the would-be lovers who ached and squirmed but still hadn't. From our contortions in doorways, on stairwells, and in the bucket seats of cars we could have composed a *Kama Sutra* of interrupted bliss. It must have been that might when I recalled all the other times of walking home after seeing you, so that it seemed as if I was falling into step behind a parade of my former selves — myself walking home on the night we first kissed, myself on the night when I unbuttoned your blouse and kissed your breasts, myself on the night that I lifted your skirt above your thighs and dropped to my knees — each succeeding self another step closer to that irrevocable moment for which our lives seemed poised.

But we didn't, not in the moonlight, or by the phosphorescent lanterns of lightning bugs in your backyard, not beneath the constellations that we couldn't see, let alone decipher, nor in the dark glow that had replaced the real darkness of night, a darkness already stolen from us; not with the skyline rising behind us while the city gradually decayed, not in the heat of summer while a Cold War raged; despite the freedom of youth and the license of first love — because of fate, karma, luck, what does it matter? — we made not doing it a wonder, and yet we didn't, we didn't, we never did.

TONY EARLEY

The Prophet from Jupiter

FROM HARPER'S MAGAZINE

MY HOUSE, the dam keeper's house, sits above the lake on Pierce-Arrow Point. The dam juts out of the end of the point and curves away across the cove into the ridge on the other side of the channel. On this side is the water, 115 feet deep at the base of the dam, and on the other side is air: the gorge, the river starting up again, rocks far down below, a vista. There are houses on 100-foot lots all the way around the lake, and too many real estate brokers. Sometimes at night, the real estate brokers pull up each other's signs and sling them into the lake.

A family on Tryon Bay has a Labrador retriever that swims in circles for hours, chasing ducks. You can buy postcards in town with the dog on the front, swimming, swimming, the ducks always just out of reach. There is a red and white sign on the Tryon Bay bridge that says NO JUMPING OR DIVING FROM BRIDGE, and I could drop the water level down a foot and a half any summer Saturday and paralyze all the teenage boys I wanted. Sometimes rednecks whoop and yell *nigger!* and throw beer bottles at Junie Wilson, who walks up and down Highway 20 with a coat hanger around his neck. Junie drops a dollar bill into the water every time he crosses the bridge. The Prophet from Jupiter brings his five young sons to the bridge to watch the Lab swim. The six of them stand in a line at the guardrail and clap and wave their arms and shout encouragement for the dog. Down in the water, the ducks let the dog get almost to them before they fly away. They fly maybe thirty, forty yards, that's all, and splash back down. The townies call the dog Shithead. You may not believe me, but I swear I have heard ducks laugh. Shithead, as he paddles around the bay, puffs like he is dying. This is where I live and this is what I think: a dam is an unnatural thing, like a diaphragm.

The most important part of my job is to maintain a constant pond level. But the lake rises all night, every night; the river never stops. When I drive below town, coming back toward home, I'm afraid I'll meet the lake coming down through the gorge. When Lake Glen was built, it covered the old town of Uree with eighty-five feet of water. As the dam was raised higher and higher across the river, workmen did not tear down the houses. Fish swim in and out of the open doors. Old Man Bill Burdette left his 1916 chain-drive Reo truck parked beside his house when he moved away.

The diver who inspected the dam in 1961 told the Mayor that he saw a catfish as big as a man swimming by the floodgates. The fish is a local legend. At night I fish for it, from the catwalk connecting the floodgates, using deep-sea tackle and cow guts for bait. The fish hangs in the water facing the dam, just above the lake's muddy bottom, and listens to the faint sound of the river glittering on the other side of the concrete. The Prophet from Jupiter says, *When you pull your giant fish out of the water, it will speak true words.* When they tell history, people will remember me because of the fish, even if I don't catch it.

The Prophet from Jupiter's real name is Archie Simpson. He sold real estate and made a fortune in Jupiter, Florida, until nine years ago when God told him that he was the one true prophet who would lead the Christians in the last days before the Rapture. The Prophet says his first words after God finished talking were, *Jesus Christ, you gotta be kidding.* He is not shy about telling the story, and does not seem crazy. He has a young wife who wears beaded Indian headbands and does not shave under her arms.

Old Man Bill Burdette's four sons hired divers and dragged their father's Reo truck out of the lake fifty years to the day after the water rose. The Burdette boys spent $6,000 restoring the old Reo and then said to anyone who would listen, *I don't know why Daddy left it. It was just like new.* Bill Jr., the eldest son, drives it in the town parade every Fourth of July, the back loaded with waving grandchildren. The oldest ones look embarrassed. In town, in front of the Rogue Mountain Restaurant, there is a plywood cutout of a cross-eyed bear. The bear holds up a red and white sign that says EAT.

Before I start fishing, I pour ripe blood from the bottom of my bait bucket into the water. I use treble hooks sharp as razors. A reel like a winch. Randy, the assistant dam keeper, is an orderly at the hospital in Hendersonville and fishes with me after he gets off work. He does not believe the story about the fish as big as a man. I fish all night. Sometimes small catfish, ripping intestines from the treble hooks, impale themselves and make a small noise like crying when I pull them out of the water. I hold them by the tail and hit their heads against the rail of the catwalk and toss them backward over the edge of the dam.

At dawn, I open the small gate that lets water into the turbine house, throw the generator switches, and go to bed. The Town of Lake Glen makes a million dollars a year selling electricity. Everybody who works for the Town of Lake Glen has a new town truck to drive. The Prophet from Jupiter makes miniature ladder-back chairs that he sells wholesale to the gift shops on the highway. His young wife braids long bands of cowhide into bullwhips and attaches them to clean pine handles. With a hot tool she burns a small cross and the words LAKE GLEN, NORTH CAROLINA on the sides of the handles. She once said to me, *I know that what my husband says about God is true because every time we make love he fills me with the most incredible light.* The bullwhips she makes hang like snakes in front of the gift shops, and tourists stop and buy them by the dozen. It is inexplicable. Once, during lunch in the Rogue Mountain Restaurant, the Prophet from Jupiter looked down into his bowl of vegetable soup and said, *You know, in the last days Christians won't be able to get corn.* The high-voltage wires leading away from the turbine house, you can actually hear them hum.

Sometime during the afternoon — cartoons are on television, the turbines have spun all day, in the town hall they are counting money, the skiers are sunburned in their shining boats, and the fishermen are drunk — the water level drops back down to where I try to keep it and the alarm goes off. I get out of bed and go down the narrow stairs to the turbine house and close the gate. All around Lake Glen it is brilliant summer: the town policemen park beside the beach and look out from under the brims of their Smokey the Bear hats at the college girls glistening in the sun. The night of the Fourth of July, the main channel of the lake fills up with boats, and the running lights on the dark water glitter like stars. The fireworks draw lines on the sky like the ghosts of the veins in your eyes after you have stared into the sun.

People who should know better play jokes on Junie Wilson. If they tell him that hair spray will scare away ghosts, he carries a can with him everywhere he goes, like Mace, until somebody tells him differently. If they tell him that ghosts at night drive ski boats, he will not walk by the marina for days or get within 200 yards of a fast boat. The Prophet from Jupiter says that Junie has the gift of true sight. The Mayor gives Junie rides to keep him out of trouble.

This is what it's like to live on Lake Glen: in the spring the sun shines all the way through you and you twist down inside yourself, like a seed, and think about growing. There are red and white signs on the water side of the dam that say DANGER! MAINTAIN A DISTANCE OF 200 YARDS, but you can't read them from that far away. In April the wind blows down out of the mountains and across the cove toward my house, and the sun and the water smell like my wife's hair. Along the western shore in the summer, in the campgrounds beside the highway, gas lanterns glow like ghosts against the mountains. Boys and girls who will never see each other again, and somehow know it, make desperate promises and rub against each other in the laurel; they wade in their underwear in the cold river. In the summer night, bullwhips pop like rifles.

Lake Glen was built between the mountains — Rogue Mountain and Rumbling Caesar — in 1927 by the Lake Glen Development Company. They built the dam, the municipal building, and a hotel with 200 rooms before the stock market crashed. My wife's name is Elisabeth. She lives, until I leave Lake Glen, with her mother in Monte Sano, Alabama, and has nothing to say to me. Twice a day the town tour boat stops 200 yards from the dam and I can hear the guide over the tinny loudspeaker explain how it would be dangerous to get any closer. Two summers ago the town made a deal with the family on Tryon Bay to keep Shithead penned until the tour boat came to the bay at ten and two. The ducks, however, proved to be undependable. In his pen Shithead became despondent. The problem was that the ducks swim on Tryon Bay every day, you just never know when. Elisabeth says that for years I had nothing to say to her and that I shouldn't expect her to have much to say to me. There are hurricane-fence gates at each end of the

dam, and only Randy and the Mayor and I have keys. When
fishermen approach it in boats I stand in the kitchen and ring the
alarm bell until they leave. They shout at me perched on top of a
cliff of water. This is something they do not consider.

The old people say that when Aunt Plutina Williams left her
house for the last time before the lake was flooded, she closed her
windows and shut and locked the door. Some of the streets in the
Town of Lake Glen still have the old Development Company
names: Air Strip Road. Yacht Club Drive. H. L. Mencken Circle.
Elisabeth, before she left, taught the church preschool class every
other Sunday. One year she brought her class here for an Easter
egg hunt, and when she unlatched the gate on the front porch
they tumbled in their new clothes down the grassy slope toward
the lake. Elisabeth followed me down to the turbine house once
and over the roar of the generators screamed into my ear, *Why
won't you talk to me? What are you holding back?* The new police chief
asked for a key to the hurricane-fence gates, but the Mayor refused
to give him one.

The Lake Glen Hotel is sold and renovated about every five
years, and banners are hung across the front of it on the days it
reopens. A crowd gathers and old men sit and watch from the
shade under the arches of the municipal building. A Florida Yankee makes a speech about the coming renaissance in Lake Glen.
The Mayor cuts the ribbon and everybody claps. But the Town of
Lake Glen doesn't have an air strip or a yacht club: the hotel never
stays open longer than a season. Most of the time, the signs of
every real estate broker in town are lined up in front of it like stiff
flags.

Elisabeth stood in the lake that Easter in a new yellow dress; the
water was up over her calves. The children squealed on the bank.
Maybe then, watching Elisabeth, I believed for a minute in the
risen Christ. This is what has happened: my wife, Elisabeth, is
pregnant with the new police chief's child. Randy never mentions
my misfortune, unless I mention it first. I am grooming him to be
the new dam keeper. From the catwalk at night we see in the
distance across the channel the lights of the town. There is no
reason to come here and stay in a hotel with 200 rooms. There is
no reason to stay here at all.

Randy fishes for crappie with an ultralight rod that is limber as
a switch and will some nights pull seventy-five, a hundred out of

the dark water, glittering, like nickels. He fishes in his white orderly clothes. He smells disinfected and doesn't stay all night. This is what I have done: I took the passenger-side shoulder harness out of my Town of Lake Glen truck and bolted it with long screw anchors into the side of the dam, behind the catwalk. I buckle up when I fish. I don't want to be pulled into the water.

Randy is twenty years old and already has two children. He is not married. His girlfriend is tall and skinny and mean-looking. Randy says she fucks like a cat. The old people say that the morning of the day the water came up, somebody asked Aunt Plutina why she closed her windows and locked her doors, and she said, *Why you never know. Sometime I just might want to come back.* Junie Wilson has seen her. I am afraid that someday I will see her, too. The last time I slept with Elisabeth, two hearts beat inside her.

Randy will go far in this town. Sometimes I can see Elisabeth bending her back into the new police chief. Randy says don't think about it. He is an ex-redneck who learned the value of cutting his hair and being nice to Floridians. He someday might be mayor. He brought his girlfriend to the town employee barbecue and swim party at the Mayor's glass house, and her nipples were stiff, like buttons. My shoulder harness is a good thing: sometimes late at night I doze, leaning forward against it, and dream of something huge, suspended in the water beneath me, its eyes yellow and open. At the party I saw Randy whisper something into his girlfriend's ear. She looked down at the front of her shirt and said out loud, *Well, Jesus Christ, Randy. What do you want me to do about it?*

During the summers in the thirties the Lake Glen Hotel was a refuge for people who could not afford to summer in the Catskills anymore. Down the road from the hotel, where the Community Center is now, there was a dance pavilion built on wooden pilings out over the bay. Elisabeth stood in the lake in a new yellow dress, holding a jar. The kids from the Sunday school squatted at the edge of the water and looked for tadpoles. The Mayor was diagnosed with testicular cancer in the spring and waits to see if he had his operation in time.

From my dam I have caught catfish that weighed eighteen, twenty-four, and thirty-one pounds: just babies. Randy said the thirty-one-pounder was big enough. I think I scare him. I got my picture in the paper in Hendersonville, holding up the fish. My

beard is long and significant; the catfish looks wise. I mailed a copy
to Elisabeth in Monte Sano. The new police chief drives up to the
hurricane-fence gate after Randy goes home, and shines his spotlight on me. I don't even unbuckle my harness anymore. The
Mayor is not running for reelection. I will stay until inauguration
day. The new police chief will live with Elisabeth and their child
in the dam keeper's house; Randy's girlfriend is pregnant again
and the house isn't big enough for three kids.

The dance pavilion orchestra was made up of college boys from
Chapel Hill and black musicians who had lost their summer hotel
jobs up north. The college boys and the black men played nightly
for tips, in their shirtsleeves on the covered bandstand, tunes that
had been popular during the twenties. On the open wooden floor
out over the water the refugees danced under paper lanterns
and blazing mosquito torches. Bootleggers dressed in overalls and
wide-brimmed hats drove their Model Ts down out of the laurel
and sold moonshine in the parking lot.

The new police chief came here from New York State and is
greatly admired by the Florida Yankees for his courtesy and creased
trousers. I try to hate him, but it is too much like hating myself
for what I have done, for what I have left undone. Florida Yankees
have too much money and nothing to do. They bitch about the
municipal government and run against each other for Town Council. They drive to Hendersonville wearing sweat suits and walk
around and around the mall. Randy will not express a preference
for Town Council candidates, not even to me. He will go far. His
girlfriend will be the first lady of the Town of Lake Glen.

The Mayor came here on summer break from Chapel Hill in
1931 and never went back. He played second trumpet in the Lake
Glen orchestra. He took his trust fund and bought lakefront land
for eighteen cents on the dollar. At the end of the night, the Mayor
says, after the band had packed up their instruments and walked
back to the hotel, the last of the dancers stood at the pavilion rail
and looked out at the lake. Fog grew up out of the water. Frogs
screeched in the cattails near the river channel. The Mayor says
that the last dancers would peel off their clothes and dive white
and naked into the foggy lake. He says that when they laughed he
could hear it from the road as he walked away, or from his boat as
it drifted between the mountains on the black lake before first .
light. Some nights I think that if I drove over to the Community

Center and turned off my lights I could see them dancing on the fog. Junie Wilson has taught me to believe in ghosts. The music I hear comes from a distance: I can never make out the tune. I remember that Elisabeth used to put her heels against the bed and raise herself up — she used to push her breasts together with her hands. *Ghosts is with us everywhere,* Junie Wilson says.

The old people say that the town of Uree held a square dance on the bank of the river the night before the water came up. They say that Jim Skipper, drunk on moonshine, shit in the middle of his kitchen floor and set his house on fire. This is something that happened: Elisabeth and I tried to have a baby for seven years before we went to see a fertility specialist in Asheville. The old people say that the whole town whooped and danced in circles in front of Jim Skipper's burning house, and that boys and girls desperate for each other sneaked off and humped urgently in the deserted buildings, that last night before the town began to sink. All the trees around the town of Uree had been cut. They lay tangled where they fell.

During the Second World War the government ran the Lake Glen Hotel as a retreat for Army Air Corps officers on leave from Europe. The Mayor says that the pilots — the ones who were not joined at the hotel by their wives — lay in still rows on the beach all day, sweating moonshine. At night they went either to the dance pavilion, where they tried to screw summer girls or the girls who walked down out of the laurel in homemade dresses, or they went to the whorehouse on the second floor of the Glen Haven Restaurant, where the whores were from Charleston, some of them exotic and Gullah, and the jukebox thumped with swing. The house specialty was fried catfish and hush puppies made with beer. The Prophet from Jupiter and his young wife live with their five sons in the Glen Haven building because the rent is so cheap. There are ten rooms upstairs, five on each side of a narrow hall. One Sunday morning in the early spring, the Prophet's son Zeke told Elisabeth that he dreamed Jesus came to his house and pulled a big bucket of water out of a well and everybody drank from it.

The fertility specialist, Dr. Suzanne Childress, said that I had lethargic sperm. *I knew it wasn't me,* Elisabeth said, *I knew it wasn't me.*

Dr. Suzanne Childress said, *Your sperm count is normal. They just do not swim well enough to reach and fertilize Elisabeth's ovum.*

They say that Jim Skipper camped out under his wagon for three

weeks beside the rising lake. He borrowed a boat from the Lake
Glen Development Company and paddled around the sinking
houses. He looked in the windows until they disappeared, and then
he banged on the tin roofs with his paddle. He said he did not
know how to live anywhere else. They say that before Jim Skipper
shot himself, he stood in his borrowed boat and pissed down Old
Man Bill Burdette's chimney.

Elisabeth said, *You always thought it was me, didn't you?*

Dr. Suzanne Childress said, *I think that perhaps we can correct your
problem with dietary supplements. Vitamins. Do you exercise?*

Elisabeth said, *I'm ovulating right now. I can tell.*

Dr. Suzanne Childress said, *I know.*

They closed the dance pavilion for good in 1944 when a moon-
shiner named Rudy Thomas, in a fight over a Glen Haven whore
named Sunshine, stabbed a B-27 pilot from New York eleven times
and pushed him into the lake. Rudy Thomas died of tuberculosis
in Central Prison in Raleigh in 1951. They say that Jim Skipper
was a good man but one crazy son of a bitch.

Several nights a week during his second summer in town the
Mayor leaned a chambermaid named Lavonia over the windscreen
of his 1928 Chris-Craft and screwed her until his legs got so weak
that he almost fell out of the boat. Junie Wilson says that the boxes
on the sides of telephone poles — if the ghosts have turned them
on — make him so drunk that he is afraid he is going to fall into
the lake. The coat hanger around Junie's neck protects him from
evil spirits. *Sweet Lavonia,* the Mayor says, *had the kind of body that a
young man would paint on the side of his airplane before he flew off to
fight in a war.*

The young Mayor took off his clothes as he drove his boat fast
across the dark lake. Lavonia waited between two boulders on the
shore near Uree Shoals. The Mayor cut the engine and drifted
into the cove. Lavonia stepped out from between the rocks, pulled
her skirt up around her waist, and waded out to the boat. The
white Mayor glowed in the darkness and played gospel songs on
his trumpet while she walked through the water. There wasn't a
house or a light in sight. Lavonia told him every night while he
squeezed her breasts, *You're putting the devil inside of me.* The boat
turned in the water, and the Mayor owned everything he could
see. Randy in his orderly clothes, jigging for crappie, tells me there

is nothing wrong with me, that to make a woman pregnant you have to fuck her in a certain way, that's all, you have to put your seed where it will take.

Junie Wilson woke me up one morning yelling, *Open the gate. Open the gate.* One of the town cops had told him that ghosts wouldn't walk across a dam, that walking across a dam was the way for a man to get rid of his ghosts once and for all. Junie sees three ghosts in his dreams: he sees a man standing in a boat, he sees a woman looking out the window of a house under water, and he sees his mama wading out into the lake. This last dream torments Junie the most, because he doesn't know how to swim. He stands on the bank and yells for her to come back. We walked across the dam, water up close beside Junie, the air falling away beside me. Junie said, *She better get out of that water if she knows what's good for her.* What my wife said is true: I never thought it was me. After we made love Elisabeth kept her legs squeezed tight together, even after she went to sleep. *Ghosts is keeping me awake,* Junie said. *I got to get rid of these ghosts so I can get me some sleep. Ghosts is crucifying me.*

Something's wrong with me, Elisabeth whispered. *I can't have a baby.* I said, *I still love you. Shhh.*

Before we went to see Dr. Suzanne Childress, I liked to sit astride Elisabeth, hard and slick between her breasts. Lavonia tried to kill the baby inside her by drinking two quarts of moonshine that she bought from a bootlegger named Big Julie Cooper in the pavilion parking lot. Junie didn't speak until he was four. Ghosts began to chase him when he was twelve. The first time Lavonia saw Junie touching himself, she whipped him with a belt and told him that if he ever did that again a white man would come with a big knife and cut it off. Elisabeth, when I was finished, wiped her chest and neck off with a towel.

Bugs fly like angels into the white light of the gas lantern and then spin and fall into the water. Randy jabs the air with his index finger: *It's special pussy, man, way back in the back. It burns like fire.* The Mayor gave Lavonia a little money every month until she died three years ago. He does not give money to Junie because Junie drops dollar bills off the Tryon Bay bridge. He does it so that the ghosts won't turn on their machines when he walks by telephone poles. The Mayor says, *Jesus Christ, if I gave that boy a million dollars, he'd throw every bit of it off that damn bridge.*

Randy says, *Man, women go crazy when you start hitting that baby spot. They'll scratch the hell out of you. You gotta time it right, that's all. You gotta let it go when you hit it.* He slaps the back of one hand into the other. *Bang. You gotta get the pussy they don't want you to have.*

Junie Wilson and I walked back and forth across the dam until the alarm went off and I had to close the gate and shut down the generators. I didn't tell Junie about the machines in the turbine house. Elisabeth said over the phone from Monte Sano, *I know you won't believe it now, but all I ever wanted was for you to pay attention to me.* In a sterile men's room in the doctor's office, I put my hands against the wall and Elisabeth jerked me off into a glass bottle. Junie Wilson said that he did not feel any better, and I said that walking across the dam does not always work.

In August the air over the lake is so thick you can see it, and distances through the haze look impossible to cross. The water is smooth and gray, and the Town of Lake Glen shimmers across the channel like the place it tried to be. At the beach, policemen sit in their station wagons with their air conditioners running. The college girls are tanned the color of baseball gloves. Randy's girlfriend is starting to gain weight and Randy fishes less; the crappie have all but stopped biting. The Prophet from Jupiter winks and says that in hot weather his wife smells like good earth and that God has blessed him in more ways than one. In the hot summer the ghosts keep their machines turned on all the time, and Junie Wilson staggers through town like a drunk. If there is one true thing I know to tell you, it is this: in North Carolina, even in the mountains, it takes more than a month of your life to live through August.

September is no cooler, but the sky begins to brighten, like a promise, and the town begins to pack itself up for leaving. The college girls go first, their tans already fading, and motor homes with bicycles strapped to their backs groan up out of the campgrounds to the shimmering highway. Boys and girls damp with sweat sneak away to say goodbye in the laurel and make promises one last time. Around the lake, family by family, summer people close up their houses and go back to where they came from in June. The Florida Yankees have mercifully decided among themselves who the new mayor will be, but the council candidates drive

around town at night and tear down each other's campaign posters. My beard is down to the middle of my chest. Junie Wilson
walks through town with his hands held up beside his face like
blinders, to keep from seeing the bright faces stapled to the telephone poles. One afternoon I slept in front of a fan and dreamed
it was spring: Elisabeth waded in the lake and I sat on the porch
and held a baby whose hair smelled like the sun. I dialed a 1-900
phone-love number and charged it to the Town of Lake Glen, and
a woman named Betty said she wanted me to come in her mouth.
In the closed-up summer houses, burglar alarms squeal in frequen-
cies only bats can hear and the lights burn all night, turned on
and off by automatic timers, but the rooms are empty and still.

In the fall the wild ducks fly away after the summer people in
great, glittering V's. Weekend tourists drive up from Charlotte and
Greenville to point at the leaves and buy pumpkins. The ducks
skim low over the channel in front of my house, their wings
whistling like blood, and then cross the dam, suddenly very high
in the air. The Floridians burn leaves in their yards and inhale the
smoke like Mentholatum. Randy said, *Man, I hope there ain't going
to be any hard feelings,* and stopped coming to fish. Early one morning
my line stiffened and moved through the water for twenty yards.
When I set the hook, the stiff rod bent double against a great
weight. And then it was gone. The next night the new police chief
sat outside the gate in his Jeep and played an easy-listening radio
station over his loudspeaker. In the town of Uree, Aunt Plutina
Williams sits and looks out the window of her house. Jim Skipper
wanders in and out of the houses. A giant fish moves through the
air like a zeppelin. The new police chief said over the loudspeaker,
Look, chief, I just — and then stopped talking and backed up and
drove away.

In November 1928 the Lake Glen dam almost washed away. A flash
flood boiled down out of the mountains after a week of rain, and
the dam keeper did not open the floodgates in time. The water
rose and filled the lake bed like a bowl before it spilled over the
top of the dam. Old Man Bill Burdette drove down the mountain
in his new truck to warn people downstream: the lake had turned
itself back into a river and was cutting a channel through the earth
around the side of the dam. They say that the men of the Lake

Glen Development Company construction crews hauled six heavy freight wagons of red roofing slate from the hotel site and threw it over the side of the gorge. Local men came down out of the laurel and worked in the rain filling sandbags and tossing them into the hole. But still the water ran muddy around the side of the dam and over the tops of the sandbags and the roofing. The workers rolled the six empty wagons in on top of the pile. They carried all of the furniture and both stoves out of the dam keeper's house and threw it in. They pushed three Model T Fords belonging to the company, as well as the superintendent's personal Pierce-Arrow, into the channel the river cut around the side of the dam. But the water still snaked its way through the wreckage, downhill toward the riverbed.

This October, Town of Lake Glen workmen hung huge red and yellow banners shaped like leaves from wires stretched between the telephone poles. They built cider stands and arts-and-crafts booths and a small plywood stage in the parking lot in front of the Lake Glen Hotel. The Chamber of Commerce called the whole thing ColorFest! and promoted it on the Asheville TV station. Hundreds of tourists showed up, wearing bright sweaters, even though it was warm. I saw townies look at me when they thought I wasn't looking, and their eyes said: I wonder what he's going to do. My beard is a torrent of hair. A high school clogging team from Hendersonville stomped on the wooden stage. Little boys stood at the edge of the stage and looked up through the swirling white petticoats of the girl dancers. Shithead's owners walked him through the crowd on a leash. The Prophet from Jupiter and his wife sold miniature ladder-back chairs and bullwhips from a booth, and gave away spiritual tracts about the coming Rapture. Junie Wilson, crying for somebody to help him before the white man came to get him, showed his erection to three of Old Man Bill Burdette's great-granddaughters, who were sitting in the back of the 1916 Reo truck.

In 1928 the workers at the collapsing dam looked at each other in the rain. Everything seemed lost. The superintendent of the Lake Glen Development Company produced a Colt revolver and a box of cartridges. Big Julie Cooper took the superintendent's gun when nobody else would and one at a time shot twenty-four Development Company mules right between the eyes. The workers threw the dead and dying mules in on top of the cars and the wagons and the red roofing slate and the furniture and the stoves, before the rain slacked and the water retreated back to the lake side of the dam. Then the superintendent threw his hat into the gorge and danced a jig and said, *Boys, you don't miss your water until your dam starts to go.* When the roads dried out, the Development Company brought a steam shovel to cover the debris and the mules with dirt and rock blasted from the sides of the mountains, but not before the weather cleared and the mules swelled and rotted in the late autumn sun. They say that you could smell the mules for miles — some of them even exploded — and that workmen putting the roof on the hotel, at the other end of the channel, wore kerchiefs dipped in camphor tied around their faces. They say that a black funnel cloud of buzzards and crows spun in the air over the gorge and that you could see it a long way away. At night bears came down off of Rumbling Caesar and ate the rotting mules. Big Julie Cooper said, *By God, now let me tell you something. That son of a bitch liked to of went.*

When Old Man Bill Burdette's three great-granddaughters screamed, the new police chief twisted Junie Wilson's arm behind his back. Junie screamed, *Jesus. Jesus. Oh God. Please don't cut me,* and tried to get away. The whole ColorFest! crowd ran up close and silently watched while Junie and the new police chief spun around and around. *I'm not going to hurt you, Junie,* the new police chief said. Two other town cops showed up and held Junie down while the new police chief very efficiently handcuffed Junie and tied his legs together with three bullwhips the Mayor brought from the Prophet from Jupiter's booth. The new police chief covered Junie's erection with a red ColorFest! banner shaped like a leaf. Junie's coat hanger was bent and twisted around his face. The new police chief pulled it off and handed it to the Mayor. Junie screamed for his mother over and over until his eyes rolled back in his head and his body began to jerk. Shithead howled. The high school clogging team from Hendersonville the whole time stomped and spun, wild-eyed, on the flimsy plywood stage.

The first Monday after Thanksgiving, I raised one of the floodgates halfway and lowered the lake eight feet. Randy will fill the lake back up the first Monday in February. It will be his job to maintain a constant pond level. Every day I try to piss off the river side of the dam in a stream that will reach from me to the bottom of the gorge, but it is impossible to do. When the lake level is down, the exposed pilings of the boathouses are spindly like the legs of old men. Randy's girlfriend has started to show and her breasts are heavy. The new police chief spends three days in Monte Sano with my wife every other week. The hotel is dark and for sale and locked up tight.

When the water is down the people who live here year-round replace the rotten boards on their docks and the rotten rungs on their uncovered ladders. All around the lake circular saws squeal. The water over the town of Uree seems darker somehow than the rest of the lake, and I've always wanted to drop the lake down far enough to see what is down there. At the end of that last night, when Jim Skipper's house had burned down to a glowing pile of ashes, the people of the town of Uree sang "Shall We Gather at the River" and then stood around, just looking at their houses and barns and sheds, wishing they had done more, until the sun came over the dam at the head of the gorge. The Mayor stays mostly in his house now. His successor has been elected. Randy wore a necktie and a sport coat and met with the mayor-elect to discuss ways to generate electricity more efficiently. The Mayor keeps his thermostat set on eighty-five and still cannot get warm. The word from the state hospital in Morganton is that Junie Wilson has no idea where he is or what has happened and screams every time he sees a white doctor.

The lake began to freeze during a cold snap the week before Christmas. There were circles of whiter ice where part of the lake thawed in the sun and then refroze again at night. The temperature dropped fast all day Christmas Eve, and the ice closed in and trapped a tame duck on Tryon Bay. Shithead, going out after the duck, broke through a soft spot in the ice and could not get back out.

In fifteen minutes most of the town of Lake Glen was on the Tryon Bay bridge screaming, *Come on, Shithead. Come on, boy, you can do it.* Nobody could remember who had a canoe or think of how to rescue the dog. The Prophet from Jupiter, before anyone could stop him, ran across the frozen mud and slid head-first out onto the ice. The duck frozen to the lake in the middle of the bay flailed its wings. I stood beside the new police chief on the bank and screamed for the Prophet to *Lie still! Lie still!* that we would find a way to save him.

The Prophet from Jupiter moved his lips and began to inch his way forward across the ice. It groaned under his weight. Cracks in the ice shot away from his body like frozen lightning. The Prophet kept going, an inch at a time, none of us breathing until he reached forward into the hole and grabbed Shithead by the collar and pulled him up onto the ice. It held. The dog quivered for a second and skittered back toward shore, its belly low to the frozen lake.

We opened our mouths to cheer, but there was a crack like a gunshot, and the Prophet from Jupiter disappeared. He came up, once — he looked surprised more than anything else, his face deathly white, his mouth a black O — and then disappeared again and did not come back up. On the bridge the Prophet's five sons ran in place and screamed and held their arms toward the water. Randy's girlfriend kept her arms wrapped tight around the Prophet's wife, who shouted, *Oh Jesus! Oh Jesus!* and tried to jump off of the bridge. By the time we got boats on the lake, and broke the ice with sledgehammers, and pulled grappling hooks on the ends of ropes through the dark water and hooked the Prophet and dragged him up, there was nothing even God could do. The duck frozen to the lake had beaten itself to death against the ice. The new police chief sat down on the bank and cried like a baby.

Elisabeth's water broke that night. The new police chief called the Mayor and left for Monte Sano, and the Mayor called me. I walked back and forth and back and forth across the dam until all the ghosts of Lake Glen buzzed in my ears like electricity: I saw the Prophet from Jupiter riding with Old Man Bill Burdette, down the streets of Uree in a 1916 Reo truck, toward the light in Aunt Plutina Williams's window; I saw catfish as big as men, with whiskers like bullwhips, lie down at the feet of the Prophet and speak in a thousand strange tongues; I saw dancers moving against each other in the air to music I had never heard; I saw Lavonia, naked and beautiful, bathing and healing Junie in a moonlit cove; I saw Elisabeth standing at the edge of the lake in the spring, nursing a child who smelled like the sun; I saw the new police chief in a boat watching over his family; I saw the Mayor on his knees praying in

Gullah with Charleston whores; I saw Jim Skipper and Rudy Thomas and Big Julie Cooper driving a bleeding pilot beside the river in a wagon pulled by twenty-four mules; I saw the Prophet from Jupiter and his five sons shoot out of the lake like Fourth of July rockets and shout with incredible light and tongues of fire, *Rise, children of the water. Rise and be whole in the kingdom of God.*

CAROLYN FERRELL

Proper Library

FROM PLOUGHSHARES

BOYS, MEN, GIRLS, children, mothers, babies. You got to feed
them. You always got to keep them fed. Winter summer. They
always have to feel satisfied. Winter summer. But then you stop and
ask: Where is the food going to come from? Because it's never-end-
ing, never-stopping. Where? Because your life is spent on feeding
them and you never stop thinking about where the food is going
to come from.

Formula, pancakes, syrup, milk, roast turkey with cornbread
stuffing, Popsicles, love, candy, tongue kisses, hugs, kisses behind
backs, hands on faces, warmth, tenderness, Boston cream pie,
fucking in the butt. You got to feed them, and it's always going to
be you. Winter summer.

My ma says to me, Let's practice the words this afternoon when
you get home, baby. I nod to her. I don't have to use any words
with her to let her know I will do what she wants. When family
people come over and they see me and Ma in the kitchen like that
with the words, they say she has the same face as the maid in the
movies. She does have big brown hands like careful shovels, and
she loves to touch and pat and warm you up with them. And when
she walks, she shuffles. But if anyone is like the maid in the movies,
it is Aunt Estine. She likes to give mouth, 'specially when I got the
kids on my hands. She's sassy. She's got what people call a bad
attitude. She makes sure you hear her heels clicking all the time,
'specially when you are lying in bed before dawn and thinking
things in order, how you got to keep moving, all day long. Click,

click. Ain't nobody up yet? Click. Lazy-ass Negroes, you better not be 'specting me to cook y'all breakfast when you do get up! Click, click. I'm hungry. Click. I don't care what time it is, I'm hungry y'all and I'm tired and depressed and I need someone to talk to. Well, the hell with all y'all. That's my last word. Click, click, click.

My ma pats her hands on my schoolbag, which is red like a girl's, but that's all right. She pats it like it was my head. The books I have in it are: Biology, Woodworking for You, Math 1, The History of Civilization.

I'm supposed to be in Math 4, but the people keep holding me back. I know it's no real fault of mine. I been teaching the kids Math 4 from a book I took out of the Lending Mobile in the schoolyard. The kids can do most of Math 4. They like the way I teach it to them, with real live explanations, not the kind where you are supposed to have everything already in your head and it's just waiting to come out. And the kids don't ask to see if I get every one right. They trust me. They trust my smart. They just like the feel of the numbers and seeing them on a piece of paper: division of decimals, division of fractions. It's these numbers that keep them moving and that will keep them moving when I am gone. At school I just keep failing the City Wide Tests every May and the people don't ask any questions: they just hold me back. Cousin Cee Cee said, If you wasn't so stupid you would realize the fact of them holding you back till you is normal.

The kids are almost as sad as Ma when I get ready to go to school in the morning. They cry and whine and carry on and ask me if they can sit on my lap just one more time before I go, but Ma is determined. She checks the outside of my books to make sure nothing is spilled over them or that none of the kids have torn out any pages. Things got to be in place. There got to be order if you gonna keep on moving, and Ma knows that deep down. This morning I promise to braid Lasheema's hair right quick before I go, and as I'm braiding, she's steady smiling her four-year-old grin at Shawn, who is a boy and therefore has short hair, almost a clean shave, and who can't be braided and who weeps with every strand I grease, spread, and plait.

Ma warns me, Don't let them boys bother you now, Lorrie. Don't let 'em.

I tell her, Ma, I have not let you down in a long time. I know what I got to do for you.

She smiles but I know it is a fake smile, and she says, Lorrie, you are my only son, the only real man I got. I don't want them boys to get you from me.

I tell her because it's the only thing I can tell her, You cooking up something special tonight?

Ma smiles and goes back to fixing pancake mix from her chair in the kitchen. The kids are on their way to forgetting about me 'cause they love pancakes more than anything and that is the only way I'll get out of here today. Sheniqua already has the bottle of Sugar Shack Syrup and Tonya is holding her plate above her nappy lint head.

Tommy, Lula Jean's Navy husband, meets me at the front door as I open it. Normally he cheers me up by testing me on Math 4 and telling me what a hidden genius I am, a still river running deep, he called it one time. He likes to tell me jokes and read stories from the Bible out loud. And he normally kisses my sister Lula Jean right where I and everybody else can see them, like in the kitchen or in the bedroom on the bed, surrounded by at least nine kids and me, all flaming brown heads and eyes. He always says: This is what love should be. And he searches into Lula Jean's face for whole minutes.

I'm leaving for Jane Addams High School and I meet Tommy and he has a lady tucked under his arm and it ain't Lula Jean. Her hair is wet and smells like mouthwash and I hate him in a flash. I never hate anybody, but now I hate him. I know that when I close the door behind me a wave of mouths will knock Tommy and this new lady down but it won't drown them. My sister Anita walks into the room and notices and carries them off into the bathroom, quick and silent. But before that she kisses me on my cheek and pats her hand, a small one of Ma's, on my chest. She whispers, You are my best man, remember that. She slips a letter knife in my jacket pocket. She says, If that boy puts his thing on you, cut it off. I love you, baby. She pushes me out the door.

Layla Jackson who lives in the downtown Projects and who might have AIDS comes running up to me as I walk out our building's door to the bus stop. She is out of breath. I look at her and could imagine a boy watching her chest heave up and down like that and suddenly get romantic feelings, it being so big and all, split like two kickballs bouncing. I turn my eyes to hers, which are crying.

Layla Jackson's eyes are red. She has her baby Tee Tee in her arms but it's cold out here and she doesn't have a blanket on him or nothing. I say to her, Layla, honey, you gonna freeze that baby to death.

And I take my jacket off and put it over him, the tiny bundle.

Layla Jackson says, Thanks Lorrie man I got a favor to ask you please don't tell me no please man.

Layla always makes her words into a worry sandwich.

She says, Man, I need me a new baby sitter 'cause I been took Tee Tee over to my mother's but now she don't want him with the others and now I can't do nothing till I get me a sitter.

I tell her, Layla, I'm going back to school now. I can't watch Tee Tee in the morning but if you leave him with me in the cafeteria after fifth period I'll take him on home with me.

She says, That means I got to take this brat to Introduction to Humanities with me. Shit, man. He's gonna cry and I won't pass the test on Spanish Discoverers. Shit, man.

Then Layla Jackson thinks a minute and says, Okay, Lorrie, I'll give Tee to you at lunch in the cafeteria, bet. And I'll be 'round your place 'round six for him or maybe seven, thanks, man.

Then she bends down and kisses Tee Tee on his forehead and he glows with what I know is drinking up an oasis when you are in the desert for so long. And she turns and walks to the downtown subway, waving at me. At the corner she comes running back because she still has my jacket and Tee Tee is waving the letter knife around like a flag. She says that her cousin Rakeem was looking for me and to let me know he would be waiting for me 'round his way. *Yes.* I say to her, See you, Layla, honey.

Before I used to not go to Jane Addams when I was supposed to. I got in the habit of looking for Rakeem, Layla's cousin, underneath the Bruckner Expressway, where the Spanish women sometimes go to buy oranges and watermelons and apples cheap. He was what you would call a magnet, only I didn't know that then. I didn't understand the different flavors of the pie. I saw him one day and I had a feeling like I wanted him to sit on my lap and cradle me. That's when I had to leave school. Rakeem, he didn't stop me. His voice was just as loud as the trucks heading towards Manhattan on the Bruckner above us: This is where your real world begins, man. The women didn't watch us. We stared each other in the eyes. Rakeem taught me how to be afraid of school and of people watching us. He said, Don't go back, and I didn't. A part of me was saying that his ear was more delicious than Math 4. I didn't go to Jane Addams for six months.

On the BX 17 bus I see Tammy Ferguson and her twins and Joe Smalls and that white girl Laura. She is the only white girl in these Bronx projects that I know of. I feel sorry for her. She has blue eyes and red hair and one time when the B-Crew-Girls were going to beat her butt in front of the building, she broke down crying and told them that her real parents were black from the South. She told them she was really a Negro and they all laughed and that story worked the opposite than we all thought. Laura became their friend, like the B-Crew-Girls' mascot. And now she's still their friend. People may laugh when she ain't around but she's got her back covered. She's loyal and is trying to wear her thin flippy hair in cornrows, which in the old days woulda made the B-Crew, both boys and girls, simply fall out. When Laura's around, the B-Crew-Girls love to laugh. She looks in my direction when I get on the bus and says, Faggot.

She says it loud enough for all the grown-up passengers to hear. They don't look at me, they keep their eyes on whatever their eyes are on, but I know their ears are on me. Tammy Ferguson always swears she would never help a white girl, but now she can't pass up this opportunity, so she says, You tight-ass homo, go suck some faggot dick. Tammy's kids are taking turns making handprints on the bus window.

I keep moving. It's the way I learned: keep moving. I go and sit next to Joe Smalls in the back of the bus and he shows me the Math 3 homework he got his baby's mother Tareen to do for him. He claims she is smarter now than when she was in school at Jane Addams in the spring. He laughs.

The bus keeps moving. I keep moving even though I am sitting still. I feel all of the ears on us, on me and Joe and the story of Tareen staying up till 4 A.M. on the multiplication of fractions and then remembering that she had promised Joe some ass earlier but seeing that he was sound asleep snoring anyway, she worked on ahead and got to the percent problems by the time the alarm went off. Ha ha, Joe laughs, I got my girl in deep check. Ha ha.

All ears are on us, but mainly on me. Tammy Ferguson is busy slapping the twins to keep quiet and sit still, but I can feel Laura's eyes like they are a silent machine gun. Faggot faggot suck dick faggot. Now repeat that one hundred times in one minute and that's how I am feeling.

Keep moving. The bus keeps rolling and you always have to keep moving. Like water like air like outer space. I always pick something for my mind. Like today I am remembering the kids and how they will be waiting for me after fifth period and I remember the feel of Lasheema's soft dark hair.

Soft like the dark hair that covers me, not an afro but silky hair, covering me all over. Because I am so cold. Because I am so alone. A mat of thick delicious hair that blankets me in warmth. And therefore safety. And peace. And solitude. And ecstasy. Lasheema and me are ecstatic when we look at ourselves in the mirror. She's only four and I am fourteen. We hold each other smiling.

Keep moving. Then I am already around the corner from school while the bus pulls away with Laura still on it because she has fallen asleep in her seat and nobody has bothered to touch her.

On the corner of Prospect Avenue and East 167th Street where the bus lets me out, I see Rakeem waiting for me. I am not supposed to really know he's there for me and he is not supposed to show it. He is opening a Pixie Stick candy and then he fixes his droopy pants so that they are hanging off the edge of his butt. I can see Christian Dior undies. When I come nearer he throws the Pixie Stick on the ground next to the other garbage and gives me his hand just like any B-Crew-Boy would do when he saw his other crew member. Only we are not B-Crew members, we get run over by the B-Crew.

He says, Yo, man, did you find Layla?

I nod and listen to what he is really saying.

Rakeem says, Do you know that I got into Math 3? Did you hear that shit? Ain't that some good shit?

He smiles and hits me on the back and he lets his hand stay there.

I say, See what I told you before, Rakeem? You really got it in you to move on. You doing all right, man.

He grunts and looks at his sneakers. Last year the B-Crew boys tried to steal them from him but Rakeem screamed at them that he had AIDS from his cousin and they ran away rubbing their hands on the sides of the buildings on the Grand Concourse.

Rakeem says, Man, I don't have nothing in me except my brain that tells me: Nigger, first thing get your ass up in school. Make them know you can do it.

I say, Rakeem, you are smart, man! I wish I had your smart. I would be going places if I did.

He says, And then, Lorrie, I got to get people to like me and to stop seeing me. I just want them to think they like me. So I got to hide *me* for a while. Then you watch, Lorrie, man: *much* people will be on my side!

I say to him, Rakeem, you got Layla and baby Tee Tee and all the teachers on your side. And you got smart. You have it made.

He answers me after he fixes his droopy pants again so that they are hanging off exactly the middle of his ass: Man, they are whack! You know what I would like to do right now, Lorrie? You know what I would like? Shit, I ain't seen you since you went back to school and since I went back. Hell, you know what I would like? But it ain't happening 'cause you think Ima look at my cousin Layla and her bastard and love them and that will be enough. But it will never be enough.

I think about sitting on his lap. I did it before but then I let months go by because it was under the Bruckner Expressway and I believed it could only last a few minutes. It was not like the kind of love when I had the kids because I believed they would last forever.

He walks backwards away and when he gets to the corner, he starts running. No one else is on the street. He shouts, Rocky's Pizza! Ima be behind there, man. We got school fooled. This is the master plan. Ima be there, Lorrie! *Be there.*

I want to tell Rakeem that I have missed him and that I will not be there but he is gone. The kids are enough. The words are important. They are all enough.

The front of Jane Addams is gray-green with windows with gates over all of them. I am on the outside.

The bell rings first period and I am smiling at Mr. D'Angelo and feeling like this won't be a complete waste of a day. The sun has hit the windows of Jane Addams and there is even heat around our books. Mr. D'Angelo notices me but looks away. Brandy Bailey, who doesn't miss a thing, announces so that only us three will hear:

Sometimes when a man's been married long he needs to experience a new kind of loving, ain't that what you think, Lorrie?

For that she gets thrown out of the classroom and an extra day
of in-school suspension. All ears are now on me and Mr. D'Angelo.
I am beyond feeling but I know he isn't. And that makes me happy
in a way, like today ain't going to be a complete waste of a day.

He wipes his forehead with an imported handkerchief. He starts
out saying, Class, what do we remember about the piston, the stem,
and the insects? He gets into his questions and his perspiration
stops and in two minutes he is free of me.

And I'm thinking: Why couldn't anything ever happen, why does
every day start out one way hopeful but then point to the fact that
ain't nothing ever going to happen? The people here at school
call me ugly, for one. I know I got bug eyes and I know I am not
someone who lovely things ever happen to, but I ask you: Doesn't
the heart count? Love is a pie and I am lucky enough to have
almost every flavor in mine. Mr. D'Angelo turns away from my desk
and announces a surprise quiz and everybody groans and it is a
sea of general unhappiness but no one is more than me, knowing
that nothing will ever happen the way I'd like it to, not this flavor
of the pie. And I am thinking: Mr. D'Angelo, do you know that I
would give anything to be like you, what with all your smarts and
words and you know how to make the people here laugh and they
love you. And I would give anything if you would ask me to sit on
your lap and ask me to bite into your ear so that it tingles like the
bell that rips me in and out of your class. I would give anything.
Love is a pie. Didn't you know that? Mr. D'Angelo, I am in silent
love in a loud body.

So don't turn away. *Sweat.*

Mrs. Cabrini pulls me aside and whispers, My dear Lorrie, when
are you ever going to pass this City Wide? You certainly have the
brains. And I know that your intelligence will take you far, will open
new worlds for you. Put your mind to your dreams, my dear boy,
and you will achieve them. You are your own universe, you are your
own shooting star.

People 'round my way know me as Lorrie and the name stays.
Cousin Cee Cee says the name fits and she smacks her gum in my

face whenever she mentions that. She also adds that if anyone ever wants to kick my ass, she'll just stand around and watch because a male with my name and who likes it just deserves to be watched when whipped.

Ma named me for someone else. My real name is Lawrence Lincoln Jefferson Adams. It's the name on my school records. It's the name Ma says I got to put on my application to college when the time comes. She knows I been failing these City Wide Tests and that's why she wants to practice words with me every day. She laughs when I get them wrong but she's afraid I won't learn them on my own, so she asks me to practice them with her and I do. Not every day, but a whole lot: look them up and pronounce them. Last Tuesday: Independence. Chagrin. Symbolism. Nomenclature. Filament. On Wednesday, only: Apocrypha. Ma says they have to be proper words with proper meanings from a dictionary. You got to say them right. This is important if you want to reach your destiny, Ma says.

Like for instance the word Library. All my life I been saying that "Liberry." And even though I knew it was a place to read and do your studying, I still couldn't call it right. Do you see what I mean? I'm about doing things, you see, *finally* doing things right.

Cousin Cee Cee always says, What you learning all that shit for? Don't you know it takes more than looking up words to get into a college, even a damn community college? Practicing words like that! Is you a complete asshole?

And her two kids, Byron and Elizabeth, come into the kitchen and ask me to teach them the words too, but Cee Cee says it will hurt their eyes to be doing all that reading and besides they are only eight and nine. When she is not around I give them words with up to ten letters, then they go back to TV with the other kids.

When we have a good word sitting, me and Ma, she smoothes my face with her hands and calls me Lawrence, My Fine Boy. She says, You are on your way to good things. You just got to do things the proper way.

We kiss each other. Her hands are like the maid in the movies. I know I am taken care of.

Zenzile Jones passes me a note in History of Civilization. It's the part where Ptolemy lets everyone know the world is round. Before

I open it, I look at her four desks away and I remember the night when I went out for baby diapers and cereal and found her crying in front of a fire hydrant. I let her cry on my shoulder. I told her that her father was a sick man for sucking on her like that.

The note says, Please give me a chance.

Estine Smith, my mother's sister who wants me and the kids to call her by both names, can't get out of her past. Sometimes I try on her clothes when I'm with the kids and we're playing dress-up. My favorite dress is her blue organza without the back. I seen Estine Smith wear this during the daytime and I fell in love with it. I also admired her for wearing a dress with the back out in the day, but it was only a ten-second admiration. Because then she opens her mouth and she is forever in her past. Her favorite time to make us all go back to is when they lynched her husband, David Saul Smith, from a tree in 1986 and called the TV station to come and get a look. She can't let us go one day without reminding us in words. I never want to be like her, ever. Everybody cries when they are in her words because they feel sorry for her, and Estine Smith is not someone but a walking hainted house.

Third period. I start dreaming about the kids while the others are standing in line to use the power saw. I love to dream about the kids. They are the only others who think I am beautiful besides Ma and Anita. They are my favorite flavor of the pie, even if I got others in my mind.

Most of the time there are eight but when my other aunt, Samantha, comes over I got three more. Samantha cries in the kitchen and shows Ma her blue marks and it seems like her crying will go on forever. Me, I want to take the kids' minds away. We go into Ma's room where there is the TV and we sing songs like "Old Gray Mare" and "Bingo Was His Name O" or new ones like "Why You Treat Me So Bad?" and "I Try to Let Go." Or else I teach them Math 4. Or else I turn on the TV so they can watch Bugs or He-Man and so I can get their ironing done.

Me, I love me some kids. I need me some kids.

Joe Smalls talks to me in what I know is a friendly way. The others in Woodworking for You don't know that. They are like the rest of the people who see me and hear the action and latch on.

Joe Smalls says, Lorrie, man, that bitch Tareen got half the percentage problems wrong. Shit. Be glad you don't have to deal with no dumb-ass Tareen bitch. She nearly got my ass a F in Math 3.

I get a sad look on my face, understanding, but it's a fake look because I'm feeling the rest of the ears on us, latching, readying. I pause to heaven. I am thinking I wish Ma had taught me how to pray. But she doesn't believe in God.

Junior Sims says, Why you talking that shit, Joe, man? Lorrie don't ever worry about bitches!

Perry Samson says, No, Lorrie never ever thinks about pussy as a matter of fact. Never ever.

Franklin says, Hey, Lorrie, man, tell me what you think about, then? What can be better than figuring out how you going to get that hole, man? Tell me what?

Mr. Samuels, the teacher, turns off the power saw just when it gets to Barney Moore's turn. He has heard the laughter from underneath the saw's screeching. Everybody gets quiet. His face is like a piece of lumber. Mr. Samuels is never soft. He doesn't fail me even though I don't do any cutting or measuring or shellacking. He wants me the hell out of there.

And after the saw is turned off, Mr. Samuels, for the first time in the world, starts laughing. The absolute first time. And everybody joins in because they are afraid of this and I laugh too because I'm hoping all the ears will go off me.

Mr. Samuels is laughing Haw Haw like he's from the country. Haw Haw. Haw Haw. His face is red. Everyone cools down and is just smiling now.

Then he says, Class, don't mess with the only *girl* we got in here! Now it's laughter again.

Daniel Fibbs says, Yeah, Mr. Samuels is *on!*

Franklin laughs, No fags allowed, you better take your sissy ass out of here 'less you want me to cut it into four pieces.

Joe Smalls is quiet and looking out the window.

Junior Sims laughs, Come back when you start fucking bitches! Keep moving, keep moving.

I pick up my red bag and wade towards the door. My instinct is the only thing that's working, and it is leading me back to Biology. But first out the room. Inside me there is really nothing except for Ma's voice: *Don't let them boys.* But inside there is nothing else. My bones and my brain and my heart would just crumble if it wasn't for that swirling wind of nothing in me that keeps me moving and moving.

Perry laughs, I didn't know Mr. Samuels was from the South.

With his eyelashes, Rakeem swept the edges of my face. He let me know they were beautiful to him. His face went in a circle around mine and dipped in my eyes and dipped in my mouth. He traveled me to a quiet place where his hands were the oars and I drifted off to sleep. The thin bars of the shopping cart where I was sitting in made grooves in my back, but it was like they were rows of tender fingers inviting me to stay. The roar of the trucks was a lullaby.

Layla Jackson comes running up to me but it's only fourth period because she wants to try and talk some sense into Tyrone. She hands me little Tee Tee. Tyrone makes like he wants to come over and touch the baby but instead he flattens his back against the wall to listen to Layla. I watch as she oozes him. In a minute they are tongue kissing. Because they are the only two people who will kiss each other. Everyone says that they gave themselves AIDS and now have to kiss each other because there ain't no one else. People walk past them and don't even notice that he has his hand up her shirt, squeezing the kickball.

Tee Tee likes to be in my arms. I like for him to be there.

The ladies were always buying all kinds of fruits and vegetables for their families underneath the Bruckner Expressway. They all talked Spanish and made the sign of the cross and asked God for forgiveness and gossiped.

Rakeem hickeyed my neck. We were underneath the concrete bridge supports and I had my hands on the handle of a broken shopping cart, where I was sitting. Don't go back, Rakeem was telling me, don't go back. And he whispered in my ear. And I thought of all the words I had been practicing, and how I was planning to pass that City Wide. Don't go back, he sang, and he sat me on his lap and he moved me around there. They don't need *you*, he said, and *you* don't need *them*.

But I do, I told him.

This feeling can last forever, he said.

No, it can't, I said, but I wound up leaving school for six months anyway. That shopping cart was my school.

I am thinking: It will never be more. I hold Tee Tee carefully because he is asleep on my shoulder and I go to catch the BX 17 back to my building.

Estine Smith stays in her past and that is where things are like nails. I want to tell her to always wear her blue organza without the back. If you can escape, why don't you all the time? You could dance and fling your arms and maybe even feel love from some direction. You would not perish. *You* could be free.

When I am around and she puts us in her past in her words, she tells me that if I hada twitched my ass down there like I do here, they woulda hung me up just by my black balls.

The last day Rakeem and I were together, I told him I wanted to go back, to school, to everyone. The words, I tried to explain about the words to Rakeem. I could welcome him into my world if he wanted me to. Hey, wasn't there enough room for him and me and the words?

Hell no, he shouted, and all the Spanish women turned around and stared at us. He shouted, You are an ugly-ass bastard who will always be hated big time and I don't care what you do; this is where your world begins and this is where your world will end. Fuck you. You are a pussy, man. Get the hell out of my face.

Ma is waiting for me at the front door, wringing her hands. She says it's good that I am home because there is trouble with Tommy again and I need to watch him and the kids while she goes out to bring Lula Jean home from the movies, which is where she goes when she plans on leaving Tommy. They got four kids here and if Lula Jean leaves, I might have to drop out of school again because she doesn't want to be tied to anything that has Tommy's stamp on it.

I set Tee Tee down next to Tommy on the sofa bed where I usually sleep. Tommy wakes up and says, Hey, man, who you bringing to visit me?

I go into the kitchen to fix him some tea and get the kids' lunch

ready. Sheniqua is playing the doctor and trying to fix up Shawn,
who always has to have an operation when she is the doctor. They
come into the kitchen to hug my legs and then they go back in
the living room.

Tommy sips his tea and says, Who was that chick this morning,
Lorrie, man?

I say I don't know. I begin to fold his clothes.

Tommy says, Man, you don't know these bitches out here nowadays. You want to show them love, a good time, and a real deep
part of yourself and all they do is not appreciate it and try to make
your life miserable.

He says, Well, at least I got Lula. Now that's some woman.

And he is asleep. Sheniqua and her brother Willis come in and
ask me if I will teach them Math 4 tonight. Aunt Estine rolls into
the bedroom and asks me why do I feel the need to take care of
this bum, and then she hits her head on the doorframe. She is
clicking her heels. She asks, Why do we women feel we always need
to teach them? They ain't going to learn the right way. They ain't
going to learn shit. That's why we always so alone. Click, click.

The words I will learn before Ma comes home are: Soliloquy,
Disenfranchise, Catechism. I know she will be proud. This morning before I left she told me she would make me a turkey dinner
with all the trimmings if I learned four new words tonight. I take
out my dictionary but then the kids come in and want me to give
them a bath and baby Tee Tee has a fever and is throwing up all
over the place. I look at the words and suddenly I know I will know
them without studying.

And I realize this in the bathroom and then again a few minutes
later when Layla Jackson comes in cursing because she got a 60
on the Humanities quiz. She holds Tee but she doesn't touch him.
She thinks Tyrone may be going to some group where he is
meeting other sick girls and she doesn't want to be alone. She
curses and cries, curses and cries. She asks me why things have to
be so fucked. Her braids are coming undone and I tell her that I
will tighten them up for her. That makes Layla Jackson stop crying.
She says, And to top it off, Rakeem is a shit. He promised me he
wouldn't say nothing but now that he's back in school he is
broadcasting my shit all over the place. And that makes nobody
like me. And that makes nobody want to touch me.

I put my arm around Layla. Soon her crying stops and she is thinking about something else.

But me, I know these new words and the old words without looking at them, without the dictionary, without Ma's hands on my head. Lasheema and Tata come in and want their hair to be like Layla's and they bring in the Vaseline and sit around my feet like shoes. Tommy wakes up still in sleep and shouts, Lula, get your ass on in here. Then he falls back to sleep.

Because I know I will always be able to say the words on my own. I can do the words on my own and that is what matters. I have this flavor of the pie and I will always have it. Here in this kitchen I was always safe, learning the words till my eyes hurt. The words are in my heart.

Ma comes in and shoves Lula Jean into a kitchen chair. She says, Kids, make room for your cousin, go in the other room and tell Tommy to get his lame ass out here. Layla, you can get your ass out of here and don't bring it back no more with this child sick out his mind, do your 'ho'ing somewhere out on the street where you belong. Tommy, since when I need to tell you how to treat your wife? You are a stupid heel. Learn how to be a man.

Everybody leaves and Ma changes.

She says, I ain't forgot that special dinner for you, baby. I'm glad you're safe and sound here with me. Let's practice later.

I tell her, Okay, Ma, but I got to go meet Rakeem first.

She looks at me in shock and then out the corner of my eye I can tell she wants me to say no, I'll stay, I won't go to him. Because she knows.

But I'm getting my coat on and Ma has got what will be tears on her face because she can't say no and she can't ask any questions. Keep moving.

And I am thinking of Rocky's Pizza and how I will be when I get there and how I will be when I get home. Because I am coming back home. And I am going to school tomorrow. I know the words, and I can tell them to Rakeem and I can share what I know. Now he may be ready. I want him to say to me in his mind: Please give me a chance. And I know that behind Rocky's Pizza is the only place where I don't have to keep moving. Where there is not just air in me that keeps me from crumbling, but blood and meat and strong bones and feelings. I will be me for a few minutes behind Rocky's Pizza and I don't care if it's just a few minutes. I pat my hair down in the mirror next to the kitchen door. I take Anita's letter knife out my jacket pocket and leave it on the table next to where Tommy is standing telling his wife that she never knew what love was till she met him and why does she have to be like that, talking about leaving him and shit? You keep going that way and you won't ever know how to keep a man, bitch.

JOHN ROLFE GARDINER

The Voyage Out

FROM THE NEW YORKER

TONY HOSKINS, at twelve, was an intellectual child, wary of
sensation. Not a prodigy exactly, but at the head of his form at
Cacketts School. He could declaim on several tales from Chaucer,
and on the paths of the planets, even on the curious journeys of
human sperm and ovum, although he hadn't a clue about finding
a girlfriend or about what might be asked of him in pleasing one.

On this day he was saying all the wrong things. First to his father:
"Daddy, at least I'll be sailing on a British ship, under a British
flag."

"Actually not," he was told. "It's an American vessel. You'll be all
right."

This was before the German began to aim his torpedoes at
Yanks, before his subs began to hunt in wolfpacks.

"Not to worry," his father went on. "You'll be in convoy."

Why a convoy if no need to worry? His father, in Royal Army
lieutenant's uniform, bare of medals, could not answer.

Hoping to put his religion in order before embarkation, Tony
looked to his mother. "Tell me again, what's the Trinity?" he said
unexpectedly just before the ship pulled out.

"Tiresome boy," she said. "Three in one and one in three. If you
don't understand that, you shan't have a chocolate."

Again he was confused; his mother's simplistic formulation seemed
at odds with her piety. Hardly off the gangplank, his legs rubbery
with fear, he didn't want candy, only assurance that this huge and
blunt-prowed merchant ship with a woman's name, the Ellen Reilly,
riding high in the water, would come to safe port across the
Atlantic and that his new school would be tolerable.

He saw other parents retreating, crying into handkerchiefs, stumbling off the boat and along the dock, giving their boys up to the sea and a new world. The drawn lips of his father and mother began to quaver as they turned away. And enemies appeared beside him, his second-form mates Booth and Jeffries, full of questions:

"Do the lifeboats have engines?"

"Is it daytime in Canada?"

"Will we take a secret course to avoid submarines?"

The same boys who despised him in the classroom, who had called him "twit" and "wonkie" for his privileged conversations with the masters, were hovering around him. Why should he nurse their fears?

And here came Rasson-Pier, who was older, a fifth former who had once caned Tony for impudence. Rasson-Pier told them all to shut up. He said the lot of them should be ashamed for leaving their country in wartime. And if it were up to him he'd be in uniform, not in retreat.

"Hoskins, you're in my cabin," he announced. "See that the beds are made taut."

Rasson-Pier, tall, well muscled, and lording it over the others from Cacketts, with gray eyes under blond bangs, and sufficient beard to be permitted a razor in his kit.

Riding down the channel from Folkstone, Tony tried to use his father's advice: "Think of the ship as the floating island of a country still at peace." Over on their left was France, which he knew to be alive with Germans; on the right, his own island, which, after dark, would be under attack again from the air.

Only three weeks earlier, Tony's headmaster, strolling across his playing fields at night, had been killed by a bomb far off its city target. A miraculous and devastating event, a direct hit on school morale. In the ensuing rearrangements of the school year, Tony and six other boys, and Mr. Pardue, history master of the stunned academy, had been booked on this empty supply ship — refugees for resettlement in a Canadian boarding school.

The Ellen Reilly came clear of the coast and swung to the west. There was no convoy, only open sea. Tony took the blank journal his father had given him that morning (with the advice of writing five hundred words a day at bedtime) and threw it over the side.

"You mustn't be angry," Pardue admonished. "It will only be fourteen days." But Tony gestured at the zigzag wake of the ship, the pattern of fear they were leaving on the sea behind them.

"Never mind," Pardue told him, "you'll be at their organ in two weeks. Maybe some of your Chopin, eh?"

"Maybe some of his Chopin, eh?" The other boys played with the line, but anxiety cracked their voices.

In the boys' new school, an oddity of brick and stone nestled in farm fields to the west of Toronto, they came to be known as "The Boys from Cacketts," or "The Boys from Cacketts Minus One," after the tragedy at sea, while their teacher shepherd became "Pastor Pardue" among his new colleagues, who found him to be a total loss as an instructor, and a fount of useless homily: "There are no ifs in history."

They were set apart as a curious subculture among the relatively coarse population of Canadian boys — a little band with a higher order of fealty to the King, and led in intellect by the youngest, the pale scholar Tony. He was allowed into the school chapel each afternoon to practice at the organ, while the others were led off to a field to fight over a leather ball or flail away with cricket bats. Tony had come with two copies of his medical excuse, proof of his asthma — one to be filed in the school infirmary, and the other for his pocket. Thus reprieved from athletic torment, he was free to demonstrate his case that the body's only sensible purpose is to carry around the brain.

On October 28, 1941, Lieutenant Gerald Hoskins dashed off a note, from his office in the London Cage, to his son, Tony, at the Charter Bridge School:

Dearest Tony,

Horrible, horrible. We had the awful news before your letter arrived. There are not enough tears in the world to answer for the loss of a child. And such a well-favored boy by all reports. You must be numb. Our only response to such an untimely death can be surpassing love for those who survive. Try to think of our love for you.

You say the Trinity was revealed to you on the crossing. Very well, but remember you are stuck to the planet by gravity,

and from an Oriental perspective you may be upside
down, worshipping the devil. But no more — the Colonel is
calling.

P.S. No, we don't keep animals here. Nor are there Nazis in
dank cells. "London Cage" is simply the informal name given to
this interrogation center. From time to time I will write you
from my office here, where I won't have your mother looking
over my shoulder. The address here must remain unknown to
you. Your letters should be posted home.

A second letter from the lieutenant to his son, dated November
15, 1941:

Dearest Tony,

Nothing from you this month. Our assumption must be that
you have settled in and found a schedule suited to your
special needs. We have a report from Dean Hastie, who tells us
your academic proficiency is "not balanced by contribution
to community."

While offering the excuse of your harrowing journey, he cites
you for sarcastic remarks about the Canadian students, for shirking
work in the school garden, and resisting dress regulations.

Though your mother and I agree that shorts are not suited to
the climate, the answer is to bundle heavily on top. Wear the
sweater, scarf, and cap as prescribed in the school manual. You
know that long trousers come in the third form, just as they do
at Cacketts.

You may have heard on the wireless that we are managing
quite well in the air. When I am not translating or writing
interrogation reports, they have me reading prisoners' mail.
There, I've told you a little secret, and you must keep it to yourself.

A sympathy committee has been got up here. We take turns
visiting the Rasson-Piers. When you have a moment you will
write them whatever you can muster of David's last days.
Perhaps something you found heroic in him, or you could
express your wonder at his potential. As the last to see him you
are a target of their curiosity. They have questions beyond the
police type, which they are too discreet or grief-bound to ask.
It will be your job, now or later, to anticipate and console.

It's too awful to think he might have been showing off

acrobatically so close to the side. Showing off for whom? one asks, since no one saw him go overboard. So dreadful for all of you, wondering if he were hiding somewhere or actually lost at sea.

We hope the investigation has ended and we pray for your happiness. Or, I should say, your mother prays and I beg of fate. Have you been faithful to your journal? It will be a revelation to you in time to come.

After the blank journal had gone over the side, Mr. Pardue had gone to his cabin to fetch a substitute, another bound notebook with marbled cover.

"Your father told me how much this means to him," he said to Tony. "I've put in some starter lines for you." He pointed to the first page:

> For every trouble under the sun,
> There be a remedy or there be none.
> If there be one, try and find it,
> If there be none, never mind it.

"You take it from there," he said, smiling.

Before they left the channel someone had puked. And now the boys' stomachs felt the rise, fall, and side shift of the Atlantic's heavy quartering waters. The first officer promised only more discomfort. "That's right — we're empty," he announced on the boat deck. "And the higher she rides, the further she rolls."

He had come from the bridge to lay down ship's rules for the Cacketts boys. At mealtime they would go to the mess deck, officers' side. The rest of the day they would remain in their cabins doing schoolwork. For exercise, they could walk the main deck, but only with Mr. Pardue's supervision. The bridge and hold of the ship were off-limits. The boys must stay out of the crew's cabins and out of the galley, or risk losing a hand to the steward's cleaver.

The officer had no sooner turned back when Rasson-Pier performed the first of his handstands on the ship's railing. Upside down, he had winked at Tony as the ship rocked in a rising swell.

"See that, Hoskins?" The older boy's hand was on Tony's shoulder as they went to their cabin. "You can count on me, you see. I'll be watching out for you. You have nothing to fear from the chaps in Canada."

*

Dean Hastie at the Charter Bridge School to the parents of Tony
Hoskins in Brasted, Kent, November 30, 1942:

We normally write to parents of the boys from Cacketts at the
end of each term. However, the head and I felt it would be
wrong to delay in reporting that Tony is in a fair way to
surpassing school records for third-form boys in Mathematics,
Latin, and History of the Empire. He might achieve similar
distinction in Composition if he could be kept to assigned topics.

We should recommend your son for immediate advancement
to fourth form if his social and emotional maturity were up to
the same marks. As you know, at Charter Bridge we strive to
develop the fully rounded boy. We had expected that in his
second year here Tony would have put new-boy diffidence behind
him and joined with a will in some extracurricular pursuit.

Perhaps Tony has mentioned the motto cut in stone over
our chapel door. "Remember Now Thy Creator in the Days of
Thy Youth." We take the charge seriously, so you must not
misunderstand when I say the religious conversion your son
experienced on his journey here is troubling in its intensity.
Our chaplain cannot shake him from his testimony that the
Trinity was revealed to him on the ocean as three glowing
balls. We see no joy in his faith.

I must tell you that the transfer has not been a complete
success. The boys from Cacketts tend to remain a clique,
though they sometimes quarrel among themselves. Your son
does not seem to be a member, even of this separate band. We
sense a residual grieving here for the loss of their young idol,
and a weight of unfinished business. One boy has suggested
that Tony's original account of the events at sea may not be
reliable. And now, more than a year after the fact, our Mr.
Pardue comes forward to say that your son may have kept a
journal which might clear him of all suspicion. We wouldn't
think of invading his privacy without warrant. Perhaps you
would advise him to open relevant pages to our scrutiny.

A brighter note. Our music instructor is leaving Charter
Bridge this month, and we are asking Tony to fill in as chapel
organist for Sunday service and Wednesday vespers. It's our
little scheme to get him more involved.

*

On the journal's first page Pardue's verse has been scribbled over
and splashed with ink:

Sept. 23, 1941. Aboard the Ellen Reilly: The ship is black, red,
and rusty. Sailed 1420 Greenwich. R.-P.'s stunt behind Pardue's
back takes everyone's breath. Supper: mashed potatoes, bright-
yellow gravy of uncommon viscosity, and salty fish, white and
cooked to a mush like the potatoes. One serving of greens a
day; we missed them by coming aboard too late for lunch.

Tonight Jeffries came into our cabin crying. He wanted to
know why I was put with R.-P. R.-P. said wouldn't the Germans
love to see him like that. Jeffries left snivelling. R.-P. asked me
down from my upper to play cards on his bunk. Twenty-one. No
money, playing for favors, he said. I lost terribly, what do I owe
him? R.-P. has torch with extra dry cells. He will allow me to use
it to keep my notes. Says he's at sea in Latin. Quite so! And
I, a second former, might help.

Booth came in shaking with fear. The idiot thinks he heard a
torpedo propeller passing under us. No one can sleep.

A year after the crossing, the notebook was more useful to Tony
as a chronology of odd particulars than as a thoroughgoing journal
— a skeleton on which his memory hung the dangerous flesh, the
things he would never have written down. For example, the way
Rasson-Pier's tone had changed after lights-out, from cold command
to simpering — as if he were taking the part of a woman in a play.

With the notion of water rushing in to drown him in his sleep,
Tony had sneaked out of his cabin in the middle of the first night
and wandered through dim-lit passages, down metal stairways, into
empty cargo compartments. Somewhere close to the throbbing center of the ship he heard a horse whinny and a lion roar. Alarmed
by what he took to be his own inventions, he became confused in
retreat, and spent an unconscionable time finding his cabin again.

From Lieutenant Gerald Hoskins at the London Cage to Tony
Hoskins at the Charter Bridge School, April 13, 1943:

Yes, we support your refusal to show any part of the journal.
Violation of your private thoughts is tantamount to rape of
the spirit.

There is mischief here, too. I'm sorry to say we are no longer
speaking with the Rasson-Piers since they find more comfort
in the gossip of the Jeffrieses, passed along by their son Arthur.
A poisonous little chap, I'd guess, but you would know better
than I.

Yes, traits in an individual can be correlated with national
origin, the pieties of Mr. Pardue to the contrary
notwithstanding. It's quite possible that the impulsive and
vainglorious side of David Rasson-Pier was passed along by the
father's French parents. As to the question of cultural
distinction, consider the opening lines of two letters which
crossed my desk this week, the first from a German: "Dear
Mother, The most awful thing has happened. We have been
captured by the English and are being held in Oran, waiting
transfer to a prison camp in America."

The second from an Italian: "Dear Mama, The most
wonderful thing has happened. We have been captured by the
English and will soon be on our way to the United States."

Don't mistake me. I'm not advocating one attitude over the
other. But if your Pardue doubts the relevance of my example,
I suggest he visit the prison camp in Bowmanville. I'm told the
Germans there are goose-stepped by their officers to the mess
hall, where Italians happily prepare the food and banter about
the women waiting for them in the town.

No, we do not hold it against the Dean for denying you
further use of the chapel organ. Really! A two-octave glissando
at the end of "God Save the King" while the school waited for
amen! Did you expect to get away with that?

Guard your journal.

September 25, 1941, aboard the Ellen Reilly:

This whole ship trembles with the thump of its engines.
Diesels, I'm told. Above this constant drumming is the daylong
rattle of electric paint chippers as the crew works at their
endless chore of scraping and painting. They'll go from bow
to stern, then start all over again.

No one actually studied today. In spite of the din, fell asleep
over my books. R.-P. woke me before Pardue came in. Anyone
caught napping during study time gets twenty-four-hour

cabin confinement. I've been made tutor of second and third
formers. Pardue says those not prone to seasickness must
minister to those who are. He is. So is Jeffries. I am not.

Booth apologized for rudeness. As R.-P. has taken my part,
others are shifting colors, too, seeking my favor. At present,
most of them are unable to function. While they moan in their
bunks, I explore.

Dolphins weaving under the prow. Watching them for most
of an hour before slipping below again. One of the crew stopped
me. Only wanted to talk. This was Sam, an able-bodied seaman,
who is missing two fingers, and limps. Asked did I know there
were unfortunates below. Heard animals again in lower cargo
compartments. Couldn't find them.

Night walk. The deck was dark but for moonlight. No outside
lights permitted. Passageways only faintly lit. Memorized
numbers on doors and did not get lost. No one believes I saw a
black-haired girl in bathing costume. She was rattling a cup of
coins and chanting something sad, as if practicing to be a
beggar. Someone called from another compartment, *"Raklo!
Raklo!"* and she stood still as a stone. If R.-P. doesn't believe any
of this, why does he keep asking how old the girl was and what
she looked like? Very young. Her skin a mottled ochre.

Someone filched my breakfast orange. R.-P. boxed Booth's
ear. Doesn't matter who did it, he says, just doesn't want it
happening again.

Tony had put aside pen and notebook when Rasson-Pier offered
his soft invitation.

"Do you want to come down to my bunk?" All the courage and
bluster vanishing again.

"No."

"For a little visit?"

"No."

"You're to be kind to those who aren't feeling well."

He didn't believe the older boy was sick, only dodging the books
for another day, with the sympathy of Pardue.

"No."

From Dean Hastie at the Charter Bridge School to the parents of
Tony Hoskins in Brasted, Kent, May 21, 1943:

Looking toward vacation, we are suggesting that Tony not
remain in dormitory with Mr. Pardue and the other boys from
Cacketts. We would not want a repeat of last summer's incident.
With your permission, Tony will spend the interim at the
Croyston farm, which provides the school with milk and eggs.

A picture of the family is enclosed. In truth, I think the Croystons
would welcome an appropriately innocent companion for their
shy daughter, Margaret, and your son seems well suited for the
job. Though the family won't provide intellectual stimulation,
they keep a wholesome life, devout yet not without humor.

Tony will be expected to help with farm chores, perhaps just
the thing for the continuing melancholy. A break from the high
academic standard to which he holds himself, and from his
difficult religion. May I quote him? "The faith at Charter Bridge
is to true faith as water is to wine." Perhaps the justification
for his little musical joke on the school.

We have not discounted homesickness — the long, unnatural
separation from the two of you. Too, the Rasson-Pier case will
not go away. As I explained months ago, the initial investigation
produced little but tears and mystery. Should we discourage the
family from persisting? So many loose ends. From their distance
can they be sure the appropriate questions were asked? Our
Cacketts boys have kept the stew at a boil.

You ask again for the facts free of the children's fantasy.
The ship's log reported the child missing on October 1, 1941.
Captain Andrew Shad made inquiries and established that
David had been given to reckless displays of daring. He
concluded one of these must have been the boy's final act.

The Ellen Reilly made its first port, Halifax, on October 7.
Our boys disembarked and were detained there two days for
questioning, first by the R.C.M.P., later by a visiting magistrate
from London. Before the investigation was completed and
the Captain's finding upheld, the ship had already taken on
grain and tinned food, and sailed the night of October 8 for
Baltimore. There the loading of war supplies was completed.
With the same officers and crew the boat turned back for
England on October 14.

We now believe there was another element on board the
Ellen Reilly between England and North America, a group kept
apart from legitimate ship's company but sighted several times

if we are to believe the Jeffries boy and your own child. A band
of Polish performers? Gypsies? Lithuanian Jews? How they came
to be on the ship and where they disembarked are as open to
speculation as their nationality.

We had, too, the crass report of a seaman named Sam, put
off the boat in Halifax for the theft of a pair of shoes. He was
a rough sort who befriended several of our boys and
entertained them with bawdy talk in his quarters, which they
knew were off-limits.

This Sam testified to having seen passengers in the hold. He
fouled his account with details of a dark young lady, little more
than a child by his word, offering her favors to several of the
crew. If people didn't believe him, he said, they could ask our
boys what she'd do.

As to the mysterious travellers, whether Captain Shad gave
them passage as a humanitarian gesture or for his own profit
is unclear. Their arrival was not recorded by Canadian
immigration. Shad, who survives as a master in the merchant
marine (the Ellen Reilly went down in January, off the Azores),
does not deny that such a group could have been stowaways
during his command.

We are told that the docks in Halifax are too closely patrolled
for any such band to have disembarked without papers. They
may never have come ashore in North America unless they were
spirited off the ship in Baltimore. The United States was not yet
at war, and security was doubtless lax. This seems a remote
possibility but so does their very existence on board. Given the
curious tatterdemalion migrations and urgencies of wartime,
their passage is not beyond belief. Perhaps sympathy, reinforced
by coin, eased the path into America.

Again we ask you to urge your child to come forward with
his journal, if it exists, and any relevant information that might
soothe the family. We have again advised the Rasson-Piers
against a crossing.

Though we find Tony a difficult boy, the faculty is interested
by him, and, if I may say so, fond of him. We would see nothing
unnatural in an infatuation he may have had for David Rasson-
Pier. These things are common as hiccups among schoolboys,
and are left behind as naturally as they arrive.

Our comptroller reminds me that we have not received your

share of reparations for the water damage in Tony's room last August. We appreciate your faith in Tony's innocent part. However, a clear culprit was not found, and all the boys from Cacketts must share the cost of repair.

September 26, 1941, aboard the Ellen Reilly:

Ocean calm but Sam says we're headed into "weather to pump the boys' stomachs again." Complimented me for my sea legs. Told him R.-P. is faking it to avoid the books. If he were sick, how could he use the ship's rail for a gymnast's horse? He spins his legs right around over the side. Jeffries, Phillips, and Booth have all seen him do it. Gives me the willies. Booth said he wouldn't care if R.-P. lost his balance.

Found another route to the forward cargo bay. Hid in a crate and watched the show. Bales of hay set out in a circle. There appears to be a family circus travelling with us. Preparing its act for America? A small black bear was brought in, muzzled and growling softly. Is this the noise I took for a lion's roar? Can bears survive on ship's rations? There is also a miniature pony that whinnies like a full-grown horse.

I suppose the man must throw knives every day or get out of practice. Tonight the girl was pitiable, with her chin fallen to her chest, and her arms stretched wide, like Christ on the cross, and surrounded by the steel blades delivered in rapid order. By her father? Her brother?

A woman unleashed the bear and placed it on the seat of a small bicycle. Maybe upset by the motion of the ship, it could not keep the pedals going and tumbled over.

R.-P. says I must pay my gambling debt. I'm sure he cheated me.

Tony had recorded nothing of what happened the next day, or the following night when, after lights-out, Rasson-Pier had climbed into the upper bunk with him, whispering urgently, "The others needn't know."

He wrote nothing of his haunted sleep, of this famous athlete poking around behind him with his stupidly swollen thing.

*

From Captain Gerald Hoskins at the London Cage to Tony Hoskins
at the Charter Bridge School, September 20, 1943:

Dearest Tony,

Your mother and I would transfer you to another school in
an instant if it were reasonably within our power. Our distance,
our ignorance of alternatives, and the Dean's reluctance to
recommend "some inferior academy" all work against us. It is
an outrage that your notebook was stolen. We have demanded
an apology from Hastie. He seems to us a great blandifier.
Believe me, you have nothing to fear from him but his
dangerous good will.

It is out of the question for you to return to England now.
The Americans have only just begun to appreciate the logic of
convoys. In the meantime their coastal waters have become a
continent-long fireworks display, with U-boats sinking tankers
and supply ships at will. Hardly a time to play "Red Rover, Red
Rover, Let Tony Come Over."

There is nothing to be ashamed of in your account of the
crossing save the occasional grammatical lapse, though eyebrows
are raised at the mention of gambling. The hounds have what
they've bayed for, a dry bone. Now let them bury it.

The Dean says you worked admirably for the Croystons and
amazed their church youth fellowship with the force of your
testimony. I know your mother's letters are full of admiration
for your spiritual awakening. She warns me not to disrupt your
faith with petty sophistry. Still, I can't approve a dogma which
condemns to perdition all those beyond its pale. This is *entre nous*.

It's no special boast to tell you I've been promoted to
Captain. All officers here at the Cage have taken one step up.
So, nothing heroic, though I am credited with devising a new
purgative for the tight-lipped Germans. I stamp their papers
N.R. (*Nach Russland,* to Russia) and their mouths run a torrent.

From Dean Hastie at the Charter Bridge School to the parents of
Tony Hoskins in Brasted, Kent, January 24, 1944:

Again the school offers its full apology to you and your
son. That Tony's journal should have been taken from his

room is altogether unacceptable. That pages were copied and distributed is despicable.

We don't know who stole the notebook. It appeared in the office of our school paper, the *Charter Sentinel,* where the editor, one of our senior boys, cut a stencil of certain pages and ran them off on the mimeograph machine. This misguided chap, who comes to us from Detroit with a warped notion of press freedom, has been relieved of all journalistic duty.

I now believe it was a mistake to badger Tony for his record of the voyage. The notes have only raised the anxiety of the Rasson-Piers, who insist they could not be the work of a twelve-year-old. In their new anguish they suspect the cruel mischief of an adult — a post-dated fabrication supporting the police report of a foolhardy, self-inflicted death.

The family's theory was reinforced by your son's admission that the notebook was not the original, lost at sea, but a substitute provided by Mr. Pardue. Thus, he too is a subject of suspicion. The evidence of a missing page, the ragged edge in the journal, where a sheet was torn from it, adds to our confusion. The more so, since this was apparently part of the entry for October 2, 1941, the day after David's disappearance was first recorded.

We have assured the family that the original notes are in Tony's skilled hand, and that your son is capable of the vocabulary and sentiment, even the occasional poetic flourish. We couldn't swear to the dating of the entries, but have no reason to doubt their honesty. The headmaster and I were disturbed by references to gambling, punishable at Charter Bridge by immediate expulsion. However, we accept Tony's word that nothing of value was to be exchanged, only favors.

That the mysterious travellers below-decks are transformed into a Gypsy circus seems a wild leap of imagination. Our school physician advises me that the mind under stress (all the Cacketts boys have acknowledged their numbing terror of submarines) may take refuge in illusion.

A copy of the mimeographed notes is now in the hands of the police, who have asked to speak with Tony once more. Be assured that the school's attorney will again be on hand to prevent investigative bullying. If Tony chooses to tell them he

remembers nothing, that will suffice. We pray for a return to
academic tranquillity.

September 28, 1941, aboard the Ellen Reilly:

   The rattle of the paint chippers stopped for a merciful hour
this morning. Pardue took advantage of the relative quiet,
calling a meeting in his cabin to rally spirits. He never rose
from his bunk. The air was horrid.
   Our workbooks will be collected tomorrow, though there
is not a word or cipher in most of them. Took Pardue some
tea this morning and was caught out by Phillips watching from
the door of his room. Phillips says it will all come out
when we reach Canada, all the broken rules. And there will
be whippings. Told him there is no corporal punishment at
Charter Bridge. He seemed much relieved. He asked what R.-P.
talks about and does he do stunts in the cabin.
   Pardue whined pitifully for me to take his tray away. The
smell of toast and margarine was making him ill again. Jeffries
tried to trip me at his doorway. Called me "suck-bottom."
   I can tolerate the pitch and roll of the ship. Also, the further
one descends through the lower decks, the less one notices the
roll. Sam says the people below are stealing food. The galley
is missing a dozen tins of beef. Bear provender? Captain Shad
is furious and says we've been roving through his ship against
orders. I'm the one. I suppose the others would rather die in
their cabins.
   I have seen a periscope like a black needle in the waves
behind us.

October 1, 1941, aboard the Ellen Reilly:

   R.-P. did not return to the cabin last night. A search for him
began this morning. Certain we won't find him.

   There followed a line obliterated, washed over with ink. How
many times had he been asked, "If you wrote 'certain,' were you
not certain?" And "Why did you cross this out?" Why should he
tell them, "I did not cry with the rest"?

                                    *

On the evening of September 29, Rasson-Pier followed Tony down through the maze of passages to the performance chamber, complaining repeatedly of the grease stains the metal stairways were leaving on his trousers.

"Periscope? Girl in a bathing costume? What next, Hoskins?"

"Why didn't Pardue put Phillips with you?" Tony asked him. "Someone more your age."

"I asked for you," he said. "Thought it might give you a boost."

The hero of the Cacketts playing fields had asked for *him?* Anxious about displeasing Rasson-Pier again, he prayed the girl would be there.

She was sitting on a bale, with her back to them. A long black dress appliquéd with red and orange rings gave the effect of contouring her ample young figure in tight-fitting bracelets.

"Run along," Rasson-Pier ordered. "I'll speak to her alone."

"She doesn't speak English," Tony said. "I could try a little French for you."

Why had he wanted to be helpful? He was only pushed aside.

The girl turned and stared at them without modesty. Before Rasson-Pier could sit beside her, she had risen, taken his arm, and was leading him away through the hatch at the far end of the compartment. Perhaps a fortune-teller, Tony thought, leading him to a private place to read his palm.

From Dean Hastie at the Charter Bridge School to the parents of Tony Hoskins, Brasted, Kent, January 26, 1944:

I dare to presume a friendship has developed between us in our pursuit of your son's welfare. This letter following close on the heels of the last is prompted by a surprising turn in the Rasson-Pier case. There is now a theory the boy may be alive.

We are told by the police that there was a family row before the voyage, a shouting match in which David called his parents such names as "pale cowards" and "funny little people." He threatened never to come back if they packed him off to Canada. This was followed by one of his acrobatic demonstrations, a walk on his hands down a stone stairway in front of their home in Kent. Certainly a thoughtless display in front of his troubled parents.

The imaginations of the Rasson-Piers must be racing along

with the flow of news and rumor from the families of our
Cacketts contingent. I'm told that "Gypsy circus" is oxymoronic,
that, while Gypsy children are often sent out to beg, the families
never perform or work for money, unless it be in telling the
future.

The Rasson-Piers now cling to the frail chance that a
rebellious David might have been drawn to, or charmed away
by, this band that must have intended to land in America.
That they may have seen profit in his gymnastic virtuosity. But
who is to say they were Gypsies? Haven't they also been called
Lithuanian Jews and Polish performers?

I turn again to Tony's situation. Why do the other children
continue to torment him? If the authorities don't trust his
written account, how will they credit his oral testimony?

Your child has taken refuge in his faith. All worthy counsel,
he avers, comes from the three-person God, though we know he
looks daily to his letter box for guidance from you. Your son
has lost weight. We try to see that he eats well.

From Captain Gerald Hoskins at the London Cage to Tony Hoskins
at the Charter Bridge School, February 15, 1944:

Dearest Tony,

We're proud of you. Stick to your guns, and ask yourself this:
Why would they have you impeach yourself? What good could
come of it? Can the lost boy be brought back? If you find
yourself in a compromising box, don't jump out in public. If
there is something to say that can cause only humiliation, take
it to this higher being of yours, all three of him if necessary.
I am dead serious. Take proper nourishment, and hold on. You
will cross this way in victory the moment the Atlantic is secure.

Early on September 30, Rasson-Pier had come back to the cabin
quite exhausted.

"They don't wash, you know," he said. He sighed and fell asleep.
Tony covered for him through the morning, calling "Studying,
please" when the others knocked for their morning chats.

At noon, Rasson-Pier was awake and irritable.

"Who doesn't wash?" Tony asked him.

But the older boy was looking into the future. "If you say anything of what's happened in this cabin, I'll report your funny business when I caned you at Cacketts."

"What business?"

"The way you enjoyed it. Even more without trousers."

"I never. Whatever do you mean?"

"Yes, well, who will they believe?" He fell back on his bunk. "Perhaps I'll tell them anyway," he said.

He slept again for several hours, woke, and asked, "What if she's given me the disease?"

"What disease?"

"You sap. The one that takes your brain."

"I believe there's a cure for that."

The older boy nodded slowly.

"Don't look for me tonight" was the last Tony heard him say.

If the girl's odor displeased him, if he thought her infected, why had he gone to see her again? Goatish, Tony had heard his mother say, but would not a goat demand exclusively a mate of opposite gender?

The October 1 journal entry had concluded: The ship went a drunken path through the glowing sea when the sky was torn into three ragged black sheets by lightning.

Tony had stayed out on the open deck that evening in order to avoid his roommate. Standing at the stern, he watched the serpentine course of the ship recorded in the roiled wake. With the first bolt of lightning, he swung around and saw a figure far up the deck, balanced upside down and turning with his hands on the rail, his legs, at that instant, over the side. And someone was standing there, close to him, perhaps the girl. All went black and a moment later they were all brilliantly lit by a second bolt. The spinning body was disconnected from the rail, floating out into the night.

So obvious of Rasson-Pier. Showing off for the girl. Performance was the only language they had in common. Tony made his way forward in the dark, but the two of them had vanished. No time to applaud the trick; the next act of his floating circus had already begun. A spectral ball was gliding down the stay that ran from antenna mast to the bow. It split into two glowing spheres, and then there were three of them, evenly spaced, moving back and forth along the taut metal line. He watched for several minutes until they merged into one again and disappeared.

October 2, 1941, aboard the Ellen Reilly:

Is he pestering the dolphins? Sawn into rude portions by sharks? Have I seen the spirit of God in triplicate?

The next page had been torn from the notebook.

From Tony Hoskins at the Croyston farm to his parents in Brasted, Kent, August 23, 1944:

The summer has flown. I am two inches taller. Six feet! The second haying is finished. I was allowed to work the rake, an old-fashioned thing once pulled by a horse, this season by an ancient tractor, petrol being available. For two weeks, I've been sitting on the metal seat of the rake and lifting its tines at each windrow with a hand lever. As a result my right arm is appreciably muscled, and I must do something to bring the left into balance.

Yesterday a man came to replace some rotten boards in the north end of the haymow. I was asked my estimate of the barn's height at the point of the gable. I could tell them quite precisely, I said, by measuring the shadow of the barn and that of a pole of known length, then applying simple geometry. By the time I gave my answer, Mr. Croyston had made a calculation of his own and the carpenter was on his way to the lumber- yard. My figure was off by half a foot, Mr. Croyston's correct to the inch. So my fancy education is a thing of some amusement here, though Margaret is keen to share my books and ideas.

Last Thursday I was asked to escort her to a "young people's" in the village. It's not the social gathering it sounds. There is some flirtation, but only so much as is possible when you are seated in church pews under the eyes of a preacher.

Between hymns, each boy and girl is expected to rise, in turn, and share a faith-affirming experience. I think I blushed awfully when the minister's eyes fell on me, but I was able to stand and tell again of the three balls of fire over the deck of the Ellen Reilly. By the end of my story the pastor's eyes were brimful, and *I* was embarrassed for *him*. Margaret, seated to my right, took my hand when I sat down again.

From Captain Hoskins at the London Cage to Tony Hoskins at the Charter Bridge School, September 10, 1944:

A note to tell you that civilians are crossing again! Given proper escort, it appears to be safe. I've made inquiries, and will find a berth for you the moment space is available on a secure ship. You've been so long there under brutish circumstances. It would be cruel of us to leave you longer than is prudent for your safety. We know that there is still talk of your journal's missing page. I fear the gossips will never give it up.

From Tony Hoskins at the Charter Bridge School to his parents in Brasted, Kent, October 5, 1944:

Please do not book passage for me. I'm content and intend to finish here.

Fair questions have been raised, and there is something I want to clear up about the voyage out. When I saw David Rasson-Pier spinning above the ship's rail, I thought he'd learned a new trick. It never occurred to me he was out of control. Not until it was far too late to give an alarm.

The following day I returned to the same place on the deck. Looking down, I saw a row of three lifeboats suspended over the side. One could speculate about David's having possibly fallen onto the canopy covering one of these and climbing back onto the deck below. But the chance is so minuscule. Believe me, he perished at sea. It's too late to raise another slim hope that can only give anguish.

If you must know, the page torn from my journal held my thoughts on the family belowdecks. Particularly the girl, and Rasson-Pier's use of her. I did not invent the girl. Think of her under a rain of knives, and try to imagine throwing knives at me for a living.

The Dean is quite mistaken about Gypsies. They frequently take itinerant work, and are known for their rapport with animals, notably as trainers of circus acts. And when I went down in the ship, I heard *"Raklo! Raklo!"* called out like a crow's

warning. It's the Gypsy word for a non-Gypsy boy. I doubt I will
see her again, or know what befell her, but we were all Gypsies
on that voyage, I now believe, and I would cry *"Raklo!"* now to
those who did not make the crossing. Our chaplain says the
war has blown seed, good and bad, to all points of the compass,
and it remains to be seen what will germinate. High hopes for
me. But what of the rootless Gypsies? I like to think of the girl
and her family moving across America, performing, escaping,
from one camp to the next.

I'm confident her troupe survives. Almost as certain as I am
that David Rasson-Pier is dead. The passage of time has not
weakened my resolve not to write to his family. You will have to
guess at my reasons.

About my "hard faith," as Hastie calls it. You shouldn't think
I ever believed the fireballs over the ship's deck were the
actual embodiment of the Trinity. I took them, rather, as a
phenomenal sign of Mother's faith. No more periscopes after
that. They helped me complete the crossing without going mad.
And why should that sign be erased now, by some scientific
explanation? Really, for men who profess faith, some of my
instructors are quite hopelessly literal.

For all that, I like the teachers here quite as well as the
masters at Cacketts. The Atlantic may, as you say, be secured for
Allied shipping. Nevertheless, I don't wish to return to England
before graduating from Charter Bridge.

From Dean Hastie at the Charter Bridge School to the parents of
Tony Hoskins in Brasted, Kent, November 20, 1944:

We shall never hope to understand this war's random terror,
why we are spared here in our snug academy while refugees
from all walks are driven pillar to post. I do believe we can now
take hope in these few boys from Cacketts who were washed
up on our shores. I am their Dean, yet I sense that they are
children no more. The heat of war has fired them, and they
shine with a new hardness and brilliance. Especially your son.

You would not recognize Tony. His second summer on the
Croyston farm did wonders. He is quite filled out in athletic
proportion, and happy as we have never seen him. It will please
you to hear, too, that your son has found common ground

with students and masters alike, and can be seen on occasion
roughhousing and joking with his mates from Cacketts.

Something has cleared the air. There is less ostentation in his
religious assertion. I don't think the other boys ever believed he
was guilty of any complicity in the Rasson-Pier tragedy. Rather,
they resented his claim to a private audience with God on
the voyage out. Without boasting, we give our faculty credit
here, in particular our Department of Physical Science. Mr.
Theonel believes his lecture on electricity was responsible. As he
says, "Knowledge must rush in where dispelled superstition leaves
a vacuum." Tony now concedes that the three balls of light he
saw on the ship's antenna must have been static electricity, the
phenomenon called "St. Elmo's fire."

We think it gave him comfort to learn from our History
instructor that early mariners also believed they witnessed holy
bodies in the rigging of their ships — the *corpus sancti,* or
corposants, as they called them. Tony will be returning to you
with a new maturity. Once more, he has our permission to
practice his music on the chapel organ. Eventually, I'm sure,
he'll be trusted to play for our services again.

The third anniversary of David Rasson-Pier's disappearance
will not have escaped your notice. It was observed here by a
special prayer at evening vespers, and a reading of this note
from the family: "We believe our son perished at sea by his own
dangerous devices. To those children who survive, we offer our
blessing. Your useful lives must be our monument to David's
memory." The school is much relieved by their sad but sensible
resignation.

The Charter Bridge students filing in to the final chapel service
of the year were surprised to see Tony Hoskins seated at the organ.
Excited, they squirmed and whispered in their pews, as if assured
of a sacrilege to spice the imminent summer rebellion.

They were disappointed to hear scarcely a hint of the expected
irreverence. Buttercup's theme floated over "Faith of Our Fathers," so cleverly hidden in tempo and contrapuntal disguise that
no one but the new music instructor was wise to it. From the choir
he winked approval at his richly gifted student.

DAVID GATES

The Mail Lady

FROM GRAND STREET

1

I WAKE AGAIN in our bedroom, vouchsafed another day. May I
use it to Thy greater glory. In the dimness, a throbbing line of
sunlight along the bottom of the window shade stabs the eye. So the
rain has stopped at last. (Memory spared. Reason spared, too, seemingly.) When I turn away, my sight is momentarily burned black,
and I can't be certain whether I'm truly *seeing* Wylie's features in
the photograph on the nightstand or simply remembering them.
I close my eyes again, and in afterimage the fierce light reappears.

The radio's on downstairs and I hear that sweet song, now what
on earth is that called? Sweet sweet song. Our station comes all
the way from Boston, and seems to be the one certain refuge
anywhere on the dial. We still try the classical station from time to
time — back in Woburn, we never deviated from WCRB — but
now find it awfully heavy going. (I have it: "Edelweiss.") Now I hear
a rustle of sheets. Alice is in here, making her bed. And checking
on me. I don't open my eyes. A pat to her pillow and she's gone.

In the first weeks after my shock, I slept fourteen, sixteen hours
a day, they tell me. The brain, as they explain it, shutting down in
order to repair itself. It's the queerest idea: one's body simply
shoving one aside. Lately I'm down to eight or nine hours (plus
my nap in the afternoon), so I assume that much of what could
be done has now been done. The thing is to be thankful for what's
come back. But try as I will, it frets me: I had been, for my age, an
active man. Taking care that each season's duties be done. Trees

and shrubs pruned in the spring, leaves raked and burned in the fall. I would sleep six hours a night, seldom more, and wake up — if not refreshed, at least ready for what might be required. Now, in effect, I'm a child again, put to bed early and hearing the grown-ups through a closed door. Like a child, too, with these sudden storms of weeping. I'm told they could still come under control.

Stroke: a stroke of the lash, for chastisement and correction. Yet something gentle in the word as well.

The next thing I hear is Alice down in the kitchen, so I must have dozed off again. Or, God help me, had a vastation. I can hear the stove making that snapping sound, like a dangerous thing. Then it goes silent again, or nearly so, when it lights. I say nearly so because I seem to hear the ceaseless exhale of gas and the rumble of blue flame burning. Just after my shock my hearing became strangely acute (unless I was imagining it), as if in compensation for what I can only describe as the cubist way I was seeing things. Yet although my eyesight has returned to normal (thank you, Lord), that acute sense of hearing seems not to have been repossessed. So perhaps something else is being compensated for. I pray it's not some cognitive function that I'm too damaged to understand has been damaged.

Still, sharp as my hearing may be, it's impossible, isn't it, that I could hear a gas stove burning all the way down in the kitchen? Or — terrible thought — is what I'm hearing (or think I'm hearing) the hiss of unignited gas racing out the ports, spreading, expanding, filling the house? Well, and what then? Would I shout for Alice — who, being downstairs, may have been overcome already? Would I struggle up out of bed and make my way down the stairs after my new fashion, bad foot scraping along after good foot and cane? Or would I simply lie here and breathe?

Well, hardly a cheerful reflection to begin the day.

And good cheer — not mere resignation — is required of us. *To be unhappy is to be in sin* — I'm certain I've read that somewhere or other, though perhaps it was the other way around. Certainly easier to swallow it the other way around — to be in sin is to be unhappy — but that makes it so trite I don't see why it would have made an impression. Now what was my point? Good cheer. I had wanted to say, it is available to us. Freely offered. We need to know where to look, is all. And where not to. Back when Wylie was a little girl and Alice and I would have our troubles (I would like to believe we never allowed them to darken her childhood), I used to say to myself, *But on the other hand, you have Wylie.* Though there were times when even that didn't mean what it ought to have meant, and at such times I would have to be stern with myself and say, *You must think of Wylie.* This was before the Lord came into my life.

It's been many years, of course, since Wylie has lived at home. And many years, too, since Alice and I have had words. So things happen as they were meant to, and in the Lord's good time. Though I dread sometimes that I will pass on before I know, with my whole heart, that this is true. When in a more hopeful frame of mind, I think the Lord would never allow it, and that His plan for me includes revelations yet in store.

Certainly Alice hasn't presumed to question (in my hearing) the dispensation that now binds her to a piece of statuary in the likeness of her husband. (Now that, I'm sorry to say, smacks of self-pity.) *In sickness and in health,* she must tell herself daily. She has never complained about being unable to leave me alone. Or about the friends who have stopped visiting. (We have seen the Petersons *once!*) Her strength shames me, much as I like to think that these past months have made shame a luxury. (I have even been, God help me, incontinent.) And from little things I over-hear, I gather she's quietly making her plans for afterwards. I'm afraid to ask about the details, and ashamed that I'm afraid. Isn't this something she's owed: a chance to talk with her husband about what must be on her mind constantly? What may in fact have been on her mind for years, since even before my illness (as she calls it) the actuarial tables were on her side. Although we've always taken pride (I know it's blamable) in not being like the generality of people.

It was my conversion, of course, that made me odd man out for many of my working years. Research chemists tend to be a skeptical lot anyway, and our company was particularly forward-thinking. (We were one of the first, you know, to have moved out to Route 128.) Eventually I decided it was best to steer clear of certain discussions; *As much as lieth in you,* Paul tells us, *live peaceably with all men.* Poor Alice, meanwhile, has had to go from being the wife of a hot-tempered drinker to being the wife of a religious nut, so-called. I remember one day, shortly after my life had been transformed, I walked in on her ironing one of Wylie's school skirts with the telephone wedged between ear and shoulder. "I'll tell you, June," she was saying, "I don't get it quite, but I don't look a gift horse in the mouth." Then she noticed me in the doorway and drew a hissing in-breath as her arms shrank into her ribs and the receiver clunked to the floor.

Up here we've found our neighbors more congenial politically than the old crowd from work, if not so well informed. The mail lady has told Alice that no one in town gets so many magazines. The people we know here, other retirees mostly, take *Modern Maturity* and *Reader's Digest*. The younger people, I imagine, scarcely read a newspaper; Alice was dismayed to learn that only two families in town get *Time*. But of course she can make conversation with anybody, right down to the neighbor woman, that Mrs. Paquette, whose talk even in the summertime is mostly about how she can no longer stand New Hampshire winters. She was over again the other morning — or was it earlier this morning? — for coffee and chitchat. Which is what her life amounts to, as far as I can see, though what can my life seem in her eyes? I could hear them all the way downstairs.

"Well, if anything should happen to Lew," Alice was saying, "Florida's the *last* place I'd go. And I would certainly not go out and inflict myself on Wylie and Jeff."

I thought about the word *anything*.

I thought about the word *if*.

"I think I'd try and get myself one of those new little apartments over in Concord," she said. "Have you been by there?"

I knew the place she meant. Brown brick and brown window glass. I had had no idea it loomed so large for her.

I wake again when Alice comes in and sets my tray on the dresser. How long have I been asleep this time? I struggle up to a sitting position — now that's something I couldn't have done a while ago! — she wedges the triangular pillow behind me and I collapse back on it. She's taken to saying that I live the life of Riley, getting my breakfast in bed. Can she think I don't understand (and don't understand that *she* understands) the truth of what has happened to me? To which cheer is still the only adequate response — but true cheer, not this life-of-Riley business. She hands me my eyeglasses, then walks over and tugs down on the string with the lace-covered ring at the end. Up goes the shade, and there I sit blinking like a nasty old owl (I can picture myself), the white hairs of my knobby chest curling out between the lapels of my pajamas. How can she stand this, unless she looks with the eyes of love? Or unless she no longer truly looks. She places the tray across my thighs, the living and the dead. Orange juice, Postum, All-Bran, and half a pink grapefruit, its sections sliced away from the sides, ready for the spoon. And this morning, a gaudy blossom — from one of her gloxinias? — floating in a juice glass.

"Austerity breakfast," I say. Yesterday was a bacon-and-eggs day; I am not allowed two in a row.

"Posterity?" she says.

"Aus-ter-i-ty," I say, furious. I point to the food. "Austere," I say.

"Ah," she says, giving me a too energetic nod. Can't tell if she's understood or not.

"On in the world," I say, a question.

"The world?" she says. "The news? Oh, they had the most awful thing this morning."

"Hear TV going," I say, meaning *I didn't.*

"The TV?" she says. "Yes, they were talking more about that airplane."

"Jet with a bomb," I say. We'd seen the report last night.

"Well now they're saying that those people who were sucked out of that hole?" She makes parentheses in air to suggest a hole three feet across. "They're saying that they apparently were *not* killed when it went off. They found out they were alive all the way down."

"Out you're alive," I say. Meaning *Well that's one way to find out you're alive.* I was making a joke out of her *theys.* Which I suppose was heartless. Though whom, really, could it hurt? Who, for that matter, could understand it? Alice cocks her head and squints, then just barges on. "And that poor woman was pregnant," she says.

Enough and more than enough of the world news roundup. I want her out of here now. Smear my food all over my face in peace.

"I'm going to let you eat your breakfast before it gets cold," she says, though there's nothing to get cold but the Postum. "Do you need anything else, dear?"

I don't bother answering. But when I see her going through the door, going away from me, I find that I'm weeping. It's one of the peculiarities of this thing: my body's heaving with sobs, the tears are rolling down my cheeks and off my jaw, yet really I feel nothing. Or so it seems to me. I command the crying to stop: no use. Something undamaged inside me is observing all this, but can't get out of its own silent space to intervene. Quite a study in something, if I could get it across to anyone.

After the fit passes, I take my time eating. Obviously. (Now there's a joke at *my* expense!) What I mean is, I'm dawdling to put off the process of dressing myself and getting myself downstairs. Dr. Ngo (you pronounce it like the fellow in James Bond) had suggested to Alice that she convert the dining room into a bedroom, but I wouldn't hear of it. And Mrs. Midgely backed me right up. (These therapists call you by your first name, but as soon as I was able to make myself understood I let it be known that it was to be *Mr. Coley* and *Mrs. Midgely.*) "If he can do it once," Mrs. Midgely said, "he can do it every day." Going up and down stairs and dressing yourself are what they're keenest on your learning.

Most days, though, it hardly seems worth the struggle — a way I must fight against thinking. I'll sit in the living room and look at the television, or read a magazine, or work a crossword puzzle. A great mercy that my vision has straightened out again: at first I saw only parts of things, and letters and words refused to stay in their proper order. A mercy, too, that I was muddled enough in my thinking at the time so this didn't alarm me. Nowadays I'm able to read everything from the *National Review* to our local newspaper. I even read the Neighbors page, about people we don't know being visited by their grown children from out of state, and the notices of church suppers and bingo games we can no longer attend. Not that we ever attended them. To have ended up in a town where our next-door neighbors live in a trailer (it *is* kept up nicely) with a Virgin Mary sheltering in a half-buried bathtub — it's not what we had expected of life.

Now stop right there and listen to yourself: will you ever awaken to your abundant blessings? Which *continue* to be abundant. That, I have come to believe, is part of what the Lord means to tell me. My stroke is part of our long conversation.

I'm sitting on the bed trying to pull on my socks one-handed when I hear a car slow up. I grip the four-footed aluminum cane with my good hand, rock a little to get me going, shudder up to a standing position, and go thump-scrape, thump-scrape over to the window. When I finally get over there, I see the mail lady pulling away from our mailbox in her tall, big-tired pickup truck. Toolbox on it the size of a child's coffin. Sometime during the winter, I'm not clear just when, it was while I was still in the hospital, I remember Alice telling me about the mail lady towing that rough-neck Bobby Paquette's car out of the snow on Lily Pond Road. (This is the neighbor woman's nephew.) Alice says her truck's equipped with a winch and I don't know what all. A male lady indeed. Mrs. Laffond looks like a movie cowboy, sun-scorched and slitty-eyed. And that short hair doesn't help matters. Now Wylie when she was growing up was something of a tomboy too, but always looked feminine. An outdoor girl, perhaps it's better to say. Always enjoyed bicycling, played softball on the girls' team. If back then there'd been the agitation you see today over the Little League (and now even on into the high schools in some places), Wylie would've been first in line, I'm sure. But for the sake of being modern, not mannish. This Mrs. Laffond, though. It's nothing to see her in garageman's getup: green gabardine shirt and the trousers to match. There was a Mr. Laffond, but he left for parts unknown. Supposedly he drank. (Small wonder, wouldn't you say?) It would be their own business, of course, if there weren't children involved. Two little girls and a boy, Alice says. The one thing these people seem able to do is breed, if that's not an un-Christian observation.

"The mail's here," Alice calls from down in the kitchen, over the top of the music. "Are you done your tray?"

She'll find out whether or not I'm *done my tray,* as she puts it, when she comes back upstairs, not sooner. I won't have all this hollering in the house.

2

When I finally do get myself down to the living room, I find Alice working away with her plant mister.

"Don't *you* look spruce this morning," she says. I have on a pink oxford shirt and my gray wool slacks, neither spruce nor otherwise. "You know," she says, "I was thinking. You've been cooped up in

here for days with the rain and all. Why don't we bundle you up
warm and walk down together and get the mail? I think the fresh
air would do you good."

"Sea a mud," I say. Just look at that driveway. They ought to have
brought a load of traprock last fall, but they didn't come and didn't
come, which seems to be par for the course up here. And then the
ground froze, and then I had my shock.

"Such a beautiful day," she says.

It's one of those early spring days when you begin to smell the
earth again. Painfully bright blue sky and the sun giving a false
warmth. The branches of the bare trees seem silvery. Once I get
down the steps, I stop and work open the buttons of my overcoat
to let the air at my body, though what's wrong has nothing to do
with the body. Halfway down the driveway I stop to rest, take Alice's
arm to steady me, and poke the muddy wheelrut with one of my
cane's rubber-tipped spider legs.

"Get in out," I say, meaning *You'll never be able to.* "Moon vehicle
need the moon vehicle."

"Moon vehicle?" says Alice. "Why are you saying a moon vehicle,
dear?"

"Truck the truck," I say. What I'm trying to get across is the mail
lady's pickup truck. I float my good hand up to show the tall tires.
No use. Oh, I hate this business where Alice thinks I'm making no
sense when I *am* making sense. But this is serious business, this
situation here with the driveway. To keep out of the mud, Alice has
been driving along the edge of the grass, which is tearing up the
lawn, and now we're going to have *that* on our hands, getting
someone in to reseed it and roll it. On *her* hands, I suppose I mean.

The mail lady has brought a telephone bill, a letter from Wylie,
and the new *Smithsonian.* Good: there's this afternoon taken care
of. Alice tucks the envelopes inside the *Smithsonian* and we start
back. It's become our custom to save the opening of the mail for
when we get back to the house.

"Why I think that's a robin," says Alice as we start for the house
again. "See? In that maple tree? No, over there — that's an oak tree."

Something or other flies off in the direction of the Paquettes'.

"I'm certain that was a robin," she says.

"So be it," I say. The way my mouth works now, I seem to be
saying *Soviet.* This walk will have been enough and more than
enough. I make her stop to rest three times on the way back.

When we've finally gotten my things off — I manage the coat all right, but the overshoes prove too much — we go into the living room so we can sit comfortably over the mail. I open the telephone bill, and she opens Wylie's letter. Our old division of responsibilities: the human side for her. Though my side is now only ceremonial.

The telephone bill is sixty-eight dollars!

I study it and study it. Most of the calls are to Wylie. One to Phoenix, which must be Alice's sister Sylvia. Framingham (her friend June Latham), Taunton (her brother Herb), Taunton again. Oh I suppose it's correct. I've long given up trying to make sense of all those pages in the phone bill. I lay the thing down and look out the window.

"Wylie say?" I ask Alice. It looks like such a long way down there to the mailbox. How had I managed it? The trees are dead motionless, even in their smallest branches, but beyond them, in the pure blue, a small cloud riddled with blue gaps is traveling steadily from left to right. Its shape slowly changes as it moves. On a high branch of our apple tree is perched a bird — a robin, if it pleases Alice to think so — lifting its throat and opening its beak. Singing, apparently. A tiny speck drops straight, swift, and silent from below its tail. This simple process is not an occasion for shame. At least among those of His creatures who are not accountable.

Alice has not answered me. I turn away from the window and she's holding the letter out to me with an expression I don't know what to make of. Glad, but something else, too. It's the expression she had when she first watched me, cheered on by Mrs. Midgely, lurch up a flight of steps. I take the letter with my good hand. Like all Wylie's letters, it is written in blue felt-tip on lined notebook paper. Since they never taught penmanship at that school of hers — I came near to pulling her out of there because of it — her handwriting, part script, part print, still looks like that of a child. Nearly as bad as mine now looks. As for her style, so-called, we also have progressive education to thank.

Dear Mom & Dad,
  I thought I would tell you this in a letter instead of on the phone because I thought you might like having this letter to keep. Not to keep you in suspense anymore, you are going to be grandparents! I am having a baby sometime the beginning of December. We found out today and are so thrilled. I sort of wanted you to know right off by phone but thought this best. Please do phone though when you get

this, but I decided you would like having this letter to keep. Jeffrey
sends his love.

> Love you alot,
> Wylie

Well, my first reaction is, why all this folderol about sentimental
keepsakes when the plain truth of it is, Wylie can no longer bear
talking to me on the telephone. And of course such a piece of
news might well have rendered me more than usually — what shall
we say? — unpredictable.

I tried to feel something more appropriate. I mean, good heavens, a grandchild.

"Oh I'm so glad," says Alice. "I thought she didn't *want* children."

"Trend the trend now the trend," I say.

"The trend?" she says. "I don't like to think of Wylie as part of
any trend," she says.

I wave my good hand and say, "Shining individual," meaning
Fine, have it your way. Alice cocks her head: more gabble she won't
bother trying to decode. She looks at her wristwatch.

"Almost noon," she says. "So it's about nine o'clock." She picks
up the phone.

It's so quiet in our house that I can hear the purr of the
telephone ringing on the other end. Save this letter! Save it for
when, for pity's sake? Things like this make you realize that Wylie
still thinks of us as we were when she was a child. Take the time,
a couple of years ago, when she was still living in New York and we
came down to visit and she walked Alice's legs off shopping. More
to the point, look at her decision to move a continent away from
us. The pace was slower out there, she said. The air was better. The
air was better! I blame Jeffrey in part. Of course this was before
my shock; would she make the same choice today? I don't know.
I don't suppose I want to know.

As Alice listens to the phone ring and ring, her smile becomes
less and less a smile. Finally it is not a smile at all. She lays the
receiver back down. Here we are.

3

It's a thing I try not to dwell on, but at times — talk to myself as I
will, pray as I will for understanding — I can see no spiritual

significance whatever in my ruin. And let's for heaven's sake not
be mealy-mouthed about it: I am ruined, in this life. No appeal,
no going back. Dragging half a dead body from room to room,
numb lips and steak-thick tongue refusing to move as I command.
If I am of use at all anymore, it can only be as an example of patient
endurance. Or, more likely, of the perils of cholesterol. Since I was
neither a smoker nor (at least in recent years) a drinker, it keeps
coming back to that, doesn't it? Apparently I have thrown away my
birthright — the everyday miracle of a functioning human body
— for the sake of two eggs, every morning for forty years, over
easy. For the sake of two strips of bacon, wet with fat, laid parallel
next to the eggs, and the whole thing set before me like the
four-and-twenty blackbirds baked in a pie. Initially in love and ignorance, then later, as the magazine articles began to come out,
in love alone.

"He's saying you can't teach an old dog new tricks," Alice said
to Dr. Ngo, translating for me. "He hates the breakfasts."

"Ah," said Dr. Ngo, who plainly didn't know enough English to
understand even our most common idioms. I sat there stony with
shame.

"He's been so used to his bacon and eggs," she said.

"Ah," said Dr. Ngo. "Two time a week it not hurt him you
understand?"

I understood. This meant: why not pop off a little sooner with
a few familiar comforts, since pop off I must?

"I am of more value than my pleasures," I said, or tried to say.
What drunken smear of vowels came out I'm unwilling to remember. What I meant was that I mattered and must persist.

"Say again, dear?" said Alice.

I shook my head no and swatted the air with my good hand, *Go
away go away*. What I had tried to say bordered on blasphemy: it
went without saying, did it not, that I was to have life everlasting?

4

But since my purchase on *this* life (though no one will say so)
seems none too certain, it has been decided that we must waste
no time in wishing Wylie joy in person. Decided, I need not add,
by Alice and Wylie. These days I'm doing well to get a *What do you
think, dear?* And since Wylie is not to travel — in fact, must spend

much of her time lying down — we are to come to them. So it's
heigh-ho for Seattle. What do you think, dear?

What I think is, I'll do as I'm bid. If I can be wheeled onto an
airplane, I can certainly sit for six hours. What else do I do? These
terrorists hold no terrors for me, not because I'm armed in faith
particularly — I wish I could say I were — but because no place
seems safer than any other anymore. When we left Woburn there
was a bad element moving in. In Florida you have your drug lords,
and people shooting at you from the overpasses on I-295. Our
problem up here is the roughnecks who ride the back roads in
loud cars. They listen to the metal music.

Alice keeps asking, aren't I looking forward to seeing Wylie. The
aim is to keep me looking forward. Of course what can I say but
yes. But much as I love her — and I *do* look forward — I must say
that Wylie can be trying. She has become one of those people who
put bumper stickers on their automobiles — at one point, I recall,
she had replaced *Visualize Peace* with *Teach Peace,* which seemed to
me at least a small step away from delusion — and who believe we
can communicate with the plants and the dolphins. I blame Bard
College. And I imagine Jeffrey encourages it. I used to tell her,
You'd best forget the dolphins and learn to talk to your Savior. I've come
to accept that these things sink in if and when He wills them to
sink in, so I try to soft-pedal that. Now some Christians — our
minister up here is one — will tell you that the whole what they
call New Age is of the devil. We'll know someday: *Every man's work
shall be made manifest.* But who can be sure today that it's a distrac-
tion and a time waster — spiritual danger enough right there, it
seems to me. *The night cometh when no man can work.* Alice says that
Wylie says she's already begun talking to the baby inside her. I hope
it takes what it's hearing with a good-sized grain of salt! I think
Wylie imagines that this visit will have given her child at least this
much acquaintance with its grandfather. Covering herself, don't
you see.

I'm ashamed to say I think about it too. As if I were clutching
at a moving train, crying *At least remember me.* (Keep me mindful
that another home is prepared for me and that I shall have a new
body, incorruptible.) I remember my own grandfather. Or at least
I remember remembering him. He used to tell about the Civil War;
he was twelve, I believe, when it ended. Now *his* father had been
an abolitionist — a Unitarian, he was — and when the news came

that President Lincoln was dead he had all the children dressed up in mourning. And my grandfather had a fistfight with a neighbor boy whose family hated the colored. The Coleys lived in Westerly in those days. And still lived there, in the old house, until my father died in '41, and still went to the Unitarian church. You know the saying, how the Unitarians believe in one God at most. Supposed to be a joke. But it chills me now to remember that beautiful white church-house from which the Holy Spirit was so resoundingly absent. Back then, of course, I liked the hymn-singing and that was that.

I thought of my grandfather's story about President Lincoln the other night when we saw Aretha Franklin on the television, singing a song about the turnpike of love, I think it was, and lifting her fleshy arms above her head. A woman of her age and size ought not to be seen in a sleeveless dress. It seemed impossible that I could have lived so long as to have known someone who'd been alive when Abraham Lincoln freed the slaves. I don't recall how we came to be watching such a thing; Alice and I used to enjoy Mahalia Jackson, but this one is too screechy. Sometimes we'll be watching one program and then find ourselves watching the next program and the program after without meaning to. Up here we still get all three networks, of course. And PBS, if you can put up with their political slant. But those people on the local news programs! So young and so coarse-looking. And so poorly spoken, as if they had all just come out of two-year colleges. That's un-Christian of me, I suppose. My own ruined speech is appropriate chastisement.

Just as my having had no son — I've often thought this — may have been chastisement for my pride in family. (There is only one family: the family of His saints.) Though perhaps it's another, more malignant, form of pride to believe myself singled out for chastisement. But for whatever reason, I am the last of the Coleys. There are other people named Coley, of course, but of our Coleys I am the last. We have become a branch of the family tree of people named Gunderson. We're often asked — or *were* often asked, back when we socialized — if Wylie is a family name. I would always say *Why how'd you guess?* to make light of the unusualness. The Wylies are my mother's people. (Alice, of course, is a Stannard.) We knew the name might sound awkward with Coley, so we gave her the middle name Jane as a sort of buffer. When I was a boy I knew a

Mary Carey who called herself Mary Jane — she hadn't been so christened — so we thought Wylie Jane Coley would sound all right. Naturally we couldn't have foreseen that the other children would call her Wylie Coyote and tease her by yelling "Beep-beep" and running away from her. (It had to do with some show on the television.) I'm afraid it didn't mollify her when I told her that one of her Wylie forebears had been at the first Constitutional Convention! From when she was eight or nine until she went away to college, she called herself Jane; by then, she must have decided that "Wylie" would put her one up on the Wendys and Jennifers.

Though she hardly needed such help: even as a little girl she was always the prettiest in a group. Or so her father always thought. She was almost plump in grade school. When I first went over to the Paquettes' — and if there's a silver lining to this whole business, it's that I'm no longer able to go over to the Paquettes' — I was reminded of her little belly by that wooden Buddha or whatever it is on top of their television set. (This in a supposedly Christian home! Naturally they're Roman Catholics.) When she was about twelve, though, she began to starve herself and hasn't stopped to this day. Now I don't mean that she was ever in danger of going the way of that other singer, Karen something. (Alice and I watched that poor soul on television along toward the last, and we could both see she wasn't well.) But even two summers ago, when Wylie came east, I noticed her ribs under her T-shirt when she bent to tie her running shoes. (Carpenter, of course. Now you wouldn't think a Christian would forget Carpenter!) Alice, in fact, is concerned about the baby on this account. Another reason for our trip, though naturally she's not saying so to Wylie.

The story I always tell about Wylie (or always told) is the time we went to Alice's brother's house down in Taunton for Christmas. Herb had married a Roman Catholic girl and nothing would do but we had to go to their Christmas Eve mass. Well when we got into the church they had the biggest darned crucifix you ever saw hanging over the altar. The Christ wasn't quite life-size, but it must have been a good three or four feet long, with skin the color of a Band-Aid and a white-painted loincloth. The eyes wide open on it. Believe you me, Wylie's eyes opened pretty wide too: we of course had just the plain gold cross in our church. "Mommy?" she said, loud enough for everybody in the place to hear. "How come he's got diapers on?" To this day, Wylie hates to have that one told on her, though it's a perfectly harmless story.

I now wear a diaper.

The story I never tell about Wylie is this. One afternoon I surprised her and a little girlfriend behind the garage, both of them with their pants down. (This was at our house in Woburn.) I can still remember that little girl's name, Myra Meyers. Speaking of names somebody ought to have thought twice about. I sent her about her business, and grabbed Wylie by the arm and marched her right inside and whaled the living daylights out of her. They say now, of course, that you're not accountable: that you are what you are and not what you make up your mind to be. That it's all genetic: drinkers, too, like the mail lady's husband. That you're helpless to change yourself and certainly can't do anything for anybody else and never mind what God tells us in His word. Well, I believe I changed Wylie that day. Or at least helped her on toward the life she has now, with a husband (though not someone we might have chosen) and about to begin a family (however late). And away from — the old-fashioned word is *abominations,* but I'll say *abnormalities.* (My own theory is, that's what's wrong with the mail lady, children or no children.) I don't imagine Wylie realizes to this day — if she ever thinks of it — that each stroke burned with my love for her. But the day is coming when all that is hidden shall be revealed.

5

When I think back about the first great intervention in my life (I count my shock as the second), I'm ashamed to remember how long I tried to hold out. I first sought the conventional remedy for a man of my background and education (Brown, '39). One takes one's child to see *Fantasia,* one dreams that night of the devil, one's terror does not abate the next morning, nor the next, nor the next. After two weeks of this, off one scurries to a psychiatrist. To whom one is induced to complain about one's own childhood. One is talked around into trying to believe one had such and such feelings about one's father and one's mother: the so-called family romance. (Oh yes, I know the jargon.) It is pointed out to one that the word *abate* is in itself a not insignificant choice. The terror still does not abate.

Then one has a quote unquote chance encounter with a friend who quote unquote just happens to be a Christian.

This was a fellow named John Milliken, whom I'd known when we were both graduate students at Stanford. He actually took his Ph.D.; I'd had to leave and go back to New England when my father died. The little money Alice made at the library was barely enough for the two of us, and now there was Mother to think of. Eventually I was lucky enough to catch on with what was then a scrappy new company (a shoestring operation really in those days, right after the war), willing to hire a young chemist without an advanced degree. Well, Milliken, to make a long story short, ended up working for an outfit we did some business with and living just over in Arlington. So he and I would get together two or three times in the course of a year. We might have seen more of each other, but I was a new father and he was a bachelor. And Alice never warmed up to him, before *or* after.

One Saturday night, probably a month into my troubles, Milliken and I sat late at the bar of the old Parker House and I opened up to him. Alice by this time had taken the baby and gone to stay with Herb and Evelyn in Taunton; we were not calling it a separation. Desperate as I was, I would hardly have told Milliken about it had I not been drinking. In fact, I was hoping he'd call it a night so I could slip over to Scollay Square, to a certain bar I had discovered and wanted to know more about. (The thought of which terrifies me to this day.) But Milliken kept sitting there, nursing his one Manhattan, nodding, putting in a word or two. More or less, I'm bound to say, in the manner of the doctor I'd been seeing. Except kindly.

"Well Lew," he said when I told him about my dream and the terror that wasn't going away, "has it occurred to you to take this thing seriously?"

"Christ sake, what do you *think* I'm doing?" I said.

He shook his head. "Why don't I swing by your house tomorrow morning," he said. "I've got the hangover cure to end all hangover cures. Are you all right to drive, by the way?"

I was not. The room, in fact, looked tilted and seemed to be going silent. I was not all right to live.

"I think you'd best let me drop you," he said. "We can always pick up your car tomorrow. Unless you're afraid to be by yourself tonight. In which case, I've a fold-out sofa you're welcome to."

Years later, when I came to read C. S. Lewis — so often a help to me, and I wish I had the strength of mind to read him now — I was struck by what he said about his conversion. I believe I still have it by heart. *When we set out* — he was riding to the zoo in London in the sidecar of somebody's motorcycle — *I did not believe that Jesus Christ was the Son of God, and when we reached the zoo I did.* That's what it was like, riding to John Milliken's house: it was like riding to John Milliken's house. True, he did begin to pray aloud as we were passing over the Longfellow Bridge, with its stone towers like a castle keep. But around me it was quiet, and the faraway tune his voice was making seemed to blend in with something else that was happening. Out Main Street we flew and onto Massachusetts Avenue, and the people on the sidewalks seemed to pass each other in comradely fashion, like the angels in Jacob's dream — a thing I hadn't thought about, I'm sure, since I was a boy in Sunday school — moving up and down the ladder which reached from earth to heaven. They began to be surrounded by a throbbing radiance, and I thought I saw some of them passing right through others. It didn't strike me as out of the ordinary. I looked over at John Milliken: his profile glowed along its edge from hairline to Adam's apple; light frosted his gnarly eyebrows. His lips were moving. I looked to his hands, gripping the wheel, his bulging knuckles imperfectly mirroring the wheel's knuckled underside, a patch of hair on the top of each finger. I closed my eyes, and sounds rushed back in: the rubbery rapid-fire whapping of tire treads on pavement, John Milliken's voice saying *And in Jesus Christ's name we* something something something, a sweet-toned car horn off somewhere. When I opened my eyes again, there we were: just a couple of fellows in a car heading out Massachusetts Avenue.

But the whole point of Jacob's dream, as I now understand it, is that it's a *dream.* The door between this world and the spiritual world has closed, I have come to believe, and will remain closed until the heaven and the earth shall be made new. This is where I part company, not just with the Wylies of the world, but with the John Millikens. I soon shied away from the so-called spirit-filled church he brought me to that morning, where grown men and women stood blinking and babbling in no language, and he and I lost touch. He must be an old man now. I ended up with the Baptists

— imagine what Great-grandfather Coley would say to *that!* — and have mostly felt at home there. With the doctrine if not always with the people.

Of course there are Baptists and Baptists. The fellow up here, for instance, turned out to be — not a modernizer, exactly, but more missionary than pastor. Collecting cans of food is all well and good, but need we congratulate ourselves by stacking the cartons right there in the sanctuary? And where, meanwhile, was the spiritual food? Alice and I hardly need sermons against the metal music. I told him straight out, I said I'd sooner sit home and read God's word. His answer to that was that it was a changing world. Well there you go, I said. I said, Isn't that all the more reason? Talking to a wall. He's a young man, with the same haircut as the television people and a suit that's too tight on him. He shaves so close his jowls gleam. He was probably glad to see the back of me. I suppose he must have said to himself, *Talking to a wall.*

So that was more or less the end of our churchgoing, except for Easter Sunday, when you still stand a fighting chance of hearing a sermon instead of a public-service message. Easter falls early this year; we'll still be in Seattle. (God willing.) I wonder if Wylie couldn't be talked into going to services with us. How she used to plead, when she was a teenager, to be left at home: what if her friends saw her! I sometimes fought down a mean impulse to tell her it was like going to a bar where sailors met businessmen: anyone who saw you there had a guilty secret too.

But that secret was mine, to live with as best I could. They'll never persuade me I was wrong not to have burdened Alice with details of the danger I'd been in. *Bring it to the Lord in prayer,* the song says. It doesn't say, *Bring it to your wife in guilt.* Very much out of fashion, I know, the idea that certain things are between you and the Lord, period. And yes: that morning, in Everett, Massachusetts, in that shabby wainscoted church — the church smell comes back to me, the smell of varnish, the smell of musty hymnals — I made confession. But before a crowd of strangers, whose care was for a soul that could have been anybody's.

6

It's Wednesday morning, and we're about ready to be on our way. Alice has locked the cellar door and the toolshed, carried her gloxinias to the bathtub, plugged the reading lamp into the timer, and set the thermostats (except in the bathroom) down to forty. And I have spent the morning trying to compose a letter. It may be the last piece of business I'll do, formally handing down to my daughter what remains, and I chose to do this last thing without Alice's help. It may also be foolishness — our plane will probably not go down, I will probably live on until the cost of my care eats up all our money — but I felt the need.

Dearest Wylie,
   Airplanes I think are not so dangers but I am put in this today what you need to know and send by itself. Our lawyer Mr. Plankey who can explain. He is our will and his card you put away when you need it.
   A day goes by with you and my prayers. When you look after your own child you remember He died and still looks after.
                                                          Loving father,
                                                          Lewis Coley

Oh, this is all wrong, preaching away as I've sworn a hundred times not to do. But no time now: let it go as it is. I lick the envelope — even pulling an envelope across the tongue (and at the same time moving the head in the opposite direction) takes analytic thinking — and put it with the bills to be left in the mailbox.

In our forty years of marriage, Alice has always done our packing, but never before has she handled the bags. I sit at the kitchen table and watch her out the window, struggling, dragging her right leg along in unison with the avocado-green Samsonite suitcase braced against her calf, her head bowed to avoid the branches of the little cherry tree. I ought to have pruned it last year. I must have assumed there would be time.

And, again, I find that I am weeping. It's the sight of her walking away from me. I hear the car trunk slam: I must stop this before she comes back to get me, though I don't know the way to stop. Hardly a cheerful beginning to our trip.

She pulls the car up onto the grass by the back door, but lets me do the steps by myself. There are more steps here than at the front door, but these are easier: a couple of years ago, I had a fellow come around and put up a railing. Nothing fancy, just pressure-treated two-by-fours. Back when breaking a hip in icy weather was the worst I could imagine. Gripping the rail with my good hand

and hanging the cane from the crook of my arm like some antique gentleman, I make it down the steps all right. But by the time I've gotten myself into the car and the door closed, I'm done in. Enough and more than enough. And now there's the ride all the way down to Logan yet to do, and after that whatever's involved in getting a crippled man through a modern terminal and after that the hours in the air and after that the journey's unimaginable other end.

We start down the driveway, Alice keeping one wheel up on the strip of grass between the muddy wheel ruts and the other wheel on the lawn.

"Forget the mailbox," I say, meaning *Don't*. I'm making a joke on myself, the joke being that I'm an old fussbudget.

Alice just fetches a sigh. So I sigh too, and look out the window, beating the fingers of my good hand on my good knee, for all the world like a stroke patient. Though deep down I can't believe it, I remind myself this may be the last time I'll see this lawn, such as it is, with its untrimmed shrubs and the rocks I used to hit with the lawn mower. I try to give it the looking-at it deserves. And fall short as always. This was what we had worked toward, and we came too late to love it.

"Why don't I pull over close to the mailbox," says Alice, "and you just put down your window and pop the things in."

"Get stuck," I say.

"Good heavens," she says, "Mrs. Laffond goes in and out of here every day."

She gets the car over so that my mirror almost scrapes the mailbox and I feel my whole side of the car go down. Oh brother. I roll down my window as if nothing were wrong — trying to work magic, in spite of all I know and believe! — pull open the mailbox, stick the envelopes in, push the thing shut, and flip up the flag. As I roll the window back up, I look over at Alice, who looks at her watch and then at the dashboard clock. Her mouth is twitching. She steps on the gas: the wheels just whine and spin. She cuts the steering hard to the left, guns it, and we sink deeper.

"No no no no," I say. Doesn't the woman know you want to keep your wheels straight?

She jams it into reverse, guns it again, and the back tires just spin deeper.

"Cut your wheels!" I cry, meaning *Don't*. So of course she does, except she can't because we're in so deep. "Rock have to rock." Damn it she has to rock the damn car if it'll even rock.

"I don't know what you're saying," she says.

"You car rocking!" I holler. She slams it back into drive, the wheels spin, and she glares over at me.

I say, "Damn fuck."

"Well why don't *you* try it then," she says. Then she says, "I'm sorry, Lew, I didn't mean that." Well the harm is done: the next thing you know I'm sitting here bawling like a big angry baby.

"Lew," she says. "I'm so sorry. It's truly my fault." I entertain the thought that I'm weeping to punish her. Which may be so, but I try and can't stop it now.

"Lew," she says. "Now listen to me a minute. Try and listen. Will you be all right to sit here while I go back up to the house?"

"Do what?" I say.

"I can't understand you, dear."

I try harder. "You what to you do?" I say.

"I guess I'm going to try to raise somebody on the phone," she says. "Maybe one of the boys from the Shell station would come up."

I've got the blubbering stopped now. "Plane make the plane," I say, meaning *We'll never.*

"Well, Lew, *I* don't know what else to do," she says. "I'll leave the motor running so you can have the heater."

I don't turn to watch her walking up the driveway for fear it'll set me off again. I put the radio on, just in time to catch the end of some bouncy tune from way way back. Can it have been "The Dipsy Doodle"? But then the announcer comes on to say it's 10:08 and I snap the thing off again: the last thing I need is to be hearing what time it is every two minutes. The dashboard clock says 10:07. What to believe. I take a glove out of my pocket, fold it over, and put it on the dashboard to block my view of the clock. I stare out the windshield at the road we should be on and listen to the motor humming away. We've been very happy with the Lumina.

An idling engine consumes a gallon of gasoline an hour. Or used to years ago. (It said so in the owner's manual of some car we had and it stuck in my mind for some reason.) An hour. Be a good hour before anybody got here if they ran true to form. Oh brother.

Well, there's not a thing you can do about it. I go back to the hum of the motor.

But wait now. Sunk in mud, motor running: couldn't this clog the tailpipe, make carbon monoxide seep in? Isn't this what they do, trapped and Godless men going out to the garage with the hose from the vacuum? In fact it's beginning to seem to me that I'm starting to feel sleepy, that something's woozy with my thoughts. You better reach over, cut that switch.

I let it run.

Before shutting my eyes I decide I'll take a last look around at things. And when I turn my head I see somebody pulling up in front of the Paquettes'. I see them sit there a second, then pull out again, coming right at me. If it's a car full of roughnecks I'm helpless out here. I spot Alice, but she's far away, she's on the doorstep, she's opening the door. They're still coming. I stretch over with my good hand and blow the horn. But she's in the house. They're halfway here, coming fast now. And now I see this thing is too high up off the ground to be a car. Oh, I'd rather the roughnecks than what's going to happen now. It's the mail lady in her moon vehicle. And we are saved.

BARRY HANNAH

Nicodemus Bluff

FROM THE CAROLINA QUARTERLY

THAT OLD WOMAN has money, we know it, old withered dugs,
used to teach high school. They say she even taught me thirty years
ago but I'm not sure, I was mostly away on drugs. One thing about
my body or bloodflow or whatall, I'm twice as put away as anybody
else on a drug, always have been. I declare that I stayed away from
the world thirty years and more. So when I saw the old woman on
her porch chair as we ran by — running out the drugs of three
decades — I just saw a new crone, not somebody I'd ever known.
She was sitting up there taking up space and money, the leaves of
the tree limbs reaching over her head looking like money itself,
green. Say she used to teach me. I wonder what.

They stood me up and walked me when I was on those 'ludes
and reds. No man ever liked a 'lude or red better than this man.
They walked me around the high school halls and set me in the
benches and showed me food, I guess, in the cafeteria. It is amazing what I never knew, amazing. I accompanied people. I was a
devoted accomplice, accompanier, associate, minion, stooge. The
term *et al.* was made for me. But I can't remember how. We would
be in church or jail. I would just look around and take stock of
the ten or so feet of box — a cube, I guess — around me and see
what was in it, my "space," yes really. My space ended at ten feet
wide, deep, and high. Couldn't tell you further what was out there.
It could be bars or a stained glass picture of Saint John baptizing
Jesus Christ in the Jordan River, boulders and olive trees hanging
over the water.

What was going on I wanted to be away from I believe was my

father and his friends years ago at the deer camp in Arkansas.
Something happened when I was out there. My father died that
next week but it's like not only is he not dead but he is hanging
at the border — the bars, the church window — of my space, that
ten-foot cube — bloody and broken up and flattened in the nose,
a black bruise on his cheekbone because of what happened to him
with those others years ago down in the swamps.

We used to be better folks even though my father's people had
nothing. My mother was a better sort, a secretary to a wealthy
lawyer in town. There seemed to be hope of our rising in the
community. It's vague how you get to be "somebody" but mainly
it has to do with marrying the right woman, then they honor you.
Acts of kindness or neighborliness do not really count. I have seen
people do acts of kindness over and over and although people
smile, looking at them in their yard and thanking them, "much
obliged" — this circle of doing for folks and making them "much
obliged" is funny, don't you think? the way payback must forever
continue amongst world citizens, kind to kind — they'd not think
the man of any esteem. What made esteem was not acts of kindness
but money, clothes, car, house, posture, lawn. You knew where you
belonged in that time, and we were on the edge of being respected
"gentlefolk" of the town (not my term but Dr. Debord's, the
preacher friend and chairman of the sociology department at the
Methodist college in town who helped me for a while. He wouldn't
like my thoughts about the old crone as we run by, the old crone
with her nice lawn, expensive auto, elegant house). That old woman
is like time and my dog, how awful. My dog had its whole lifetime
in my youth. Time was tearing it to pieces. Once out of one of my
early drug stupors I looked at it and it was suddenly dilapidated
and ancient and I started crying. Said she was a looker and I had
a crush on her. Tried to write stories to get her attention. Now look
at her. I am looking at all my drug time, decrepit, sitting on the
porch. My mother had an easy gracious manner and dressed well
naturally although she was not of moneyed people. She was a
person of "modest understated grace," Mr. Kervochian told me
once, wanting me not to forget what a valuable woman she was, so
I'd have something to get up in the morning for. I run around the
block again and again, gasping "success, success."

Dr. Debord had certainly tried everything else. However, getting me to admit the story was tough and deep, the story about my father — Gomar, he was called — so as to get up and be about my work at the animal shelter; my father that week among those new acquaintances who were going to be his new and lasting crowd — up from the failed farmers, the beer-for-breakfast mechanics, loiterers and petty-thieving personnel who were his people. Yay for him, some people were saying. To bring himself up into genteel society. I think most people approved of his rise. In the old days the whole county knew each other, don't doubt it, and you might have thought there was some god placed in an office with account books where he let out the word on the social worth of all citizens hereabouts, keeping tab on these as rose, fell, or simply trod down the rut that was left by the prior generations; the word went around and was known.

But at ten years old what did I know when my father and the rest of them were out at the lodge? I did not know my father had borrowed heavily from Mr. Pool and that was why we had a nice house, lawn, two cars, even a yard man who rode a riding mower, a Negro man named Whit who was nice to me. Whit cut himself chopping down a tree for us and I recall thinking that his blood might be bluer and was surprised. Why do people live here at all, I ask. They must know this is a filthy, wrong, haunted place. Even the trees that are left look wrong or wronged, beat up. The red dirt is hopeless. The squirrels are thin and there is much — you can't get around it — suicide on the part of possums, coons, armadillos, and deer who tried to exist in the puny scratch but leap out on the highway. Also there are no stories of any merit to come out of this place. The only good woods are near the base of the little mountain. (Let me tell you something about all the drug pushers around here. They are no mystery to me. They are just country sorry, like my father's people. They aren't a new wave of punk. Country sorry.) Someone had a house and land and saved the woods at the west base of the little mountain (805 ft.). This person would shoot trespassers, hunters, and fishermen. (There was a deep black pond in the middle.) Nobody went in. The woods were saved. They were thick and dark with very high great oaks and ashes and wild magnolias, even bamboo, like nothing else around. Thicker, much, even than the woods over at the deer camp near the Mississippi River in Arkansas, with sloughs and irrigation ditches where the ducks come down too. Also you could catch winter crappie in the oxbow lakes if you could sit still in the cold. (Allow me to express myself about those woods near the mountain here. They were owned by a doctor who was an enormous dealer in drugs. Well I know.) In Arkansas it was sportsman's paradise. The only thing better I would see would be (later) the marijuana plantation at the state university where they grew it legal for government experimentation. I saw that once driving by with somebody when I was seventeen and almost came out of my cube of space to get them to stop the car. (No, I could never drive; didn't learn to drive until I was twenty and that is when I finished high school too. All of this delay, I believe, is because of what they did to my father.)

My father then had these acquaintances: a banker, an insurance man, a clothing store owner, a lawyer (employer of my mother), an owner of a small company that made oil pumps for aircraft engines, a medical doctor. Then there was Mr. Kervochian, a druggist, who turned out to be the kindest and the one who told me the whole story years later when he was dying of pancreatic cancer. My father — we had the lawn, the porch, the two cars, the nice fishing boat, the membership in the country club — I say again was lent heavily some money by three of these men. They told him it was a new kind of loan they were practicing with, a way to help really deserving men from the country who wanted to better themselves. It was agricultural rates interest, very low. It was "special" money on collateral of his personality and promise; and it entailed his being close by to aid these men at some business schemes; close by like at beck and call, said Mr. Kervochian. My father would get nice things immediately and pay it off so that he could enjoy the good life and pay along for it, not waiting until he was old like many men did, left only a few years to enjoy their station and bounty after a lifetime of work. They liked my mother and they thought my father was admirable the way he tried to sell real estate out in the country where the dead farms were. He knew them when they were dying and could be had.

He managed to get Mr. Pool and Mr. Hester a piece of land from a crazy man for almost nothing. The man went down to Whitfield, the asylum at Jackson. The land they used for turkey houses. That's where I came in: at age ten I went out there twice a day on my bicycle to feed and water the turkeys. I had a job, I was a little man. I was worthy of an invitation to the deer hunt. Everything was fitting together. My father had some prestige. He was arriving and I was well on the way to becoming a man of parts myself.

I can't remember why I was the only boy out at the deer camp in Arkansas. But I went along with my father, Gomar, and had my own gun, a little .410 single shot, for the delta squirrels, very fat, if I saw them, which I did but could not hit them much, at age ten. Something would happen when a live squirrel showed up in the bead at the end of the barrel. The squirrel would blur out and I'd snap the gun to the side, missing all of it. I think I embarrassed my father. A boy around here should be able to shoot at ten. The rest of them weren't hunting yet. They were in the lodge drinking and playing cards. I could hear the laughter getting louder and how it changed — louder and meaner, I guess — while I was out in those short stumps and wood chips on the edge of the forest. I remember seeing that cold oily-looking water in a pool in one stump and felt odd because of the rotten smell. They didn't know why I was frowning and missing squirrels out there, and had gone back in to laugh harder, drinking. I could smell the whiskey from where I was and liked it. It smelled like a hospital, where I was once to have a hernia repaired.

The large thing I didn't know was that my father owed all this money to the three men, and he was not repaying it on time. I thought there were just his new friends, having them in this sort of club at the lodge, which was as good as a house inside or better, with polished knotty pine walls and deer heads and an entire bobcat on a ledge. Also a joke stuffed squirrel with its head blown off, as I couldn't do out there smelling that rotten water, standing in the wet leaves in rubber boots made for a man, not my own, which I was saving for dry big hunting. I remember in December everything was wet and black. They said flash floods were around, water over the highway, and we were trapped in until the water went down. Then it began to get very cold. I went inside, without much to do. I came back outside with a box of white-head kitchen matches and started licking them on the head, striking them and sailing them out so they made a trail like rockets, then hit and flamed up before the wet took care of them. I thought the future belonged to rockets — this had been said around — and I was very excited to get into the future. My father was providing a proud place for me to grow and play on our esteemed yard. One night I was watching television, an old movie with June Allyson. Her moist voice reached into me and I began crying I was so happy — she favored my mother some. But my father owed all this money, many years of money. It seemed the other two, Mr. Hester and Colonel Wren, weren't that anxious about it. But the banker, Mr. Pool, who owned the lodge, was a different kind.

The trouble was, Mr. Kervochian told me, as he died of pancreatic cancer, that my father thought he had considerably reduced the debt by getting that piece of land from that insane man for almost nothing. This provided grounds for a prosperous turkey farm for the men. Twenty or more houses of turkeys it would be. My father supposed that he had done them a real turn, a very handy favor, and he felt easy about his lateness of payment. He assumed they had taken off several thousand dollars from it and were easy themselves. He thought things had been indicated more than "much obliged." It was riling somebody, though. Just the money — considerable — wasn't all of it. Something else very terrible was mixed in.

I didn't catch on to much except their voices grew louder and here and there a bad word came out. My father asked me to go back to my bunk in another room. There wasn't anything to do back there but read an R encyclopedia. I could read well. Almost nothing stopped me. My father could read but it was like he learned the wrong way. He took forever and the words seemed to fly off on him like spooked game. He held his finger on the page and ran it along like fastening down the sounds. My mother taught me and I could not see the trouble. I was always ahead of the teacher. I felt for my dad when I saw him reading. I knew this feeling wasn't right, but I wanted to hold his hand and read for him. It almost made me cry. Because it made me afraid, is what it did. He wasn't us.

The terrible thing mixed in it was that my dad was good at the game of chess and vain about it. He had no degree at all — I don't believe he had finished high school, really, unlike Mr. Pool, who had college and a law degree. He had never played Mr. Pool but he had whipped some other college men and he was apt to brag about it. He would even call himself "country trash," winking, when he boasted around the house, until Mother asked him to quit, please, gloating was not character. But Mother did not know that my father, when he played chess, became the personality of a woman, a lady of the court born in the eighteenth century (said Mr. Kervochian). The woman would "invest" Dad and he would win at chess with her character, not his own man's person at all. Mr. Kervochian took a long time explaining this. The chess game, as it went on, changed him more and more into a woman, a crafty woman. He began sitting there like a plain man, but at the end of the game he couldn't help it, the signs came out, his voice went up, and his arms and hands were set out in a sissy way. He was all female as the climax of his victory neared. He would rock back and forth nervously and sputter in little giggles, always pursing his lips. It wasn't something you wanted to look at and those he defeated didn't want to remember it. It unnerved them and made them feel eerie and nervous to have been privy to it, not to be talked about. I didn't know what was going on, with the noise out there in the great "den" of the lodge. Mr. Hester and Colonel Wren, the doctor (Dr. Harvard) and the oil pump company owner (Ralph Lovett), with Mr. Kervochian just leaning near them, drinking, were playing poker that night. Only two of them had gone out to hunt a little in the rain and vicious cold but come back. My father and Mr. Pool were at the other end playing chess very seriously. My father's feet became light, tapping on the floor as with princess slippers. All through the other quiet I heard them.

Mr. Kervochian, dying of cancer, told me it was not clear how my father's change came about or even where he learned to play chess, which was a surprise — his chessmanship — unto itself. He was not from chessly people. They were uneducated trash and sorry — even my grandmother Meemaw, a loud hypochondriac, a screamer — had failed on the farm and in town both and lived between them, looking both ways and hating both of what they saw. But Gomar, my dad, knew chess, maybe from one month in the Army at the time of the Korean conflict, after which he came back unacceptable because of something in his shoulders (is what he said when I asked him once). My mother looked at the floor. She hated war and was glad he'd never been in one. But I wanted him to have been in the war. Mr. Kervochian believed somebody in the service taught him, but where he came in contact with the "woman" he does not precisely know. But early on he was playing chess with the circuit-church-riding minister at the church near Meemaw's home. Sometime somewhere the woman in him appeared. It was a crafty, clever, "treacherous" woman, a "scheming, snooty, snarling" woman, rougher than a man somehow in spitefulness. She knew the court and its movements and chess was a breeze for her. She'd take him over about mid-game or when things got tough. It would lurch into him, this creature, and nobody could beat him. He beat a college professor, a hippie who was a lifetime chess bum that lived at a bohemian café; a brilliant Negro from New Orleans; two other town men who thought they were really good. Something was wrong, terrible about it. He wasn't supposed to be that good.

He might have picked up the woman who inhabited him from somebody in the Army, or from that preacher whose religion had its strange parts, its "dark enthusiasms," Mr. Kervochian said, weakly speaking from his cancer. We don't know, but it led to that long rain of four days at the deer camp, the matter of the owed money, and Mr. Pool, the banker, who professed himself a superior, very superior chess player.

Voices were short but loud and I heard cursing from the "den" where the men were. They were drunk and angry about the rain. When I peeped out I saw the banker looking angrily into my father's face. My father's face was red, too. He saw me at the door and told me to go back in the room.

I said, Daddy there's nothing to do. He brought our guns over to me and said, Clean them, without looking at me. Then he shut the door. It was only me, the R encyclopedia, and the guns with their oil kit. I went on reading at something, I think Rhode Island, which was known for potatoes. The doctor, Dr. Harvard, I could hear complaining and very concerned about the rain cutting us off, although we had plenty of food. I recall he wasn't drinking and was chubby with spectacles, like an owl, looking frightened, which wasn't right. I didn't like a doctor acting frightened about the weather. My father and Mr. Pool were in a trance over the board of pieces. Mr. Kervochian was drinking a lot, but he wasn't acting odd or loud. This I saw when I cracked the door and peeked again. Mr. Kervochian had a long darkish foreign face with heavy cheek whiskers. He stared out the window at the white cold rain like a philosopher, sad. He liked Big Band music — there was some he had brought on his tape machine — and I learned later that he wrote some poetry and might be a drug addict. He seemed to be a kind man, soft, and would talk with you (me), a kid, straight ahead. He never made jokes or bragged about killing game like the others, my father too. I remembered he had given me a box of polished hickory nuts. They were under the bed and I got them out and started playing with them.

The thing was, Mr. Pool did not believe any of my father's chess victories. Something was wrong, or fluked, he thought. It couldn't be that a man from my father's circumstances could come forth with much of a chess game, to Mr. Pool, who, with his law degree and bankership, hunting, golf, and chess, thought of himself as a "peer of the realm," Mr. Kervochian said later. "A renaissance man, a Leonardo of the backwater." There was a creature in Mr. Pool, too, Mr. Kervochian said, hoarse and small because of his cancer. Mr. Pool owned the lodge and midway (*"media res,"* said Mr. Kervochian) in his affairs he began thinking to own people too. He had a "dormant serfdom" in his head. His eyes would grow big, his tongue would move around on his teeth, and he would start demanding things, "like an old czar." Thing was, there was nobody to "quell" him when he had these fits. He did pretty much "own" several people, and this was his delight. People were "much obliged" to him left and right. Then he would have a riot of remembering this. He would leer "like Rasputin leching on a maid-in-waiting." Mr. Kervochian knew history. Pool was "beside himself" as the term had it: "himself outside the confines of his own psyche." Like he was calling in all his money and the soul attached to it. I could hear they had been talking about money and Mr. Pool was talking over all the conversation. My father's point was that the purchase transfer from the old loony man was worth a great deal as a piece of work and should make some favorable patience about the loan on Mr. Pool's part. But I didn't know all that, what their voices were saying. I knew hardly anything except for the strange loudness of their voices with the whiskey in them which was an awful thing I'd never heard.

I knew my father wasn't used to drinking and did not do it well. Once the last summer when he was coming up in the world, he had bought a bag and some clubs, some bright maroon-over-white saddle-oxford golf shoes, a cart, and took me with him to try out the country club. I remember he had an all-green outfit on. This was the club where those men who were his new group played; but this was a weekday, a workday, and he wanted to come out alone (only with me) because he'd never played. So he rolled his cart into the clubhouse and we sat in a place with a bar. He began ordering glasses of whiskey almost one after the other. I went around here and there in the chairs and came back and sat, with him looking straight at me, his ears getting red and his eyes narrowing. I didn't know what was happening but the man behind the bar made me think everything was all right, saying "sure" and "certainly" when Daddy wanted another glass of whiskey. But then he, my father, wouldn't answer me at all when I asked wasn't it time to play golf. I wanted to chase the balls and had several on the floor, playing.

"You know, really. You're not supposed to bring your bag in here," said the barman, kindly.

My father looked like he didn't know what the man was talking about. I pointed at the golf bag and said, He means your club bag, Daddy.

"What?" He looked at me, whining-like at me.

Then he drank another whole glass and something happened. I watched my father fall to the side off the chair, knock over the golf cart and bag, and hit the floor, with his golf hat falling off. I got up and saw he was really down, asleep, at the other end of his saddle oxfords, maroon and white. He had passed out.

My mother came from the office of the lawyer to pick him up after the barman called. I sat in the chair and waited for him to wake up while other people came in, not helping, just shutting their eyes and looking away. I was awfully scared, crying some. It wasn't until a long time later I learned (from Mother) that he was afraid to start playing golf and embarrass himself, although there were just a few people at the course. He wasn't sure about the sticks or the count. My mother whispered this to me but I never understood why he'd go out there at all. My father, I say, had no whiskey problem, he just couldn't drink it very well and hardly ever did. My mother I don't think had any problems at all and she had high literacy and beauty.

At the deer camp the weather would not quit. I can't recall that kind of cold with that much rain. One or the other usually stops but on top of the roof the roar of water kept up and my window outside was laid on by a curtain of white, like frost alive. They were quiet in the "den" for a long, long time. I imagined they were all asleep from drinking the whiskey. I liked imagining that because what was out there was not nice, I'd seen it, even if they were only playing chess, a game I knew nothing about, but it looked expensive and serious, those pieces out there, made of marble, a mysterious thing I knew my father was very good at.

Mr. Kervochian knew the game and had watched Mr. Pool (Garrand, his first name) defeat many good ones around the town and in big cities. Mr. Pool wore a gray mustache and looked something like an old hefty soldier "of a Prussian sort," said Mr. Kervochian. You could picture him ordering people around. You could feel him staring at you, bossing. He'd hardly looked at me, though. I was not sure, again, why I was the only child out there.

It got late at night but the lights were still on out there. I had gone to sleep for a while, dreaming about those polished hickory nuts and squirrels up to your hips. When I peeped out I saw all the others asleep, but Garrand Pool and my father, Gomar, were staring at the board without a sound. They had quit drinking but were angry in the eyes and resolved on some mean victory, seemed to me. It was fearsome. The others in the chairs snoring, the rain outside. Nothing seemed right in the human world I knew. Then Mr. Pool began whispering something, more hissing maybe, as grown men I knew of never did. Pool was saying "Stop it, Stop that. Stop that, damn you!" This made my father's body rise up and he put his hand down and moved a piece. He stiffened to a proper upright posture with shoulders spread back, and then this light queer voice came from him. I didn't know, but it was the woman overcoming him. Even in his wrist — thinking back you could see a womanly draped thing. His fingers seemed to have become longer. Now this was another evil: Mr. Pool knew nothing about the woman and thought my father was mimicking him. He seemed to be getting even angrier and I shut the door. Let me tell you, it was odd but *not* like a nightmare. Another kind of dream maybe even more wicked and curious, a quality of dream where the world was changed and there was a haze to it, and you couldn't get out by opening your eyes. It made you weird and excited, my father's voice and posture and hands.

"Now hunt, old toad," he had said actually to Mr. Pool, jangling high-voiced like a woman in a church choir.

So I had to open the door a crack again.

Mr. Pool stood up and cursed him and told him something about "deadbeat white trash." But my father said something back shrilly and Mr. Pool I thought was coming out of his skin.

"Don't you mock me with that white-trash homo voice! I won't stand for it!"

The other men woke up and wanted to know what was happening. Nobody had had any supper. They ate some crackers and cheese, commented on the steady rain, then went back to their rooms to sleep. My father and Mr. Pool had never halted the chess and paid no attention to anybody else. I was very sleepy and lost-feeling (in this big lodge, like something in a state park made for tourists). I lay there in the bunk for hours and heard the female voice very faintly and was sick in my stomach through the early morning hours. Ice was on the inside of the window. I could feel the cold gripping the wall and a gloomy voice started talking in the rain, waving back and forth. It wasn't any nightmare and it was very long, the cold wet dark woods talking to me, the woman's voice curling to the room under the doorjamb.

Another whole person was out there playing chess, somebody I never knew. A woman and, I thought, somehow sin were in the lodge. Without a dream I was out of the regular world and had prickly sparking feelings like they had put you in a tub of ice and then run you through a wind tunnel.

At daybreak they were still at the game. Garrand Pool had started drinking again. He was up looking out a kitchen window and my father was leaned over studying the board, cooing and chirping. Mr. Pool was going to say something, turning around, but then he saw me in the doorway and stopped, coughing. When my father turned in the chair, I didn't recognize his face. It was longer and his mouth was bigger. His eyes were lost behind his nose. I was very glad he didn't say anything to me. He hurled back then as if my eyes hurt him. I shut the door again. Soon there was a knock on the door. I felt cold and withered.

But it was Mr. Kervochian. He told me to dress up, it was cold out, had quit raining, and he was going to take me out, bring my gun. In a few minutes the two of us walked by Mr. Pool and Daddy, frozen at the board, not looking up. Mr. Kervochian brought me some breakfast out on the porch — some coffee (my first), a banana, and some jerky. It was hurtfully cold while we sat there on the step. I could smell whiskey on Mr. Kervochian, but he had showered and combed his hair and had on fresh clothes. My boots were new and I liked them, bright brown with brass eyelets. I felt manly. I think Mr. Kervochian was having whiskey in his coffee.

"Let's go about our way and see what we can see, little Harris," he said.

"Don't you want your gun?" I asked him.

"No. Your big shooter's all we need."

I picked up the .410 single, which was heavy. He told me how to carry it safely. We walked a long time into the muddy woods, down truck tracks and then into deep slimy leaves with brown vines eye-high. I tripped once, went down gun and all with shells scattered out of my coat pocket. Mr. Kervochian didn't say anything but "That happens." We went on very deep in there, toward the river, I guess. How could cobwebs have lived through that rain? They were in my face. Mr. Kervochian, high up there with his thermos, could float on the leaves and go along with no danger, but I was all webby. He began talking, just a slight muddiness in his voice because of the drink.

"He used to have a colored man out here with us, like successful southern white men have at a deer camp. A happy coon, laughing and grinning, step and fetch it. Named Nicodemus, you know. Factotum luxury-maker. Owing so much to Pool Abe Lincoln's proclamation didn't even touch him. Measureless debt of generations. Even his pa owed Pool when he died."

"Mr. Kervochian, what's happening with my daddy and Mr. Pool back in the lodge?"

"Old Pool's calling in his debts. He always does, especially with some whiskey in him. He's that kind, perfect for a banker, gives so gladly and free, then when you don't know when, angry about the deal and set on revenge. Gives and then hates it. One of those kind that despises the borrower come any legal time to collect."

"Are they playing for money? Is that why they're so mad?"

"They could be, a lot of money if I heard right, whatall through their whispering. I don't know for sure. It's a private thing and you can be sure Pool's not going to let it go."

"It's like nobody else's in the lodge."

"Let's hunt. Tell you what: there's got to be big game down by the river."

We walked on and on. Cold and tired, stitch in the side, sleepy, was I.

We were on a little bluff and then there was just air. He caught me before I walked out into the Mississippi River. It was like a sea and I'd almost gone asleep into it, that deep muddy running water. "Watch ho, son!" he said. Then I was pulled back, watching our home state across the big water.

"You've got to watch it around here. Something's in that bluff under us. It's haunted here. This would be a very bad place to fall off."

The river was huge like a sea and angry, waves of water running. "Why is it haunted?"

"Nicodemus is under the bluff, son."

"That colored man? Why?"

"Old Pool and Colonel Wren."

"Are you drunk now, Mr. Kervochian?"

"Yes, son, I am."

"Please don't scare me."

"I'm sorry. Pay no attention to me. I can get sober in just three minutes, though, boy."

We walked back toward the lodge very slowly, the Nicodemus place behind me and the chess game going on, I guessed, ahead. We saw two squirrels, but again, I missed them. I didn't care. Mr. Kervochian said I was all right, he wasn't much of a hunter either.

"You know, all under our feet are frozen snakes, moccasins and rattlers, sleeping. All these holes in the ground around us. Snakes are cold-blooded and they freeze up asleep in the cold winter."

I didn't like to think of that at all.

Then it began raining all of a sudden, very hard, as if it had just yawned awhile to come back where it was. We were already stepping around ditches full of running water.

"Little Harris, there is a certain kind of woman," he all at once said, for what? "A woman with her blond hair pulled back straight from her forehead, a high and winsome forehead, that has forever been in fashion and lovely, through the ages. And that is your mother. Like basic black. Always in fashion. Blond against basic black and the exquisite forehead, for centuries."

I said nothing. We stopped and saw through the forest where Mr. Hester and Colonel Wren went across a cut with their guns, out trying to hunt but now caught by the rain, heading back to the lodge. We didn't say anything to them, like we were animals watching them.

"She used to come in the drugstore for her headaches. A woman like that in this town, I predicted, would always have some kind of trouble. That nice natural carriage, big trusting gray eyes."

"It's raining hard, Mr. Kervochian."

When we at last returned to the lodge my eyes were hanging down out of their holes I was so tired. There were empty plates on the bar of the kitchen and nobody in the chess seats, just empty glasses and cups on the table. Dr. Harvard said they had left off the game and finally gone to bed, thank God. He peered at the rain past us beyond the doorway and commenced fretting, almost whining about the weather and the thunder and when were we ever going to get out of here, the way the roads were flooded over. There was no telephone, and so on. To see a grown medical doctor going on like this, well, was amiss. It changed me uglily. I went right on to bed and was out a long time.

When I woke it was late into the day, and going out I saw Mr. Pool and my father were sitting there again, at it after their nap. They looked neither left nor right. My father suddenly gave a yelp, shrill, and I thought Garrand Pool had done something to him. But he was only making a move with a chess piece that must have been a good and mean one, because Mr. Pool cursed and drank half a glass of whiskey.

Mr. Kervochian took his place at the window with a new glass. He looked out into the weather as if he could see a number of people, all making him melancholy. Colonel Wren and Mr. Hester were all wet. They threw more logs on the fire and got it really blazing. They talked about more poker. Nobody knew quite what to do with all their big grown-up bodies and eyes and ears trapped in by the rain these days. Dr. Harvard nagged himself asleep again. The insurance man, Mr. Ott, came tumbling in the door holding his hand. He had cut it on an ax out there chopping wood. The blood was all over it and when he put his hand in the sink it dripped down in splotches around the drain. They woke up Dr. Harvard and he was in the kitchen with Mr. Ott a long time. Then he went out in the rain to get his bag. Mr. Ott needed stitches. I was fascinated by this, sewing up a man. Dr. Harvard worked over

Mr. Ott for a long time. Every now and then Mr. Ott would cry out, but in a man's way, just a deep *uff!* I looked over at my father and Mr. Pool. They had never even looked up during the whole hour.

Then Colonel Wren said he was going to have something, damn it all, and went outside with his gun, where in late evening it was just sprinkling rain. Everybody had read all the magazines. I found an old Reader's Digest Condensed Book and went back to read something by Somerset Maugham.

It put me to sleep although I liked the story. I guess it was after midnight when I heard them making more sound than usual out there. I went out in my pajamas. The men at the poker table were high on beer, maybe, but they were very concerned about Colonel Wren. It was raining, thundering and lightning, and he hadn't returned. One of them called him a crazy Davy Crockett kind of fool. Mr. Kervochian, sipping at the fireplace, put in, "Closer to it, Kaiser Wilhelm the Second. Shot ten thousand stags, most of them near tame. Had a feeble arm he was trying to make up for."

Then who comes in all bloody and drenched, with a knife in one hand and a spotlight in the other, but Colonel Wren. He was tracking mud in and shouting.

"There's breakfast out on the hook, by God!"

We went to the door past Mr. Pool and my father, frozen there, and saw a cleaned deer carcass hanging on the board between two trees. It showed up sparkling in the spotlight beam in all the rain.

"That's just a little doe, isn't it?" said Mr. Kervochian.

"That's all the woods gave up, help of this spotlight," said Colonel Wren very loudly. "It'll eat fine. Come that liver and eggs in the morning, partners, we'll have an attitude change here!"

I won't say again that my father and Mr. Pool paid no attention to any of this, and didn't do anything but play and take little naps for the next two days straight.

After breakfast around eleven that day, I drove out with Mr. Kervochian and Dr. Harvard to check the roads. We looked out of the truck cab and saw wide water much bigger than it used to be, the current of the creek rushing along limbs and bushes. It was frightening, not a hint of the road. Dr. Harvard was white when I looked at him. Later Mr. Kervochian explained that every man has a deathly fear and that Harvard's just happened to be water.

There was more poker and Big Band music on Mr. Kervochian's tape player, now and then a piece of radio music or weather announcement. But the next two days they argued mainly about Killarney Island. Colonel Wren said he knew the deer were all gathered there from all the flooding. And that there was an old boat, they could go out in the Mississippi and shoot all the deer they wanted. The rain shouldn't stop them. This wasn't a god-damned retirement lodge, they were all hung over and bitchy from cabin fever. He wanted to start the expedition.

"Our old boat should be right under Nicodemas Bluff," he said. There would be nothing to rowing out there.

I looked over at Mr. Kervochian. The others were arguing about whether that old boat was any good anymore, the river would be raging, it was stupid and dangerous. Mr. Kervochian, looking with meaning at me, said that was hardly any hunting at all. The deer on that island, which was only fifty yards square, would just be standing around and it would be nothing but a slaughter.

"You couldn't shoot your own foot anyway, Cavort-shun," said Colonel Wren meanly. "You're an old thought-fucked man." Then Wren looked down at me. "Sorry," he said.

But early the next morning we were all ready to get out of the place. Except for you know who, at it, in another world. Mr. Pool suddenly won a game, but he just got tight-lipped and red in the face to celebrate. I didn't want to look at my father's face. When Mr. Pool said "Checkmate, Gomar!" it sounded like a foreign name in the house.

I went along with them, taking my gun. Mr. Kervochian took a gun and his thermos. The rain was very light now in the early morning. The plan was, when they got to the island, Colonel Wren was going to scare a deer off the island just for me. It couldn't swim anywhere but almost right to me on the shore and I could blow it down. I wanted to do this. A deer was larger than the squirrels and I wasn't likely to miss. So there I was at ten all bloody in my thoughts, almost crazy from staying in the lodge around that chess tournament that who knows when it would end, both of them looking sick when I could stand to look at them.

We tracked that long way out to the bluff. They went down and found the boat and set out with the paddles, three of them. Mr. Kervochian stayed with me. He seemed to either care for me or

wanted a level place to drink. With all these people the bluff didn't
seem that fearsome, so I asked him what about Nicodemus, what
happened?

"You can't tell this around, little Harris."

"I wouldn't."

We watched them flapping and plowing the water, heading left
and north to the island, just a hump out there a half mile away.

"Looking at it several ways, it's still a wretched thing. The man
was full of cancer. Owed Pool a lifetime's money. Couldn't afford
a hospital. He asked Pool to shoot him and so they did. I don't
know which one."

"He'd been with them —"

"His whole life. You could blame Pool for the cancer too. The
way he gave, then hounded. Nicodemus, that man, still wanted 'to
keep it in the family.'"

They were hollering now out in the tan water, paddles up in the
air. Something was wrong with the boat. They turned it around
and headed back in. You could see the boat was getting lower in
the water. The going was very slow and there was a great deal of
grief shouted out. They must've been up to their knees. But my
sense of humor was not attuned correctly. I heard Mr. Kervochian
laughing. The river to me, though, looked like the worst fiercest
place to drown. They came back under the bluff, their guns under
water and their throats stuffed with rage.

Then of course the rain came on, half strong but mocking, and
you could feel the sleet in it. The wet men said almost nothing
flapping back through the woods. It took forever.

There was a shout ahead, a cackling. Down the cut I could see
some motion in those stumps in the edge of the lodge clearing.
The cackling and now a yipping called at us through the last yards,
a stand of walnuts where on the ground you crunched the ball
husks of the nuts with your boots.

Mr. Pool was beating my father on the neck with a pistol. It was
a long gun. He kept whacking it down. But my father, holding his
hands over his head and trying to dodge, kept cackling and yipping. Thing was, he was laughing, down on his knees, fingers on
top of his head, knee-walking and sloshing through the pools. It
was there where the water lay rotten-smelling in the tops of the
stumps, putrid and deep back in your nostrils.

"It's all mine, free and clear. I won it, I won it!" my father was shrieking in that woman's voice.

He couldn't know we were standing all around him. He was shrieking at the ground. Mr. Pool didn't know we were there either. He hit my father, Gomar, again. The gun made an awful fleshy *thunk* on him.

"You trash scoundrel. Stop it, stop it!"

Then Mr. Pool drew around and saw us all, then me especially. He hauled my father around facing me, on his knees. Garrand Pool was a big man and my father had gone all limp. His face was cut, his nose was smashed down. He looked horrible, the rain all over his face, and his face long, his mouth hung down gaping like frozen in a holler.

"Show him. Talk for your son. Let him see who you are."

I went up close to stop Mr. Pool. I was right in front of my father. He came up with his face, and you could tell he didn't want to, but couldn't help it. He spilled out in that cracking cackling female voice.

"I won! I won!"

Then Mr. Pool just thrust him off and he fell on his face out there in that stinking water.

What Garrand Pool had done seemed awful, but my father almost canceled it out. Nobody could make a direction toward either one. I know how they felt.

The next morning we left. Dr. Harvard was terrified, but the water had receded some and the tall trucks whipped right out through it and to the highway.

He couldn't even look at me for days when we got home. He was all bandaged up and sore. I never saw my father full in the face again. His face would start to turn my way, then he'd shake it back forward.

Nobody, I heard from Mother, ever bothered us about payments of any sort ever again while she was a widow. We had the house, the nice lawn, the two cars, a standing membership in the country club, which I only used to get loaded at and fall in the pool over and over again, swimming long distances under water, full of narcotics, until my wrung-out lungs drove me to the surface.

My father never got it right at the country club either, you see.

The next week after the deer lodge he was walking at twilight down the road next to the golf course. The driver of the car says he swerved out suddenly, right into the nose of his car. They didn't find any alcohol in his blood, and none of it made much sense unless you had seen his eyes trying to call back that terrible woman's voice, pleading right at me.

The extra money my mother had, her legal secretary's salary free and clear, was in a way my downfall. She did not know how not to spoil me, and I always had plenty of money, more money than anybody. And Mr. Kervochian felt for me deeply, truly. I will never blame him. He was of that certain druggist's habit of thought that drugs are made to help people through hurtful times. You wouldn't call him a pusher because he meant only the kindly thing, he saw I was numbed, shocked and injured, so he provided plenty of medicine for me. He gave some to my mother too. She wouldn't take hers. So I got hers and took it. I went back and he was always a cheerful giver.

Later, he even came down to the jail and brought me out after I'd be taken in, accompanying somebody, some group, somehow an accomplice, just lugging there and near keeling over in that racing little sleep I loved. Never did I fight or even complain much. My mother never remarried. With her looks, her high brightness and carriage, you would have thought she could have a number of prominent handsome men, but she was a woman, I found out — maybe there are a few of them — who don't want but just the one marriage. They are quite all right going along alone. I was shocked, I believe when I was eighteen or thereabouts, only slightly nembied in the kitchen, when she told me she actually had loved my father very much. Then I was confused even a bit more when she said, "Your father was a good man, Harris."

"He *was?*"

This confused me, as I say. I'd hated him for being on his knees with that voice at the lodge, I'd hated him for being killed, and I was angry at him through his brother, his own country-trash brother, when I saw him at Dad's funeral in a long-sleeve black silky shirt with a gold chain on his chest. His own brother not even in a suit.

Soon I needed some more drugs and went by Kervochian's.

"My mother said my father was a good man. Is that how you saw him, Gomar Greeves?"

"Gomar? . . . Well, Harris. Frankly, I just don't know. I hadn't known him that well. But he was probably a good man."

Later, but before he got sick, Mr. Kervochian, sharing a 'lude with me, began trying to have a theory, like so: "This state is very proud of its men's men. Its football-playing, tough rough whiskey-drinking men. But I tell you, you calculate those boys at the Methodist college who come by the store here. At least *half* of them are what you call epicene — leaning toward the womanly too. The new southern man is about half girl in many cases, Harris. Now that means their mothers raised them. Their fathers didn't get into it at all. So these men, maybe Gomar was a country version, the woman came —"

"I don't want to hear that, any of that." I was thinking of that awful Meemaw.

"But it was — I watched and heard closely, closely — a brilliant courtly woman invested him, a spirit . . ."

I just walked off from him.

Of course I returned for drugs. He told me two things about Mr. Pool and one about Colonel Wren, but I hate to repeat them because here my testimony gets pushy toward life's revenge, but I'll say the real fact is, Kervochian didn't have to tell me, I saw Pool plain enough around town. The man began losing his face. It just fell down and he got gruesomer and gruesomer and at last just almost unbearably ugly. He went and had galvanized electric facial therapy — $500 — at the beautician's, but nothing would save him. The last time I saw him in a car windshield he was driving with nought but two deep eyeholes hanging on to a slab of red wrinkled tissue. He had got strange too. He had women out to the deer lodge. His wife found out about it and went over and burned it down. Then Colonel Wren, whom I never saw again, did a thing that got him "roundly mocked," said Mr. Kervochian. Wren was a veteran of Wake Island, where the U.S. soldiers had bravely held off a horde of Japanese before they were beaten down, the survivors going to a prison in China until the end of the war. Wren wrote a long article for an American history magazine, telling the true story, in which he figured modestly and with "much self-deprecation." Then in the next issue in the letter section of that magazine there was a long letter from a man who was a private at Wake with the others. He went on to say how modest the then Captain Wren was, too modest. He had exposed himself to danger over and over, carrying wounded in one arm and firing his .45 with the other, etc. The letter was signed Pvt. Martin Lewis, Portland, Oregon. All was fine until somebody found out Wren had written the letter himself.

"In his seventies, old Wren. Pathetic," smacked Mr. Kervochian.

None of these happenings raised my spirits and I am putting them in only in memory of Mr. Kervochian, who died such a long painful death, but had explained nearly the whole town to me before he passed on.

When we lap that old woman's house and see her sitting there on her porch, grand car to the side, safe and nestled in, blasted dry with age, I still say over and over, "Success, success," to my running buddy. Forever on — maybe I'll get over it — I hate a good house, a lawn, the right trees, I despise that smart gloating Mercedes in the drive, all of it. Early on, I moved out of our house, way back there, thirteen or fifteen or something like that. I believe I moved into a shack, maybe even I lived once in a chicken shack. I have missed a great deal, but as the drugs run out with each kick and step, I am beginning to see the crone, once my teacher, go back in time. My legs are pushing her back to a smoother face, a standing position, an elegant stride, a happy smile, instructing the young cheerfully and with great love.

Now there is something for tomorrow. What are women like? What is time like? Most people, you might notice, walk around as if they are needed somewhere, like the animals out at the shelter need me. I want to look into this.

THOM JONES

Cold Snap

FROM THE NEW YORKER

SON OF A BITCH, there's a cold snap and I do this number where
I leave all the faucets running because my house, and most houses
out here on the West Coast, aren't "real" — they don't have windows that go up and down, or basements (which protect the pipes
in a way that a crawl space can't), or sidewalks out in the front with
a nice pair of towering oak trees or a couple of elms, which a real
house will have, one of those good old Midwest houses. Out here
the windows go side to side. You get no basement. No sidewalk and
no real trees, just evergreens, and when it gets cold and snows
nobody knows what to do. An inch of snow and they cancel school
and the community is paralyzed. "Help me, I'm helpless!" Well, it's
cold for a change and I guess that's not so bad, because all the
fleas and mosquitoes will freeze, and also because any change is
something, and maybe it will help snap me out of this bleak post-
Africa depression — oh, baby, I'm so depressed — but I wake up
at three in the morning and think, Oh, no, a pipe is gonna bust,
so I run the water and let the faucets drip and I go outside and
turn on the outdoor faucets, which are the most vulnerable. Sure
enough, they were caking up, and I got to them just in the nick
of time, which was good, since in my condition there was no way
I could possibly cope with a broken water pipe. I just got back from
Africa, where I was playing doctor to the natives, got hammered
with a nasty case of malaria, and lost thirty pounds, but it was a
manic episode I had that caused Global Aid to send me home. It
was my worst attack to date, and on lithium I get such a bad case
of psoriasis that I look like alligator man. You can take Tegretol

for mania but it once wiped out my white count and almost killed me, so what I like to do when I get all revved up is skin-pop some morphine, which I had with me by the gallon over there and which will keep you calm — and, unlike booze, it's something I can keep under control. Although I must confess I lost my medical license in the States for substance abuse and ended up with Global Aid when the dust settled over that one. God's will, really. Fate. Karma. Whatever. Anyhow, hypomania is a good thing in Africa, a real motivator, and you can do anything you want over there as long as you keep your feet on the ground and don't parade naked on the president's lawn in Nairobi and get expelled (which I did and which will get you expelled; O.K., I lied, you can't do *anything* — so sue me). On lithium, while you don't crash so bad, you never get high, either, and all you can do is sit around sucking on Primus beer bottles, bitching about how hot it is when there's so much work to do.

While I'm outside checking my faucets, I look my Oldsmobile over and wonder was it last year I changed the antifreeze? Back in bed, it strikes me that it's been three years, so I go out and run the engine and sit in the car with my teeth chattering — it's thirteen below, jeez! And pretty soon the warm air is defrosting the car and I drive over to the hardware section at Safeway and get one of those antifreeze testers with the little balls in it. At four in the morning I'm sitting in my kitchen trying to get it out of the plastic jacket, and it comes out in two parts, with the bulb upside down. No doubt some know-nothing Central American put it in upside down for twenty cents an hour in some slave factory. I know he's got problems — fact is, I've been there and could elucidate his problems — but how about me and my damn antifreeze? I mean, too bad about you, buddy, how about me? And I'm trying to jury-rig it when I realize there is a high potential for breaking the glass and cutting my thumb, and just as that voice that is me, that is always talking to me, my ego, I guess, tells me, "Be careful, Richard, so you don't cut your thumb" — at that instant, I slice my thumb down to the bone. So the next thing you know I'm driving to the hospital with a towel on my thumb thinking, A minute ago everything was just fine, and now I'm driving myself to the emergency room!

Some other guy comes in with this awful burn because a pressure cooker exploded in his face, and he's got this receding hairline, and you can see the way the skin is peeled back — poached-looking. The guy's going to need a hairpiece for sure. A doctor comes out eating a sandwich, and I hear him tell the nurse to set up an IV line and start running some Dilaudid for the guy, which he deserves, considering. I would like some for my thumb, but all I get is Novocain, and my doctor says, "You aren't going to get woozy on me, are you?" I tell him no, I'm not like that, but I have another problem, and he says, "What's that?" and I tell him I can't jack off left-handed. Everybody laughs, because it's the graveyard shift, when that kind of joke is appropriate — even in mixed company. Plus, it's true.

After he stitches me up, I'm in no pain, although I say, "I'll bet this is going to hurt tomorrow," and he says no, he'll give me some pain medication, and I'm thinking, What a great doctor. He's giving me *pain medication*. And while he's in a giving mood I hit him up for some prostate antibiotics because my left testicle feels very heavy.

"Your left testicle feels *heavy?*" he says skeptically.

Yeah, every guy gets it, shit; I tell him my left nut feels like an anvil. I mean, I want to cradle it in my hand when I'm out and about, or rest it on a little silk pillow when I'm stationary. It doesn't really hurt, but I'm very much conscious of having a left testicle, whereas I have teeth and a belly button and a right testicle and I don't even know. I tell him I don't want a finger wave, because I've been through this a thousand times. My prostate is backing up into the seminal vesicles, and if you don't jerk off it builds up and gets worse, and the doctor agrees — that does happen, and he doesn't really want to give me a finger wave, especially when I tell him that a urologist checked it out a couple of months back. He puts on a plastic glove and feels my testicle, pronounces it swollen, and writes a script for antibiotics, after which he tells me to quit drinking coffee. I was going to tell him that I don't jerk off because I'm a sex fiend; I have low sex drive, and it's actually not that much fun. I just do it to keep the prostate empty. Or should I tell him I'm a doctor myself, albeit defrocked, that I just got back from Africa and my nut could be infected with elephantiasis? Highly unlikely, but you never know. But he won't know diddle about tropical medicine — that's my department, and I decide I will just shut my mouth, which is a first for me.

The duty nurse is pretty good-looking, and she contradicts the doctor's orders — gives me a cup of coffee anyhow, plus a roll, and we're sitting there quietly, listening to the other doctor and a nurse fixing the guy with the burned forehead. A little human interaction is taking place and my depression is gone as I begin to feel sorry for the guy with the burn, who is explaining that he was up late with insomnia cooking sweet potatoes when the pressure cooker blew. He was going to candy them with brown sugar and eat them at six in the morning and he's laughing, too, because of the Dilaudid drip. After Linda Ronstadt sings "Just One Look" on the radio, the announcer comes on and says that we've set a record for cold — it's thirteen and a half below at the airport — and I notice that the announcer is happy, too; there's a kind of solidarity that occurs when suffering is inflicted on the community by nature.

My own thing is the Vincent van Gogh effect. I read where he "felt like a million" after he cut off his ear. It only lasted for a couple of days. They always show you the series of four cats that he painted at different times in his life as his mental condition went progressively downhill. Cat One is a realistic-looking cat, but as life goes on and his madness gets worse he paints Cat Four and it looks as though he's been doing some kind of bad LSD, which is how the world had been looking to me until I cut my thumb. It gave me a three-day respite from the blues, and clarity came into my life, and I have to remind myself by writing this down that all the bad stuff does pass if you can wait it out. You forget when you're in the middle of it, so during that three-day break, I slapped this note on the refrigerator door: "Richard, you are a good and loving person, and all the bad stuff does pass, so remember that the next time you get down and think that you've always been down and always will be down, since that's paranoia and it gets you nowhere. You're just in one of your Fyodor Dostoyevski moods — do yourself a favor and forget it!"

I felt so good I actually had the nerve to go out and buy a new set of clothes and see a movie, and then, on the last day before the depression came back, I drove out to Western State and checked my baby sister, Susan, out for a day trip. Susan was always a lot worse than me; she heard voices and pulled I don't know how many suicide attempts until she took my squirrel pistol and put a .22 long-rifle slug through the temple — not really the temple, because at the last minute you always flinch, but forward of the temple, and it was the most perfect lobotomy. I remember hearing the gun pop and how she came into my room (I was home from college for the summer) and said, "Richard, I just shot myself, how come I'm not dead?" Her voice was calm instead of the usual fingernails-on-the-chalkboard voice, the when-she-was-crazy (which was almost always) voice, and I realized later that she was instantly cured, the very moment the bullet zipped through her brain. Everyone said it was such a shame because she was so beautiful, but what good are looks if you are in hell? And she let her looks go at the hospital because she really didn't have a care in the world, but she was still probably the most beautiful patient at Western State. I had a fresh occasion to worry about her on this trip when I saw an attendant rough-handling an old man to stop him from whining, which it did. She'd go along with anything, and she had no advocate except me. And then I almost regretted going out there, in spite of my do-good mood, because Susan wanted to go to the Point Defiance Zoo to see Cindy, the elephant that was on the news after they transferred the attendant who took care of her, for defying orders and actually going into the elephant pen on the sly to be her friend.

There are three hundred elephants in North American zoos, and although Cindy is an Asian elephant and a female and small, she is still considered the most dangerous elephant in America. Last year alone, three people were killed by elephants in the United States, and this is what Susan had seen and heard on the color television in the ward dayroom, and she's like a child — she wants to go out and see an elephant when it's ten below zero. They originally had Cindy clamped up in a pen tighter than the one they've got John Gotti in down in Marion, Illinois, and I don't remember that the catalogue of Cindy's crimes included human murder. She was just a general troublemaker, and they were beating her with a two-by-four when some animal activist reported it and there was a big scandal that ended with Cindy getting shipped down to the San Diego Zoo, the best zoo in the world; I think there was some kind of escape (don't quote me on that) where Cindy was running around on a golf course in between moves, and then a capture involving tranquilizer darts, and when they couldn't control Cindy in San Diego they shipped her back up here to

Tacoma and put her in maximum-security confinement. It was pretty awful. I told Susan that over in India Cindy would have a job hauling logs or something, and there would be an elephant boy to scrub her down at night with a big brush while she lay in the river, and the elephant boy would be with her at all times, her constant companion. Actually, the elephant would be more important than the boy, I told her, and that's how you should handle an elephant in America — import an experienced elephant boy for each one, give the kids a green card, pay them a lot of overtime, and have them stay with the elephants around the clock. You know, quality time. How could you blame Cindy for all the shit she pulled? And in the middle of this, Susan has a tear floating off her cheek and I don't know if it's a tear caused by the cold or if she was touched by Cindy's plight. The reason they sent my sister to the nuthouse was that you could light a fire on the floor in front of her and she would just sit there and watch it burn. When our parents died, I took her to my place in Washington state and hired helpers to look after her, but they would always quit — quit while I was over in the Third World, where it's impossible to do anything. It was like, *Meanwhile, back in the jungle / Meanwhile, back in the States* . . . Apart from her lack of affect, Susan was always logical and made perfect sense. She was kind of like a Mr. Spock who just didn't give a shit anymore except when it came to childish fun and games. All bundled up, with a scarf over her ears, in her innocence she looked like Eva Marie Saint in *On the Waterfront*.

We drove over to Nordstrom's in the University District and I bought Suz some new threads and then took her to a hair salon where she got this chic haircut, and she was looking so good that I almost regretted it, 'cause if those wacked-out freaks at the hospital weren't hitting on her before, they would be now. It was starting to get dark and time to head back when Susan spots the Space Needle from I-5 — she's never been there, so I took her to the top and she wandered outside to the observation deck, where the wind was a walking razor blade at 518 eighteen feet, but Susan is grooving on the lights of Seattle and with her homemade lobotomy doesn't experience pain in quite the way a normal person does, and I want her to have a little fun, but I'm freezing out there, especially my thumb, which ached. I didn't want to pop back inside in the sheltered part and leave her out there, though, because she might want to pitch herself over the side. I mean, they've got safety nets, but what if she's still got some vestige of a death wish? We had dinner in the revolving dining room, and people were looking at us funny because of Susan's eating habits, which deteriorate when you live in a nuthouse, but we got through that and went back to my place to watch TV, and after that I was glad to go to sleep — but I couldn't sleep because of my thumb. I was thinking I still hadn't cashed in the script for the pain pills when Susan comes into my bedroom naked and sits down on the edge of the bed.

"Ever since I've been shot, I feel like those animals in the zoo. I want to set them free," she says, in a remarkable display of insight, since that scar in her frontal lobes has got more steel bars than all the prisons of the world, and, as a rule, folks with frontal-lobe damage don't have much insight. I get her to put on her pajamas, and I remember what it used to be like when she stayed at home — you always had to have someone watching her — and I wished I had gotten her back to the hospital that very night, because she was up prowling, and suddenly all my good feelings of the past few days were gone. I felt crappy, but I had to stay vigilant while my baby sister was tripping around the house with this bullet-induced, jocular euphoria.

At one point she went outside barefoot. Later I found her eating a cube of butter. Then she took out all the canned foods in my larder and stacked them up — Progresso black beans (*beaucoup*), beef-barley soup, and canned carrot juice — playing supermarket. I tell her, "Mrs. Ma'am, I'll take one of those, and one of those, and have you got any peachy pie?"

She says, "I'm sorry, Richard, we haven't got any peachy pie."

"But, baby, I would sure like a nice big piece of peachy pie, heated up, and some vanilla ice cream with some rum sauce and maybe something along the lines of a maraschino cherry to put on the top for a little garnish. Nutmeg would do. Or are you telling me this is just a soup, beans, and carrot-juice joint? Is that all you got here?"

"Yes, Richard. Just soup and beans. They're very filling, though."

"Ahhm gonna have to call Betty Crocker, 'cause I'm in the mood for some pie, darlin'."

Suzie looks at me sort of worried and says that she thinks Betty Crocker is dead. Fuck. I realized I just had to sit on the couch and watch her, and this goes on and on, and of course I think I hear someone crashing around in the yard, so I get my .357 out from under my pillow and walk around the perimeter of the house, my feet crunching on the frozen snow. There was nobody out there. Back inside I checked on Susan, who was asleep in my bed. When I finally saw the rising of the sun and heard birds chirping to greet the new day, I went to the refrigerator, where I saw my recent affirmation: "Richard, you are a good and loving person," etc. I ripped it off the refrigerator and tore it into a thousand tiny pieces. Only an idiot would write something like that. It was like, I can't hack it in Africa, can't hack it at home — all I can hack is dead. So I took all the bullets out of the .357 except one, spun the chamber, placed the barrel against my right temple, and squeezed the trigger. When I heard the click of the hammer — voilà! I instantly felt better. My thumb quit throbbing. My stomach did not burn. The dread of morning and of sunlight had vanished, and I saw the dawn as something good, the birdsong wonderful. Even the obscure, take-it-for-granted objects in my house — the little knickknacks covered in an inch of dust, a simple wooden chair, my morning coffee cup drying upside down on the drainboard — seemed so relevant, so alive and necessary. I was glad for life and glad to be alive, especially when I looked down at the gun and saw that my bullet had rotated to the firing chamber. The van Gogh effect again. I was back from Cat Four to Cat One.

They're calling from the hospital, because I kept Susan overnight: "Where is Susan?" "She's watching *Days of Our Lives*," I say as I shove the .357 into a top drawer next to the phone book. "Is she taking her Stelazine?" "Yes," I say. "Absolutely. Thanks for your concern. Now, goodbye!"

Just then the doorbell rings, and what I've got is a pair of Jehovah's Witnesses. I've seen enough of them on the Dark Continent to overcome an instinctive dread, since they seem to be genuinely content, proportionately — like, if you measured a bunch of them against the general population they are very happy people, and so pretty soon we're drinking Sanka and Susan comes out and they are talking about Christ's Kingdom on Earth where the lion lies down with the lamb, and Susan buys every word of it, 'cause it's like that line "Unless they come to me as little children . . ."

Susan is totally guileless and the two Witnesses are without much
guile, and I, the king of agnostics, listen and think, How's a lion
going to eat straw? It's got a GI system designed to consume flesh,
bones, and viscera — it's got sharp teeth, claws, and predatory
instincts, not twenty-seven stomachs, like some bovine Bossie the
Cow or whatever. And while I'm paging through a copy of *Awake!*,
I see a little article from the correspondent in Nigeria entitled
"The Guinea Worm — Its Final Days." As a doctor of tropical
medicine, I probably know more about *Dracunculus medinensis,* the
"fiery serpent," or Guinea worm, than anyone in the country.
Infection follows ingestion of water containing crustacea (*Cyclops*).
The worms penetrate the gut wall and mature in the retroperi-
toneal space, where they can grow three feet in length, and then
generally migrate to the lower legs, where they form a painful
blister. What the Africans do is burst the ulcer and extract the adult
worm by hooking a stick under it and ever so gently tugging it out,
since if you break it off the dead body can become septic and the
leg might have to be removed. The pain of the Guinea worm is
on a par with the pain of gout, and it can take ten days to nudge
one out. The bad part is they usually come not in singles but in
multiples. I've seen seven come out of an old man's leg.

   If and when Global Aid sends me back to Africa, I will help
continue the worm-eradication program, and as the Witnesses
delight Susan with tales of a Heaven on Earth I'm thinking of the
heat and the bugs in the equatorial zone, and the muddy water
that the villagers take from rivers — they pour it in jugs and let
the sediment settle for an hour and then dip from the top, where
it looks sort of clean; it's hard to get through to them that *Cyclops*
crustacea may be floating about invisibly and one swallow could
get you seven worms, a swallow you took three years ago. You can
talk to the villagers until you're blue in the face and they'll drink
it anyhow. So you have to poison the *Cyclops* without overpoisoning
the water. I mean, it can be done, but, given the way things work
over there, you have to do everything yourself if you want it done
right, which is why I hate the idea of going back: you have to come
on like a one-man band.

   On the other hand, Brother Bogue and the other brothers in
the home office of Global Aid don't trust me; they don't like it
when I come into the office irrepressibly happy, like Maurice

Chevalier in his tuxedo and straw hat — "*Jambo jambo, bwana, jambo bonjour!*" — and give everyone one of those African soft hand-shakes, and then maybe do a little turn at seventy-eight revolutions per minute: "Oh, *oui oui*, it's delightful for me, walking my baby back home!" or "Hey, ain't it great, after staying out late? Zangk heffen for leetle gorls." Etc. They hate it when I'm high and they hate it when I'm low, and they hate it most if I'm feeling crazy/paranoid and come in and say, "You won't believe what happened to me now!" To face those humorless brothers every day and stay forever in a job as a medical administrator, to wear a suit and tie and drive I-5 morning and night, to climb under the house and tape those pipes with insulation — you get in the crawl space and the dryer-hose vent is busted and there's lint up the ass, a time bomb for spontaneous combustion, funny the house hasn't blown already (and furthermore, no wonder the house is dusty), and, hey, what, carpenter ants, too? When I think of all that: Fair America, I bid you adieu!

But things are basically looking up when I get Suz back to the hospital. As luck has it, I meet an Indian psychiatrist who spent fifteen years in Kampala, Uganda — he was one of the three shrinks in the whole country — and I ask him how Big Daddy Idi Amin is doing. Apparently, he's doing fine, living in Saudi Arabia with paresis or something, and the next thing you know the doc is telling me he's going to review Susan's case file, which means he's going to put her in a better ward and look out for her, and that's a load off my mind. Before I go, Suz and I take a little stroll around the spacious hospital grounds — it's a tranquil place. I can't help thinking that if Brother Bogue fires me — though I'm determined to behave myself after my latest mishap — I could come here and take Haldol and lithium, watch color TV, and drool. Whatever happened to that deal where you just went off to the hospital for a "little rest," with no stigma attached? Maybe all I need is some rest.

Susan still has those Jehovah's Witnesses on her mind. As we sit on a bench, she pulls one of their booklets out of her coat and shows me scenes of cornucopias filled with fruit and bounty, rain-bows, and vividly colored vistas of a heaven on earth. Vistas that I've seen in a way, however paradoxically, in these awful Third World places, and I'm thinking, Let them that have eyes see; and

let them that have ears hear — that's how it is, and I start telling
Suz about Africa, maybe someday I can take her there, and she
gets excited and asks me what it's like. Can you see lions?

And I tell her, "Yeah, baby, you'll see lions, giraffes, zebras,
monkeys, and parrots, and the Pygmies." And she really wants to
see Pygmies. So I tell her about a Pygmy chief who likes to trade
meat for tobacco, T-shirts, candy, and trinkets, and about how one
time when I went manic and took to the bush I stayed with this
tribe, and went on a hunt with them, and we found a honeycomb
in the forest; one of the hunters climbed up the tree to knock it
down, oblivious of all the bees that were biting him. There were
about five of us in the party and maybe ten pounds of honey and
we ate all of it on the spot, didn't save an ounce, because we had
the munchies from smoking dope. I don't tell Suz how it feels to
take an airplane to New York, wait four hours for a flight to London,
spend six hours in a transient lounge, and then hop on a nine-hour
flight to Nairobi, clear customs, and ride on the back of a feed
truck driven by a kamikaze African over potholes, through thick
red dust, mosquitoes, blackflies, tsetse flies, or about river blindness, bone-break fever, bilharziasis, dumdum fever, tropical ulcers,
AIDS, leprosy, etc. To go through all that to save somebody's life
and maybe have them spit in your eye for the favor — I don't tell
her about it, the way you don't tell a little kid that Santa Claus is
a fabrication. And anyhow if I had eyes and could see, and ears
and could hear — it very well might *be* the Garden of Eden. I
mean, I can fuck up a wet dream with my attitude. I don't tell her
that lions don't eat straw, never have, and so she's happy. And it's
a nice moment for me, too, in a funny-ass way. I'm beginning to
feel that with her I might find another little island of stability.

Another hospital visit: winter has given way to spring and the
cherry blossoms are out. In two weeks it's gone from ten below to
sixty-five, my Elavil and lithium are kicking in, and I'm feeling fine,
calm, feeling pretty good. (I'm ready to go back and rumble in
the jungle, yeah! *Sha-lah la-la-la-lah.*) Susan tells me she had a
prophetic dream. She's unusually focused and articulate. She tells
me she dreamed the two of us were driving around Heaven in a
blue '67 Dodge.

"A '67 Dodge. Baby, what were we, the losers of Heaven?"

"Maybe, but it didn't really matter because we were there and we were happy."

"What were the other people like? Who was there? Was Arthur Schopenhauer there?"

"You silly! We didn't see other people. Just the houses. We drove up this hill and everything was like in a Walt Disney cartoon and we looked at one another and smiled because we were in Heaven, because we made it, because there wasn't any more shit."

"Now, let me get this straight. We were driving around in a beat-up car —"

"Yes, Richard, but it didn't matter."

"Let me finish. You say people lived in houses. That means people have to build houses. Paint them, clean them, and maintain them. Are you telling me that people in Heaven have jobs?"

"Yes, but they like their jobs."

"Oh, God, does it never end? A *job!* What am I going to do? I'm a doctor. If people don't get sick there, they'll probably make me a coal miner or something."

"Yes, but you'll love it." She grabs my arm with both hands, pitches her forehead against my chest, and laughs. It's the first time I've heard Susan laugh, ever — since we were kids, I mean.

"Richard, it's just like Earth but with none of the bad stuff. You were happy, too. So please don't worry. Is Africa like the Garden of Eden, Richard?"

"It's lush all right, but there's lots and lots of dead time," I say. "It's a good place to read *Anna Karenina*. Do you get to read novels in Heaven, hon? Have they got a library? After I pull my shift in the coal mine, do I get to take a nice little shower, hop in the Dodge, and drive over to the library?"

Susan laughs for the second time. "We will travel from glory to glory, Richard, and you won't be asking existential questions all the time. You won't have to anymore. And Mom and Dad will be there. You and me, all of us in perfect health. No coal mining. No wars, no fighting, no discontent. Satan will be in the Big Pit. He's on the Earth now tormenting us, but these are his last days. Why do you think we are here?"

"I often ask myself that question."

"Just hold on for a little while longer, Richard. Can you do that? Will you do it for me, Richard? What good would Heaven be if you're not there? Please, Richard, tell me you'll come."

I said, "O.K., baby, anything for you. I repent."

"No more Fyodor Dostoyevski?"

"I'll be non-Dostoyevski. It's just that, in the meantime, we're just sitting around here — waiting for Godot?"

"No, Richard, don't be a smart-ass. In the meantime we eat lunch. What did you bring?"

I opened up a deli bag and laid out chicken-salad-sandwich halves on homemade bread wrapped in white butcher paper. The sandwiches were stuffed with alfalfa sprouts and grated cheese, impaled with toothpicks with red, blue, and green cellophane ribbons on them, and there were two large, perfect, crunchy garlic pickles on the side. And a couple of cartons of strawberry Yoplait, two tubs of fruit salad with fresh whipped cream and little wooden spoons, and two large cardboard cups of aromatic, steaming, fresh black coffee.

It begins to rain, and we have to haul ass into the front seat of my Olds, where Suz and I finish the best little lunch of a lifetime and suddenly the Shirelles are singing, "This is dedicated to the one I love," and I'm thinking that I'm gonna be all right, and in the meantime what can be better than a cool, breezy, fragrant day, rain-splatter diamonds on the wraparound windshield of a Ninety-eight Olds with a view of cherry trees blooming in the light spring rain?

JOHN KEEBLE

The Chasm

FROM PRAIRIE SCHOONER

IN WINTER THE glazed bunchgrass and wild oats tuft the road-sides and edges of fields. In spring the exhausted grass will be there still, a blond whiskering to the green. Through summer the dry stalks of last year's grass memorialize winter, the pale of the dead fringing the alive in this place that has become Jim Blood's country. In the heat of the summer, it takes a powerful leap of the imagination to remember the snow that covered the fields. So it is. Usually, the winters in eastern Washington are kind enough, but not too many years ago the cold came early. A northerly from the Gulf of Alaska found a trough between the mountain ranges to howl down. For a solid month record low temperatures were broken daily. Before it was done Jim found cause for the first time in years to reflect upon the small Saskatchewan town he'd come from.

That was a hard place. He remembered it as crystalline and white. He remembered voices ringing in the cold like metal. His two-year-old sister had died there. He remembered the bright sound the tiny coffin made when it struck the ice at the bottom of the grave. He remembered his parents in the graveyard, and how his father, the only minister for miles around, had conducted the service himself. He remembered how his father seemed to stand straight against this trouble, while his mother bent under it. That was then. He'd been a boy to whom the many common and uncommon things in life were equal in their power to astonish him.

Now, he lived here with his wife, Diane, and their three sons. They were trying to start up a ranch. They'd moved out to the place late last spring to finish building a house. They had few neighbors. By their driveway, the distance from the house to the county road was nearly a mile, and when they drove out they emerged from the woods onto a rise from which they could look northward to the Lanattos' place across the fields, and then the Holisters' place, the two houses and network of outbuildings that went with a dairy. To the south was the canyon. That was all. Phil Lanatto was a dentist, but he and his wife worked an alfalfa crop too. Bob Holister was a farm cooperative executive. He and his wife lived in a house near the road. Their son and daughter-in-law, Lem and Judy, lived in the back house.

It was the younger Holister's dairy operation. Lem and Judy worked as x-ray technicians in a hospital in the city. Judy worked swing, Lem graveyard, and by day they ran the dairy which they were establishing with the greatest care. Like Phil Lanatto, Lem was a veteran. Gradually, Jim had come to know how long the other two had been in Vietnam, whereabouts, and in what capacity: Lem had been a helicopter gunner and Phil a surgical dentist. When Phil and Lem talked about Vietnam, about the jungle, Jim felt an unease, and yet he felt drawn to the scorching he could almost smell on them like burnt hair.

Jim met Lem early in the summer when he dropped by the Holisters' place to introduce himself. He found Lem loading calves. A trim man with black hair and sharp eyes, Lem drove the calves into a pen, then coaxed them up the chute and into a closed, two-ton truck by clucking softly and flicking them with a switch. These were excess calves headed for a feedlot. It was June. The flies had just hatched and the air was thick with them. The calves did not balk at the loading, but crowded anxiously into the head of the box, their glossy eyes and white and black coats flashing in the dark. Jim and Lem leaned against the chute and occasionally Lem reached over with the switch to make a calf move. The two men continually brushed flies away from their faces. They spoke little. Lem grinned and said, "It's hard to talk when you have to keep your teeth closed."

Jim saw Lem again in July. Jim was doing roadwork with his old crawler tractor. The tractor had a boom on it and a blade for dozing. His road had a low spot near the front gate, a sink that became a pond in the spring and would make a hard place to plow the snow in winter. He pushed rocks into the hole, then scraped dirt off the rise to cover the rock. The blade snagged on an outcropping near the bottom and the tracks on the left side spun. He lifted the blade and tried to back the tractor off. The tracks didn't grab. He looked down and saw that he was in mud, that it wasn't just a hole or just a runoff pond he was filling, but an underground spring, and that he'd chewed off the crust with the tracks. He tried to move the tractor, forward and backward. He tried to turn it to drive it out. The left side only dug itself in. He got out to look and instantly sank knee-deep in the mire. He scrambled onto the outcropping and looked.

The side of the tractor was sinking, slowly but visibly sinking. It was not a small tractor. An antiquated behemoth, a D-14, it weighed five tons, and it was tipping. Something had to be done right away. Diane and the telephone were too far. The Lanattos' house was a half mile across the field. The Holisters' place was farther yet. If Jim tried to move the tractor, and failed, and dug it in deeper, the situation would quickly change from grave to desperate. He pictured the tractor listing until it dropped to its side. He told himself to calm down.

The tractor had two winches, one to operate a boom and the other to run a set of log tongs. One cable might be disconnected and used to winch the tractor out if he could find something to tie it to. He looked for a tree in front or in back of the tractor. They were all too small. They would snap under the weight. There was a tree to the right, a big one. He looked at it. There was no way to pull the tractor out sideways. He walked around and looked at the tractor. He could see the mud inching up the tracks on the left side. He looked at the tree again, then at the boom, which could be swiveled. As he considered this, the shiny nose of Lem's black pickup appeared.

Lem came over. "Saw you from the road," he said, then he squinted at Jim. "It's that bad?"

"It's not good."

"It won't move?"

"Down."

Lem squatted and studied the buried track, then stood and looked the tractor over. He looked at the boom, then at the tree Jim had been studying.

"You were considering the tree."

Jim nodded. "The boom."

"I'd do it."

"I don't know if the boom can lift up half of that tractor. I don't know, maybe the right side will just sink."

"The cable'll go first. Do you know anybody with a bigger Cat than this one?"

Jim looked down at his boots, covered with mud.

"If you have to hire somebody's Cat, it'll cost you a small fortune."

Jim nodded.

"You drive," Lem said.

Jim didn't like it. He didn't like the thought of the cable snapping, but he got in and swiveled the boom around to the right until it was perpendicular to the tractor body, and let down the tongs. Lem grabbed them, wrapped the cable twice around the tree, and secured it by closing the tongs onto the trunk. Jim winched in the cable, then paused. He'd seen the tongs go rigid. He didn't like the thought of anything breaking — boom, tongs, or cable — with him sitting there in the open cab. Lem grinned and gestured with his thumbs up. Jim didn't like the fear he felt, either. He wound the winch in a little more. He watched the cable cut into the bark of the tree and felt the left side of the tractor rise. He looked down at the right side. The track hadn't sunk. He winched in more. If the cable snapped, he would be in the line of fire and a whipping cable could slice him in half. He took a deep breath and winched in the cable until the left track cleared the ground. The cable held.

Lem motioned to back up. Jim got about a foot before the left track touched again because of the incline. Lem motioned to winch in more. Jim did so. They used the same method again and again, five times lifting the left track and backing up on the right until the tractor was clear. Jim let the cable out and Lem unhooked it from the tree. Jim wound it back, moved the tractor up the hill, stopped and turned it off. The silence boomed in his ears. He sat still, balancing his hands on his knees.

Lem grinned. "You had it from the start."

"I had the idea. That's all." He thought — the idea, I had the idea, but the execution of it scared me.

"Hell," Lem said, "that machine could pull itself up a tree if you found one big enough. You could hook it up to its own engine and it'd disembowel itself."

Lem and Judy had no children, but planned to adopt a baby. It had taken them three years of waiting. The baby was to arrive the Friday before Christmas. Over roughly the same period, Jim and Diane had felled trees, trimmed, hauled, peeled, milled, set and notched them to make the walls of their house. They were building with logs. When the two couples talked, they were struck by the mirroring in their lives. One couple had children, which the second couple desired. The second couple had their farming enterprise well under way, which the first couple had just begun. Though they did not spend that much time together, they had spoken of this — the waiting they shared, the expectation, the work — and a sense of luminousness that cast away their differences fell upon them.

For the first two and a half years Jim and Diane had used the nearby city as a home base and traveled to the ranch to work. They used chain saws to cut and trim the logs, and the tractor's boom to lift them, but otherwise it was an extended exercise in hand labor — socket slick, chisels, sledge, augers, froe. This was an economy, but the use of primitive methods also came from Jim's desire for the cleansing touch of simple tools and natural materials.

Diane didn't believe in such things as fervently as he did. She wished to live in this place in approximately this fashion, but she wondered why he had to do everything the hard way. She'd said that maybe what he really wanted was to vanish into the woods of north Idaho like some of the others had, to become a mountain man. "What are you trying to overcome?" she asked him one day. They were working their way through the last group of logs on the ground, peeling them with bark spuds.

Jim couldn't answer. He thought that Diane knew about the touch of the hand to things — nail, spike, bar, and wedge, the yellow pine — and about the spirits that had their roots in the material world. She was a musician, a cellist. She understood that the bow drawn across the strings activated the atoms in the air. But in another way he realized that Diane's question went deeper, that the images of impeccability he pursued were striking a crazy, precarious balance with a chaotic thing he couldn't name. He stuck the blade of his bark spud into a log and looked at Diane. She was staring deeply into him with her bright green eyes. The true answer to her question seemed just out of his reach. The answer was like a word remembered for its feel on the tongue, but which he couldn't raise to his mind.

During the second year of work, Jim's parents moved out from the Midwest. Everyone lived in Jim and Diane's rented house in the city and planned to move together to the ranch when the new house was ready. This became the plan, a closing of ranks following Jim's father's retirement. Funds were pooled. The new house expanded, then took shape, but at the same time the couples were learning that they could not live together. Relations grew strained, then fragile. The more fragile relations became, the more far-fetched were the dreams. Life together was like a web, intricately woven, but cut loose from its moorings and floating away crazily on the wind.

There was a scene. Jim's father corrected his middle grandson, a five-year-old, at the dinner table. In itself it was nothing, but Jim told his father to let the boy be. His father, one who by profession had given comfort to others, called the child despicable. Hot words were exchanged. Several months' worth of resentment suddenly broke surface: when to make noise and when not, in what order to use the bathroom, how clean to keep the kitchen, who should wash dishes . . . Jim's mother slammed a glass on the table, shattered it, cut her hand, rose and vented a flood of accusations. Who did Jim and Diane think they were to bring them to this? There were too many children here, too many people, too much junk. Her face was white and her eyes blazed in the way Jim hadn't seen since he was a boy — young-looking, blue, glinting like knives in the old face. Heedless of her bleeding hand, she cursed her son, this house and the one under construction. Why weren't they left where they were to die? Or sent away to a retirement home in California? She cursed herself, her husband, and her long life of disappointment.

The oldest boy, a nine-year-old, watched his grandmother in amazement as the room rang with her voice. The baby was silent. The five-year-old, who believed, his parents would learn, that he had caused his grandmother to cut her hand, began to cry fran-

tically. Jim felt drawn into the center of a dynamo of his own
making, and yet he was simultaneously on the edge of it, watching
as it spun and broke apart. He couldn't swallow the chunk of bread
in his mouth. His mother's blood dotted the white tablecloth like
wine. Diane, whose face showed her burden winding tight on its
spool, picked up the five-year-old and carried him away. His cries
receded and then grew louder again from behind a closed door.
They sounded piteous and made Jim's body wrench. His father
had his hands folded on the table and he stared at them with an
expression of great solemnity.

In June of the third year, Jim, Diane, and the boys moved into tents
at the ranch. Jim's parents bought a house in town. Jim threw
himself into the building. The two older boys helped as they
could. Diane managed the household, which consisted of two tents
pitched under trees, and a table, a rickety shelf, and an old wood-
burning cookstove set up on the porch of the small toolshed. She
helped with the building, but because she was a musician, there
were certain things she shouldn't do. She needed time to practice,
too, since she played with the symphony in the nearby city. For his
part, Jim had taken time off from his job to build. Sometimes
Diane practiced outside as he worked. The notes were whipped
around by the breeze. Sometimes they seemed to shatter into
pieces and to fly at him like a flock of birds bursting out of a tree.
    When the work was heavy, friends might come out. By Septem-
ber they'd completed the log raising, by October they had floors,
and by November they had half the roof up. It snowed. They spent
a great deal of time huddled around the cookstove. The two older
boys were happy to go to school where it was warm. By Thanksgiving they had electricity in the house, a door, temporary windows,
a temporary wall erected between the half of the house they would
live in and the half that would remain uninhabitable, and two
temporary chimneys, one for a potbelly stove in the bedroom and
one for the cookstove in the kitchen. They moved in. They shared
the bedroom, all five of them. Diane found a corner for practicing.
As he worked, Jim liked to feel bass notes throbbing in the wood.
    By December they had plumbing, the copper pipe run under
the house and up into the water heater, and down again, then up
into the bathroom. One night early in December everybody took

a bath, each of the boys separately, then all three together. Their
laughter rang in the house. For six months they'd bathed in the
spring. For three months the water heater had stood waiting in its
crate, an article of faith. Diane took a bath and emerged with her
flushed legs shining behind the slit in her bathrobe. Jim took a
bath and lay in it, astounded, then came out looking for Diane.
They put the boys to bed, waited for them to go to sleep, and threw
a blanket down on the subfloor in the kitchen and made love.
Afterward, Diane sat up and leaned toward Jim, grasping his leg.
Her hair was disheveled. Her eyes gleamed. She said, "It's O.K. for
you to be a mountain man, so long as you come out of your cave
once in a while."

Several nights later a hard north wind blew down the chimney
to the potbelly stove in the bedroom and the house filled with
smoke. They had to open the door to the cold. Jim went out to fix
the chimney. It was dark and the wind bit through his coat. He stood
on a twenty-foot ladder with a flashlight in his mouth while Diane
steadied the pipes from inside. He had to rejoin the sections of pipe,
then secure the whole with wires fastened to the roof. He couldn't
work with gloves on, but with them off his fingers went numb. The
flashlight stuck to his lips. Every few minutes he climbed down the
ladder, ran back into the house, and stood before the working
cookstove with his hands out.

Diane stood on a chair in order to hold up the pipe. Jim went
out and came back repeatedly. His fingers became numb more
quickly with each trip. From the cookstove, he saw that Diane had
the pipe balanced on her shoulder. She'd put on a tattered coat
over her blue nightgown and had her hands in the pockets. Her
mind had gone off somewhere else. She was dreaming. The soot
that masked her face made her look like a ceremonial creature. She
turned her eyes to him. Provoked by her calm, he swore at her.
Her eyes suddenly narrowed, and she said, "Not me. It's not me."

"Then what?" he said.

"Right now, it's you."

He went out and stayed until he had the chimney reassembled,
then moved around the snow-covered roof to secure the wires. He
lay flat and moved with great caution to keep from plummeting
off. He slipped once, but caught himself by grabbing hold of a lath
with his fingertips. He discovered himself laughing. He felt himself

surrounded by his own crazy, scared laughter. Alarmed, he stopped laughing, pulled the wires taut, tacked them down, and stayed for a moment straddling the ridge, staring at the night, listening to the vibration of the metal chimney and the wind singing in the wires.

Diane had started a fire in the potbelly stove and they sat down on the floor in front of it. The fire was hot, but their legs were cold. They'd only just begun to apply insulation. Jim's fingers were white. When he'd first come in and touched the wall with one hand he'd found the hand dead as a block of wood. He'd rubbed his hands together under a stream of cool water. Now, he had them under his armpits and he bent double with pain as blood filled his fingers. He thought about the water trench that had to be covered before the line froze and the vulnerability of the copper lines in the house. Diane touched his back under his shirt. As he bent and unbent his fingers, he apologized for swearing.

"It's hard," Diane said. They often said this to one another. To say it was to speak the truth, and so it was a ritual form of re-assurance. "But please don't take it out on me. It's not just you struggling here."

"You're right," he said. He looked over at the three boys sleeping side by side on a double mattress on the floor under layers of blankets: the oldest was now ten, the next was six, and the baby was just over a year. The two older boys slept on the outsides, the baby in the middle, snuggled up close to the six-year-old. The six-year-old slept on his side with one arm stretched out and touching the ten-year-old's head. Their faces were filled with the calm of sleep, the tenderness, the perfect innocence of youth. Jim longed for the power to keep them so forever. He looked at Diane. Firelight flickered through the vent and danced on her soot-streaked face. She smelled of carbon. It made her seem alluring.

He touched her knee. "Why are we doing this?"

She answered more quickly than he had expected. "It's like you're making a monument."

He looked down at the floor, at the plywood which was already shiny from wear. He reached out and ran his finger along a whorl in the grain. "To what?"

"When you get obsessive, the rest of us are closed out."

"The chimney had to be fixed."

"Yes."

"I have to get jacked up to take care of these things."

"But your energy's too strong. You're rushing at something. It's like you're trying to smother something, not just fix it and go forward."

Exasperated, he said, "Smother what?"

"Look," she said. "I love this place, and the garden we'll have, the fields we're supposed to plant, all of it. I don't mind the work, and even trying to bring your parents in was fine, but they're not my parents."

He thought about her parents, who were different from his, and maybe wiser in their refusal to compromise their separation from their children. It galled him to think that. He said, "It's the ideas."

"What ideas?"

"Like that. Providing for the old instead of having to send them off. Raising our kids with their grandparents around. That's why."

"It didn't work."

"But the idea was worth trying."

"All right. I supported it. I liked your parents."

"Also raising the kids in a place where they'll be in touch with nature, building our own house, and not going into debt to do it." He could have gone on. He had in his mind a litany of objectives they had dreamed of fulfilling.

"We're not hippies."

"Maybe not, but they had some good ideas. Ideas can change the world."

"Not if it doesn't fit the world. If it doesn't fit, it's destructive." Diane paused, then asked, "Is it guilt?"

Startled, he said, "Guilt?"

Diane didn't respond, but leaned up against him and grasped his arm. Though they were arguing, he felt comforted by her touch, even aroused. He stared at the stove, remembering when they'd "picked rocks" from a field the Holisters planned to seed to hay the following spring. That was September. The weeds crackled underfoot because of the long dry spell that had begun back in August. All of them were there. Judy drove a wheel tractor with a loading bucket. She kept the bucket poised so that Lem, Jim, and the two older boys could toss rocks into it. Diane drove a one-ton flatbed, and she had the baby in the cab with her. Each time Judy dumped a load into the truck, a thin cloud of dust lifted into the air. A cocoon of dust followed the tractor. It rose in tiny puffs from the footfalls of the men and boys.

When the truck had a load, the boys jumped into the back and Diane drove out of the field, down the gravel road, and along the lane to the house. Dust trailed the truck and hung above the road. Diane and the boys would unload above the house where Jim planned to build a riprap reinforcement to an embankment. It was necessary to do this to keep the bank from washing out in the spring. Lem and Judy wanted to get the rocks out of the field for the sake of avoiding damage to their bailer. In each case — Jim had thought — that present action was directed against trouble several seasons distant. It had pleased him to realize that. Even now, it made him feel better to think of it — that one good thing done.

They had established a pace in the field. The truck came and went, and returned, and waited for its load. The boys jumped out and rejoined Lem and Jim. The tractor followed the men, who sought out the rocks, the basalt, the granite. It was hot, dusty, pleasurable work in the blazing sun. Lem and Jim fell in and out of conversation. Lem talked about Vietnam. He said he could still see the jungle beneath the helicopter, the charred sectors like scars, and the green again, rushing by. There was no green in the world like it. The actual air seemed green. But the veins of the jungle ran with death.

Jim had asked how he felt about that, living through the death. "You mean guilt?" Lem said. Jim hadn't meant that at all, but Lem went on, and said that soldiers who never saw action felt guilt, the ones who went to Germany, or who came near but were spared from fighting for one reason or another. They felt guiltier than the ones who did the killing — for what they'd narrowly escaped, for what happened to the others. "I was a helicopter gunner, for God's sake," Lem said.

Jim stood there, cradling a rock against his belly. He had never considered guilt in quite this way before — that cleansing might come from entering the demon's bowels. He felt foolish.

"What about you?" Lem asked.

"I guess I was a protester."

"Of course," Lem said. He grinned. "A lot of us were torn

between wanting to waste you guys and wishing you'd get on with it and shorten up our calendars."

Jim looked down at his boots, which were coated with dust. The cuffs of his jeans were brown. Behind them, the tractor's engine rumbled. The flatbed came up the road. The two boys clung to the rack behind the cab. Jim looked back at Lem. "Some protesters were anti-soldier," he said. "I wasn't. That was a mind-fuck."

"Right," Lem said. He picked a weed and stuck the stem between his teeth. "We got burned. But you sure can't feel guilty for wasting somebody who'd waste you the first chance they got. Most everything was elusive there, but that one thing was not."

"Yes," Jim said, meaning to acknowledge that he heard. "I spent time in jail." He wanted to say that he hadn't had to do that, that it was his choice, that he'd had a child and so was exempt, practically speaking, that he was Canadian by birth, that he could have returned to Canada any time he wanted to, that he'd almost enlisted anyway, that he supposed he felt some guilt over the greater suffering of others, but that he still believed what he'd done was right. Between himself and Lem there were boundaries, and at times a certain edginess, so he didn't say any of that.

The truck pulled up. The boys jumped out and walked toward the men. When Jim threw his rock in the loader, the steel clanged. He looked over at the baby, whose mouth and chin were covered with dirt that had stuck to the juice he'd been drinking. The baby clutched the edge of the partially rolled-up truck window, bounced ecstatically up and down, and screeched at his father. "I guess we had a few things in common with the protesters, though," Lem said, grinning again. "Jimi Hendrix and the hash pipe." Jim grunted. They went on, picking rocks and tossing them into the bucket. Over toward his place, Jim could see the pine trees that encircled the hole where the tractor had almost sunk. The trees raked the sky. Heat waves pulsed above the pale earth. Dry weeds tufted the roadsides. Everything was absolutely still. There was not a breath of wind, not a drop of moisture. The dust went up and slowly came straight down.

Here in the house, in the cold, Diane said, "Forget I said that. Fuck guilt."

"O.K.," Jim said.

The stove ticked as it cooled. He swung around to his knees, pulled the stove door open, put in a chunk of wood, and shut the door. The stove sucked air. The ticking accelerated as the metal expanded with renewed heat. He sat back down and rested his hand on his oldest boy's foot. Diane put her hand on Jim's thigh. They were all touching each other, Diane and himself, the oldest boy, snuggled-up baby, and the six-year-old. They were silent, sitting that way in a chain. Finally, Jim said, "I hope the boys remember this well."

Diane sighed. "If we quit, they won't. If we keep on, at least they'll know that such things can be done. But we have to do one thing at a time and then the next."

"If we hadn't started, they wouldn't have to bother with this."

"There'd be something else. It's all right for them to know this." She stopped. Without looking at her, Jim could tell she was going to make a joke. "Maybe we are trying to be like the hippies," she said. "But what I don't understand is where they get off being so damn cheerful all the time."

They went into the bathroom and made love against the wall. He hiked her up and she wrapped her legs around him. They sank to the floor and made love there from various angles of pursuit and repose. It seemed ornate. Diane whispered, "Is this how the hippies do it?"

"This is guilt we're fucking," he said. Diane laughed. He felt the laughing like a shuddering that came all through her body to the point where they were joined.

Because of the push to make the house livable, they'd acquired no store of wood. Daily, they dug wood out of the snow, cut and chopped it, and stacked it inside to dry. Jim dozed the piles of dirt into the water trench, finishing one night when the temperature was predicted to fall to fifteen degrees. A few hours later a switch in the pumphouse froze. The pumphouse roof hadn't been insulated yet. The next day he did that and replaced the switch. The bathtub trap froze every night. He thawed it with candles, a torch, and finally worked out a dangerous system with an electric heater placed inside a makeshift tent. He insulated the floor. He cut the batts and shoved them under the house, crawled after them, dragged them around, and placed them up between the joists. It took a week. At night he coughed up the fiberglass filaments. The bottom of the house was open and the wind blew through it. A plastic vapor shield had to be stapled over the insulation. The plastic was as cold as metal and the temperature kept dropping — ten degrees, zero, ten below, twenty below.

When Jenny Lanatto called on Christmas Eve they were applying insulation to the ceiling. It was a cathedral ceiling and Jim had laid planks across the beams to sit on while he stapled insulation between rafters. Diane cut the batts and passed them up. The boys slept in a row on the floor. The Christmas tree was alight and the gifts wrapped. When Diane answered the phone Jim waited with his legs dangling ten feet above the floor. It was fine up there, heady and warm, for the insulation had begun to take effect, and it was a vantage point from which to survey the work — logs, floor, children, wood stack, and gifts. But then Diane's voice changed tone. She asked if there was anything she could do. She mentioned the Holisters. Jim thought it must have been the adopted baby girl, who had arrived the day before: the baby was unwell, or there'd been a legal complication. Diane hung up and said that Lem had been in a wreck, that in his excitement over the baby he'd hardly slept before going to work Friday night and on his way home he'd fallen asleep at the wheel. His car had been found in a ditch. His back was broken and he'd nearly frozen to death.

Jim stared blankly at the wall opposite him, then climbed down the ladder. He went over and stood next to Diane at the stove. Jim thought about Lem in the ditch, in his car. He wondered who'd found Lem. He thought about how in the country relations between neighbors grew firm when they were good, how they were like the country itself with its points to which one fastened — the house, the barn, the spring, gates to open and close, a neighbor's place, turns in the road — and how in the country the space between points was never truly disconnected, but material in differing ways, joined by earth and air as if by filaments in a web. The space was treacherous if one was hurt and alone, or when a cow out in the pasture calved in the breech. The space was made for surprise because of the detail with which one knew it. It allowed people to show their good side and for things like this to hurtle at one out of nowhere.

Diane turned her back to the stove. Jim turned. Their hips and shoulders touched. They didn't talk. Jim remembered the last time he'd seen Lem. It wasn't long after they'd moved in. Lem rode over on his horse. He'd looked the house over and spoken about the logwork in the fashion of the truly polite, of those with the power to reflect upon someone else's life and to speak kindly of it. He sat in the kitchen, drank coffee, admired the notchwork and the two-by-twelve roof joists, and joked about the overkill in the construction. "You expecting an invasion?" he'd asked, poking Jim in the arm.

Jim remembered how he'd stood out in the yard to see Lem off, and how Lem had looked going away — the straight figure of the warrior on the black horse, leather chaps, spurs on his boots, brown hat and bright blue shirt, then as he crossed a meadow of sage and straw-colored bunchgrass and climbed the rise, just black horse, hat, and blue shirt showing, and then just the blue shirt like a flag as he rode into the trees.

Jim and Diane were to drive into the city to his parents' place for Christmas. Before they left the next morning, Diane called the Lanattos to check on Lem. He'd improved during the night. At first it hadn't been thought he would walk again, but now it was thought that he would. He might be ready for visitors tomorrow. Tomorrow then, Jim decided, he would go to see Lem. The boys were waiting outside and they cried at their parents to hurry. Their voices sounded thin in the cold air.

They headed for town. Jim's parents had bought an old house on a hill. Two walls of their living room were lined with leaded glass doors. In the glass, the windows, and in the mirror over the mantel, the Christmas tree was reflected, broken up into parts and reflected again and again, scattered across the room. Jim's parents sat on the sofa near the tree and they could be seen, too, all around the room in the mirror, the windows, the glass. Their images were everywhere, lit by Christmas tree lights. Jim's mother liked light, and glass for it to shine through, and mirrors to reflect it. She liked to be surrounded by light. They ate nuts and fruit and the pastries Jim's mother prepared every Christmas — coconut drops, choco-late chip cookies, sugar cookies cut into shapes, shortbread, and fruitcake steeped in rum. But they ate in moderation because they'd seen the elaborately laid-out table in the dining room, the carrot and celery sticks, pickles, and chutney already set on the linen cloth, and the broccoli and peas in the kitchen, ready to be cooked, and the makings for Yorkshire pudding and gravy, the giblets chopped up and stewed, and they could smell the goose roasting in the oven, and potatoes, and the rich aroma of plum pudding steaming in a double boiler.

They exchanged gifts. Jim and Diane sat on the floor and watched the children. Diane was mainly silent. Jim conversed with the old ones about the cold, about the pipes that had burst and flooded the new county courthouse. Talk turned to the ranch, to that cold, those water pipes, then stopped abruptly. It was the rift between them that blunted exchange when it neared the delicate ground. It seemed that the grandparents still wished to come into the house once it was finished. This was intimated, but just when or how, and according to what agreements, was quite unclear. Jim felt hung between two worlds. In one he was father and husband, in the other a son. He knew well which one required his first loyalty, but he couldn't extricate himself from the other one. No one ever spoke directly of any of this. Surely, no one spoke of the rift itself, the wound, which was to the belly, but chose to address it by attending the extremities. It was so that Jim's mother had prepared Christmas dinner in all its detail, that Jim, Diane, and the boys were here.

The baby played with a stuffed bear, lay on his back and held the toy up with his feet. The six-year-old sat in a corner, engrossed by a set of plastic blocks. The ten-year-old had received a brass compass. He read the directions for charting a course, then looked up to ask a question, but he didn't ask, struck perhaps by the heavy silence that had fallen over the adults. His face became somber. The boy looked at his father, then at his mother. Jim followed the progression. The boy looked at his grandfather, who was staring at the rug, who despite his sixty-seven years was as hale as many men of forty-five, but who had come to need comforting more than Jim could ever remember his needing it, and yet who by his nature and the pride of his profession was a hard one to comfort. The boy looked at his grandmother. She had back troubles, she'd been plagued lately by one minor infirmity after another, her body seemed to express both her and her husband's trouble, their aging, their sense, perhaps, of their error in having come out west, and she accepted her husband's comfort so that he might be comforted in giving it. She dwelt on death. She'd become fanatic about her grandchildren's affection, like himself about the ranch, Jim thought — a fanaticism pulled taut over the rips.

Jim's father bent and picked up the directions to the compass from the floor, then sat with his elbows on his knees, reading. His mother leaned forward and smiled at her grandson in a way that seemed would break her face. The boy smiled back wanly, holding his compass. It was a crèche.

Shaken by the powerful sense of emotional wreckage, Jim leaned back and stared into a pane of glass that collected the reflection from the mirror on the mantel, and he saw all of them there, the baby, the two boys, the grandfather reading as if to answer the question the boy still hadn't asked, and the grandmother's white face locked in what seemed an aghast expression, and Diane, and himself, a reduced, doubly removed crèche. Everyone was frozen in position — waiting, waiting . . .

Jim had a glimmer of how his oldest boy saw the people — in stronger, purer outline, and not so cluttered, the old ones a little forbidding in their frailty. He considered that where he saw entanglement the boy saw obscurity, that where he saw the need for comfort, the pride, and the dwelling on death, and the quirks of character twisting toward strangeness, the boy saw a mystery, that the boy received all this, truly, and yet in his youth he still had the freedom not to judge it. Jim hung on to his glimmering of the boy's way of seeing, and kept staring into the glass, and out of this the small Saskatchewan town of G—— emerged. It rose slowly in his memory, then filled his mind: the cold, the crystalline brightness of ice and snow, the town buried to the eaves in drifts, the tunnel-like pathways shoveled from one place to the next. His body jerked when he remembered the car that was buried in a snow-filled ditch and the frozen body of a townsman that was found inside it during the spring thaw. Then he remembered the graveyard, the half-dozen icy graves pre-dug in the fall against the averages, and his sister's tiny coffin going down to the bottom of one of them, and his father, stoic and formal, a tuft of his hair rising and falling in the breeze.

It seemed to Jim that his father had conducted the funeral as if it were for anyone, not his own daughter. He remembered his mother's torment, how she clutched her arms together and bent as if she were about to dive into the grave. His father was strong, Jim supposed. In a manner of speaking, his mother was weak. But the rigid strength of his father contained his mother's weakness, and within the weakness of his mother was the love that was not afraid to show itself and so was open to assault. It made the strength of his father possible. In the strength was weakness, and rising from the weakness the greater strength. Jim remembered being in church the next Sunday and hearing the women's choir singing "Rock of Ages," and how when he had closed his eyes and leaned his head against his mother's shoulder, the voices seemed to be coming like distant laughter from the snow-covered graveyard.

He was transfixed by all he had remembered, then he felt a need to say something. No one in the room had moved. He wanted to say that it would be all right, to tell himself that, and his sons, his family. He wanted desperately to claim the substance of mystery for everyone, to draw it over the weirdness like a cloak, but he couldn't speak. He had words with which to begin the naming — death, dream, laughter — but he couldn't break the silence.

The route back home was Lem Holister's daily route to and from work. The road took them through a small town that had built up between the municipal airport and a Strategic Air Command base. Lem had crashed just beyond the town. It was night, but the town, which did nearly as much business by night as by day, was brightly lit.

The two boys slept in the back seat. The baby slept on Diane's lap. They passed the base, the atmosphere above it orange-colored from its lights, as if with fire. The hangars were dark. In daytime the B-52s could be seen poised in the "alert" compounds like huge insects with their wings drooped toward the ground. Sometimes, B-52s cruised over the ranch, tipping ponderously to turn. They drove by a place where the snow in the ditch appeared to have been gouged out by a car, a deepening of shadow in the ditch and bank. Without speaking of it, Jim and Diane had been looking for such a place. When he glanced at her she looked back with a searching expression.

He tried to tell her about the town of G——, how he'd recalled it in his parents' living room, but he stumbled on his words.

"There was a moment there," Diane said, "when you looked like you'd seen a ghost."

"It was what I was remembering."

"And?"

He couldn't go on. He was bewildered by his inability to speak sensibly.

"And your mother," she said. "You scared her, the way you looked. Did you see her face?"

"Yes. She lost a daughter there. My sister. Maybe it's a hole in her life that sucked her in and kept her. I haven't thought of it in years. I remembered it tonight."

Diane murmured, then said, "Maybe we both have to give your folks a little more room."

He stared into the rearview mirror at the fire-colored lights above the base. "You weren't exactly kicking up your heels with joy."

"I hated it," she said, "and I hated myself for hating it so. Now I feel guilty."

Jim said, "The bad thing about guilt is that it makes you into a stranger."

Diane said, "We have to give them more room. Beginning with the way we think of them."

"You're generous."

"No. It's the only alternative. Maybe it's not even as damn complicated as we're making it."

Tomorrow, he decided, he would go see Lem. He didn't want to. Or he did want to. But he didn't want to see Lem broken. They turned onto the gravel road. The way was desolate, the sky black and the earth white. When they walked in the doorway of their house the telephone was ringing. It was Jenny Lanatto calling to tell them that Lem was dead. A blood clot, she said.

The bathtub drain froze that night. The line into the water heater froze. Jim thawed them out the next day. Nothing had burst. Diane baked bread and took it over to the Holisters.

The next night they had more snow, then cold — twenty-five below — and a wind that tore down power lines. They awoke Tuesday morning to darkness and cold. The fire had burned out. They had no water. With no power, the pump had stopped. Jim started both fires in the house. The logs and rafters creaked as they expanded. The baby awoke crying. Diane stood hunched over the stove and cooked eggs.

Jim walked out to check the pumphouse. The sky was absolutely blue. The snow squeaked under his boots. In the pumphouse he crouched and shined the flashlight and ran his fingers along the pipes, seeking ice oozed out of a break, but found none. He walked to the shed, got the Coleman lantern, took it to the pumphouse, lit it and closed the door on it, hoping that when the heat thawed the pipes he would still find no breaks. He knew he'd have to crawl under the house to check the pipes. He didn't want to. When he got back to the house he crawled under, pulled down the insulation, and found what he feared.

There was ice everywhere. The piping was ruptured. He lay back and looked at the bathtub and toilet drains, dropped through the holes he'd cut in the plywood subfloor, and at the plywood itself, nailed to the joists which were attached to the stringers he'd bolted to the lower logs of the house, and the insulation, and the plastic vapor shield he'd carefully pulled taut and stapled over the insulation, all along the bottoms of the joists. Now the bathtub and toilet drains were cracked, the vapor shield bulged with ice and had torn loose, and he could see that the plywood had buckled under the toilet. Ice was packed against the joists and piled up like stalagmites on the ground. It was a cave of ice. It was cold. He felt helpless. His toes and fingers were going numb.

He crawled out, went inside, found the bottle of whiskey and took a belt.

"It's that bad?" Diane said.

"The hell with it."

"No," she said.

"The hell with the whole damn thing."

"No," she said. "Eat your eggs." She handed him his eggs. He turned his back on her. The boys were in the other room by the potbelly stove, keeping warm, eating eggs and keeping their distance. "So, what is it?" she said.

"The bathroom's wrecked."

"So?"

"So!" he said, turning to face her. "I mean wrecked. Destroyed." Wildness thrashed inside him.

"And?"

"And! What do you mean? And?"

"And what else?"

"What else, the hell."

"So what is it with you about Lem?"

Angry, he didn't respond.

"Listen," Diane said. "What happened is awful, but it's got nothing to do with the bathroom. There's no connection except the cold." The way she held the iron frying pan with both hands looked menacing. "We're lucky," she said. She looked like she was about to cry.

He didn't speak.

"Lem lived up the road," she said. "Not here. We're lucky, do you hear?"

He moved away toward a window. Behind him, the frying pan clattered violently against the stove. He stood, squinting out at the blinding world. The earth was white. The grass, weeds, and trees were encased in ice. Flakes of ice floated in the air. He thought of the day in the hay field, so unlike this day. Lem had gone on to say that sometimes when he fired on the enemy, the figures disappeared. "Just popped out of there," Lem had said, "like they were puppets." That was the worst part, he'd said — not the actual slaughter, not even the wrecked bodies of his own people, but the enemy that vanished, whose invisibility he sometimes kept on strafing, the deaths he did not witness, the deaths that may or may not have occurred, the death that was everywhere. "That's what I mean by elusive," he'd said. "Being there, you had to join the dead."

In his desolation at this moment, Jim took that to mean the death that was always near, the inescapable end of everything. He turned back to Diane and said, "I'm sorry. I can't adjust so quickly."

"Adjust! My God, we chose to chase ourselves out here half-cocked," she said. "But that's O.K. I can live with not being ready just so long as we see that taking care of these things, all these daily things as they occur, is the only path."

He took in a deep breath, then let it out. "All right."

Diane picked up the frying pan and delicately set it down again. "What happened to all the good reasons for being here?"

"They keep going into hiding."

She gazed at him, then walked into the other room to check on the boys. Jim moved to the stove and ate his egg. He thought about the Holisters, of Lem's cows, of the lack of power and the automatic waterers in their barn, of the electric milkers. He considered that he should go over there, despite their assurances that they could manage — because they had seven grown children, some of whom had wives and husbands, all of whom would come out for the funeral. He decided that he would drive over.

When Diane returned, he told her so.

"Yes," she said. "And I'm sorry. I'm upset about the bathroom, too. Truly, I am."

"No," he said. "That's fine."

"It's good to check on them."

"Look," he said. "Lem and Judy were very different from us, but I liked him. He was wise."

"All right."

"Now he's dead."

"Yes," Diane said.

"He was in the clear. Now he's dead, for God's sake. Just snipped off."

Diane reached up and held his face between her hands. "Yes, awful."

He went. The Holisters' driveway was crowded with cars. Jim went into the barn and found Bob Holister with two of his sons, his daughter, and Phil Lanatto. They were carrying water from a hydrant that was attached to a line that ran to a diesel-fueled pump at their pond. Jim found the foresight in this impressive. He thought of that — foresight, Lem's foresight, his competence. Lem, Phil Lanatto, and he had planned to go quail hunting the week after Christmas. Now they would not.

He helped carry water. A bucket was filled in one place, then emptied in another, and it was good work to calm one down. Then there wasn't anything to do. Phil and Jim stood and watched the Holisters milk. The Holisters knew what they were about. They moved from one cow to the next, and emptied the brimming pails of milk into a large stainless steel canister. Light seeped through the walls of the barn. Lem's Holsteins, standing at the troughs in four rows, were handsome animals, well built, well conditioned. The white on their flanks was as white as their milk. They stomped occasionally, and chewed, and there was the rhythmic sound of milk squirting into the four metal pails, slower or faster according to how close a cow was to being milked out. It made a counterpoint, the milk hitting the empty pails, and the tone of it deepened as the pails filled, but they didn't all fill at the same pace, so in addition to the intricate rhythm there was a melody. And there was the sound of metal clinking, and the gush when a pail was emptied into the canister, and footsteps, and the soft words of the three men and one woman, an occasional murmuring. There was that music, the very substance of mystery, a requiem. There was the sweet smell of alfalfa and straw and manure. Vapor rose from the pails, from the breath of the people, and from the ground when a cow urinated. There was an air of peace, of spiritual calm attending the work. After a time, Jim and Phil left quietly.

As they walked up to the drive to their cars, Jim glanced over at Lem and Judy's place. Just then, Judy came up to the front window. Her shape, obscured by the dimness within, moved close to the glass. She didn't seem to notice them. She was cradling a baby, holding it against her shoulder, and she seemed to be looking across the fields in the direction of the road that ran toward the trees, as if she expected to see Lem drive up it. Jim glanced at Phil. Phil was looking straight ahead. They walked on in step.

On Wednesday, Jim and Diane gathered wood, then drove through the snow to Lem's funeral mass. During the eulogy it struck Jim that dreams and personal acts — Lem and Judy's dairy, his and Diane's ranch — always left wreckage. There was hazard to a good idea, and to family. This morning, as she hugged an ice-encrusted hunk of pine, Diane had said that it would honor Lem to use him as a conduit, not as a blockage heavy as stone.

"Exactly," Jim had said. He plunged a steel pry bar through the crust of a snowbank. He hoped to find another log end hidden in there. He said, "I've been thinking that maybe my problem is that I can't face death." Diane gave him a quizzical look, as if to say, "You and who else?" It made him smile. It made him feel immeasurably grateful to her for her refusal at times to bend. He began to laugh. Diane chuckled and rocked back and forth. Jim wondered — what the hell? He probed with the pry bar, felt resistance, and leaned on the bar. There was a crack. Suddenly, the dark edge of a chunk of pine tipped up through the snow. Jim straightened. "Maybe it was my sister, the death that got slipped to me and the guilt that came with it, being a survivor of something I had little to do with except by being alive, and not understanding that, not even enough to know how to mourn her. Maybe in my head I got it mixed up with everything else just like the politicians do, sitting around with their heads up each other's butts. Lem said that Vietnam was about as real as Disneyland, only Mickey was passing out M-16s instead of balloons."

Now, Jim stared at the priest in the pulpit, scarcely hearing the words. He was thinking about how he had opposed the war in Vietnam, and yet not his comrades who suffered in it, and about how that suffering took so long to come home to him, how it would still never be truly his because there was no actual wound, but how he was required to carry what of it he could and not ever to either claim or deny it, only to hold close its pain. It was a contradiction from which there was no escape, like the war itself which opened a chasm in the nation for the charlatans to enter. It was the same with the fury he felt toward his father for the insult leveled at a five-year-old boy. He must not become a charlatan in his own chasm, must not pit himself against himself, and must not be afraid.

On Thursday it snowed, helping to bring the temperature up to ten below. Winter had scarcely begun. Jim capped off the water line to the house. They would have to use the outdoor stock hydrant until spring. As the baby napped, Diane practiced. The older boys were at school. Jim went out to plow the road with the crawler. He found a Christmas card in the mailbox at the end of the drive. The card had a note from Judy Holister, thanking them for the bread, their help, and their support.

The utter lack of bitterness in the note made him sit for a long time in the cab of the crawler tractor. The mailbox door hung open. He stared across the fields, then into the white sky that swirled with flakes. He discovered himself weeping. The singing of women came again just as he had heard it when he was a boy, the sound eerie and distant and beautiful, a music turned into laughter and back again to music coming out of ice, and then when he turned a little and looked toward the trees he saw something in the darkness, the shape of a horse, its hooves kicking shimmers of snow off the bunchgrass, and one gleaming spur and the bright blue shirt of a rider, flashing in and out of sight behind the black trunks, going southward deeper into the woods.

for Zeke

NANCY KRUSOE

Landscape and Dream

FROM THE GEORGIA REVIEW

Cows

A BARN IS a beautiful place where cows are milked together. Our
barn has many windows facing east and west. These windows have
no glass in them.

You get up early in the morning to milk cows. You pour warm
white milk into heavy gray metal cans with matching metal tops
that fit like a good hat, and these tops are very pretty, their shape
a circle with a brim over the neck of the can.

Warm cow milk has a certain smell, a from-inside-the-body smell,
the way your finger smells pulled out of your own vagina.

Women who are married to dairy farmers stand in their kitchens
at their kitchen windows and stare longingly at their husbands'
barns, but they don't go there. Barns are female places; they are
forbidden places for women. These women stand at their kitchen
windows staring at their husbands' barns because barns are beautiful female places, full of sweet-milked, happy, honey-faced cows
being milked by men's hands or by machines with cups. Cows have
rough-skinned teats, sometimes scraped and scratched, chapped
and bleeding, which fit into these cups put on by men whose hands
are not gentle.

So the wife I am talking about stands at her kitchen window
facing east. She has no one to be with. Unlike the cows and the
men in the barn (her husband and her son, who helps his father
for a while), she is alone. I, the daughter, am in the barn, too —
young enough to be there a little while longer. But I would like

for the wife, my mother, to leave the farmer, to go away from the farm and the barn and this warm longing for cows.

Our barn is a cold place in winter with only the heat of cows to warm you. You stand very close to their large bodies so that you won't frost over like the windows of the kitchen where you stare, looking for your mother to see if she is watching you.

On the other side of the barn, the east side, are the hill and the lake at the bottom of the hill and the gray-brown grass that holds this hill in place in winter. Tiny slivers of ice float on the lake in winter, at dusk and during the night, and they melt each morning when the sun comes up. Our cows slide through mud to drink cold morning water, because even though they're full and ready to be milked, their mouths are saliva machines with licorice-colored tongues, thick and dark with cud and the need for water. I see them standing by the side of the lake, their knees bent a little, bracing themselves as they lean over the icy water, mud rising up their delicate sweet ankles. *Hurry, drink fast,* I say. *Hurry, hurry.*

Seeing them like this makes me want to be a cow, but which kind would I be? There are dainty, needle-brown Jerseys, big woolly Guernseys, and the large, black-and-white-spotted, famous-for-milk Holsteins. There is also the plain black cow.

When cows come to the barn to be milked, it's a happy, sloppy time of day for them, and I am there waiting. They all push in at once, rushing toward me as I stand at the far end of the barn — in case one goes wild I will stop her — and running, some of them, because their favorite food is waiting there (that delicious grainy mixture of oats and wheat and barley and who knows what else that I myself eat along with them out of cupped hands). They are running toward me, looking at me, and then abruptly turning in, one by one, each into her own place, and someone will close the stanchions around their necks for milking, because you can't have them visiting — wandering around and disturbing each other during milking — of course not. Each one has her own place, her own stanchion, and she remembers it; out of fifty or sixty stalls, each cow knows her own. How: Smell? Number of footsteps from the door to the slippery spot at the entrance to her place? Or rhythm — how many sways of the heavy stomach, the bloated udder, back and forth to the stall that is hers?

I remember how it was to be inside the barn with all those

steamy, full-of-milk, black-and-white cows, with their sweet, honey-barn faces and their clover-alfalfa breath. And their beautiful straight backbones that you could rub between your fingers across the length of their bodies, a delicate spine for all that weight underneath. And light falling through the windows. I washed their udders, washed them all with the same brown cloth soaked in disinfected water, their teats covered with dirt, and sometimes I didn't get it all off they were so swollen (of course, I didn't know how it felt, not for years did I know how that felt), but they didn't mind. No words were spoken there in the barn — or if they were, they weren't between me and the men. I didn't feel it so much then — well, maybe more than I thought — but I felt the bodies of cows, dozens of them, their big, sloppy, breathy faces and sighs in the barn with me.

In the kitchen, it isn't a happy time of day: cooking breakfast, half moon, half dark. My mother stands there waiting. Anyone could come, even cows could come to her flower bed outside the kitchen window, could lie down and wait with her for the farmer — and the daughter — to return. There is nothing to stop them from coming to her, coming to her window, nothing at all.

The Farmer

Sometimes men beat their dairy cows. Sometimes they hit them with lead pipes, and the cows fall down; they slide down in their cow shit on the floor of the barn, fall down on their bones into shit puddles while the daughter is standing at the barn door staring for a very long time at the floor, at the slick running cow pee that has soaked everything the cow was standing on and is now lying in, on her bones, and she is crying.

Is the cow crying? Heaving, trying to stand up on her feet (her feet are so pretty — little hooves like tiny irons), which slip again every time he hits her.

Her head's in the stanchion, her head's trapped, but she can stand up. *Please don't get up again,* I tell her, but it makes no difference: he hits her again. I hope cows don't feel pain; I hope they don't have brains. I hope they have fires in their hearts. If they had brains, I would have to hold them and kiss them and tell my mother at the window what has gone on — not just in her garden but here in her husband's barn. I would have to tell her I hope that the next time the tractor turns over, the farmer is under it.

When a man is beating a cow, a young cow, what is he thinking? Does he think how beautiful she is, struggling to stand? Does he think how she will never stand again unless he lets her, *unless he lets her?*

I am talking about cows which sometimes aren't so beautiful to look at. They love to bathe in slushy red mud, get covered in dirt. Their brains are made of salt licks and saliva so they won't feel pain, you see what I mean? What kind of puzzle could a cow solve? Not the kind a word would solve, a kind word. That's what I mean.

I am talking about women like my mother who watch barns, waiting, because they cannot stop watching with their eyes and hearts, as if smoke will arise, as if smoke will come out of that barn, as if the men and cows will be burned, as if she can stop her daughter from being there in the barn, in the fire, as if she can hold her daughter back, can close the barn door with the power of her eyes — but this will not be enough. The mother watches her daughter move in slowly toward the barn where she will become a cow, where nothing can stop her, where the cow she becomes is the cow her father beats with a metal pipe over and over on her back, on her shoulders and her stomach, on her whole brown bony small body, and the daughter hides inside the cow's body and screams, *Stop, stop.*

But do you think he hears, or — if he hears — that he believes what has become of his daughter? What will the farmer tell his wife? What will the daughter tell her mother? Nothing. She will hear nothing about it, for remember, this is a young girl watching her father, and he's beating the cow with a pipe that's long and gray and hollow; he holds it with both his hands. The cow is young like the daughter who's watching. What can she possibly have done to deserve such a beating? Did the young cow kick the girl's father? Being young, she might not have known better, but the girl sees no blood on her father. She looks at his arms and his face and sees nothing but rage — his mouth is clamped shut and his eyes are huge and still swelling in his head. (He has taken off his glasses, and the daughter notices this: that her father isn't wearing his glasses and she can see his eyes.) He looks strange to her. He could be holding back tears, she thinks. He is holding back something, but look at all that is coming out.

The girl looks toward her house, which is across the road from the barn; she searches for her mother in the window to see if she is watching the way she sometimes does. It is too far and too dark to tell. And so the daughter looks back at the barn, at her father in the barn, this man who without his glasses has eyes she hardly knows. This young cow is called, she knows, a heifer. What else should she know?

The Kitchen

We had a chair in our kitchen that was so large I could sit in it doubled up and still have room for my brother and a tub of peas for me to shell. On my right as I sat in the chair, I could see the pasture in front of our house, out the kitchen window, where animals sometimes grazed — cows and horses. The sky was bluer here than anywhere else. Behind the pasture was a semicircle of pine trees, a screen which blocked my view of anything beyond it and formed the limits of my world.

It was on this pasture of grass that phantom men, invaders, conquerors, arose from the earth one day, riding on dusty brown horses, circling the field, riding toward our house. These horsemen wore dusty red scarfs on their necks and blankets on their backs. Dirt from deep inside the earth all about them was kicked up by their horses' feet as we sat, my mother and I, inside the kitchen, waiting for them to surround us, to terrify us, to tell us what they wanted, what crimes they were going to commit. Of course, I opened the door; this was long before I began, in later dreams, to slam and lock all doors and windows against strange men. Tribesmen from deep inside the earth — what could be better? What had they come for? For me, of course. They had come to take me away, or to tell me the secrets of life — whichever, I was ready. I am sure my mother knew, could see that I was ready.

I looked at my mother and wondered what she thought about and if she loved cows the way I loved them. I am the one who watched her, and watching her was all in the world I did for years.

Like her I became a cow and I became a mother. I became the barn and the hill behind the barn, the lake and the water cows drink from the lake, the salt and saliva in their mouths. I became, for a while, entirely these things — nothing more. And this is not enough.

Fur

FROM PLOUGHSHARES

FEI LO NOTICED the new clerk right away, a persimmon in a basket of oranges. Three letters on a gold-toned plaque spelled out her name. So as to make no mistake, the old gentleman wrote it in his notebook, FUR. He liked to know the names of all the women tellers, as he flirted with each in turn; he had even when his wife was alive. The clerks indulged him, they treated him with deference, they called him *Ah Goong*, Old Grandfather. Behind his back they said, without derision, *Fei Lo*, Fat Man.

Fei Lo tipped his hat.

Fur said good morning, and she called him Ah Goong.

"Your name, very pretty."

She smiled. "I chose it myself."

Her mother had named her Four Fragrance. When American-born Chinese made fun of her nonsense name, she changed it to Fur, something she coveted more than any perfume. She tried first Mink, then Sable, but never Chinchilla, since it had too many syllables for Chinese. She finally settled on the all-encompassing Fur, and while it made no more sense than Four Fragrance, the other tellers let it go.

"Yes. Fur. Very distinctive."

Fur gave the old gentleman her full attention.

Fei Lo smiled, too.

He would offer a proposition. She only had to wait. "Something I can do for you today?"

Fei Lo could tell by the shift of her weight that she had stepped out of her shoes. He tapped his breast pocket where he kept his deposit.

"Guess," he said. "Guess the amount of my deposit, within ten percent, and I will sign my check over to you."

Fur pressed her bunions back into her shoes, she rolled her tongue over her teeth. The clerks on either side stopped in mid-motion but did not look up.

Back-room eavesdropping had told her about the rotund flirt, his large appetites and even larger deposits — monthly totals of some $20,000 in Hong Kong rents, shack storefronts, three dollars a square foot. She quickly calculated the ten percent error and added a chunk. She did her best imitation of shooting in the dark.

"$23,199!"

Fei Lo's eyes narrowed. He glanced about. The other women made busy. He did some calculating himself as he pulled out his check.

"Pretty good guess. But you are off about fifteen percent. Still, pretty good guess."

"No! So close? Let me see!" Fur examined the front and back of the check as she stamped it. "Maybe next time I'll be more lucky." She grinned.

"Hmmm. Maybe."

The next time Fei Lo came into the bank, Fur timed her transactions to coincide with his arrival at the head of the line. "Ah Goong, you are a traveled man. You ever been to Las Vegas?"

"Oh, many times. But Tahoe is nicer."

"Better than Vegas?"

"Umm. Like gold is better than paper."

"You win?"

"Win! Of course, win. Even when I lose, I win. Consider our hotel, very reasonable, very nice. Dining room — out of this world. Menu thick like a book, and every dish ready at your fingertips." He passed his hand over the counter so elegantly Fur lifted up on her toes to see. "Lovely pink crab, prime rib, five different ways to eat potatoes —"

"Any desserts?"

"On a table of their own! Meringue pies, sweet cream cakes —"

"Chocolates?"

"Ah, chocolates." Here he reflected. "Yes, chocolates. Even on your pillow, chocolates."

Fur framed a smile and lowered her eyes. She could even blush on demand.

"Twelve dollars," he said, staring straight at her. "All you can eat."

The bank clerk and the old man regarded each other. Between them, the tellers' counter laid end to end with food only they could see.

"I don't go anymore."

"Why not?"

"Wife died. She didn't like to go."

"Oh, sorry, Ah Goong. I didn't know." Fur knew. She had read his entire file. "But Goong, what's to keep you, now that you are a free man?"

"No. Can't. It's no fun without her."

Fur nodded. "Yeah, yeah, I understand."

Fei Lo reached into his breast pocket. He tried to keep it light. "*Něih séung mhséung heui?*" You want to go?

"*Séung!*" she said. "You bet. I'm going, yes, I am." The bank clerk tilted her head toward a sign promoting the opening of new certificates of deposit, $1,000 minimum. "Twenty new accounts and I win a free trip." She winked. She drummed her fingernails, red painted over chipped.

Fei Lo turned away long enough to read the large print. "And how many you have so far?"

"Nineteen," she said, as if giving her age. He laughed out loud. The clerk on her right shot a glance, the one on the left harrumphed.

He pulled out his deposit and pushed the check toward her. She saw his knowing smile.

"Oh no, Ah Goong, you get much more interest if you add this to your existing account. Oh, but you are such a kind man. Really, I mean it. Don't worry, before the day is over I will get my trip to Las Vegas. I'm a good salesman."

Fei Lo was thrown. "Hmmm."

Fur punched in his account number, then stopped. "Ah Goong, you want me to be happy?" She tapped the check on the counter.

Ah, he thought, here it comes after all. "I want all you young women to be happy."

"You have been so kind to me, since the very first day. I want to take you to lunch. Will you let me, please?"

The bank clerk herded the fat man into the most expensive restaurant in Chinatown, one with valet parking and a doorman. Her eyes worked the room, studying, memorizing the choice of wallpaper, the recessed lights, the antique screens — scholar on a donkey, painted silk in a teak surround.

"Oh no, Ah Goong." She pulled the paper insert out of his hand. "No rice-plate specials for you today. It's my birthday and we are having only the finest food on the menu." *"Oh! Yin wō!"* She lay her hand on his arm. "I've never had bird's nest soup. Can we have that? I mean, would you enjoy it?"

Fei Lo glanced at her hand. She removed it and giggled.

A fiftyish woman in a wool crepe suit bumped Fur's shoulder and made a point of apologizing. Fur never had a lady apologize to her, and this woman was deft. She managed within the same breath to greet her friends three tables away, tossing her hand in an effortless wave. As she passed, Fur caught the surprise of her shoes, faux leopard with an open toe, the flash of red, as if a woman's power and every secret resided in the feet. Fur rubbed the top of her own pump against the back of her other leg, a quick, dry polish under the table.

Fei Lo was staring at her. "So, how old are you today?"

"Oh! How old do you think I am?" She crossed her legs and leaned forward on her elbow. She giggled. She swung her free leg carelessly.

Fei Lo got a little warm. He giggled, too. He steadied his hands on the menu and studied. He tried to consider balance and contrast, spice and subtlety, texture, methods of preparation, a soup, a fish, a fowl, some green vegetables to cleanse. He peered over his bifocals at her.

She flipped back and forth in the eight-page menu, her eyes scanning down the right-hand column as if doing addition. She smiled. "Remember, it's my treat."

It's my treat was repeated three more times during the meal. They ordered as if for a wedding banquet. Fei Lo was smitten to finally find a woman not afraid to eat. He didn't know Fur had not eaten since breakfast the day before, but he had already guessed that she couldn't afford such a meal on her salary and that, in the end, they both expected him to pay. By the time the oysters arrived, sizzling, practically leaping off the hot cast-iron plate, he also deduced it wasn't really her birthday.

Fei Lo parked his Lincoln Continental next to the chapel, got his things out of the trunk, and started up the hill. He enjoyed the approach to the gravesite and didn't want to rush. He liked the walking, the tulip beds in spring, the tall stalks of summer, grass that stained the hems of his pants, proof of his participation. He liked reading the names on the house-like tombs, miniature temples adorned with columns. He, too, owned one of these stone houses, enough space for an extended family, guarded by an iron gate. If he drove up to the site, he might feel compelled to drop off the flowers and just go. Soon he might not come at all. Their children rarely came — at Christmas, her birthday, maybe Mother's Day, in alternating turns that smacked of arrangement.

He set his things down and used both hands to open his folding stool. He unlocked the gate and opened it wide, letting into the crypt every possible ray of sun. He hung his coat on the gate and said hello to his wife. "Hear that?" The crunch of leaves fueled his appetite. "Indian summer." He sighed. He sat down on the folding canvas.

From a plaid thermos he poured some fragrant hot tea. He fanned himself with the Chinese daily. When the tea cooled, he unwrapped the towel he used as insulation and untied the string around the square pink box, enough *dím sām* for a family: parchment chicken, pink shrimp in translucent dresses, sweet rice studded with three treasures and bound with shiny *ti* leaves, sweet black bean paste in a golden seeded pouch. From the tens of offerings from the *dím sām* tray, Fei Lo always chose those that came wrapped up like gifts.

The sun warmed his back and he did not sweat. Fei Lo chewed his toothpick into a flat pulp. He didn't look at his wife's grave. With effort he could get through the entire visit without mentioning the bank clerk's unusual name, or the number of times they'd had dinner since the "birthday" lunch.

He held the newspaper upright and turned a bit away from the gate. This was not the way he had imagined it, him sitting here talking to her. The vision that had come most frequently to him, in the years before her death, was of her, her approaching with plants and flowering shrubs, working on hands and knees, she, who would finally discover in widowhood the meditation of horticulture.

"Young Woo died last week," he relayed.

Young Woo was the seventy-three-year-old son of Old Woo, who
was still living, in his own home, in his own bed. Young Woo had
built from a corner stand, selling hand-knotted brushes, a chain
of hardware stores stretching up and down the peninsula. He
made Old Woo very comfortable. His last act was to step on wet
dog excrement. Young Woo saw the droppings as he was taking
the wheelchair from the trunk, and he was very careful while
helping his father sit down. A car double-parked behind him and
banged his bumper. In his excitement, Young Woo let go of the
wheelchair. It rolled, he lunged, he slipped, and broke his hip,
from which he never recovered. Young Woo had built from nothing, yet this the ladies at the bank would soon forget, as quickly as
they would forget his name, recalling only a man who was killed
by dog droppings. Fei Lo unbuttoned his vest. He knew what men
feared. Men feared acts of foolishness. Women had no trouble with
this. They only feared being unvalued.

The air chilled. The widower lifted his head just in time to see
the last of the fall sunset, a pulsing ovoid tangent to the Pacific,
the sky seared orange and red. As on recent days, he thought he
could see with his naked eye, even at this distance, ribbons of fire
eject from the surface, streamers from a departing vessel. She
burned, his sun, day and night, witnessed or not, she burned.

"What a fine view we have. A splendid view. Splendid."

And, as he did at the end of each visit, Fei Lo watched until the
colors bled from the sky. Then he slowly packed up to go.

"I'm looking for investors."

They had warned him she would ask for money, it was just a
matter of time. Fei Lo wanted to give it to her. Whatever she asked.
But his son said, *No.* His daughter said, *No.* They said, *We don't want
it, Dad, but you need it to live on. And why would you want to give it to
this woman with no family?* Fei Lo had wondered how he could have
raised such children. And yet, when a certain woman had asked
Young Woo for a loan, Fei Lo had offered similar advice.

Fur laid her chopsticks across her rice bowl, she nudged her
plate aside. She had barely eaten.

"Ah Goong" — she spaced her words — "I'm not a clever person. Some people have good ideas every day. Me, I only have so
many good ideas. Not every day. This is my good idea. A beauty

shop for hair. No permanents. No color. No nails. Just wash and cut. Look, look at our beautiful hair."

Fur whipped out her drugstore compact and shoved the mirror under his nose. Fei Lo had a view of the top of his head, spare gray strands parted low on one side and combed over to the other. "Thick, straight, and black. The most desirable hair in the world. Why make it something different?" She snapped the compact shut and tapped it on the table. "Wash and cut." She amended as she went. "More than a cut, a shape, a frame for the face. A high class." She inhaled with care. She looked him in the eye. "Partners. Fifty-fifty."

He stared at her, chopsticks poised. The rice was getting cold.

Fur wet her lips. "You like my idea, yes or no?"

Fei Lo hated talking business over food. He wished she had asked for fun money. He gladly would have given that, even a monthly allowance, whatever she wanted, for a little silk scarf, a sumptuous dinner, car payments. But this was an investment, and while the actual dollars might end up being the same, or even less, he had to think it out. Real estate he knew, but not shopkeeping. He asked himself, Is it good business? Does she know about hair? Has she any talent?

As if from behind his ear the bank clerk pulled out a card, the name of a salon, someone else's salon. "I'm there Thursday nights, all day Saturday and Sunday until four." Whenever she wasn't at the bank.

Fei Lo considered Fur's own hair, which was chemically curled and had never struck him as anything special. But then he was not a judge. He tried to calculate how many women would want their hair cut by her. Would his wife have gone to her? Would the ladies at the bank? And there came to him a startling realization. "Women don't like you."

He spoke with such carelessness, as if comparing coats in a store window, that Fur, too, saw herself with detachment. "That's right. Women don't like me. I don't fit, do I? But men like me fine. And men get their hair cut three times more often than women."

Fei Lo nodded. "Then what you really want is a barbershop."

"No, no, no. No barbershop. *Beauty* shop. Barbers charge a fraction what hairdressers charge." She marked off the tip of her index finger with her thumb to indicate how small a fraction she had in mind. "Barbers don't wash. I wash. I wash very good, very gentle. Men like that. You come sometime, I show you."

They stared at each other.

Fei Lo thought about more shrimp, salty, crusty, pan-fried little devils in their bed of lettuce.

Fur let her gaze wander about the room. She tinked her glass with her chopsticks. When the waiter approached, she got up to go to the restroom.

Fei Lo caught her eye. "Let me think about it."

She nodded once and smiled, knowing that he wouldn't.

The bank clerk made a detour by the bar and talked to three different men, men she knew well enough to touch their shoulders. There was laughter, eyes that did not move, glancing hands, codes he had long forgotten. When she continued on to the bathroom, the men watched through half-closed lids. Heads inclined in her direction. Someone made a joke. They all laughed.

Fur took her time returning. Fei Lo stood up and held out her chair, but she did not sit. She took her jacket in one arm and said, "I should take you home now. It's a long drive for me back to Fremont."

"But I can take a cab. Please, sit down, we haven't finished our dinner."

"Oh, no, I couldn't let you take a cab. You are my dearest friend. I'll wait. Please. Sit down. Eat."

She sat and did not look about, did not eat, did not fidget. She was more silent than even his wife had been on her most quiet days.

Fei Lo lost appetite. He didn't ask for the leftovers.

They drove, and the silence sat between them like cold fat. Chinatown blurred into downtown, blurred into the lakefront, manmade, polluted, and fringed with high-rises. A wall of glass separated them from a dinner party halfway up a building, sparkling stemware, red wine and white. A family ate in silence. Another tasted from cartons passed back and forth. Others were locked down for the night in front of TVs that etched them in a pulsing blue light. On the top floor, darkness, except for one low light, a night light. As their car rounded the bend, Fei Lo could make out a form. A child too young to stay alone pressed her palms into the glass and kissed her own reflection.

"Is it true, what they say about your father?" And as soon as the words came out, he regretted.

Fur tapped the brakes. "Who, they? What do they say?"

"The women at the bank. They say —" Fei Lo blushed. "They say your father had two wives."

The women had circulated a story about young Four Fragrance, some said twenty, some said eighteen. One woman said she was barely fourteen, with a dead mother and the address in America of a father she had never met. They spiced it up with his car, all fins and angles, his quick drive up to the curb, a hand that extruded only to slap her face, the motor running. They iced it with his parting line: "I have no daughter. Don't call me again."

Fur said nothing, and Fei Lo wondered if she had heard him. She drove straight to his house with no instruction from him. She pulled right up the curved driveway, as if she did it every day, and parked behind his garaged Lincoln Continental. She killed the engine and looked out at nothing in particular.

"Rumors, Ah Goong, are like the bamboo. Planted and left alone they will multiply into a forest that blocks out all light. They weave a root system you cannot destroy. The tiniest splinter can cause unbearable pain. And every day the bamboo sways, it bangs one into its neighbor. It wails its song, it clanks its tune, and makes you deaf to all other music." She turned and smiled at him. "Or so my mother used to tell me. You believe this?"

They sat some. The windows frosted.

He asked, "You want to come in?"

She didn't answer, but when he came around and held open her door, she got out.

Fur sat cross-legged on the bathroom carpet, reading outdated decorating magazines. Her eyes stopped on an advertisement of metal spiral staircases. She tore out the page and tossed it with other torn sheets, ragged ideas for a dream salon.

Fei Lo was a few steps away when he thought he heard something rip. He tapped the door. "Is everything all right?"

She didn't answer.

He unlocked the bar and set out his favorite liqueurs, substituting brandy for port and French for domestic until he felt he got it right. He went back and asked if she would like a drink. She turned a page and said without shouting, "I can't hear you. I'll be out soon."

When Fur finally emerged, the TV was on. Fei Lo had fallen asleep, his head hung on his chest. A fire raged in downtown San Francisco. Glass exploded. A barefoot woman half in flames stumbled from the building. The fire seized her like a jealous husband. Fur nudged the old man with her finger. His lips fluttered.

She walked along his mahogany bookcases, dragging that same finger along the shelves. No dust. Even now, though *she* was dead, no dust. Not many books, either. Some statement in simplicity. But each spare shelf was anchored by an object, things she probably picked out.

Above the bar were a pair of lions, one facing east and one west, carved from jade so rare the stone was almost white. She picked one up and almost dropped it. Much too heavy to slip into a pocket. On another shelf — arranged so precisely as to discourage touching — what looked like shoehorns. Fur flipped one over. They *were* shoehorns. Here, in the front room. Carved ivory, no two alike, untouched by human feet. A pair of this, a dozen of that, nothing was collected singly, as if Fei Lo's wife had been shoring up against a day of enormous need. Fur understood that urge.

Here, sterling bowls, graded to nest, so shiny with polish they sang. The hollows of each were lacquered a different color — ruby, emerald, sapphire. Fur pulled a bobby pin from her hair, bit off the coated tip, and ran the sharp end against the ruby hollow of one. She was surprised that it did scratch. She glanced at Fei Lo, then wet a finger with saliva and tried to repair the damage. She shrugged, picked up another.

This bowl was filled with chocolates, individually wrapped in foil and molded into assorted sea shells. Fur put a fat fistful in her pocket and continued her tour of Fei Lo's house, saving the master bedroom for last.

From the dim hall light, Fur could see her, Fei Lo's dead wife, captured as a young woman of forty, sitting in the shade of a backyard tree, framed for all eternity in sterling. Even seated, the woman looked uncommonly tall. Fur flopped down in the middle of the bed. She wondered what kind of woman would wear a suit in her own backyard.

Two doors flanked the oversized bed. One led to Fei Lo's closet, the other to an enormous walk-in, perhaps once a study or a nursery, and finally refitted as a temple of adornment. On either side of the door, identical dressers, gloss white with cut-glass pulls. Opposite was a matching cabinet for shoes, shoes for every season and social occasion, including shoes in which to be alone in the house. Handmade of glove leather, not one pair would redefine the toes, or hinder flight from a difficult situation.

Fur stepped in. She opened drawers, she fingered lingerie several sizes too large. Around her neck she wound a rope of pearls.

On the vanity lay an engraved silver tray filled with everything a woman needed to enhance, mask, or preserve. She picked up a crystal atomizer and misted behind each ear, then tried to fan away the sticky perfume. *Luster, Bedazzle, Remembrance* — lipsticks that gave no clue to their color but attested to some state of mind — *Promise.* She wiped off her own lipstick and drew a new mouth. The vivacious pink favored by older women barely covered lips stained dark red. The corners of her mouth where the tissue had missed formed sharp little brackets around her smile. She looked all wrong and told herself it was lovely.

Initials were carved into the matching brush. Fur tossed her hair. *One, two, three . . . one hundred strokes a day for a dazzling shine.* In the dusty gutters between the bristles, the hairs of two women matted into a loose felt. Fur rested her forehead against the mirror. It refreshed. When the glass beneath her warmed, she rolled her forehead to the next cool spot. A little breath escaped. She opened her eyes. Pink lips, so close to her own they almost touched. She leaned, a small but deliberate move, and much less effort than holding the distance, she pressed her lips against the glass.

When she turned to go, she saw it.

In the back of two long racks of dresses — a zippered cotton bag. Dark brown hairs poked through the neck, their glisten subtle but distinct. Fur walked over. She unzipped. There it was, Fei Lo's dead wife's coat — mink, past the knees.

The gold paper was stamped with a pattern of ridges and spines, a miniature nautilus wrapped around dark imported chocolate. Unlike cheap candy that clawed and irritated, this confection slipped down the throat and satisfied.

The gold paper was subtly textured, and, like fine damask, when angled just so to the light, it revealed secret designs — diamonds — iridescent and intermittent. Opened flat, the foil was about a three-inch square. It never failed to amaze Fei Lo how boxes and bags could be knocked down to a flat piece of hard paper with notches and missing corners. But the spines that formed this shell design could not be flattened. They were hot-stamped into the paper almost permanently, giving the wrapped chocolate its crisp elegance. Fei Lo turned the foil over. A shard of chocolate fell free from the crease. He stared at it before knocking it into his mouth.

In the restaurant, he would watch his daughter fold the long, flat envelope her chopsticks came in, first twice along its length, then diagonally across one end. She would turn the paper over, and fold, turn, and fold, butting one crease up against its neighbor, a process that gave the translucent paper thickness and integrity. Then she would hook the ends together and make a ring on which to rest her chopsticks. She made one for him and one for herself, her fingers busy while they discussed the menu. He had watched her do this many times, and still he could not duplicate the process.

He tried it now with this square of gold foil, knowing the proportions were wrong and his fingers no longer deft. He inhaled, his breath whistled, but he refused to breathe through his mouth. Only children, asthmatics, and dying dogs breathed through their mouths. He also refused to talk to himself. He would not do that. So it was largely in silence, broken by this whistling breath, that he folded and refolded the gold paper, patiently trying to transform a flat square into a standing ring, as he waited for Fur to call.

It was Thursday when he found the foil, almost two weeks after their last dinner. The gold paper lay scrunched in the hallway outside his daughter's old bedroom, a room last used by his wife as her private refuge. She could have sat in their raked rock garden, or in the living room overlooking the creek, but she preferred to spend her afternoons in her daughter's old room, which faced east and was cool. What she did in there he never asked, and she never volunteered. He occasionally passed the door just after she went in. If he shut his eyes, a pattern of sound would return: the flap of a shade, a book scraping the shelf, a lamp switch at midday.

He wouldn't have stopped outside the door, but there was this piece of litter, this scrap of gold. He bent over, and from that stooped position he could see light under the door to a room unvisited except by the housekeeper.

Fei Lo opened the door.

It wasn't the overhead, but a table lamp in the middle of the room. He walked over in such a hurry to walk out again, he was already turning away as he reached for the switch. The hot socket stung. He recoiled and slipped on something slick — opened books, half shoved under the club chair.

"What the goddamn."

Afraid of moving his feet, Fei Lo leaned on the table, setting his considerable weight on his forearm. He turned the light up another notch. More books lay on the carpet, almost as if arranged.

Fur.

In here. She had been in here — here, where his child used to sleep. Fei Lo spun as if he heard a thief. Not just in here. No. She had gone into each of the twelve rooms of his house. He could imagine her, nosing around, touching everything, her eyes eating up whatever they wanted, greedy, hungry animal, while he slept, while he snored, the indignity. What had she ever wanted that he had not given? He wanted to ask, he wanted to know, What kind of girl you are you come into my house and look while I sleep? He dialed. Her phone rang, rang, rang. Had he slept with his mouth open? He angled his watch face to the light. Ten P.M. He hung up and redialed. Hung up again. Call the police. He laughed. And tell them what? That she ripped up some magazines? That she dared to sashay in here in her, her *sà chàhn* way, here where his wife always shut the door? Fei Lo took out his handkerchief and wiped his forehead. Robbed. He was sure of it. His son had been right. His daughter had been right. Surely, she had taken something.

He walked around until he was standing where he imagined her sitting. But he was mistaken. Photo albums, not books. He traced the trail back to the bookcase, shelves tight with albums, a rack as high as a hatted man, as wide as a marrying couple.

The old man slumped into the overstuffed chair and just as reflexively jerked his feet back, as if at the last moment he saw her sitting here, cross-legged on the floor, her skirt inching, inching, surrounded by these musty photographs — birthday parties, horses, a succession of bigger houses and better neighborhoods. And when her legs became numb she had stood up and stretched. While he slept in the front room, she had kicked off her shoes, tucked naked legs under, and sat, in this same chair, in this very room where his daughter shut the door, where she talked in hushed tones with girlfriends, where his wife used to nap, where the two of them brushed each other's hair while his son wheeled around on his tricycle, head back, hair flying behind, caught forever in the streak of being two years old.

Funny, Fei Lo did not remember his son having a tricycle. But every child had a tricycle.

He got out his glasses. He pulled the lamp close and sat down. The album was edge-stitched with brown yarn. Roy Rogers waved from his horse and smiled the *So long* smile. Fei Lo wiped the cover with a handkerchief, sneezed, and turned the page. A square of foil slipped out. And another. A cascade of gold.

He dropped the book.

He stood up faster than his blood could recover and he lumbered across the room. The doorframe boxed him. Seal it up. Let the housekeeper tidy it. He slammed the door. It popped open again. Fei Lo steadied himself in the dim hall, willing some cooperation between heart and lung.

In time, the eye adjusts. Pupils dilate. A table lamp and a comfortable chair were what he saw. Together they defined a space and scale for intimacy. Yes, he could imagine them here, his daughter, his wife, even Fur. Nothing had happened. She had been looking, only looking. It could just as easily have been like that.

Fei Lo thought about cold chicken and *jūk,* thick rice soup, hot and cleansing. He thought about bed and forgetting. But the widower went back in, as if his life depended on it.

If there were ten albums on the floor, there were another eighty or ninety still on the shelves, no two alike. The books on the top shelf documented the youth of his wife, until she married; then she almost disappeared. There were few pictures of him or of the two of them, fewer yet of the entire family. And what pictures there were of the four of them showed events he could little recall, as if his participation had been aural and after the fact.

Here — something familiar. On their wedding day, his mother
had broken her toe and brothers jostled for the privilege of carrying her. *Her* mother was relieved to find for her gangly daughter
a decent and equally tall husband. He turned a page. His bride
could not believe how skinny he was, coming from such ample
parents. And after she had gotten used to skinny, she could not
believe how quickly he could grow. With each return trip to Hong
Kong, he would multiply their wealth, hers, and come back dis-
playing it to the world around his middle. That day, she had loved
him handsome in a top hat, and said he should own one. With
that passing remark, she had inspired in him a taste for acquisition
as a measure of his feeling for her. That day he had kissed her for
the first time.

Fei Lo had to close his eyes, had to. For just a moment.

Over the years he had perfected the habit of falling asleep in
his chair, to awaken refreshed after everyone had gone to bed.
Then, in the company of other people's sleep, he would pad about
the house, eating whatever he wanted, wherever he wanted, admir-
ing figurines he suspected were new, thumbing through textbooks
lying about, arranging the shoes at the front door into tidy pairs.

After the children left and after his wife died, he was at liberty
to roam the house. He stayed up later and later, to bed at dawn,
to table at three. Soon he could not distinguish night from day.
He feared a tumor. His doctor laid a hand on his shoulder and
said it was grief, and would pass.

Christmas, 1962. His wife posed in her new ranch mink, the top
of her head cut off, her eyes red from the flash, making her seem
alien. He had admired her coat when she came to pick him up.
*You like it? Just a little something I bought on my way home from the
airport. Perhaps it could be my Christmas present.* Each year, he returned three, four times to Hong Kong, to inspect their properties,
to visit their mothers. But he only ever missed that one Christmas.

He thought he saw his wife last week, in San Francisco, going
up the alley-like Commercial Street. Or rather, her mink coat. A
woman walking away, in a fur coat, and on a fairly mild day. The
warm weather and the coat's vague familiarity distracted him,
because the walk he knew very well. He had spent many evenings
watching Fur walk away.

Fei Lo slipped a finger beneath his bifocals and rubbed. He
didn't have to go to his wife's closet to check, he knew.

A fur coat. She wanted a fur coat. For a damn coat she made herself into a thief.

Dinner, she had written. *Next Saturday. Someplace new. All you can eat.* Then she had kissed him before leaving. He could just taste her lipstick when he woke.

Fei Lo pushed himself up from the chair and made his way to bed, overcome with the fatigue of a hiker who realizes, as he reaches the peak too late in the day, that his rest will be inadequate, and his descent will have to be made mostly in the dark.

Dusk and the lighting of the city appeared hand in hand. Thousands of amber lights came up in the special stillness that occurs only in dead winter. The city shimmered.

Of all the views of this city, Fei Lo loved best this one, at night from Treasure Island. From the island, the city's spires seemed to rise straight out of the Pacific in defiance of gravity. These buildings were set upon precious square footage and thrown up to the skies, maximizing the total number of rooms that could command rent. Under these towers lay a scattering of human-sized buildings. One of them was new and sprawling, built in flagrant disregard of cost.

With reluctance, Fei Lo got back on the bridge and continued on to San Francisco. He arrived and drove three times around the same blocks until a street spot opened up, half hoping for failure and an excuse to go home.

A single restaurant occupied the entire new structure, a building so flat an expanse it spread out like a stain, this restaurant launched by a Hong Kong entrepreneur eager to reinvest, eager to put both the Empress and the Mandarin to shame. Every lavishness had been pursued. That was the talk. And to guarantee good fortune, the owner had staged a parade, he hired a dragon, he chose a name of promise and called it The Forbidden Palace.

Fei Lo hated this kind of restaurant, where overplush carpets absorbed all gaiety, where autographed pictures defined who you weren't and men felt more at ease without their families. Gloved waiters served with discretion. Deals were negotiated in a subtle mélange of tranquility and artful consumption. Right hands clasped, left hands remained on the table. Why come to a restaurant if not to eat? Fei Lo could not comprehend. Yet he had attended the grand opening and returned each subsequent Saturday night, arriving early, staying late, eating, drinking, hoping for a glimpse, a chance encounter to set Fur straight.

But opening night belonged to the wife, the mother of the owner's sons. The following Saturday, to the owner's favorite mistress, not the youngest, but the most ruthless. With each succeeding week, Fei Lo had felt both a petty victory and some small embarrassment for Fur, whose one claim in the hierarchy was to be novel.

Tonight he should have stayed home. Or gone to the Economy Cafe in Oakland — run by a Chinese granny in constant sport of very dark glasses to filter out what the grill on the windows could not. For a fraction of what he would be leaving here for a tip, he could have had a fine bowl of Granny's *jūk*. The rice soup soothed as it meandered through one's system, happily carrying away with it all impurities. His stomach was in need of rest.

Fei Lo arranged and rearranged his utensils. From a deposit slip, he tried once again to fold a paper ring, ignoring the ceramic one that matched in design the plates and bowls and the solid brass door handles. He canted the ubiquitous chopsticks — here, ebony.

He was tired and was contemplating leaving, going home to lie down, just getting up and going, now, before the waiter arrived, when Fur finally walked in.

She was preceded, however slightly, by the men in tuxedos, the owner and his towering guards. Fei Lo knew S.K., a man of questionable alliances on both sides of the Pacific. During the Japanese War, he had tried to buy up a quarter-mile section of Tsim Sha Tsui, including property once owned by Fei Lo's wife.

S.K. conferred with his men, his eyes swept the room. He pointed with discretion and the young men nodded as one. The group began to move on, having forgotten Fur. Very soon she was standing all alone. And yet she continued to wait for one of the men to come back, to help her out of her coat, to hand it to the checker, this fur that had belonged to an Amazon of a Cantonese and that she clutched to her breast as if it protected against some as yet undiscovered element.

Fei Lo went past the bar, past the bank of telephone booths, past several doors marked PRIVATE and down the broad, curving stairs, following arrows that pointed the way. On the door to the men's room was a hand-lettered sign: *The management regrets . . . Please, use the Ladies' Room.* Fei Lo could hear voices, arguments about specifications and fulfillments punctuated by banging pipes and gurgling water. He added percussion of his own as he turned away — his shoes squished the carpet.

The door to the ladies' room was propped open. Fei Lo hesitated. His intestines beckoned. Inside, two more doors faced each other. One led to a washroom. He turned to the other and was startled to see a sickish old man, equally startled, staring back at him. It was himself, reflected in a mirror. He was standing in a generous powder room faced with enormous sheets of silvered glass, ceiling to floor and wall to wall. Relief came where one expanse of glass was sheared by a slab of peach-veined marble. Fei Lo was now supporting his gut with one hand. He shouldn't have ordered for two, shouldn't have then tried to eat it. Some men came out of the washroom after first allowing a woman to pass. It seemed all right to go in.

He rushed through the washroom to the toilet room and locked himself in the first free cabinet. Despite the warm tones and textured wallpaper, he still felt the chill, the damp.

By the time the old man finished his business, the washroom had emptied out. He removed his jacket and hung it on a gleaming hook.

The hall door creaked open and swung shut.

"Don't turn around."

Someone was standing in the powder room. While she herself couldn't be seen, her reflection could. His heart contracted.

The old man worked the pink soap into a lather. "Don't turn? Why not?"

Fur tried to make it light. "I have to fix my slip."

Without her coat, he could see she had lost weight. He missed her fleshiness, the suggestion of abundance. Her smart black sheath and stilettos only emphasized her gaunt frame. She looked worn, as if from the strain of standing erect.

"Are you well?"

She waited until he looked up again before answering. "Why didn't you stop me?"

He purposely misunderstood. "But you were with your party."

Fur arranged and rearranged a wayward curl. "He's asked me to marry him."

"Congratulations."

Neither of them mentioned the golden anniversary wife, the litter of mistresses.

"Do you love him?"

Her smile was a fine line in her face. "Did you marry for love? What do you and I know about it? You've been in America too long."

The old man leaned heavily against the sink, seized by sharp pains in his stomach. He paled. Fur started to go in, then stopped. She wasn't used to helping. She didn't know where to begin. When he straightened up, she busied herself with the contents of her purse.

She finally blurted out, "What about the coat?"

The old man cupped some water to his mouth. "Your fur coat? It looks very nice on you."

"Don't be a fool. It's not *my* fur coat."

He had to laugh.

"Aren't you going to call the police?"

"And say to them what?"

"Your wife's coat has been stolen!"

There. She had said it. Almost. But where was the satisfaction?

Fei Lo wet his handkerchief and applied it to the back of his neck. His convulsions had almost subsided. "To call the police I would first have to go home to my wife's closet, where I never go, and discover that her fur coat is missing. If the coat is not missing, what will the police do for an old fat fool?"

In the other room, Fur's eyes darted here and about. Everywhere she looked she could see only herself. "You won't go into her closet?"

It had never before occurred to him that his death could be sudden. He could very well die tonight. Even right here, down in S.K.'s basement toilet. No one would remember the fortune he had built, from nothing, shacks. They would remember only another old man who died without his family.

"In order to find the coat is missing I would have to violate my wife's sanctuary. I would have to think of my friend as a thief. And I would have to consider myself indifferent to a life I can't fully comprehend. That would be the cost to me." He looked for the towel dispensers and found in their place monogrammed linens. "And the gain? I might get back a coat my wife can't wear, a coat my daughter won't wear. A political coat, she says." He tossed his used towel in a basket. "Besides, it's not the coat that I miss."

The hall door opened. A young man filled the frame. He glanced at Fur. She was drawing a generous outline around her lips. The man continued through the washroom with keen dispassion. From the toilet room came the snap of heels, the bang of doors. Down the aisle. Back. Fei Lo managed to produce a comb. Fur was filling in her lips with a sable brush, an even darker shade of red than she used to wear. She puckered. She blotted. The young man paused at the door.

"Five minutes," he said, and he left without haste.

Fur was flushed with color, as if the threat excited. All these weeks Fei Lo had mistakenly thought his desperation to find her was to chastise.

"Fur, you are the boss. Of your own life, you are the boss." If only they were in the same room. "Please, learn to make better opportunities."

"Opportunity! Always the deal! You and he were torn from the same womb, you think I'm a deal to be made?"

"Please. I meant no disrespect." Fei Lo shook his head. He wanted to sit down. "A man cannot change the eyes through which he views the world. Opportunity, it's just my way of speaking. What do I know of fancy words? I just want for your happiness."

She tossed her tissue and kissed the air in front of her. "Maybe it's not just *my* happiness that concerns you."

Fei Lo blushed. "Oh! You are an impossible girl! S.K. will ruin you. Without regret!"

"I have a top-floor apartment, a view of the Golden Gate so wide I have to turn my head to see it all. He visits two or three times a month. I regret nothing."

"And your name is on the deed?"

She gave no answer.

"You have a driver? Wherever you go, he goes?"

"I live like an empress."

"An empress is *protected* by those who watch her."

"And with you, life could be so different?"

"Yes! Of course different, because *I* am different."

"Here's how you are different. You hang on to all those shacks in Tsim Sha Tsui when you could have bought in Victoria, like S.K., be a millionaire many times over."

His color deepened. "Anyone can take valuable property and turn a profit. Where is the challenge in that? I have taken what others discard as worthless and made that into something valuable."

"I am no chunk of land to be improved. I am not worthless. I will not be discarded."

"No. Of course not." Fei Lo hung his head. He went back over their times together and pondered all the things he might have done differently, knowing that the course of a person's life is all but unalterable. Yet he was unwilling to give up hope, or the desperate optimism one can acquire in increasing abundance the nearer one gets to the end of life.

As if she could read his mind, she said, "Nothing you do will change things."

"What I do is of no consequence, you are right. But what you do can determine the rest of your life."

"Mine is a good life, Ah Goong. No better." She spoke with little conviction.

He nodded. "I fear you will beat me to the grave." From an abundance of names, *gā jē, múi, gū mā, bíu jé* — precise nouns that left no ambiguity as to whether a sister was older or younger, a cousin was male or female, an aunt was single or not, related by blood or marriage, and on which side of the family — from the hundred names which evoked the exact relationship between two family members, he could find not one that might describe what he felt about her. And he had come to think of Fur as family. "We could have had something fine, something that honored us both, a relation not unlike what I had with my wife, or daughter, or sister, or even my mother. Something quite — fundamental."

Fur rolled her tongue over her teeth. She snapped her tiny clutch.

Fei Lo flinched and made no move to hide it.

She avoided his gaze, steadfast and genuine, but she could not avoid the ring of his words: mother, sister, daughter, wife. Something fine, he said. Something fundamental. Something, she felt, completely foreign to them both. He might as well have invited her to jump off the boat. For what?

The minutes ticked. Four, five.

Mother, sister, daughter — if she could hold still for just a moment, the brilliance would surely fade. The beckoning would pass.

Her voice was barely audible. "I'm a good girl, Ah Goong. You believe me?"

He nodded, with conviction. She did not see.

"I was a fool to take the coat. And you had invited me into your home."

Fei Lo's heart caught.

Fur stepped out into the room, a little unsteady, as if on first-time legs. Her determination remained, but not the steel. He could imagine her in the center of other cold rooms, awkward, young, toughing it out, coached from the side by a mother who wanted her child to practice standing alone.

Fei Lo shifted to turn.

Fur held a finger to her lips, at once kiss and admonition: *Don't . . . turn.*

He ached to turn, to speak to her, face to face.

She moved decisively toward the door. He struggled. She hesitated. The hall door squealed open. Fur stepped through.

He would not remember going up to the street. Nor would he remember the people he passed, any more than they would remember him. He would recall instead the lightness of her steps.

Fei Lo climbed the stairs and walked through the restaurant, stopping only when he reached the sidewalk. The stars seemed especially bright and plentiful tonight. Not a wisp of cloud in the sky. Not one.

He had to laugh. All these years he had been gazing at the skies at the wrong time of day, so dazzled was he by the sun, so thankful for its warmth on his back. All those nights he knocked about his house while his family slept, he could just as easily have stepped outside his door, and looked up. *Bāk Dáu Chāt Sīng, Sīn Hauh Chóh,* the Big Dipper, Cassiopeia, the stars were the same no matter what they were called, constant in the firmament, whether or not he looked, there to give definition to the space that could be seen, and hint at what could not.

Fei Lo shielded his eyes from the streetlights, and he counted, taking special delight in the faintest sparks, stars that might indeed be small, but could just as easily dwarf his sun while being much farther away. So far away that some already may have burned out, even though their light was just now reaching his eyes. So far away that numbers were incomprehensible. So far away that faith was prerequisite.

He counted all the stars that he could see, and when he was finished, he felt confident that if he stood there a bit longer he would spot another. And another. The price for such clarity was just the cold, the pure cold of a clear night. Fei Lo paused to savor its kiss and sting.

Melungeons

FROM STORY

DEPUTY GOINS SAT in his office and watched the light that seeped beneath the door of the jailhouse. When it reached a certain pock in the floor, it would be time to go home. Monday was nearly over. In the town of Rocksalt, the deputy doubled as jailer to balance each job's meager pay. Goins had come in early to free his prisoners in time for work at the sawmill. They'd left laughing, three boys who'd gotten drunk through the weekend. Goins had spent all day in the dim office. He was tired.

Something outside blocked the light and Goins wished the county would buy a clock. A man opened the door.

"Time is it?" Goins said.

The man shrugged. He peered into the dark room, jerking his head like a blackbird on a fence rail. He looked older than Goins, who was sixty-three, and Goins thought he'd probably come for a grandson.

"Nobody here," Goins said. "Done turned them loose."

"I heard tell a Goins worked here."

"That's me. Ephraim Goins."

"Well, I'm fit for the pokey. What's a man got to do to go?"

"Drunk mostly."

"Don't drink."

"Speeding."

"Ain't got nary a car."

"Stealing'll do it."

"I don't reckon."

The man kept his head turned and his eyes down. Goins decided that he was a chucklehead who'd wandered away from his family.

"Why don't you let me call your kin," Goins said.

"No phone." The man jerked his chin to the corridor where the cells were. "What if I cussed you?"

"I'd cuss back."

"Ain't they nothing?"

"Let's see," Goins said. "Defacing public property is on the books, but it'd be hard to hurt this place."

The man walked to the door and stood with his back turned. "Come here a minute," he said.

Goins joined him. The man had unzipped his pants and was urinating on the plank steps leading to the door. Goins whistled low, shaking his head.

"You've force put me, sure enough," he said, hoping to scare the man away. "Looks like you're arrested. Lucky they ain't no lynch mob handy."

The man inhaled deeply and hurried down the hall to a cell. Goins opened the heavy door. The man stepped in and quickly pulled it shut behind him.

"Name?" said Goins.

"Desser. Haze Desser."

He lifted his head, showing blue eyes in rough contrast with his black hair and smooth, swarthy skin. They watched each other for a long time. The name Desser was like Goins, a Melungeon name, and Goins knew the man's home ridge deep in the hills. He glanced along the dim hall and lowered his voice.

"Say you're a Desser?"

"Least I ain't the law."

"What's your why of getting locked up?"

"You been towned so long," Desser said, "I don't know that I can say. I surely don't."

"Why not?"

"Don't know which way you're aimed at these days."

Goins stepped close to the bars.

"You know," he said. "If you're a Desser, you do. But you ain't making it easy."

"It never was."

Desser lay on the narrow cot and rolled on his side, turning his back to Goins. A mouse blurred across the floor.

"I'm a done-talk man," Desser said.

Goins returned to his desk and stared through the window at

the courthouse. He remembered his fourth-grade teacher threaten a child who was always late to school. "If you don't get up on time," the teacher had said, "the Melungeons will get you."

Melungeons weren't white, black, or Indian. They lived deep in the hills, on the most isolated ridges, pushed from the hollows two centuries back by the people following Boone. The Shawnee called them "white Indians" and told the settlers that they'd always lived there. The pioneers left them alone. Melungeons continued to live as they always had.

Goins wasn't born when the trouble started between the Desser and Brownlow clans, but he'd felt the strain of its tension all his life. Members of his family had married both sides. To avoid the pressure of laying claim to either, Goins had volunteered to serve in Korea. Uniforms rather than blood would clarify the enemy.

When a dentist noticed that his gums were tinged with blue, the army assigned Goins to an all-black company. Black soldiers treated him with open scorn. The whites refused to acknowledge him at all. Only one man befriended him, a New Yorker named Abe, whom no one liked because he was Jewish.

On a routine patrol Goins became separated from the rest and was not missed until the sound of gunfire. American soldiers found him bleeding from two bullet holes and a bayonet wound. Five enemy lay dead around him. Goins was decorated with honor and returned to Kentucky, but stayed in town. He didn't want to live near killing. Out of respect for its only hero, the town overlooked which hill he was from. Now the town had forgotten.

Goins rose from his desk and walked to Desser's cell, his boots echoing in the dark hall. The smell of human waste and disinfectant made his nose sting. The walls were damp.

"How long you aim to stay?" Goins said.

"Just overnight. Hotel's too risky."

"Why stay in town at all?"

"Man gets old," Desser said. "You don't know who I am, do you?"

"No," Goins said. "I ain't been up there in thirty years."

"Longer for me. I'm the one that left and went up north."

"Plenty of work?"

"As many taxes they got laying for a man, it don't hardly pay to work."

"What'd they take you for up there?"

"Went by ever who else was around. Italian mostly. Couple times

a Puerto Rican till they heard me talk. Sometimes it never mattered."

"Why come back?"

"I got give out on it," Desser said. "I'm seventy-six years old.
Missed every wedding and funeral my family had."

"Me too."

"By choice." The man's voice was hard. "You can walk back out
your ridge any day of the year. Don't know why a man wouldn't
when he could."

Goins gripped the cell door with both hands the way prisoners
often stood, shoulders hunched, head low. He didn't hunt or fish
anymore, had stopped gathering mushrooms and ginseng. Being
in the woods was too painful when he didn't live there. The last
few times he'd felt awkward and foreign, as if the land was mocking
him. He wondered if Desser's exile was easier without the constant
reminder of what he'd lost.

Goins unlocked the cell and pulled the door open an inch.
Desser's face twisted in a faint smile. One side of his mouth was
missing teeth.

"I'm leaving," said Goins.

"I'll be here come daylight."

"Hope you know what you're doing."

"Some of my grandkids have got kids," Desser said. "You don't know
what it's like to see them all at once. And them not to know you."

"You were up to the mountain?" Goins said.

The man nodded.

"Bad as ever?"

"Not as much as it was. They're all married in now and don't
bother with it no more. The kids have got a game of it, play-acting.
I look for it to stop when the next bunch gets born. Still ain't full
safe for me. I'm the last of the old Dessers left alive."

He moved to face the wall again. Goins walked quietly away,
leaving the cell open, hoping Desser would change his mind. He
left the front door unlocked. The dusk of autumn cooled his face
and he realized that he'd been sweating. The fading sun leaned
into the hills with a horizontal light that made the woods appear
on fire.

A gibbous moon waned above the land when Beulah Brownlow
left her house. Though she hadn't been off the mountain in fifty

years, she found the old path easily, and followed it down the final
slanting drop to the road by the creek. The road was black now,
hard and black. She'd heard of that but never seen it. Beulah
stayed on the weedy shoulder, preferring earth for the long walk
to Rocksalt. The load she carried was easier on flat terrain.

Beulah had never voted, or paid taxes. There was no record of
her birth. The only time she'd been to town, she'd bought nails
for a hogpen. Her family usually burned old buildings for nails,
plucking them hot from the debris, but that year a spring flood
had washed them away. Beulah had despised Rocksalt and swore
never to return. Tonight she had no choice. She left her house
within an hour of learning that Haze was on the mountain. He'd
slipped away, probably after hearing that she was still alive, and
headed for town. Beulah walked steadily. The air was day-white
from the moon.

Sixty years before, five Brownlow men were logging a hillside at
the southern edge of their property when a white oak slipped
sideways from its notch. The beveled point dug into the earth.
Instead of falling parallel with the creek, the oak dropped onto
their neighbor's land and splintered a hollow log. Dislodged tree
leaves floated in the breeze. When the men crossed the creek, they
found a black bear crushed to death inside the hollow log. They
built a fire for the night and ate the liver, tongue, and six pounds
of greasy fat.

In the morning, a hunting party of Dessers discovered the camp.
The land was theirs and they demanded the meat. Since the
Brownlows had already butchered the bear, they offered half. The
Dessers refused. Three men died in a quick gunfight. The rest
slank through the woods, leaking blood from bullet wounds. Over
the next decade, twenty-eight more people were killed.

Ground fog rose to the eastern sky, streaked in pink like lace.
Beulah's face was dark as a ripe pawpaw. Checkered gingham
wrapped her head, covering five feet of gray hair. She wore a bulky
riding duster that smelled of duck oil and concealed her burden.
Her legs hurt. A flock of vireos lifted from a maple by the creek,
a thick cloud of dark specks that narrowed at the end like a
tadpole. Beulah watched them, knowing that winter would arrive
early.

She scented town before she saw the buildings, a foul smell.

Rocksalt was bigger now, had spread like moss. Frost in the hills was heavy enough to track a rabbit, but here the ground was soft. Town was suddenly all around her. Beulah moved downwind of a police car. She couldn't read, but knew that an automobile with writing on its side was like a tied dog. Whoever· held the leash controlled it. She stalked the town from the shade. Her shins were damp from dew.

Railroad Street was empty. The muddy boardwalk was gone, and the cement sidewalk reminded her of a frozen creek, shiny and hard in the shade. Beulah leaned against the granite whistle post in the morning sun. On her last trip this had been the center of town, bristling with people, wagons, and mules. Now the tracks were rusty and the platform was a bare gantry of rotted wood. Beulah looked past it to the treeline, listening to a cardinal. The hollow was glazed by mist like crystal. She turned her back and headed into the silence of improvement.

Sunlight crept down the buildings that faced east. She walked two blocks out of her way to avoid a neon diner sign glowing in the dawn. No one here would take Haze in. There was only one place he could go for safety.

In front of the jail was a bench with one side propped on a concrete block. She stepped past it to shade and leaned against the southern wall. She was eighty-four years old. She breathed easily in the chill air.

Goins slept rough that night, listening to the building crack from overnight cold. At dawn he rose and looked at the hills. He missed living with the land most in autumn, when the trees seemed suddenly splashed with color, and rutting deer snorted in the hollows. There were walnuts to gather, bees to rob. Turkeys big as dogs jumped from ridgelines to extend their flight.

He rubbed his face and turned from the window, reminding himself of why he'd stayed in Rocksalt. Town was warm. It had cable TV and water. He was treated as everyone's equal, but his years in town had taught him to hide his directness, the Melungeon way of point-blank living.

After breakfast, he reached under his bed for a cigar box that contained his Purple Heart and Bronze Star. They were tarnished near to black. Beneath them was an article he'd cut from a Lex-

ington paper a few years back. It was a feature story suggesting that
Melungeons were descendants of Madoc, a Welsh explorer in the
twelfth century. Alternate theories labeled them as shipwrecked
Portuguese, members of Hernando de Soto's band, or one of Israel's lost tribes. It was the only information Goins had ever seen
about Melungeons. The article called them a vanishing race.

He slipped the brittle paper in his pocket and walked to work.
Strands of mist haloed the hills that circled the town. The jailhouse
door was unlocked, and Goins hoped the cell would be empty.

Inside, Desser sat silently on his bunk, making a cigarette. Goins
gave him a cup of coffee, watching him take it in two hands for
warmth. The cigarette hung from his mouth. Once lit, he never
touched it.

"Sleep good?" Goins said.

"My back hurts like a toothache."

Goins unfolded the newspaper article and handed it through
the bars. Desser read it slowly.

"Don't mean nothing," he said. "They're just fighting over who
come to America first. Damn sure wasn't you and me."

"I kindly favor that Lost Tribe of Israel idea."

"You do."

"I've give thought to it. Them people then moved around more
than a cat. Your name's off Hezekiah and mine's Ephraim. I
knowed a Nimrod once. Got a cousin Zephaniah married a Ruth."

Desser shook his head rapidly, sending a trail of ash to the grimy
floor.

"That don't make us nobody special," he said.

"We're somebody, ain't we?"

"We damn sure ain't Phoenicians or Welshes. We ain't even
Melungeons except in the paper. It don't matter where we upped
from. We're what we are now, right now."

"Man can study on it if he's a mind to."

"You're a Goins."

"I'm a deputy."

"And I'm a Desser. Ain't a damn thing else to it."

Goins returned to his desk. He wanted to ask for the article back
but decided to wait until the man wasn't twitchy as a spooked
horse. A preacher had donated a Bible for the prisoners. Goins
hunted through Genesis for his namesake, the leader of the Lost

Tribe who never made it to the land of milk and honey. He hoped it was hilly. He turned to Exodus and thought of Abe, his army buddy from New York. Goins wondered if he had a phone. Maybe Abe knew where the lost tribes went.

The jail's front door slowly creaked open and a woman's form eclipsed the light that flowed around her. She stepped inside. Goins became very still, mouth dry, armpits suddenly wet. He didn't know her, but he knew her. It was as if the entire mountain itself had entered the tiny room, filling it with earth and rain, the steady wind along the ridge. She gazed at him, one eye dark, the other yellow-flecked. Between the lines of her face ran many smaller lines like rain gullies running to creeks. She'd been old when he was young.

"You look a Goins," she said.

He nodded. He could smell the mountain on her.

"They a Desser here?" she said.

Goins nodded again. He swallowed in order to speak, but couldn't.

The woman shifted her shoulders to remove a game bag. Inside was a blackened pot, the lid fastened with moonseed vine. She looked at him, waiting. He opened a drawer for a plate and she removed the lid to reveal a skin of grease that covered a stew. She scooped a squirrel leg onto his plate, then a potato. The musk of fresh game pushed into the room. Her hands were misshapen from arthritis but she used them freely, her lips clamped tight as bark to a tree. Goins understood that she was following the old code of proving the pot contained no file or pistol. He relaxed some. She wasn't here for trouble.

The woman shifted her head to look at him. The blink of her eyes was slow and patient. She stood as if she could wait a month without speech and movement, oblivious to time or weather. Goins tried to speak. He wanted to ask her where they'd all come from, but knew from looking at her that she wouldn't know or care.

When he realized what she was waiting for, he opened his pocketknife, sliced some meat from the leg, and lifted it to his mouth. It tasted of wild onion and the dark flavor of game. He nodded to her. She straightened her back and faced the hall and did not look at him again.

She walked to the cells, moving stiffly, favoring her left side as if straining with gout. The long coat rustled against her legs like brush in a breeze. Goins pivoted in his chair to give them privacy. He looked at the strip of light below the door, knowing that as the sun passed by, the light would get longer, then shorter, before he could leave. Outside, a clerk laughed while entering the court-house. A car engine drowned the sound of morning birds. Goins stared at the closed door. He swallowed the bite of meat.

Behind him he heard the woman say one word soaked in the fury of half a century. Then came the tremendous bellow of a shotgun. The sound bounced off the stone walls and up the hall to his office, echoing back and forth, until it faded. Goins jerked upright in the chair. His legs began to shiver. He held his thighs tightly and the shivering traveled up his arms until his entire body shook. He pressed his forehead against the desk. When the trem-bling passed, he turned toward the hall.

Gun smoke stung his eyes and he could smell cordite. The left side of the woman's coat was hiked across her hip where she'd kept the hidden gun. Its barrel was shiny and ragged at the saw cut. Her legs were steady. She tossed the weapon into the man's cell, looked at Goins and nodded once, her expression the same as before.

He used the wall to support himself as he walked to Desser's cell. The cigarette still trailed smoke. Blood covered the newspaper article and flowed slowly across the floor. The woman stepped to the next cell. She folded her coat back down and waited while Goins unlocked the door. Her face seemed slightly softer. She stepped inside. When the door clanked shut, her shoulder stiff-ened, and she lifted her head to the gridded square of sky visible through the small window.

Courthouse workers were running outside. Someone shouted his name, asking if he was hurt. Goins used the phone to call an undertaker who doubled as county coroner. It occurred to him that coroner was a better job than jailer. The coroner would receive twenty-five dollars for pronouncing the man dead, but Goins got nothing extra for cleaning the cell.

He put the Bible away and found the prisoners' log and wrote *Brownlow*. Under yesterday's date he wrote Desser. Goins rubbed his eyes. He didn't write Haze because the man was down to a body now, and the body was a Desser. Goins covered his face with his hands. It was true for him as well.

He opened the door and stepped into the sun. People ducked for cover until recognizing him. He looked at them, men and women he'd known for thirty years, but never really knew. Beyond them stood the hills that hemmed the town. He began walking east, toward the nearest slope. There was nothing he needed to take. The sun was warm against his face.

Mr. Sumarsono

FROM THE ATLANTIC MONTHLY

OH, MR. Su*mar*sono, Mr. Su*mar*sono. We remember you so well. I wonder how you remember us.

The three of us met Mr. Sumarsono at the Trenton train station. The platform stretched down the tracks in both directions, long, half-roofed, and dirty. Beyond the tracks on either side were high corrugated-metal sidings, battered and patched. Above the sidings were the tops of weeds and the backs of ramshackle buildings, grimy and desolate. Stretching out above the tracks was an aerial grid of electrical-power lines, their knotted, uneven rectangles connecting every city on the eastern corridor in a dismal, industrial way.

My mother, my sister, Kate, and I stood waiting for Mr. Sumarsono at the foot of the escalator, which did not work. The escalator had worked once; I could remember it working, though Kate, who was younger, could not. Now the metal staircase towered over the platform, silent and immobile, giving the station a surreal air. If you used it as a staircase, which people often did, setting your foot on each movable, motionless step, you had an odd feeling of sensory dislocation, like watching a color movie in black-and-white. You knew something was wrong, though you didn't know just what.

Mr. Sumarsono got off his train at the other end of the platform from us. He stood still for a moment and looked hesitantly up and down. He didn't know which way to look, or for whom he was looking. My mother lifted her arm and waved: we knew who he was, though we had never seen him before. It was 1959, and Mr. Sumarsono was the only Indonesian who got off the train in Trenton, New Jersey.

Mr. Sumarsono was wearing a neat suit and leather shoes, like an American businessman, but he did not look like an American. The suit was brown, not gray, and it had a slight sheen. And Mr. Sumarsono was built in a different way from Americans: he was slight and graceful, with narrow shoulders and an absence of strut. His movements were diffident, and they seemed to have extra curves. This was true even of simple movements, like picking up his suitcase and starting down the platform toward the three of us, standing by the escalator that didn't work.

Kate and I stood next to my mother as she waved and smiled. Kate and I did not wave and smile: this was all my mother's idea. Kate was seven and I was ten. We were not entirely sure what a diplomat was, and we were not at all sure that we wanted to be nice to one all weekend. I wondered why he didn't have friends his own age.

"Hoo-hoo," my mother called, mortifyingly, even though Mr. Sumarsono had already seen us and was making his graceful way toward us. His steps were small and his movements modest. He smiled in a nonspecific way, to show that he had seen us, but my mother kept on waving and calling. It took a long time, this interlude: encouraging shouts and gestures from my mother, Mr. Sumarsono's unhurried approach. I wondered if he, too, was embarrassed by my mother; once, he glanced swiftly around, as though he were looking for an alternate family to spend the weekend with. He had reason to be uneasy: the grimy Trenton platform did not suggest a rural retreat. And when he saw us standing by the stationary escalator, my mother waving and calling, Kate and I sullenly silent, he may have felt that things were off to a poor start.

My mother is short, with big bones and a square face. She has thick dark hair and a wide, mobile mouth. She is a powerful woman. She used to be on the stage, and she still delivers to the back row. When she calls "Hoo-hoo" at a train station, everyone at that station knows it.

"Mr. Su*mar*sono," she called out as he came up to us. The accent is on the second syllable. That's what the people at the UN told her, and she made us practice, sighing and complaining, until we said it the way she wanted: Su*mar*sono.

Mr. Sumarsono gave a formal nod and a small smile. His face was oval, and his eyes were long. His skin was very pale brown, and smooth. His hair was shiny and black, and it also was very smooth. Everything about him seemed polished and smooth.

"Hello!" my mother said, seizing his hand and shaking it. "I'm Mrs. Riordan. And this is Kate, and this is Susan." Kate and I cautiously put out our hands, and Mr. Sumarsono took them limply, bowing at each of us.

My mother put out her hand again. "Shall I take your bag?" But Mr. Sumarsono defended his suitcase. "We're just up here," my mother said, giving up on the bag and leading the way to the escalator.

We all began to climb, but after a few steps my mother looked back.

"This is an *es*calator," she said loudly.

Mr. Sumarsono gave a short nod.

"It takes you *up*," my mother called, and pointed to the roof overhead. Mr. Sumarsono, holding his suitcase with both hands, looked at the ceiling.

"It doesn't work *right now*," my mother said illuminatingly, and turned back to her climb.

"No," I heard Mr. Sumarsono say. He glanced cautiously again at the ceiling.

Exactly parallel to the escalator was a broad concrete staircase, with another group of people climbing it. We were separated only by the handrail, so for a disorienting second you felt you were looking at a mirror from which you were missing. This intensified the feeling received from climbing the stopped escalator — dislocation, bewilderment, doubt at your own senses.

A woman on the real staircase looked over at us, and I could tell that my mother gave her a brilliant smile: the woman looked away at once. We were the only people on the escalator.

On the way home Kate and I sat in the back seat and watched our mother keep turning to speak to Mr. Sumarsono. She asked him long, complicated, cheerful questions. "Well, Mr. Sumarsono, had you been in this country at all before you came to the UN, or is this your first visit? I know you've been working at the UN for only a short time."

Mr. Sumarsono answered everything with a polite unfinished nod. Then he would turn back and look out the window again. I wondered if he was thinking about jumping out of the car. I wondered what Mr. Sumarsono was expecting from a weekend in the country. I hoped it was not a walk to the pond: Kate and I had

planned one for that afternoon. We were going to watch the
mallards nesting, and I hoped we didn't have to include a middle-
aged Indonesian in leather shoes.

When we got home, my mother looked at me meaningfully. "Susan,
will you and Kate show Mr. Sumarsono to his room?" Mr. Sumarsono looked politely at us, his head tilted slightly sideways.

Gracelessly I leaned over to pick up Mr. Sumarsono's suitcase,
as I had been told. He stopped me by putting his hand out, palm
front, in a traffic policeman's gesture.

"No, no," he said with a small smile, and he took hold of the
suitcase himself. I fell back, pleased not to do as I'd been told, but
also impressed, almost awed, by Mr. Sumarsono.

What struck me was the grace of his gesture. His hand extended
easily out of its cuff and exposed a narrow brown wrist, as narrow
as my own. When he put his hand up in the Stop! gesture, his hand
curved backward from the wrist, and his fingers bent backward
from the palm. Instead of the stern and flat-handed Stop! that an
American hand would make, this was a polite, subtle, and yielding
signal, quite beautiful and infinitely sophisticated, a gesture that
suggested a thousand reasons for doing something, a thousand
ways to go about it.

I let him take the suitcase and we climbed the front stairs, me
first, Kate next, and then Mr. Sumarsono, as though we were
playing a game. We marched solemnly, single file, through the
second-floor hall and up the back stairs to the third floor. The
guest room was small, with a bright hooked rug on the wide old
floorboards, white ruffled curtains at the windows, and slanting
eaves. In the room was a spool bed, a table next to it, a straight chair,
and a chest of drawers. On the chest of drawers was a photograph
of my great-grandmother, her austere face surrounded by faded
embroidery. On the bedspread was a large tan smudge, where our
cat liked to spend the afternoons.

Mr. Sumarsono put his suitcase down and looked around the
room. I looked around with him, and suddenly the guest room,
and in fact our whole house, took on a new aspect. Until that
moment I had thought our house was numbingly ordinary, that it
represented the decorating norm: patchwork quilts, steep narrow
staircases, slanting ceilings, and spool beds. I assumed everyone

had faded photographs of Victorian grandparents dotted mournfully around their rooms. Now I realized that this was not the case. I wondered what houses were like in Indonesia, or apartments in New York. Somehow I knew: they were low, sleek, modern, all on one floor, with hard, gleaming surfaces. They were full of right angles and empty of allusions. They were the exact opposite of our house. Silently and fiercely I blamed my mother for our environment, which was, I now saw, eccentric, totally abnormal.

Mr. Sumarsono looked at me and nodded precisely again.

"Thank you," he said.

"Don't hit your head," Kate said.

Mr. Sumarsono bowed, closing his eyes.

"On the ceiling," Kate said, pointing to it.

"The ceiling," he repeated, looking up at it too.

"Don't hit your head on the ceiling," she said loudly, and Mr. Sumarsono looked at her and smiled.

"The bathroom's in here," I said, showing him.

"Thank you," he said.

"Susan!" my mother called up the stairs, "tell Mr. Sumarsono to come downstairs when he's ready for lunch."

"Come-downstairs-when-you're-ready-for-lunch," I said, unnecessarily. I pointed graphically into my open mouth and then bolted, clattering rapidly down both sets of stairs. Kate was right behind me, and our knees and elbows collided as we rushed to get away.

Mother had set four places for lunch, which was on the screened-in porch overlooking the lawn. The four places meant a battle.

"Mother," I said mutinously.

"What is it?" Mother said. "Would you fill a pitcher of water, Susan?"

"Kate and I are not *having* lunch," I said, running water into the big blue and white pottery pitcher.

"And get the butter dish. Of course you're having lunch," my mother said. She was standing at the old wooden kitchen table, making deviled eggs. She was messily filling the rubbery white hollows with dollops of yolk-and-mayonnaise. The slippery egg halves rocked unstably, and the mixture stuck to her spoon. She scraped it into the little boats with her finger. I watched with distaste. In a ranch house, I thought, or in New York, this would not happen. In New York food would be prepared on polished manmade surfaces. It would be brought to you on gleaming platters by silent waiters.

"I told you Kate and I are *not* having lunch," I said. "We're taking a picnic to the pond." I put the pitcher on the table.

Mother turned to me. "We have been through this already, Susan. We have a guest for the weekend, and I want you girls to be polite to him. He is a stranger in this country, and I expect you to *extend* yourselves. Think how *you* would feel if *you* were in a strange land."

"Ex*tend* myself," I said rudely, under my breath, but loud enough that my mother could hear. This was exactly the sort of idiotic thing she said. "I certainly wouldn't go around hoping people would *extend* themselves." I thought of people stretched out horribly, their arms yearning in one direction, their feet in another, all for my benefit. "If I were in a strange country, I'd like everyone to leave me alone."

"Ready for lunch?" my mother said brightly to Mr. Sumarsono, who stood diffidently in the doorway. "We're just about to sit down. Kate, will you bring out the butter?"

"*I* did already," I said virtuously, and folded my arms in a hostile manner.

"We're having deviled eggs," Mother announced as we sat down. She picked up the plate of them and smiled humorously. "We call them 'deviled.'"

"Dev-il," Kate said, speaking very loudly and slowly. She pointed at the eggs and then put two forked fingers behind her head, like horns. Mr. Sumarsono looked at her horns. He nodded pleasantly.

My mother talked all through lunch, asking Mr. Sumarsono mystifying questions and then answering them herself in case he couldn't. Mr. Sumarsono kept a polite half smile on his face, sometimes repeating the last few words of her sentences. Even while he was eating, he seemed to be listening attentively. He ate very neatly, taking small bites, and laying his fork and knife precisely side by side when he was through. Kate and I pointedly said nothing. We were boycotting lunch, though we smiled horribly at Mr. Sumarsono if we caught his eye.

After lunch my mother said she was going to take a nap. As she said this, she laid her head sideways on her folded hands and closed her eyes. Then she pointed upstairs. Mr. Sumarsono nodded. He rose from the table, pushed in his chair, and went meekly back to his room, his shoes creaking on the stairs.

Kate and I did the dishes in a slapdash way and took off for the pond. We spent the afternoon on a hill overlooking the marshy end, watching the mallards and arguing over the binoculars. We had only one pair. We had once had a second pair; I could remember this, though Kate could not. Our father had taken the other set with him.

Mother was already downstairs in the kitchen when we got back. She was singing cheerfully and wearing a pink dress with puffy sleeves and a full skirt. The pink dress was a favorite of Kate's and mine. I was irritated to see that she had put it on as though she were at a party. This was not a party: she had merely gotten hold of a captive guest, a complete stranger who understood nothing she said. This was not a cause for celebration.

She gave us a big smile when we came in.

"Any luck with the mallards?" she asked.

"Not really," I said coolly. A lie.

Kate and I set the table, and Mother asked Kate to pick some flowers for the centerpiece. We were having dinner in the dining room, Mother said, using the white plates with gold rims from our grandmother. While we were setting the table, Mother called in from the kitchen, "Oh, Susan, put out some wineglasses, too, for me and Mr. Sumarsono."

Kate and I looked at each other.

*Wine*glasses? Kate mouthed silently.

"Wineglasses?" I called back, my voice sober for my mother, my face wild for Kate.

"That's right," Mother said cheerfully. "We're going to be festive."

Festive! I mouthed to Kate, and we doubled over, shaking our heads and rolling our eyes.

We put out the wineglasses, handling them gingerly, as though they gave off dangerous, unpredictable rays. The glasses, standing boldly at the knife tips, altered the landscape of the table. Kate and I felt as though we were in the presence of something powerful and alien. We looked warningly at each other, pointing at the glasses and frowning, nodding our heads meaningfully. We picked them up and mimed drinking from them. We wiped our mouths and began to stagger, crossing our eyes and hiccuping. When Mother appeared in the doorway, we froze, and Kate, who was in the process of lurching sideways, turned her movement into a pirouette, her face clear, her eyes uncrossed.

"Be careful with those glasses," my mother said.

"We are," Kate said, striking a classical pose, the wineglass held worshipfully aloft like a chalice.

When dinner was ready, Mother went to the foot of the stairs and called up, "Hoo-hoo!" several times. She heard no reply, and after a pause she called, "Mr. Sumarsono! Dinner. Come down for dinner!" We began to hear noises from overhead, as Mr. Sumarsono rose obediently from his nap.

When we sat down, I noticed that Mother was not only in the festive pink dress but also bathed and particularly fresh-looking. She had done her hair in a fancy way, smoothing it back from her forehead. She was smiling a lot. When she had served the plates, my mother picked up the bottle of wine and offered Mr. Sumarsono a glass.

"Would you like a little *wine*, Mr. Sumarsono?" she asked, leaning forward, her head cocked. We were having the dish she always made for guests: baked chicken pieces in a sauce made of Campbell's cream of mushroom soup.

"Thank you." Mr. Sumarsono nodded, and pushed forward his glass. My mother beamed, and filled his glass. Kate and I watched her as we cut up our chicken. We watched her as we drank from our milk glasses, our eyes round and unblinking over the rims.

We ate in silence, a silence broken only by my mother. "Mr. Sumarsono," she said, having finished most of her chicken and most of her wine. "Do you have a *wife? A family?*" She gestured first at herself, then at us. Mr. Sumarsono looked searchingly across the table at Kate and me. We were chewing, and stared solemnly back.

Mr. Sumarsono nodded his half nod, his head stopping at the bottom of the movement.

"A wife?" my mother said, gratified. She pointed again at herself. She was not a wife, and hadn't been for five years, but Mr. Sumarsono wouldn't know that. I wondered what he did know. I wondered if he wondered where my father was. Perhaps he thought that it was an American custom for the father to live in another house, spending his day apart from his wife and children, eating his dinner alone. Perhaps Mr. Sumarsono was expecting my father to arrive ceremoniously after dinner, dressed in silken robes and carrying a carved wooden writing case, ready to entertain his guest with tales of the hill people. What did Mr. Sumarsono expect of us? It was unimaginable.

Whatever Mr. Sumarsono was expecting, my mother was determined to deliver what she could of it. In the pink dress, full of red wine, she was changing before our very eyes. She was warming up, turning larger and grander, rosy and powerful.

"Mr. Sumarsono," my mother said happily, "do you have photographs of your family?"

Silence. My mother pointed again to her chest, plump and rosy above the pink dress. Then she held up an invisible camera. She closed one eye and clicked loudly at Mr. Sumarsono. He watched her carefully.

"Photo of wife?" she said again, loudly, and again pointed at herself. Then she pointed at him. Mr. Sumarsono gave his truncated nod and stood up. He bowed again and pointed to the ceiling. Then, with a complicated and unfinished look, loaded with meaning, he left the room.

Kate and I looked accusingly at our mother. Dinner would now be prolonged indefinitely, her fault.

"He's gone to get his photographs," Mother said. "The poor man, he must miss his wife and children. Don't you feel sorry for him, thousands of miles away from his family? Oh, thousands. He's here for six months, all alone. They told me that at the UN. It's all very uncertain. He doesn't know when he gets leaves, how long after that he'll be here. Think of how his poor wife feels." She shook her head and took a long sip of her wine. She remembered us and added reprovingly, "And what about his poor children? Their father is thousands of miles away! They don't know when they'll see him!" Her voice was admonitory, suggesting that this was partly our fault.

Kate and I did not comment on Mr. Sumarsono's children. We ourselves did not know when we would see our father, and we did not want to discuss that either. We longed for all this to be over, this endless, messy meal, full of incomprehensible exchanges.

Kate sighed discreetly, her mouth slightly open for silence, and swung her legs under the table. I picked up a chicken thigh with my fingers and began to pick delicately at it with my teeth. This was forbidden, but I thought that the wine and excitement would distract my mother from my behavior. It did. She sighed deeply, shook her head, and picked up her fork. She began eating in a dreamy way.

"Oh, I'm glad we're having rice!" she said suddenly, pleased. "That must make Mr. Sumarsono feel at home." She looked at me. "You know that's all they have in Indonesia," she said in a teacherly sort of way. "Rice, bamboo, things like that. Lizard."

Another ridiculous statement. I knew such a place could not exist, but Kate was younger, and I pictured what she must imagine: thin stalks of rice struggling up through a dense and endless bamboo forest. People in brown suits pushing their way among the limber stalks, looking around fruitlessly for houses, telephones, something to eat besides lizards.

Mr. Sumarsono appeared again in the doorway. He was holding a large leather camera case. He had already begun to unbuckle and unsnap, to extricate the camera from it. He took out a light meter and held it up. My mother raised her fork at him.

"Rice!" she said enthusiastically. "That's familiar, isn't it? Does it remind you of *home?*" She gestured expansively at our dining room. Mr. Sumarsono looked obediently around, at the mahogany sideboard with its crystal decanters, the glass-fronted cabinet full of family china, the big stern portrait of my grandfather in his pink hunting coat, holding his riding crop. Mr. Sumarsono looked back at my mother, who was still holding up her rice-heavy fork. He nodded.

"Yes?" my mother said, pleased.

"Yes," Mr. Sumarsono said.

My mother looked down again. Blinking in a satisfied way, she said, "I'm glad I thought of it." I knew she hadn't thought of it until that moment. She always made rice with the chicken-and-Campbell's-cream-of-mushroom-soup dish. Having an Indonesian turn up to eat it was just luck.

Mr. Sumarsono held up his camera. The light meter dangled from a strap, and the flash attachment projected from one corner. He put the camera up to his eye, and his face vanished altogether.

My mother was looking down at her plate again, peaceful, absorbed, suffused with red wine and satisfaction.

I could see that my mother's view of all this — the meal, the visit, the weekend — was different from my own. I could see that she was pleased by everything about it. She was pleased by her polite and helpful daughters, she was pleased by her charming farmhouse with its stylish and original touches. She was pleased by her delicious and unusual meal, and, most important, she was pleased by her own generosity, by being able to offer this poor stranger her lavish bounty.

She was wrong, she was always wrong, my mother. She was wrong about everything. I was resigned to it: at ten you have no control over your mother. The evening would go on like this, endless, excruciating. My mother would act foolish, Kate and I would be mortified, and Mr. Sumarsono would be mystified. It was no wonder my father had left: embarrassment.

Mr. Sumarsono was now ready, and he spoke. "Please!" he said, politely. My mother looked up again and realized this time what he was doing. She shook her head, raising her hands in deprecation.

"No, no," she said, smiling, "not me. Don't take a picture of me. I wanted to see a picture of your wife." She pointed at Mr. Sumarsono. "Your wife," she said, "your children."

I was embarrassed not only for my mother but also for poor Mr. Sumarsono. Whatever he had expected from a country weekend in America, it could not have been a cramped attic room, two sullen girls, a voluble and incomprehensible hostess. I felt we had failed him, we had betrayed his unruffled courtesy, with our bewildering commands, our waving forks, our irresponsible talk about lizards. I wanted to save him. I wanted to liberate poor Mr. Sumarsono from this aerial grid of misunderstandings. I wanted to cut the power lines, but I couldn't think of a way. I watched him despondently, waiting for him to subside at my mother's next order. Perhaps she would send him upstairs for another nap.

But things had changed. Mr. Sumarsono stood gracefully, firm and erect, in charge. Somehow he had performed a coup. He had seized power. The absence of strut did not mean an absence of command, and we now saw how an Indonesian diplomat behaved when he was in charge. Like the Stop! gesture, Mr. Sumarsono's reign was elegant and sophisticated, entirely convincing. We suddenly understood that telling Mr. Sumarsono what to do was no longer possible.

"No," Mr. Sumarsono said clearly. "You wife." He bowed firmly at my mother. "You children." He bowed at us.

Mr. Sumarsono stood over us, his courtesy exquisite and unyielding. "Please," he said. "Now photograph." He held up the camera. It covered his face entirely, a strange mechanical mask. "My photograph," he said in a decisive tone.

He aimed the camera first at me. I produced a taut and artificial smile, and at once he reappeared from behind the camera. "No smile," he said firmly, shaking his head. "No smile." He himself produced a hideous smile, and then shook his head and turned grave. "Ah!" he said, nodding, and pointed at me. Chastened, I sat solemn and rigid while he disappeared behind the camera again. I didn't move even when he had finished, the flash over; I listened to the clicks of lenses and winding sprockets.

Mr. Sumarsono turned to Kate, who had learned from me and offered up a smooth and serious face. Mr. Sumarsono nodded, but stepped toward her. "Hand!" he said, motioning toward it, and he made the gesture that he wanted. Kate stared, but obediently did as he asked.

When Mr. Sumarsono turned to my mother, I worried that she would stage a last-ditch attempt to take over, that she would insist on mortifying us all.

"Now!" Mr. Sumarsono said, bowing peremptorily at her. "Please." I looked at her, and to my amazement, relief, and delight, my mother did exactly the right thing. She smiled at Mr. Sumarsono, in a normal and relaxed way, as though they were old friends. She leaned easily back in her chair, graceful — I could suddenly see — and posed. She smoothed the hair back from her forehead.

In Mr. Sumarsono's pictures, the images of us that he produced, this is how we look:

I am staring solemnly at the camera, dead serious, head-on. I look mystified, as though I am trying to understand something inexplicable: what the people around me mean when they speak, perhaps. I look as though I am in a foreign country where I do not speak the language.

Kate looks both radiant and ethereal, her eyes alight. Her mouth is puckered into a mirthful V: she is trying to suppress a smile. The V of her mouth is echoed above her face by her two forked fingers, poised airily behind her head.

But it was the picture of my mother that surprised me the most. Mr. Sumarsono's portrait was of someone entirely different from the person I knew, though the face was the same. Looking at it gave me the feeling that the stopped escalator did: a sense of dislocation, a sudden uncertainty about my own beliefs. In the photograph my mother leans back against her chair like a queen, all her power evident, and at rest. Her face is turned slightly away: she is guarding her privacy. Her nose, her cheeks, her eyes are bright with wine and excitement, but she is calm and amused. A mother cannot be beautiful, because she is so much more a mother than a woman, but in this picture it struck me that my mother looked, in an odd way, beautiful. I could see for the first time that other people might think she actually was beautiful.

Mr. Sumarsono's view of my mother was of a glowing, self-assured, generous woman. And Mr. Sumarsono himself was a real person, despite his meekness. I knew that; I had seen him take control. His view meant something. I could not ignore it. And I began to wonder.

We still have the pictures. Mr. Sumarsono brought them with him the next time he came out for the weekend.

JIM SHEPARD

Batting Against Castro

FROM THE PARIS REVIEW

IN 1951 YOU couldn't get us to talk politics. Ball players then would just as soon talk bed-wetting as talk politics. Tweener Jordan brought up the H-bomb one seventh inning, sitting there tarring up his useless Louisville Slugger at the end of a Bataan Death March of a road trip when it was 104 degrees on the field and about nine of us in a row had just been tied in knots by Maglie and it looked like we weren't going to get anyone on base in the next five weeks except for those hit by pitches, at which point someone down the end of the bench told Tweener to put a lid on it, and he did, and that was the end of the H-bomb as far as the Philadelphia Phillies was concerned.

I was one or two frosties shy of outweighing my bat and wasn't exactly known as Mr. Heavy Hitter; in fact me and Charley Caddell, another Pinemaster from the Phabulous Phillies, were known far and wide as such banjo hitters that they called us — right to our faces, right during a game, like confidence or bucking up a team-mate was for noolies and nosedroops — Flatt and Scruggs. Pick us a tune, boys, they'd say, our own teammates, when it came time for the eighth and ninth spots in the order to save the day. And Charlie and I would grab our lumber and shoot each other looks like we were the Splinter himself, misunderstood by everybody, and up we'd go to the plate against your basic Newcombe or Erskine cannon volleys. Less knowledgeable fans would cheer. The organist would pump through the motions and the twenty-seven thousand who did show up (PHILS WHACKED IN TWI-NIGHTER; SLUMP CONTINUES; LOCALS SEEK TO SALVAGE LAST GAME OF HOME

STAND) wouldn't say boo. Our runners aboard would stand there like they were watching furniture movers. One guy in our dugout would clap. A pigeon would set down in right field and gook around. Newcombe or Erskine would look in at us like litter was blowing across their line of sight. They'd paint the corners with a few unhittable ones just to let us know what a mismatch this was. Then Charley would dink one to second. It wouldn't make a sound in the glove. I'd strike out. And the fans would cuff their kids or scratch their rears and cheer. It was like they were celebrating just how bad we could be.

I'd always come off the field looking at my bat, trademark up, like I couldn't figure out what happened. You'd think by that point I would've. I tended to be hitting about .143.

Whenever we were way down, in the 12-to-2 range, Charley played them up, our sixth- or seventh- or, worse, ninth-inning Waterloos — tipped his cap and did some minor posing — and for his trouble got showered with whatever the box seats didn't feel like finishing: peanuts, beer, the occasional hot-dog roll. On what was the last straw before this whole Cuba thing, after we'd gone down one-two and killed a bases-loaded rally for the second time that day, the boxes around the dugout got so bad that Charley went back out and took a curtain call, like he'd clubbed a round-tripper. The fans howled for parts of his body. The Dodgers across the way laughed and pointed. In the time it took Charley to lift his cap and wave someone caught him in the mouth with a metal whistle from a Cracker Jack box and chipped a tooth.

"You stay on the pine," Skip said to him while he sat there trying to wiggle the ivory in question. "I'm tired of your antics." Skip was our third-year manager who'd been through it all, seen it all, and lost most of the games along the way.

"What's the hoo-ha?" Charley wanted to know. "We're down eleven–nothing."

Skip said that Charley reminded him of Dummy Hoy, the deaf-mute who played for Cincinnati all those years ago. Skip was always saying things like that. The first time he saw me shagging flies he said I was the picture of Skeeter Scalzi.

"Dummy Hoy batted .287 lifetime," Charley said. "I'll take that anytime."

The thing was, we were both good glove men. And this was the

Phillies. If you could do anything right, you were worth at least a spot on the pine. After Robin Roberts, our big gun on the mound, it was Katie bar the door.

"We're twenty-three games back," Skip said. "This isn't the time for bush league stunts."

It was late in the season, and Charley was still holding that tooth and in no mood for a gospel from Skip. He let fly with something in the abusive range, and I, I'm ashamed to say, became a disruptive influence on the bench and backed him up.

Quicker than you could say Wally Pipp, we were on our way to Allentown for some Double A discipline.

Our ride out there was not what you'd call high-spirited. The Allentown bus ground gears and did ten, tops. It really worked over those switchbacks on the hills to maximize the dust coming through the windows. Or you could shut the windows and bake muffins.

Charley was across the aisle, sorting through the paper. He'd looked homicidal from the bus station on.

"We work on our hitting, he's got to bring us back," I said. "Who else has he got?" Philadelphia's major league franchise was at that point in pretty bad shape, with a lot of kids filling gaps left by the hospital patients.

Charley mentioned an activity involving Skip's mother. It colored the ears of the woman sitting in front of us.

It was then I suggested the winter leagues, Mexico or Cuba.

"How about Guam?" Charley said. "How about the Yukon?" He hawkered out the window.

Here was my thinking: the season was almost over in Allentown, which was also, by the way, in the cellar. We probably weren't going back up afterwards. That meant that starting October we either cooled our heels playing pepper in Pennsylvania or we played winter ball. I was for Door Number Two.

Charley and me, we had to do something about our self-esteem. It got so I'd wince just to see my name in the sports pages — before I knew what it was about, just to see my name. Charley's full name was Charles Owen Caddell, and he carried a handsome suitcase around the National League that had his initials, C.O.C., in big letters near the handle. When asked what they stood for, he always said, "Can o' Corn."

Skip we didn't go to for fatherly support. Skip tended to be hard on the non-regulars, who he referred to as "you egg-sucking noodle-hanging gutter trash."

Older ball players talked about what it was like to lose it: the way your teammates would start giving you the look, the way you could see in their eyes, Three years ago he'd make that play, or, He's lost a step going to the hole; the quickness isn't there. The difference was, Charley and me, we'd seen that look since we were twelve.

So Cuba seemed like the savvy move: a little seasoning, a little time in the sun, some señoritas, drinks with hats, maybe a curve ball Charley *could* hit, a heater I could do more than foul off.

Charley took some convincing. He'd sit there in the Allentown dugout, riding the pine even in Allentown, whistling air through his chipped tooth and making faces at me. This Cuba thing was stupid, he'd say. He knew a guy played for the Athletics went down to Mexico or someplace, drank a cup of water with bugs in it that would've turned Dr. Salk's face white, and went belly-up between games of a double-header. "Shipped home in a box they had to *seal*," Charley said. He'd tell that story, and his tooth would whistle for emphasis.

But really what other choice did we have? Between us we had the money to get down there, and I knew a guy on the Pirates who was able to swing the connections. I finished the year batting .143 in the bigs and .167 in Allentown. Charley hit his weight and pulled off three errors in an inning his last game. When we left, our Allentown manager said, "Boys, I hope you hit the bigs again. Because we sure can't use you around here."

So down we went on the train and then the slow boat, accompanied the whole way by a catcher from the Yankee system, a big bird from Minnesota named Ericksson. Ericksson was out of Triple A and apparently had a fan club there because he was so fat. I guess it had gotten so he couldn't field bunts. He said the Yankee brass was paying for this. They thought of it as a fat farm.

"The thing is, I'm not fat," he said. We were pulling out of some skeeter-and-water stop in central Florida. One guy sat on the train platform with his chin on his chest, asleep or dead. "That's the thing. What I am is big boned." He held up an arm and squeezed it the way you'd test a melon.

"I like having you in the window seat," Charley said, his Allentown hat down over his eyes. "Makes the whole trip shady."

Ericksson went on to talk about feet. This shortened the feel of
the trip considerably. Ericksson speculated that the smallest feet in
the history of the major leagues belonged to Art Herring, who wore
a size 3. Myril Hoag, apparently, wore one size 4 and one size 4½.

We'd signed a deal with the Cienfuegos club: seven hundred a
month and two-fifty for expenses. We also got a place on the beach,
supposedly, and a woman to do the cleaning, though we had to
pay her bus fare back and forth. It sounded a lot better than the
Mexican League, which had teams with names like Coatzacoalcos.
Forget the Mexican League, Charley'd said when I brought it up.
Once I guess he'd heard some retreads from that circuit talking
about the Scorpions, and he'd said, "They have a team with that
name?" and they'd said no.

When Ericksson finished with feet he wanted to talk politics. Not
only the whole Korean thing — truce negotiations, we're on a
thirty-one-hour train ride with a Swedish glom who wants to talk
truce negotiations — but this whole thing with Cuba and other
Latin American countries and Kremlin expansionism. Ericksson
could get going on Kremlin expansionism.

"Charley's not much on politics," I said, trying to turn off the
spigot.

"You can talk politics if you want," Charley said from under his
hat. "Talk politics. I got a degree. I can keep up. I got a B.S. from
Schenectady." The B.S. stood for Boots and Shoes, meaning he
worked in a factory.

So there we were in Cuba. Standing on the dock, peering into
the sun, dragging our big duffel bags like dogs that wouldn't co-
operate.

We're standing there sweating on our bags and wondering where
the team rep who's supposed to meet us is, and meanwhile a riot
breaks out about a block and a half away. We thought it was a block
party at first. This skinny guy in a pleated white shirt and one of
those cigar-ad pointed beards was racketing away at the crowd,
which was yelling and carrying on. He was over six feet. He looked
strong, wiry, but in terms of heft somewhere between flyweight and
poster child. He was scoring big with some points he was making
holding up a bolt of cloth. He said something that got them all
going and up he went onto somebody's shoulders, and they pa-
raded him around past the storefronts, everybody shouting "Castro!
Castro! Castro!" which Charley and me figured was the guy's name.

We were still sitting there in the sun like idiots. They circled around past us and stopped. They got quiet, and we looked at each other. The man of the hour was giving us his fearsome bandito look. He was tall. He was skinny. He was just a kid. He didn't look at all happy to see us.

He looked about ready to say something that was not any kind of welcome when the *policía* waded in, swinging clubs like they were getting paid by the concussion. Which is when the riot started. The team rep showed up. We got hustled out of there.

We got there, it turned out, a few weeks into the season. Cienfuegos was a game down in the loss column to its big rival, Marianao. Charley called it Marianne.

Cuba took more than a little getting used to. There was the heat: one team we played had a stadium that sat in a kind of natural bowl that held in the sun and dust. The dust floated around you like a golden fog. It glittered. Water streamed down your face and back. Your glove dripped. One of our guys had trouble finding the plate, and while I stood there creeping in on the infield dirt, sweat actually puddled around my feet.

There were the fans: one night they pelted each other and the field with live snakes.

There were the pranks: as the outsiders, Charley and me expected the standards — the shaving-cream-in-the-shoe, the multiple hotfoot — but even so, never got tired of the bird-spider-in-the-cap, or the crushed-chiles-in-the-water-fountain. Many's the time, after such good-natured ribbing from our Latino teammates, we'd still be holding our ribs, toying with our bats, and wishing we could identify the particular jokester in question.

There was the travel: the bus trips to the other side of the island that seemed to take short careers. I figured Cuba, when I figured it at all, like something about the size of Long Island, but I was not close. During one of those trips Ericksson, the only guy still in a good mood, leaned over his seat back and gave me the bad news: if you laid Cuba over the eastern United States, he said, it'd stretch from New York to Chicago. Or something like that.

And from New York to Chicago the neighborhood would go right down the toilet, Charley said, next to me.

Sometimes we'd leave right after a game, I mean without showering, and that meant no matter how many open windows you were able to manage, you smelled bad feet and armpit all the way there and all the way back. On the mountain roads and switchbacks we counted roadside crosses and smashed guardrails on the hairpin turns. One time Charley, his head out the window to get any kind of air, looked way down into an arroyo and kept looking. I asked him what he could see down there. He said a glove and some bats.

And finally there was what Ericksson called A Real Lack of Perspective. He was talking, of course, about that famous South of the Border hotheadedness we'd all seen even in the bigs. In our first series against Marianao after Charley and I joined the team (the two of us went two for twenty-six, and we got swept; so much for gringos to the rescue), an argument at home plate — not about whether the guy was out, but about whether the tag had been too hard — brought out both managers, both benches, one or two retirees from both teams, a blind batboy who kept feeling around everyone's legs for the discarded lumber, a drunk who'd been sleeping under the stands, reporters, a photographer, a couple of would-be beauty queens, the radio announcers, and a large number of interested spectators. I forget how it came out.

After we dropped a double-header in Havana our manager had a pot broken over his head. It turned out the pot held a plant, which he kept and replanted. After a win at home our starting third baseman was shot in the foot. We asked our manager, mostly through sign language, why. He said he didn't know why they picked the foot.

But it was more than that, too: on days off we'd sit in our hammocks and look out our floor-to-ceiling windows and our screened patios and smell our garden with its flowers with the colors from Mars and the breeze with the sea in it, and we'd feel like DiMaggio in his penthouse, as big league as big league could get. We'd fish on the coral reefs for yellowtail and mackerel, for shrimp and rock lobster. We'd cook it ourselves. Ericksson started eating over, and he did great things with coconut and lime and beer.

And our hitting began to improve.

One for five, one for four, two for five, two for five with two doubles: the box scores were looking up and up, Spanish or not. One night we went to an American restaurant in Havana, and on the place on the check for comments I wrote, *I went 3 for 5 today.*

Cienfuegos went on a little streak: nine wins in a row, fourteen out of fifteen. We caught and passed Marianao. Even Ericksson was slimming down. He pounced on bunts and stomped around home plate like a man killing bees before gunning runners out. We were on a winner.

Which is why politics, like it always does, had to stick its nose in. The president of our tropical paradise, who reminded Charley more of Akim Tamiroff than Harry Truman, was a guy named Batista, who was not well liked. This we could tell because when we said his name even in our cracked Spanish our teammates would repeat it and then spit on the ground or our feet. We decided to go easy on the political side of things and keep mostly mum on the subject of our opinions, which we mostly didn't have. Ericksson threatened periodically to get us all into trouble, or worse, a discussion, except his Spanish was even more terrible than ours, and the first time he tried to talk politics everyone agreed absolutely with what he was saying and then brought him a bedpan.

Neither of us, as I said before, were much for the front of the newspaper, but you didn't have to be Mr. News to see that Cuba was about as bad as it got in terms of who was running what: the payoffs got to the point where we figured that guys getting sworn in for public office put their hands out instead of up. We paid off local mailmen to get our mail. We paid off traffic cops to get through intersections. It didn't seem like the kind of thing that could go on forever, especially since most of the Cubans on the island didn't get expense money.

So this Batista — "Akim" to Charley — wasn't doing a good job, and it looked like your run-of-the-mill Cuban was hot about that. He kept most of the money for himself and his pals. If you were on the outs and needed food or medicine it was pretty much your hard luck. And according to some of our teammates, when you went to jail — for whatever, for spitting on the sidewalk — bad things happened to you. Relatives wrote you off.

So there were a lot of protests, *demostraciones,* that winter, and driving around town in cabs we always seemed to run into them, which meant trips out to eat or to pick up the paper might run half a day. It was the only non-fineable excuse for showing up late to the ballpark.

But then the demonstrations started at the games, in the stands. And guess who'd usually be leading them, in his little pleated shirt and a Marianao cap? We'd be two or three innings in, and the crowd out along the third-base line would suddenly get up like the chorus in a Busby Berkeley musical and start singing and swaying back and forth, their arms in the air. The first time it happened Batista himself was in the stands watching the game, surrounded by like forty bodyguards. He had his arms crossed and was staring over at Castro, who had *his* arms crossed and was staring back. Charley was at the plate, and I was on deck.

Charley walked over to me, bat still on his shoulder. I'm not sure anybody had called time. The pitcher was watching the crowd, too. "Now what is this?" Charley wanted to know.

I told him it could have been a religious thing, or somebody's birthday. He looked at me. "I mean like a national hero's, or something," I said.

He was still peering over at Castro's side of the crowd, swinging his bat to keep limber, experimenting with that chipped-tooth whistle. "What're they saying?" he asked.

"It's in Spanish," I said.

Charley shook his head and then shot a look over to Batista on the first-base side. "Akim's gonna love this," he said. But Batista sat there like this happened all the time. The umpire straightened every inch of clothing behind his chest protector and then had enough and started signaling play to resume, so Charley got back into the batter's box, dug in, set himself, and unloaded big time on the next pitch and put it on a line without meaning to into the crowd on the third-base side. A whole side of the stands ducked, and a couple people flailed and went down like they were shot. You could see people standing over them.

Castro in the meantime stood in the middle of this with his arms still folded, like Peary at the Pole, or Admiral Whoever taking grapeshot across the bow. You had to give him credit.

Charley stepped out of the box and surveyed the damage, cringing a little. Behind him I could see Batista, his hands together over his head, shaking them in congratulation.

"Wouldn't you know it," Charley said, still a little rueful. "I finally get a hold of one and zing it foul."

"I hope nobody's dead over there," I said. I could see somebody holding up a hat and looking down, like that was all that was left. Castro was still staring out over the field.

"Wouldn't that be our luck," Charley said, but he did look worried.

Charley ended up doubling, which the third-base side booed, and then stealing third, which they booed even more. While he stood on the bag brushing himself off and feeling quite the pepperpot, Castro stood up and caught him flush on the back of the head with what looked like an entire burrito of some sort. Mashed beans flew.

The crowd loved it. Castro sat back down, accepting congratulations all around. Charley, when he recovered, made a move like he was going into the stands, but no one in the entire stadium went for the bluff. So he just stood there with his hands on his hips, the splattered third baseman pointing him out to the crowd and laughing. He stood there on third and waited for me to bring him home so he could spike the catcher to death. He had onions and probably some ground meat on his cap.

That particular Cold War crisis ended with my lining out, a rocket, to short.

In the dugout afterwards I told Charley it had been that same guy, Castro, from our first day on the dock. He said that that figured, and that he wanted to work on his bat control so he could kill the guy with a line drive if he ever saw him in the stands again.

This Castro came up a lot. There was a guy on the team, a light-hitting left fielder named Rafa, who used to lecture us in Spanish, very worked up. Big supporter of Castro's. You could see he was upset about something. Ericksson and I would nod, like we'd given what he was on about some serious thought, and were just about to weigh in on that very subject. I'd usually end the meetings by giving him a thumbs-up and heading out onto the field. Ericksson knew it was about politics so he was interested. Charley had no patience for it on good days, and hearing this guy bring up Castro didn't help. Every so often he'd say across our lockers, "He wants to know if you want to meet his sister."

Finally Rafa took to bringing an interpreter, and he'd find us at dinners, waiting for buses, taking warm-ups, and up would come the two of them, Rafa and his interpreter, like this was sports day at the UN. Rafa would rattle on while we went about our business, and then his interpreter would take over. His interpreter said things like, "This is not your tropical playground." He said things like, "The government of the United States will come to understand the Cuban people's right to self-determination." He said things like, "The people will rise up and crush the octopus of the North."

"He means the Yankees, Ericksson," Charley said.

Ericksson meanwhile had that big Nordic brow all furrowed, ready to talk politics.

You could see Rafa thought he was getting through. He went off on a real rip, and when he finished the interpreter said only, "The poverty of the people in our Cuba is very bad."

Ericksson hunkered down and said, "And the people think Batista's the problem?"

"Lack of money's the problem," Charley said. The interpreter gave him the kind of look the hotel porter gives you when you show up with seventeen bags. Charley made a face back at him as if to say, Am I right or wrong?

"The poverty of the people is very bad," the interpreter said again. He was stubborn. He didn't have to tell us: on one road trip we saw a town, like a used car lot, of whole families, big families, living in abandoned cars. Somebody had a cradle thing worked out for a baby in an overturned fender.

"What do you want from us?" Charley asked.

"You are supporting the corrupt system," the interpreter said. Rafa hadn't spoken and started talking excitedly, probably asking what'd just been said.

Charley took some cuts and snorted. "Guy's probably been changing everything Rafa wanted to say," he said.

We started joking that poor Rafa'd only been trying to talk about how to hit a curve. They both gave up on us, and walked off. Ericksson followed them.

"Dag Hammarskjöld," Charley said, watching him go. When he saw my face he said, "I read the papers."

But this Castro guy set the tone for the other ballparks. The demonstrations continued more or less the same way (without the burrito) for the last two weeks of the season, and with three games left we found ourselves with a two-game lead on Marianao, and we finished the season guess where, against guess who.

This was a big deal to the fans because Marianao had no imports, no Americans, on their team. Even though they had about seven guys with big league talent, to the Cubans this was David and Goliath stuff. Big America vs. Little Cuba, and our poor Rafa found himself playing for big America.

So we lost the first two games, by ridiculous scores, scores like 18–5 and 16–1. The kind of scores where you're playing out the string after the third inning. Marianao was charged up and we weren't. Most of the Cuban guys on our team, as you'd figure, were a little confused. They were all trying — money was involved here — but the focus wasn't exactly there. In the first game we came unraveled after Rafa dropped a pop-up that went about seven thousand feet up into the sun, and in the second we were just wiped out by a fat forty-five-year-old pitcher that people said when he had his control and some sleep the night before, was unbeatable.

Castro and Batista were at both games. During the seventh-inning stretch of the second game, with Marianao now tied for first place, Castro led the third-base side in a Spanish version of "Take Me out to the Ball Game."

They jeered us — Ericksson, Charley, and me — every time we came up. And the more we let it get to us, the worse we did. Ericksson was pressing, I was pressing, Charley was pressing. So we let each other down. But what made it worse was with every roar after one of our strikeouts, with every stadium-shaking celebration after a ball went through our legs, we felt like we were letting America down, like some poor guy on an infantry charge who can't even hold up the flag, dragging it along the ground. It got to us.

When Charley was up, I could hear him talking to himself: "The kid can still hit. Ball was in on him, but he got that bat head out in front."

When I was up, I could hear the chatter from Charley: "Gotta have this one. This is where we need you, big guy."

On Friday Charley made the last out. On Saturday I did. On Saturday night we went to the local bar that seemed the safest and got paralyzed. Ericksson stayed home, resting up for the rubber match.

Our Cuban skipper had a clubhouse meeting before the last game. It was hard to have a clear-the-air meeting when some of the teammates didn't understand the language, and were half paralyzed with hangovers besides, but they went on with it anyway, pointing at us every so often. I got the feeling the suggestion was that the Americans be benched for the sake of morale.

To our Cuban skipper's credit, and because he was more contrary than anything else, he penciled us in.

Just to stick it in Marianao's ear, he penciled us in the 1-2-3 spots in the order.

The game started around three in the afternoon. It was one of the worst hangovers I'd ever had. I walked out into the Cuban sun, the first to carry the hopes of Cienfuegos and America to the plate, and decided that as a punishment I'd been struck blind. I struck out, though I have only the umpire's say-so on that.

Charley struck out too. Back on the bench he squinted like someone looking into car headlights. "It was a good pitch," he said. "I mean it sounded like a good pitch. I didn't see it."

But Ericksson, champion of clean living, stroked one out. It put the lid on some of the celebrating in the stands. We were a little too hung over to go real crazy when he got back to the dugout, but I think he understood.

Everybody, in fact, was hitting but us. A couple guys behind Ericksson, including Rafa, put together some doubles, and we had a 3–0 lead which stood up all the way to the bottom of the inning, when Marianao batted around and through its lineup and our starter, and went into the top of the second leading 6–3.

Our guys kept hitting, and so did their guys. At the end of seven we'd gone through four pitchers and Marianao five, Charley and I were regaining use of our limbs, and the score was Cuba 11, Land of the Free 9. We got another run on a passed ball. In the ninth we came up one run down, with the sun setting in our eyes over the center field fence and yours truly leading off. The crowd was howling like something I'd never heard before. Castro had everybody up and pointing at me on the third-base side. Their arms went up and down together like they were working some kind of hex. Marianao's pitcher — by now their sixth — was the forty-five-year-old fat guy who'd worked the day before. The bags under his eyes were bigger than mine. He snapped off three nasty curves, and I beat one into the ground and ran down the first-base line with the jeering following me the whole way.

He broke one off on Charley, too, and Charley grounded to first. The noise was solid, a wall. Everyone was waving Cuban flags.

I leaned close to Charley's ear in the dugout. "You gotta lay off those," I said.

He shook his head. "I never noticed anything wrong with my ability to pull the ball on an outside pitch," he said.

"Then you're the only one in Cuba who hasn't," I said.

But in the middle of this local party, with two strikes on him Ericksson hit his second dinger, probably the first time he'd had two in a game since Pony League. He took his time on his home-run trot, all slimmed-down 260 pounds of him, and at the end he did a somersault and landed on home plate with both feet.

For the Marianao crowd it was like the Marines had landed. When the ball left his bat the crowd noise got higher and higher pitched and then just stopped and strangled. You could hear Ericksson breathing hard as he came back to the bench. You could hear the pop of the umpire's new ball in the pitcher's glove.

That sent us into extra innings, a lot of extra innings. It got dark. Nobody scored. Charley struck out with the bases loaded in the sixteenth, and when he came back to the bench someone had poured a beer onto the dugout roof and it was dripping through onto his head. He sat there under it. He said, "I deserve it," and I said, "Yes, you do."

The Marianao skipper overmanaged and ran out of pitchers. He had an outfielder come in and fling a few, and the poor guy walked our eighth and ninth hitters with pitches in the dirt, off the backstop, into the seats. I was up. There was a conference on the mound that included some fans and a vendor. Then there was a roar, and we stretched forward out of the dugout and saw Castro up and moving through the seats to the field. Someone threw him a glove.

He crossed to the mound, and the Marianao skipper watched him come and then handed him the ball when he got there like his relief ace had just come in from the pen. Castro took the outfielder's hat for himself, but that was about it for uniform. The tails of his pleated shirt hung out. His pants looked like Rudolf Valentino's. He was wearing dress shoes.

I turned to the ump. "Is this an exhibition at this point?" I said. He said something in Spanish that I assumed was, "You're in a world of trouble now."

The crowd, which had screamed itself out hours ago, got its second wind. Hurricanes, dust devils, sandstorms in the Sahara — I don't know what the sound was like. When you opened your mouth it came and took your words away.

I looked over at Batista, who was sitting on his hands. How long was this guy going to last if he couldn't even police the national pastime?

Castro toed the rubber, worked the ball in his hand, and stared in at me like he hated everyone I'd ever been associated with.

He was right-handed. He fussed with his cap. He had a windmill delivery. I figured, let him have his fun, and he wound up and cut loose with a fastball behind my head.

The crowd reacted like he'd struck me out. I got out of the dirt and did the pro brushoff, taking time with all parts of my uniform. Then I stood in again, and he broke a pretty fair curve in by my knees, and down I went again.

What was I supposed to do? Take one for the team? Take one for the country? Get a hit, and never leave the stadium alive? He came back with his fastball high, and I thought, enough of this, and tomahawked it foul. We glared at each other. He came back with a changeup — had this guy pitched somewhere, for somebody? — again way inside, and I thought, forget it, and took it on the hip. The umpire waved me to first, and the crowd screamed about it like we were cheating.

I stood on first. The bases were now loaded for Charley. You could see the Marianao skipper wanted Castro off the mound, but what could he do?

Charley steps to the plate, and it's like the fans had been holding back on the real noisemaking up to this point. There are trumpets, cowbells, police whistles, sirens, and the god-awful noise of someone by the foul pole banging two frying pans together. The attention seems to unnerve Charley. I'm trying to give him the old thumbs-up from first, but he's locked in on Castro, frozen in his stance. The end of his bat's making little circles in the air. Castro gave it the old windmill and whipped a curve past his chin. Charley bailed out and stood in again. The next pitch was a curve, too, which fooled him completely. He'd been waiting on the fastball. He started to swing, realized it was curve breaking in on him, and ducked away to save his life. The ball hit his bat anyway. It dribbled out toward Castro. Charley gaped at it and then took off for first.

I took off for second. The crowd shrieked. Ten thousand people, one shriek. All Castro had to do was gun it to first and they were out of the inning. He threw it into right field.

Pandemonium. Our eighth and ninth hitters scored. The ball skipped away from the right fielder. I kept running. The catcher'd gone down to first to back up the throw. I rounded third like Man o' War, Charley not far behind me, the fans spilling out onto the field and coming at us like a wave we were beating to shore. One kid's face was a flash of spite under a Yankee hat, a woman with long scars on her neck was grabbing for my arm. And there was Castro blocking the plate, dress shoes wide apart, Valentino pants crouched and ready, his face scared and full of hate like I was the entire North American continent bearing down on him.

CHRISTOPHER TILGHMAN

Things Left Undone

FROM THE SOUTHERN REVIEW

ON THE MORNING his son was born, Denny McCready walked out to the banks of the Chesapeake to see the dawn. As a farmer does on his endless spirals, lost in meditation to the tractor's unwavering drone, he had been picturing and repicturing this moment for some months. Just as he had imagined, the first yellow light dappling the water was full of promise; he could breathe in the textured Bay air and smell the sharp fragrance of the honeysuckle growing along the fence lines behind him. But his heart was not suddenly filled with the majesty of it all. He looked down at his stained hands, resting without task at his side, and they reminded him of season after season, drought followed by too much rain, sickness and health. He took one last glance across the water to Hail Point, a fragile stand of loblolly pines slowly being undermined by the tides and storms, and then he turned, feeling almost as if his love had been found insufficient even as his son was wet from his first reach lifeward.

Denny began to feel better when he settled in on the telephone, working through the list of friends and family that Susan had prepared weeks ago. On his way through the farmyard he had stopped by the milking parlor, found his father and the hired man, and received a round of congratulations, pats on the back. The baby was named Charles after Denny's father. The sun-creased scowl on the old man's face relaxed for a time into a smoother reflection of satisfaction: it was right for a man to have children, and grandchildren, just as it was right for a farmer to have a dog. The moment was over fairly quickly — it was time to move the milkers to the cows on the other aisle — but as Denny left the others to their labors, he looked back with the sensation that these familiar routines were no longer his, that his life had now slipped slightly out of his control.

A few hours later, showered and shaved, he was back at the hospital. Susan's eyes showed black rings of fatigue, but she had demanded the baby and he lay at her side.

"I don't know how you could sleep at a time like this," she said, assuming that he had. Denny's big round face seemed to eclipse the sun at her window; she could smell the farm on his clothes, a pungent sweetness in contrast to all these metallic fumes. It seemed odd, and wonderful to her, that the future of this rough and self-reliant man would now be softened by a child.

He did not want to tell her about visiting the rivershore. "Why did I have to call Jack Hammond?" he asked. "He seemed surprised and not happy to be woke up."

"He's your uncle," she said.

"My uncle? I haven't seen him since before we graduated. I had to tell him my last name."

"Shh." She looked down at the small bundle, a pointy old man's face rimmed with a red rash, shrouded in a light blue blanket. The baby's eyes were now closed, and when the nurse came in and took him to be checked over by the pediatrician he was so firmly bound in his blanket that he looked stiff, like a mummy.

"Why are you being so ornery?" Susan asked when they were alone.

He wondered why, and he looked around this hospital room, pleasant by any standard he could think of, a whiteness that spoke of hope and a busy hum that sounded like rest. He looked at Susan, drifting off in this borrowed bed; she seemed as haggard and puffy as his mother had when she was dying of cancer, perhaps even in this very same room, nearly ten years earlier. He had the sudden feeling that for families as well as hospital rooms, birth and death were really the same thing. He banished these thoughts, wondering what was next and why it was taking so long, and then the door opened and a trio of doctors walked in. One of them had a sort of pleased look on his face, as if he had just been proven right. When Susan was again alert, the doctors told them that the boy had cystic fibrosis, that his insides and lungs were already plugged, that he might not survive the week, and if he did he would probably not live long enough to enter kindergarten. The doctors — even the smug one — said it kindly, over the period of an hour or so, but that is what they said.

For the first months of his son's life, Denny could barely bring himself to touch him. He heard air passing through those small lips and pictured his lungs as blackened ruins dripping with tar. He watched Susan happily nursing the boy, passing her hand over the smooth contours of his silky head, luxuriating in the weight of the child in her arms. It surprised him that she seemed, at these moments, so satisfied with her baby, despite all that awaited them. On late afternoons, when Denny came home from the fields, he usually found Susan and the baby in the kitchen. Sometimes, even before he entered the house, he could hear the deep jarring thud, thud, thud, of Susan's firm hands on the baby's back, the pre- scribed regimen for loosening what Denny thought of as the crusts and plugs of tar. The boy never seemed to mind this; Susan had learned how to drive the blow through the small body, and not to let it hit with a slap on his skin. But even so, Susan always ended the procedure by rubbing and massaging him, which made him giggle and coo. In time it became part of a sensuality between them, a kind of game, starting her hand down for one more blow, stopping just short and then folding into a caress, her broad palms covering his entire back. When Charlie had begun to talk, he said to his mother, "Smooth me," and Denny watched, almost embar- rassed, as she passed her flesh — the inside of her forearms, her cheeks — over his body.

Back when Charlie was still a newborn, when the first untrou- bled and unknowing smiles began to appear, Denny prayed that this could all happen quickly, before he gave too much of his love, before he surrendered too much of his hope. It took almost to the end of Charlie's life for Denny to realize that this prayer was monstrous, that he had asked for an end of his own pain in the place of a cure for his son. Susan would make him pay for this. But by then Denny had also learned that of all the pain a human can endure, not allowing oneself to feel love is the worst; that denying love to oneself can destroy, from the inside.

In the hospital, during what they had all finally decided would be his last hours or days, Denny sat beside Charlie while Susan went home to eat and perhaps to cry in the solitude of the shower. Charlie was awake, naked except for a diaper, an oxygen tube, and an IV. He was breathing somewhat easily and his eyes were at rest on his father. Denny reached over to take his hand and then began to stroke his small chest, running his fingertips around the cushioned indent of his nipples. Charlie smiled and closed his eyes halfway. "Smooth me, Daddy," he said.

"You O.K.?" he asked. "Can you breathe good?"

"Smooth me, please."

Denny dropped his hand down to the flat, starved stomach, to the navel that had been opened too wide by the poisons concocted from his parents' mingled blood. Charlie held still for those hands, rough and work-stained as they were, as Denny traced the lines of his body. "This is what it feels like here," Denny thought, rubbing the shoulder; "this is a tickle. This is a pat." He even lightly twisted a finger until the eyes reflected irritation and discomfort. He followed the sinews of each leg and then reached the top at the elasticized leg holes of the diapers.

"Smooth me, Daddy," said Charlie, and then Denny realized what the boy was asking him to do, or was it that Denny realized that there was one gift left to bestow? What does it feel like there? What will I miss? Denny could do this for a son, not for a daughter. As the boy, in dreamy rest now, lay still on his sheet, Denny parted the tapes of the diaper and put his hand on his stomach. He traced down to the penis, to the tiny purplish tip, to the vacant scrotum. Denny looked up to Charlie, and the eyes were full of surprise and joy. Denny knew there would be no shame between them, even as the penis became erect, a slight nub of a thing. Denny imagined what he himself liked, how he liked to be touched, and he tried to do it, running his thumb up and down the bottom and closing the tip into his palm. He kept at it, lightly, not even wondering for a second what a doctor or nurse would think, and Charlie finally seemed to fall asleep, a rest full of gratitude, a relief from struggle, a life, as far as it went, full of joy.

In high school, Susan DeLorey's large frame, her big hands and feet, had made her seem heavy. No one would have, or ever did, call her cute. "Solid," they said, referring both to her body and her character. Perhaps marrying Denny, who spent most of his time in those days in bitter combat with his father, was one of the less practical things she had done. But Denny had settled down enough, taken an uneasy but consistent place as a partner in the family dairy, and he had begun to seem acceptable to the town ladies in comparison to the valedictorians and boy scouts who had long ago up and left their families with no warning. And since high school the cute girls, the short and skinny blonds, the pert and sassy ones, had busted out of their blue jeans and peroxide, while Susan's age caught up to her strong-boned features, straight posture, and thick brown hair.

Susan worked as the electric-meter reader for all "non-metro-politan" areas of the county. It took her half-time, on her own time, and if someone invited her in for a cup of coffee and a doughnut, it was her decision to make. They gave her a car, with a whip antenna for its citizen's band radio, which flexed coyly as she drove from farm to farm. She had inherited this deal from her father, and it came with her to the marriage like a dowry. When Denny was courting her, after they had both spent their twenties dating others, she sometimes worried that it was the job he had fallen in love with.

After Charlie was born she contemplated giving the job up, and Denny had persuaded her not to. He said that she needed more than ever to get out of the house and that she could bring the baby along just as they had always planned. When Charlie died she was behind by two or three months on her accounts, and two weeks after the funeral she began to work overtime. For the most part the customers, at least the ones who tended to be home during the day, were friends and admirers of hers. She came back from those first few days of meter reading in a car loaded with hams, and sticky buns, and roasted chickens, and pickled green tomatoes.

One evening, exhausted from a two-hundred-mile day, she was leaning across to gather some of these consoling gestures when she realized that her mind had slipped back in time for a moment, and that she thought she was reaching for Charlie in his car seat. She blinked past the illusion and saw that it was a casserole in her arms, and the hideous image of this food, and the shock of reliving the entire loss in a split second, gripped her in panic and she began to scream.

Denny heard her and came running out, opening the car door

to receive her kicks and punches; he staggered off dazed from a good blow to his right eye, and she came after him, trying to hurt him. The hired hand saw her standing over Denny, kicking at him, and sprinted over the width of the farmyard. They called for Dr. Taylor, and he knocked her out with a full syringe of Nembutal.

Denny was off duty for the morning milking, and he was sitting at her bedside when she woke up. Their bed was a four-poster that had been her grandmother's, and Susan had made muslin curtains with ruffles to match the canopy. She had loved to sew before Charlie was born, lacy things, feminine touches of lace here and there throughout the house as if to mark off a boundary for the odors and substances of farm life. Denny hadn't complained, but to this day, especially this day, he felt as if he slept in her private space. "How do you feel?" he asked.

"My head aches."

"So does mine," he said, rubbing his eye.

"I'm sorry, Denny." She cried rarely, and almost always for others, but this time, her face gripped by her large hands, her elbows clamped against her breasts, Denny could tell that she wept for herself.

"It's all over now. We can look ahead." He meant for these words to soothe, and he repeated them a few times. He didn't feel he needed to argue the point and therefore did not put a lot of emphasis behind them.

She snapped up from her clenched recline and opened her full face to him. "It's that simple for you? You think now that Charlie's gone I'll just let you back?"

Denny knew what she meant, and he knew it wasn't fair, not entirely. She had all too easily let him free of the pain. She had gathered everything that hurt into herself, every one of Charlie's laughs and mangled words. That's mine, she seemed to have said; I'm going to save that one for later. She had gone to each doctor's appointment loaded with questions, and night after night she studied the packets of information from parents' organizations and disease foundations. Denny could only scan these materials, squinting to screen the truths into a blur, looking for mention of a miracle cure. It seemed to Denny that everything in her mind had been backwards. Right up to the day Charlie died, she had continued to help him learn his numbers and letters. Though she must have known that the alphabet would remain half unlearned forever, she seemed capable of staring into the deep almost cheerfully. Denny used to hear her teaching Charlie lessons for use later in life, and he had to cover his ears with his hands. Denny knew what Susan was saying, but it wasn't as simple as she made it sound.

"Are you God now, Susan?"

"No. There's no word for what I am. I'm a mother who lost her child."

Denny almost argued that he was a father who had lost his, but he didn't think the loss was comparable, at least not in their house. He had often wondered what kind of father he would have been if Charlie had been healthy, and whether he would have behaved all that differently. Who knew? But this he could say to the mother who had lost her child: that he was a man who lost the person who would have become his best friend.

"I'm trying," he said finally, "to make you feel better. I want you to feel better." He spoke gingerly, not assuming too much, as if he were sharing her feelings out of kindness.

She heard these tones, and came bounding back. "Why didn't you love him? That was all he asked, to be loved by his mother and father."

Denny thought back to the last months of Charlie's life, and the last night at the hospital. How could she ask that? What could she be thinking of? He had no answer. He looked back at her blankly, and then said, "I'm trying to keep you from losing everything else."

She softened at this, even put out her hand to his. "Maybe you are. But there isn't anything you can do now." She got up, still in the T-shirt and underpants that Denny had left on her the night before. He looked at the curve of her hips and he wanted suddenly to make love, to fall back into bed like newlyweds. He could honestly picture this as something that might make things better, because it had been some years since they had really made love. For many months after Charlie was born they had not even tried, and then occasionally they had joined, and they did not have to remind each other that there was fate in their mingled fluids, they did not need to admit to each other that when Denny was done and had withdrawn, the cold drops of his poisonous semen burned on the sheet between them. They did not need to confess that anytime their flesh touched — a simple caress, a brush of the hands — their thoughts bored deep through the skin and into the code of damaged chromosomes.

Denny believed, as he watched his long-legged wife walk across the bedroom, that they could leave this behind now. He was ready, at this moment, with the sharp tremble of desire. But she closed the door of the bathroom behind her, and then turned on the shower, and when she came back out to the kitchen, she was dressed in her jeans and was holding her account book, number $2\frac{1}{2}$ pencils, a flashlight, can of Halt, and her thermos. "I might be late this afternoon," she said. "I've got to go all the way to Grangerfield."

Charlie died in May, and the long, buttery Chesapeake summer moved through plantings, through the flowering of the soybean plants toward the tasseling of the corn. Denny threw himself into this work, this nurturing, but he stopped the tractor now and again on the rivershore and thought back to that unlucky morning, back to a moment, now jumbled in his memory, when he had hoped that just beginning a life was enough to give it meaning. He made his turns on the tractor, and many times as he approached the riverbank he imagined what would happen if he simply kept going, down over the crumbling yellow clay and onto the pebbled beach, and then into the warm brackish ripples and out onto the sandbars, a mile or two into the Chester River before the water reached higher than his axles.

Susan was often away from the farm these days, even into the early evening, still catching up on her accounts, maybe, or hanging around with old high school friends to whom she'd never before paid the least attention. They all had babies, even big kids now, and after the difficulty of getting pregnant in the first place, and then Charlie, Denny could hardly imagine Susan wanting to spend time in someone else's happy chaos. But he had nothing better to offer, the gray silence of the house, the farm. As Susan said earlier in the summer, the real crop on this family farm was death. She said they weren't living there anymore as much as waiting to see who went next: the logical one — Denny's father; the unnecessary one — Susan; or the unexpected one — Denny himself. None of them had gained anything other than front-pew seats at the funerals. She said that Denny could not offer life to her, or she to him, the promise of it, and he knew well enough what she meant.

Evening after evening, after milking, Denny walked the length of the farmyard in the knowledge that the three men on the place, himself, his father, and the latest teenage hand, were all heading home to empty houses.

"It appears that your wife ain't spending too much time at home these days," said Denny's father on one of those evenings in August. They were standing in the roadway between their two houses, and the heat in the parlor had drained them both. He wasn't being hostile calling her "your wife"; he was of an older school.

"Her private affairs are her business," Denny argued.

The old man agreed. "I'm not anyone to pry."

"But what?" said Denny.

"Things have to be managed, don't they?" his father asked back. This was an old point, his refrain from the years when Denny fought against him and against the endless repetitive details of the farm life.

"You don't manage a marriage like fences and Johnson grass, Dad. There's nothing I can do."

The old man gave him the same disappointed look that he had worn during those arguments in his teenage years, and Denny simply stared back, as he had done years ago. "There is always something," said his father, his eyes filling.

Denny nodded once more, and took those words home with him, across the broad lawn, and waited up for Susan to come back. It was seven-thirty when she pulled in. She was wearing her pale green shirt, with a new satiny scarf tied over the tops of her shoulders. She was carrying a sack of groceries, and she started to put them away, a bag of flour, a few cans of corned beef hash, frozen vegetables, without greeting him. He wondered if she thought of him anymore as she walked up and down the aisles of Acme, what he liked; he could not imagine her putting much attention on shared meals, just on food, just on the common need to eat something.

"Sue," he said.

"Huh?"

"I'm not stupid. I'm trying to help." She seemed not to pick up on his invitation to confess. He added, "You can trust me."

She glanced over; the light was beginning to fade and neither of them had turned on a lamp. "I never said you were stupid."

"So where are we at?"

"I think we're just floating, as long as you ask what I think. I think I'm just waiting. I don't think anything that has happened all summer is real."

"I'm dairying," he stated. "That's real."

"Denny, as long as you ask —"

"I am," he interrupted. "I am asking."

"Well I'm seeing someone. I'm seeing someone who makes me feel better."

The truth hit his gut; he could not deny that. But he could also not deny that he and Mandy Towle, in the occasional circling and looping through lives in small towns, had fallen together a few times over the years. "Why?" he asked.

She shrugged.

"Don't think I don't know why you are doing this. Another man."

Her eyes darted, but she only shook her head and told him that he could not possibly know what she was thinking.

"You're going to leave me behind, is that it?"

"Stop."

"Throw me off like a Kleenex?"

She did not respond to this right away, but continued to lean against the kitchen counter as she considered things, and she began slowly to get more and more angry, and Denny could not divine if it was because he had located her private truth, but at last she wheeled around for something to throw at him, and came up with a canister of flour, which would have been almost funny, an explosion of white mist. Denny waited, readying himself to avoid the sharp edges of the tin, but after a few moments she put it down. "You asshole," she said, and went into her bedroom.

Denny slept, as he had been doing for a month or two, in the spare room. In the morning he leaned into her room and said, "I'm sorry. You can do what you like. That's all I wanted to say." But she was already gone.

Denny had a gift for machines. Before he was out of his teens, other farmers, even mechanics in town, began to seek him out to perform magic with a welder and metal lathe. He could do this, engineering answers not on paper but with his hands. The shop, from which these bits of genius came, was at the end of the barn complex closest to his house. It had been the granary, and the walls were still lined with rodent-proof tin. There was a single low window that looked down toward the creek, and in the afternoon, when the light came sideways, orange off the water, the grease-shined floor and tin walls glowed, a radiance that started at the feet and worked upward as the sun fell. Early in Denny's marriage, his friends used to gather in the shop on winter Saturdays, drinking beer around someone's project, and the women gathered with Susan, cooking and drinking wine and Irish Mist, and after everyone staggered home and after he and Susan had made love a little on the dirty side, Denny lay back in the four-poster and thought the future was offering itself to him not in years, which no one could predict, but in seasons, certain and always new.

The winter Susan was living in town — she had moved in with her friend Beth on Raymond Street, but spent most of her time in Chestertown — Denny closed himself into his shop. The maw of the vise stayed open, and the roller chest of Snap-On tools remained untouched. Often, at the end of milking, he went straight there, sat down in his cold Morris chair and stared out the low window across the lawn and to the creek, to the black winter water lapping at a brittle rim of tidal ice. Occasionally, when the weather wasn't too cold, Denny slept the night in that chair, and then, painfully stiff and foul-breathed, he stole over to the house for breakfast, eating quietly as if she were asleep behind the thin partition of the kitchen. Early in the fall he went into town a few times to see Mandy Towle. They'd always liked each other, and she deserved a lot better than two failed marriages, one of them to a man from Kent County who was now in jail for house-renovation schemes that preyed on the elderly. She deserved a lot better than Denny, in these circumstances, which they both understood. She sent him home the last time, back to his shop, with a sisterly hug.

His father often stopped in to check on him, and occasionally sat down to talk. They stayed on dairying, for the most part, which wasn't a subject that held a lot more cheer than the remains of Denny's family life. "Just sell the goddamn place," Denny said once; "sell out and move to Florida. You deserve it." When his father hid his eyes, Denny knew the old man still hoped for the best.

"Do you think she's going to come back?" Denny asked. He knew that Susan had called his father once or twice.

"I expect what she's going through has a shape of its own."

Denny and Susan talked when they ran into each other in the street, and people could look out the windows of Todman's Insurance or Latshaw's Jewelers or Price and Gammon Hardware and see them meeting like old sweethearts. The town was full of these almost forgotten couplings, kids who had maybe once or twice fucked each other in his father's haywagon, or all winter long in her father's Buick, and what remained was a county full of people who treated each other like siblings, with the accidental intimacy of brothers and sisters who had shared the same bathroom. That's how it felt to Denny, meeting Susan on the street, and she seemed to want it that way, as if by wiping out their marriage she could eliminate her pain. Time, after all, had run out on them, had perhaps been running out on them for years: quality time, as the doctor said, had given way to the dry consolations of memory. "Until death do us part" would perhaps, despite love, turn out to be not long enough.

Denny brought these thoughts back into his workshop, these repetitious looping stabs at reason, all these variations on history. He tried to make sense of it, but he was finally bored by this hibernation and, as if in prayer, his thoughts began to wander. He could not say exactly from where or why the idea had come to him, but as the first stirrings of warmer weather came on the March winds, he realized that he had begun to concentrate more and more on the water, of the highways it offered, down the Bay perhaps, and out to sea. His father hated the water; most farmers did. All it did was steal away land, a furrow or two between planting and harvesting in stormy summers. Kids went out on the water to drink beer. Watermen went out there to do God knew what. The Bay, that long question mark out there beyond Kent Island: Denny's father had raised him to believe the Bay was not only wet and dangerous but immoral, a slippery surface choppy with wasted money.

But the water called to Denny. It seemed to offer refreshment for his soul; it was as if he had recognized that he had been looking at only the land side of his life all these years, and had been missing what was perhaps the fuller half. He spent hours imagining boats, revarnishing and repainting the woodwork, overhauling the engine in the cooked odors of a clean bilge. He could not imagine why, up to now, he had never been curious about them. They seemed self-contained and sufficient, at once economical in space but extravagant with amenity.

In late spring Denny got in touch with the watermen at the Centreville landing, for whom he had repaired and built all sorts of labor-saving devices, and told them he wanted a workboat. The watermen were willing to help him, an intruder on the water, as long as he didn't tell anyone; when they found a good boat in Crisfield, they brought it up for him at night.

The following day, after knockoff, he drove it in the creek and dropped anchor at the farm. His father, as Denny had expected, was standing on the creekbank ten minutes later.

"What in hell is this?" the old man yelled.

Denny paddled over in a dinghy that had been thrown into the deal and stood beside his father to admire the boat. It looked like a destroyer, a dropping curve that started high and fixed at the bowsprit and then seemed to go on forever, like a view. "It's a boat," said Denny finally.

The old man was speechless; all the slack he'd given to Denny this winter, and this was what came of it, a boat? Like some god-damn rich Philadelphian? "Just tell me what in hell you mean to do with it."

"I don't know, Dad," said Denny. It was the truth. One thing Denny had learned during his winter months was to tell the truth. "Maybe I'll do some crabbing. Maybe you and me will go out and have picnics," he shouted as his father retreated back up the lawn to his house. "Maybe you and me will take it through the Narrows and down the Bay. Maybe we'll just keep going south."

For the next six or seven Sundays, through May and into the first heat of June, Denny threw himself into his project. He had never had much regard for watermen as mechanics: they tended to make repairs under way with Vise-Grips and then forget about them when they returned to port. Denny was delighted to have so much to do. His father continued to grumble for a week or two, but relented in the end to the point of putting an aluminum lawn chair under the shade of the lone mulberry tree and passing his Sundays on the bank. Occasionally they chatted with each other across the few feet of water.

One day in June, Denny had his head deep into dark thwarts of the hull when he heard the scrape of the lawn chair over the shells and pebbles of the bank. He assumed it was his father and did not come up for twenty minutes, and when he did finally it was Susan he saw. She was wearing a yellow shirt, which made her dark hair shine. Denny could not believe how lovely she looked, a wife on the shore awaiting a sailor returning from a long cruise. He poled his flat-bottomed dinghy to her.

"I see you've got yourself a project." She was humoring him, as if the boat were childish, like electric trains.

"It feels good to be fixing something, for a change." He came down hard on the last word.

She looked over at him, and betrayed no emotions. She was wearing white pants and earrings, and Denny could smell the slight shade of her perfume.

"So who you dressing up for today?" he said.

She gave him no answer, no anger, no hurt. "Denny, a lot has happened to us, hasn't it?"

He shrugged, but it was clear to him that she had said this in preparation for something. Asking for a divorce, most likely. Get the unpleasantness over with, then drive back out to Route 50 and meet up with her accountant from Chestertown, or whatever he was, the person she dressed up for.

She continued. "None of it made much sense, did it? I mean, why did Charlie have to die?"

"Charlie's dying is the only thing that made any sense at all," Denny snapped back. "He had cystic fibrosis. Remember? What happened to him started happening from the moment he was conceived. It's a disease that began millions of years ago, some cell or something that crawled out of the water ass-backwards. Who the hell knows where it come from?" Denny realized he was shouting. "Charlie made sense, Sue. It's what happened to us in the meantime that doesn't make sense."

She raised her hands, almost as helplessly as if shielding herself from a pistol shot. "O.K., O.K.," she yelled. "What happened to us. You want to whip my ass, Denny. Do it."

They looked at each other for a few minutes across the oily shine of the boat's pistons, laid out on a rag.

"What I mean is," she began again, "that we've lived through some times I never expected, and we've done things I never imagined doing."

He shrugged, but she was right enough about that, right enough to say that everything she had done or thought since Charlie was born was contrary to logic, especially treating Denny as if he were to blame for it.

"I want to come home," she said. "I haven't seen anyone since Christmas," she added.

"Why?"

"Because it doesn't make me feel better. I still want to die," she said. Her radiance, from a distance, had been an illusion. She looked very bad, haggard and worn out from within. Denny wondered if she had been looking this miserable all winter and whether he was just now noticing because he had turned the corner. But he did not want to feel sorry for her yet. He got up, grabbed a handful of oyster shells, and flung them in a spray far across the water. A heron, feeding in the green shade of the other side of the creek, took this as a sign that it ought to move on, and it leaned forward, chest almost on the water, and then kicked its long legs into the flapping of its wings. It skimmed slow, unlikely, doomed, until it busted out into the sunlight and headed out to the rivershore.

"Jesus," said Denny finally. "You've slapped me from one side of this county to the other; I'm so bruised by you that my piss is purple. There's some mercy in this somewhere, isn't there?"

She looked at him and nodded, and it was a look he had not seen in a long time. She could not have been offering herself as mercy, but as faith. Her eyes suggested, her head tipped toward the house, but still he could ignore these gestures and they could vanish as if they had been nothing. Denny did not know how to tell her yes; instead, he nodded back at her, and if she expected the beginning of caress on the way across the lawn, she did not show it. As they entered the bedroom, Denny was telling himself, as he had not done in many years, that he would soon make love to this woman in front of him.

She undressed with her back to him and turned to face him. He had forgotten the strength of her body, how broad and powerful she looked across her upper chest, how quick and nimble she looked at the tuck of her waist, how sufficient and frank she looked from the stretched points of her hipbones to the inside of her thighs. Denny had also undressed, and she gave him a little smile as they stood and looked at each other across the room. Her eyes dropped to his penis, and his to the patch of her pubic hair, and he pictured the outstretched arms of her tubes, the encyclopedia drawings with each ovary clutched at the curled extreme, and he pictured a line of eggs like pearls, some perfect, some flawed, ready to drop one by one into potential life, and then beyond. He pictured the grip of her uterus. She was looking at his penis, and he knew she also was tracing backwards to unanswered questions of that genetic disease, following on the long circuitous route to his balls, where there were sperm cells by the billions, enough to conceive an epidemic.

They stood facing each other, naked as if new, and they understood that they needed far more than pleasure to make him erect and to open her to him. And with that understanding, pleasure did come to him, and she smiled again, this time more slyly, as he stiffened.

"Hello, Denny," she said, a joke from long ago.

He said nothing — this was as always — as they finally joined on the bed. He traced her lines, and searched for wetness and warmth, and very soon she was sliding one leg under him, and he did not ask what she knew about this minute in her month, and did not ask whether she had, in anticipation of this moment, driven over with her diaphragm in place, and did not ask whether she might want him to hunt through the bedstand for a condom. He allowed himself to be guided in. They rested for a moment, centered and tied in this way. He began to move, and long before he thought he was ready for an orgasm he was ejaculating inside her, and he pictured it not as a burst but as a showering, a mist like soft rain. Susan felt him come, and she too imagined what was happening inside her body, and it was a tumbling she thought of first, like the tumbling of an egg on its passage outward, and then — though she had not expected it — pleasure came to her also, and she pictured a wall, a brick wall slowly giving way to his continued motion and to the rhythmic encouragement of her own flesh.

Two months later, on a Sunday, Susan sat on the porch and looked across the barnyard to the water. She could see out the creek, across the wide mouth of the river to Eastern Neck, and then, on clear days such as this one, across the dark line of the Bay and toward the smudged air of Baltimore. She knew Denny would be out there somewhere on his boat, but when she glanced up, she could not see him. She had a cup of coffee resting precariously on her thigh, and was reading the *Sun* in the streams of September light; she was warmed by the sensations and was happy to read the movie reviews, though she went to the show only rarely, with her friends Beth and Delia from town, and when she did the other two spent the whole time making silly cracks about how beautiful the male actors were and how skinny the women.

When Susan thought about love and men these days, and about the past year, and about her son, her thoughts came ordered like a liturgy. It was necessary, in terms of fairness, for her to start always with her own general confession, with a listing of the things she had done. She did not think having an affair with Jack Marston was a particularly kind or clever thing to do. But Susan, as she considered these things, also had to go forward and admit that she had at least taken up once again a hope for the future because of it. Once she had confessed, she could proceed to a thanksgiving, to say that she was grateful that Denny had given her what he could, freedom if not understanding; and then, because Susan did not blink at herself or at Denny or at the eternal pain losing a child had caused her, she gave thanks that Jack Marston had been there, because in retrospect, without him she might have done something even less clever, killed herself maybe. And finally, in her supplications, she could pray for the people in her life, for Denny's health and happiness, her mother and his father, for her sisters and their children. But not for herself, yet. She did not know what she wanted next; she did not know whether this move back, which she had done a few weeks after they made love, would work. She was waiting patiently for a sign. All she knew was that she feared nothing: she would never again be afraid, just a little hesitant, just a little reluctant to invite notice or comment.

She glanced down the length of the barns, silver in the morning light, and watched her father-in-law wash his car. He did this every Sunday morning in his milking clothes, before changing and then sleeping in front of the television. He had, last winter, called her a "loose woman." She had not argued with him; if she had she would have told him that ever since Charlie had been born it seemed everyone on the place simply wanted her gone, and that she had done precisely that. She might have tried to explain to him that she had taken with her all those bits of Charlie's life that needed a resting place somewhere far from the farm. But during her marriage she'd never argued with Denny's father, and he had a dim talent for her ways of thinking. Susan had always thought of her father-in-law as a child, and girl-child at that, with a front tooth missing from her occasional frightened smile, a sort of waif trapped in an old man's rough and blemished body.

When Susan came back out onto the porch from filling her coffee cup, she saw that the old man had finished with his car, had walked down the long lawn to the water and was staring out into the river. With his jug ears, his hearing had always been remarkable; he could sit in the barnyard and tell, from nothing audible to her, that the baler had broken down on the point field or that the hired hand was now in fourth gear on the Kubota and was heading for home. Perhaps he had heard Denny's boat coming in. It was a restful sight, the man under the waterside mulberry tree.

He turned slightly as she approached and then looked back out to the river.

"Is he coming in?" she asked.

"Sounded like it."

She took up her place beside him. The water was dappled gold; the slight onshore breeze was clean, clean but rich, like the air that came with the fresh-shucked oysters she used to buy for frying. She could smell the fresh milk warming on her father-in-law's clothes. "Do you see him?"

He waved his hand outward. There were several boats in view, indistinguishable to her except, perhaps, for the sailboats way over by the Narrows.

"What's he up to, with this boat?" the old man asked. He began by spitting out the words, but ended with a genuine question.

She stopped halfway around. "He likes being out on the water. He thinks it will save him."

The old man protested, this time with the beginning of a sarcastic snarl. "Save him from what? Seems to me what will save us —"

She put her hand out onto his shoulder and he stopped abruptly. They both looked at her hand, big, strong, a mother's hand, resting on his thinning frame, the white of her flesh against the green of his chino jacket. They both recognized that she had never done this before, that except for some early handshakes and the usual bumps in the narrow parlor when she filled in at milking, they had never touched in any way. A slight breeze, flavored with cattle, rose up behind them. It seemed almost miraculous for them to be joined on this small point of land.

"Denny always took things hard," he said, after she had withdrawn. "That's all I'm trying to say."

Susan thought about Denny for a second, the man high in the tractor or deep, confident with his tools, in the guts of the combine.

"I don't suspect you know that he was a soft boy. He liked to be held by his mama."

Susan had guessed this, but it made tears come to her eyes anyway.

"By the time you knew him, he was fresh enough," said the old man. He pulled out a handkerchief — a washrag they used to clean the teats before plugging them into the milkers — and held it out for her. She knew what it was, still damp with disinfectant, and she took it. "He was even softer than his sisters. One year he planted a flower garden over behind the equipment bays and he made bouquets and vases of flowers, you know, to give. It was a girlish thing to do," the man said, sounding as confused now, and as unsure, as he must have thirty years ago, a dairy farmer with a boy who loved flowers. "The teachers were partial to him."

Susan listened, and waited for more, wanted these images to do their job, feeling as if these tears could be the ones she had been waiting for all this time.

"If I had it to do over again . . ." he began, and then stopped. Neither of them needed him to describe how he had reacted to this child.

"What?" she asked. She brought her hand to her face and felt the oily release of mucus on her fingertips.

"Sometimes I look at him and I catch a glimpse of that soft boy. In his eyes, I expect. It's like he is asking me for something. I always figured he would get it from his own family, but that wasn't to be. I always hoped you could make it right."

"I —" she said, ready to tell him she couldn't do it alone, but he talked past her.

"I wish you could see the boy like I do," he interrupted.

He had ended on a sort of question, a plea perhaps, and now seemed to want her to respond. But she no longer had anything to say, no answers to a father so troubled by his son, no apologies to a father who loved his boy. They waited as she blew her nose, and they both turned their stares out to the water, as if worried Denny might sneak up in his boat and overhear this conversation.

She did not want her thoughts to turn toward sorrow. This had not helped her. To ward off the impulse, she thought back for a moment to herself as a schoolgirl, without blemish, living in the uncomplicated glow. She had always liked herself best in her Brownie uniform; because the older girls wore precisely the same costume, Susan didn't feel so awkwardly big and tall. Perhaps at some point in the past year or two, she had let the girl in the brown dress out of her grasp, let her fall away as if disappearing down a sweet but deep well. She no longer felt, as she had in her younger adulthood, that she was living as two people, the girl and the woman.

"I sometimes think all of us out here just gave up a little early," she said.

"Speak for yourself," he said, but it wasn't said harshly. It was more of an absolution than a retort.

"Oh," she said. "I've got plenty to confess. I expect that goes without saying."

The old man put up his hand to stop her. He turned to go, but seemed reluctant to leave this brilliant September day and to let this conversation stop. He looked at her, and made her realize that he believed the next step was hers.

"Charles," she said. She rarely used his name.

"What?"

"I can't fix everything. You know that. It's not as if I have any magic." She did not know why she was so certain that this was what he wanted.

"I'm not asking for magic. You've come home. That's enough to keep from offending the dead," he said finally. "The boy and my wife." He began to walk away, heading up toward his house. Susan found herself waving to him as he departed, and then turned quickly to see that Denny had entered the mouth of the creek, a tall-weather bow, unnaturally, stunningly white, plowing toward her out of the molten sunlight.

She waited on the creekbank, sitting in the dry autumn grasses. Denny caught the mooring ball and was making the line fast. He seemed in a good mood, his skin a golden reflection in the tea-colored water. He looked fine as a waterman, big-chested over the low sides of the boat. Suddenly, as she looked upon this graceful scene, from deep in her lungs came a wave of joy, a relief as if for the first time in years her whole body had relaxed. She could feel it in her chest and in her shoulders. Could it be, Susan wondered, that this morning, this very moment, was what she had been waiting for, that mourning would end with the same abruptness with which it had begun, begun with the words, out of a sleep as any parent fears it most, a strange doctor saying, "Wake up, wake up, it's about your son Charlie." But Charlie isn't even born yet, she had told herself as she roused; how can doctors be waking me up with bad news about Charlie?

"Hey," Denny called out as he poled close.

"Shhh," she said, putting a finger to her lips. She did not know why it was necessary for him not to talk. She watched him struggle for a second or two with an answer, perhaps even an angry complaint about being cut short when all he was saying was hello. Since she had moved back they had been careful with each other, and had not probed for feelings, and had sat silent for phrases or thoughts they did not understand. Asking for explanations would have done no good. Susan wished that her life and her marriage were that simple; she could hardly remember the time when it was, when words took care of what words were supposed to and touch handled the rest.

"Can you be with me here for a minute?" she asked.

He sat down beside her on the bank. He had moved a little beyond her, and when she turned in her seat to face him she saw the old man watching them from the patch of grass in front of his house. The three of them hoping for a peace or for a change, depending on her. It was maybe not much of an audience. Out of all the people she had known in her life, her own family, her girlfriends, the boys and men, her electric company customers, out of the planet's billions only these few, this assortment, looked to her. Was that enough to make any of this worth it?

"A real pretty day out there," said Denny, Denny the soft boy, the one who loved flowers.

She moved closer to him, her knees parting the grass as if she were still in school, still looking up at Denny from her spot at the senior picnic. She took his hand, spread it out between hers, attempting to flatten the natural cup of his palm with her thumbs. She could feel the pulses of blood, stunning bursts of life-giving pressure.

"It may be over," she said. She held her breath, waiting to see how this would feel, once said. A V of geese honked overhead, a cow bellowed angrily from the holding yard, a school of small fish breached the surface in front of them in a gravelly shower. She was glad to have these other voices join in with hers.

"I'm hoping so too," he answered.

She wished, for a moment, that he had not used this word. Of course she had hoped for many things, beginning with herself, things done and things left undone. She had hoped to be a mother, but for the moment, once risked, it was better to put that hope aside. Especially with the new knowledge and choices that could be revealed in a drop of her fluid, conceiving life seemed to have much too much to do with death. She had hoped not to be still thinking in such terms, but she was. She had hoped — maybe pretended would be a better word — that Denny could suddenly become someone quite different, starting with what she had learned was a slight defect, a trivial speck of dust, located on the long arm of his chromosome 7. Denny could also be more communicative, less defensive, more open to suggestion, less inter-ested in sex, more interested in love; he could not have that palm-sized birthmark on his left flank and his breath could be nicer when he awoke. Hope, in other words, seemed a little beside the point for Susan.

He said, "It didn't seem anyone did anything wrong, anyway. That's the thing. Neither of us did anything wrong."

She quieted him once more, and this time he seemed content to sit with her in the grass. She could see Denny's father disappear-ing into his house; she could see the inevitable lineup of cows beginning at the far gate, drawn by the pressure of time as they measured it. She felt Denny remove his hand from its splayed captivity, and she looked down to see him moving to pick up one of hers. She would know everything when he did. There was no way for either of them to lie on this one: the moment had come, almost five years reduced to a slight clasp of his hand. It could be a little too tight and then relax too abruptly; a sort of halfhearted greeting, something for a cousin, something to be gotten over.

That would mean that they would live out their lives side by side, but that it would never be sweet again. His grasp could be too loose, a kind of forgetful drape, the kind of thing you do to keep your balance. If so, they would drift apart in a year or two, and perhaps he would lose the farm and start drinking. Or he could run his hand into hers, flatten it against her palm and find the fit for his fingers; he could search and then, slowly, take what she gave him, herself, and he could draw the two of them together, and this is what she expects, and it will be enough, not perhaps for every man and every woman, but for her, and for him, for now.

JONATHAN WILSON

From Shanghai

FROM PLOUGHSHARES

THE ADVICE NOTE, dropped on my father's desk in the first week of September 1955, lay unread for a week. My father was away from home, resolving a dispute over burial sites in Manchester. He was a synagogue troubleshooter, the Red Adair of Anglo-Jewish inter-necine struggles, and it was his job to travel up and down the country, mollifying rabbis and pacifying their sometimes rebellious congregations. It was only when he returned to his office in Tavistock Square that he learned that a package awaited him at London docks. My father was a little confused. The note had come from the Office of Refugee Affairs, a department, now almost defunct, that he had little to do with. What could possibly be sent to him, and why?

During his lunch hour, he traveled to Tilbury, emerging by the loading dock on the river where bulky cargo vessels lined up beneath towering cranes. It took him a long time to locate the appropriate office, and even longer to find the right collection point. But my father was used to bureaucrats, and patient with them, and he chatted amiably while the papers he had brought with him were perused and stamped.

In the warehouse, he was presented, not with the brown paper parcel that he had imagined, but with two enormous crates, low-ered to his feet by a man on a forklift truck.

"What's in them?" asked my father.

"No idea, guv. They're in off the boat from Shanghai."

"I see," said my father, utterly bemused. After the usual delays and indignation, a crowbar was provided, and my father, with the reluctant aid of the forklift driver, pried open one of the wood slats on the side of the crate. The driver, his inquisitiveness aroused, tore through some thin paper wrapping.

"Looks like books," he said.

"Books?"

"Yes, mate, books."

"But who from?"

They searched the surface of the crate; the bill of lading indicated only "P.O. Box 1308, Shanghai."

"Well, I've got work to do," the driver announced, remounting his forklift and starting the engine.

My father reached into the crate and dislodged one of the books. It was a German translation of *The Collected Tales of Hans Andersen*, strongly bound in blue linen. He took out another book; it was written in a language he couldn't understand, Japanese or Chinese. The third book was, again, *The Collected Tales*, but this time in English. He tugged out five more illustrated, English-language versions of *The Fairy Tales of Hans Andersen*. My father returned to the Far Eastern text and flicked through the pages. Sure enough, there were the telltale drawings: a duckling, a nightingale, three dogs with eyes as big as saucers.

Over the next few months, more and more crates arrived, each one adding to the Andersen collection. My father arranged to have them held in a warehouse near the docks. My mother was less than pleased with the extra expense imposed upon our family by this storage of books from nowhere. After all, we had only recently been freed from the restrictions of wartime rationing: filling the larder was her priority, not the unasked-for freight of a phantom dispatch agent. But my father reacted in his usual lighthearted manner, as if we had all entered a fairy tale. From out of the blue, a gift had come our way. Who could possibly guess what the magical consequences might be?

By the end of the year, we had some twenty thousand books in storage. One winter morning, under a cold blue sky, my father took me down to the warehouse with him to view the crates. It was like a trip to the pyramids. I ventured cautiously into the dark alleyways between the wood containers, piled three high, as if these mysterious monuments held an ancient power. What on earth had we come to possess? Of course, my father had written to the P.O. box in Shanghai, but so far he had received no reply.

As we walked away from the docks, the ships grew smaller and

smaller in the distance, until they looked like the curios at the fun
fair that you could snatch up with the metal jaws of a miniature
crane. I asked my father, as I had heard my mother ask him in a
moment of frustration and anger, why we didn't sell the books.
"Because they are not ours to sell," he replied.

It was Sunday, and we were both free, for the only day of the
week, from the dual constraints of work (homework, in my case)
and synagogue. We walked all the way to Tower Bridge. A small
crowd had gathered in an open area on the wharf. Nearby, on the
river, a brightly painted houseboat, *The Artful Dodger*, had been
moored.

A small, muscular man with a shaved head and an ugly tattoo
inscribed upon his forearm — barbed wire entwining a naked
woman — was passing round a set of heavy chains for the crowd
to inspect. Shortly he bound himself up. My father, who appeared
more captivated than most, was selected to turn, and then pocket,
the key of a massive padlock that secured our escapologist. The
Artful Dodger then asked my father to gag him. After this, a
giggling woman from the audience helped the escapologist step
into a burlap sack, laid out on the flagstone next to him. This
accomplished, the woman waved to her cheering friends, and
tightened the drawstring with a flourish.

Behind the writhing sack, the black Thames flowed hastily. Two
swift Sunday morning scullers, who had taken my attention, disappeared behind a chugging tugboat. By the time they emerged, our
prisoner was free. I wasn't surprised. I knew his trick. I had read
all about Houdini in a school library book. I knew that our man
had swallowed a duplicate key before the show, and then regurgi-
tated it while in the sack. But, to my astonishment, I found myself
no less impressed. Escape, however it was accomplished, was the
glittering thing.

In the spring, my uncle Hugo arrived from Shanghai. He wasn't
really my uncle but my father's second cousin. He brought with
him his wife, Lotte, and nothing more than the clothes on their
backs. At first, of course, he was simply a stranger who walked into
my father's office one day in March, and announced that he had
come to claim both the Andersen books and a relationship.

My father took Hugo Wasserman for lunch, by which I mean
that they went to a nearby park, sat on a bench, and shared sand-

wiches. It was one of those transitional spring days, when it is warm enough in the sun but still very cold in the shade. While they sat side by side, lifting their faces to the pale medallion in the sky, Hugo told his story. He had been expelled from his home in the Austrian Burgenland in 1938. Like many others he had fled, in desperation, to the International Settlement in Shanghai, the only city in the world he could enter without a visa. A gentile friend, Artur Jelinek, a philatelist, had forwarded the Andersen books to China with money left for the purpose by Hugo. He had lived in Shanghai for fifteen years, working as a technician in a hospital laboratory. By profession he was a biologist, he had written a botanical treatise on mushrooms; by inclination he was a biblio-phile. In Austria, before the war, through penny-pinching, perse-verance, and resourcefulness, he had accumulated what he be-lieved to be the world's second largest collection of Hans Andersen books, exceeded only by the corpus owned by the Danish royal family.

My father listened. There had been, of course, a thousand refugee stories in wide circulation in the London Jewish commu-nity in the previous ten years; most reported greater hardship, some less. Hugo had escaped early. He was lucky. Of course, his life had been terribly disrupted, but he was alive, he was here, his collection was intact.

"But how did you get to me?" my father asked.

"Your cousin, Miki, the one who . . ."

My father nodded before Hugo could proceed. He already knew the details, and wanted to spare himself the pain of hearing them repeated.

"Well," Hugo continued, "before — that is, some months before he was taken, when I was about to leave, he gave me your name. He told me that you were an administrator for Jews. The address of the office I discovered in Shanghai."

"But why," my father continued, "didn't you reply to my letters?"

"Arthritis," Hugo replied, and held his misshapen hands out for my father to inspect. "I cannot hold a pen."

"But surely . . ." My father stopped. Sometimes, he told me later, an excuse, given for whatever reason, simply has to be accepted.

Hugo had met Lotte in Shanghai. Like him, she was a refugee from Hitler's Europe. But, unlike him, she was vivacious and energetic. Partly this derived from the fact that she was twenty years Hugo's junior. Although Hugo was only in his mid-fifties, he was, to my eyes, an old man, with his shock of white hair and deeply lined face. It was Lotte who enchanted me. She would arrive for Saturday night dinner in a fox-fur stole (borrowed from her neighbor) and chain-smoke through a long cigarette holder. She liked to sing, and after supper she would call my father to the upright piano in our dining room. He would accompany her in feisty, throaty renditions of songs in German that I couldn't understand, but of which both Hugo and my mother appeared to disapprove. I would stand near Lotte, in the aura of her rich, heavy perfume, and take deep breaths.

Lotte's family, miraculously, had survived the war and were now dispersed all over the world. Her parents were in America with her sister, Grete; one of her brothers was in Buenos Aires, the other in Israel. Sometimes she would bring me the latest postcards and letters that she had received, and together we would sit in the kitchen, soak the stamps off, and carefully catalogue them in my album. You might have thought that this kind of activity would have been more up Hugo's street, but he remained remarkably indifferent to me, almost cold, until the day that my father gave me the present.

Two evenings a week, my father took art classes at the adult education program of St. Martin's School of Art. The works that he produced provoked a great deal of hilarity in our household. He generally painted nudes. The teacher, not rich in imagination, seemed to demand two poses of his models. The first, a dull, straightforward, upright seated position in a high-backed chair; the second, a "sensual," provocative draping of the body over a velvet-backed chaise longue. My father, an admirer of Matisse but not a great colorist himself, would bring home to us strange light brown figures, twisted, not altogether intentionally, into expressionist poses. He would line his canvases up against a wall in the hall. My brother and I would collapse in laughter. My mother, busy with supper, barely gave the works a passing glance. To his credit, my father took our cruel responses very well. For two nights a week he seemed to enjoy playing the part, not of the overburdened synagogue administrator, but of the lonely artist struggling in a hostile, philistine world.

a serpentine *lamed* and squarish *vav* that served to represent the
After the arrival of Hugo and Lotte Wasserman, I thought I
brother and I had taken up the initials as sobriquet). I may have
been mistaken, but it seemed to me that the faces of the nudes
were coming more and more to carry Lotte's features: her full lips
and unmistakable green eyes. But whether this was the result of
my fantasies or those of "Lamed Vav" has never been clear to me.

My father had a friend at the art class, a man named Joe Kline,
who worked as a salesman for the publishing company of Eyre &
Spottiswoode. One night, my father came home with a small cardboard box packed with four hardback books. "More?" said my
mother, who was suspicious of all transactions involving bound
volumes. We were still defraying the costs of the Andersen storage
until Hugo and Lotte could "get on their feet."

"These are a gift," my father responded, "from Joe. They're
remainders, out of print, but in mint condition. It was really very
nice of him. There's a book for every member of our family,
including you."

The novel for my mother was *My Cousin Rachel*, by Daphne du
Maurier, while my brother received a how-to guide to safe chemis-
try experiments in the home. My book was, well, a brand-new, very
nicely illustrated edition of *The Collected Tales of Hans Andersen.*
"Coals to Newcastle," said my mother scornfully.

I was twelve, a little old for Hans Andersen, I thought, although
secretly I still liked the stories and soon became quite attached to
one lavish illustration in particular. It showed the beautiful princess
from "The Tinder Box," asleep on the giant dog's back, a low-cut
dress revealing the cleavage of what the illustrator had decided
would be disproportionately large breasts. This color print fed into
the fantasy connected to Evelyn, the fourteen-year-old girl whose
bedroom window faced mine across the two postage stamp–sized
lawns that abutted our homes. Recently, I had removed a round
mirror from my bicycle, bolted it to a long stick, and attached it

to one of my bedposts. In this way I was able to watch Evelyn Boone undress in her room without being observed myself. Unfortunately, most of the time Evelyn took what was the conventional precaution in our enclosed neighborhood of drawing the curtains before disrobing. So far, I had not seen any more in my magic mirror than had already been granted to me by Eyre & Spottiswoode's dubiously inspired illustrator.

From the first time he laid eyes upon it, Uncle Hugo wanted my book. In the wide world of desire, there is little that exceeds the covetousness of the collector. From a distant, unconcerned relative, Hugo was suddenly transformed into a charming, wily confrere. I was not immune to the bribery and seductiveness of adults, nor was I invulnerable to the parental cajoling that began when my father (my mild-mannered father!) decided to join in the fray and persuade me to hand over my book to Hugo. Indeed, I might have given in, were it not for the fact that what Hugo was asking for constituted, however bizarrely, a piece of the puzzle of my erotic life, one that I was unwilling to relinquish. Lotte, who seemed to have a sense that there was more than stubbornness and obstinacy to my refusal, took my side.

"You don't have enough books?" she asked her husband. "So you have to steal from a child?"

"It's not stealing," my father interposed. "Hugo has offered Michael an extremely rare and valuable first edition in return for his book. We are talking about a swap here. An exchange in which Michael will come out the winner."

The two men pressured me for a month, but I held my ground.

"Why can't he buy the book from someone else if he wants it that badly?" I whined to my father, after Hugo had left the house one day.

"Because it is unavailable in bookshops, and Uncle Hugo does not steal from libraries. What is more, buying books costs money, and, at the moment, Hugo and Lotte are trying to *save* money. You're not too young to understand that. Joe Kline tells me that they only printed a thousand copies of your edition. It didn't do well. Too many competitors on the market. It isn't valuable, but Hugo would have an impossible job tracking one down. To you, it's virtually worthless, but to Hugo, as part of a collection, it means something. Has it sunk in what Hugo is offering you in return? You could own a book worth, maybe, fifty pounds!"

Fifty pounds to give up Evelyn Boone's breasts? For, yes, I could no longer distinguish her teenage bumps from the more developed forms that belonged to the princess in the illustration. Out of the question!

For reasons of domestic propriety (perhaps my mother had noticed the Lotte heads on the naked bodies, too), the Wassermans had, sometime during the summer, been switched from Saturday nights to Sunday afternoons. Hugo and Lotte had bought a car on the HP, an old Singer with seventy thousand miles on the clock. In this distinguished vehicle, Hugo at the wheel, Lotte making hand signals because the left indicator did not work, they negotiated a slow, careful way to our house each weekend. When they pulled up at the curb, my father would look out of the window and say, "Here comes the Rolls Canardly — rolls down one side of a hill, can 'ardly get up the other."

Hugo was now a fully incorporated member of something my father called the Cheesecake Club. This organization now boasted four members, men from the neighborhood who gathered weekly to overpraise my mother's patisserie and discuss the contemporary scene. One of the men, Sidney Oberman, would arrive with the week's newspapers under his arm. It was his responsibility to select and underline topics for further discussion. The group's heroes were Winston Churchill, the late Chaim Weizmann, and Dr. Armand Kalinowski, a brilliant Jewish panelist on the popular radio show *Brains Trust.* In deference to this invisible mentor, the members of the Cheesecake Club each sported a bow tie, symbol of decorum and high thought.

Six weeks after Hugo had first held my book in his hands for examination and quiet evaluation, the Wassermans arrived, as usual, late for Sunday tea, and, as usual, in the middle of an argument. The general cause of their altercations was "The Collection." The Wassermans were poor. They lived in a tiny two-room flat in Willesden Green. Hugo had looked for laboratory work, but, he said, his strong German accent made prospective employers uneasy. The Wassermans' small income accrued from Lotte's piano lessons, offered to neighborhood children in their own homes, and from piecework (advice on fungus and fungicides) that Hugo performed as assistant to a local landscape gardener. According to Lotte, if Hugo were only to sell his books, they could live like royalty. On the other hand, if Hugo ever tried to unpack his books in her home, he would have to find another wife.

Lotte's scorn for Hans Christian Andersen and his work knew no limits. Fairy tales! What nonsense. A collection of Goethe or Tolstoy she might respect, although, in her present crisis, she would still want to sell it. But a grown man straining his eyes poring over "The Emperor's New Clothes" in twenty different languages. What a terrible waste.

When Lotte spoke this way, Hugo flushed deeply; he would look around to see if my brother and I were in earshot. When his eyes met ours, we would try to look distracted and hard of hearing. On this particular occasion, their argument appeared to have peaked shortly before the ring on our doorbell, and what I overheard as I opened the door ("You want us to remain poor all our lives." "Is this all you care about, money?") were their last tired shots, the blows of a boxer whose arms are spent, and legs wobbly.

Lotte moved shakily toward the kitchen. "I need a glass of water," she said. Hugo carefully removed his jacket and searched our hall cupboard for a hanger. Were there tears in his eyes? I wasn't sure, but suddenly I felt sorry for him. Perhaps it was the look of deep exhaustion on his face — a look I had seen before but not really registered — that softened me, or maybe it was simply the fact that, for the first time since we had begun our battle of wills, he did not say to me, "So, have you changed your mind?" Whatever the reason, I hovered around until Hugo had hung up his jacket, and then I said, "I'll swap."

The ceremonial exchange of books did not take place for more than a fortnight. It was mid-August, and time for our annual holiday. My parents would book us into some quiet, respectable boarding house in Margate or Swanage or Southbourne, making sure to order vegetarian meals in advance, in this way anticipating and surmounting problems that might arise with *kashrut.* Off we would go, packed snugly into our old Ford Prefect. After a long eighty miles or so of traffic jams, carsickness, and back-seat fights, we would arrive at someone else's house, not too different from our own, ready to read indoors while the rain fell in sheets; play crazy-golf in light drizzle; and venture out on the three or four fine, warm days that nature seemed to guarantee us, to swim the cold sea and shiver.

This year, however, we were doing something different. We had *rented* a seaman's cottage on the beach in Folkestone. High, choppy waves thundered against the retaining wall behind the little dwelling. When I lay in bed at night, I felt as if my bedroom were a ship's cabin, pitching and rolling in the summer winds. In the mornings, my brother and I explored the dunes near where the ferry came in from Boulogne. The sandy knolls and hillocks were still dotted with concrete pillboxes. We clambered inside these dry chambers, peered through their narrow window slits, and pretended to be gunners scanning the Channel for approaching German aircraft.

At the end of the first week, my father was suddenly and mysteriously called back to London. All we knew was that Lotte had phoned one day in a state of high excitement. My father had a few whispering sessions with my mother. But, after he had departed, she claimed, and she seemed to be telling the truth, that my father had told her only that Hugo and Lotte had a real emergency, not of a medical nature, but serious enough to warrant his returning home for a couple of days to help them out.

It rained for the duration of my father's three-day absence. We visited a shop that held demonstrations in toffee manufacture, went to the pictures to see Danny Kaye in *The Court Jester,* and attended a children's talent contest in the local town hall.

When he returned, late one night, my father appeared anxious and disturbed. In fact, he was so agitated that I allowed myself to imagine, for one brief flicker of a thought, that he and Lotte had perhaps, well . . . no, it was inconceivable.

The Prince of Denmark, we learned eventually, had sent an emissary to Hugo. The royal family's librarian wished to review the collection. There was genuine interest from Copenhagen. If Hugo would not agree to sell it whole, perhaps he would permit the collection to be split up?

Lotte had called on my father to help her persuade Hugo that this was a once-in-a-lifetime chance. They could escape their dreary lodgings and dead-end jobs. They could move to Golders Green; better, to Hampstead! If he wished to pursue his "hobby," Hugo could open an antiquarian bookshop. My father had spoken to Hugo, but he was powerfully resistant to the idea of selling.

"Leslie, you don't understand," he had said. "I have to hold it together. The collection has to be protected."

But then something happened. Here, my father paused in his

narrative, as if to gather strength. My mother poured him a cup of tea. Hugo had received a letter in the mail. He had not let Lotte see it, but after reading it, he had rushed out of the house. He had gone missing for a day and a night, and when he returned in the early hours of this morning, hatless, soaked through, with his teeth chattering, he had simply slumped in a chair and refused to explain himself. My father had visited the Wassermans' for lunch. Hugo had been polite, but withdrawn. He did not want to discuss the collection anymore. Perhaps, after all, he would sell; he only wanted to be left alone and given a little more "time to think."

"Well," said my mother, testily, when my father had finished speaking. "I think they've got a nerve. Interrupting a person's holiday, and then behaving in this outrageous fashion when you — and only *you* would do this — went up there to help them."

My father didn't reply. Outside, the sea swelled and surged, spraying droplets of surf against our kitchen windows. I thought, in my ignorance, that my mother had a point.

When we returned to London, my father immediately had to deal with a crisis at work: for the first time, a woman had been elected to the Board of Management of a North London synagogue, and now the entire spiritual staff — rabbi, cantor, beadle, and choirmaster — was threatening to resign. "This is the beginning of the end for Judaism," the rabbi had written back to headquarters, and added in parentheses, "'A foolish woman is clamorous: she is simple, and knoweth nothing' (Proverbs 9:13)." My father was dispatched to calm everybody down.

The school holidays were drawing to a close. I had to buy a new blazer and stock up on those sweet-smelling essentials: an eraser, a new exercise book, blue-black ink, and a fountain pen. In the subdued excitements of anticipation before a new school year, I almost forgot about Hugo and Lotte.

One evening, when an autumn chill could already be felt in the air, they turned up on our doorstep. Lotte was transformed. She was wearing a white crêpe de Chine blouse and a knee-length black satin skirt. Her hair was dressed in a chic new style. She was brimming over with joy. "He's going to sell!" she announced even before she greeted us.

Hugo followed her sheepishly into the house. It seemed that Lotte had jumped the gun. Her emphatic expectation of great wealth had led her to spend, in one brave day, the little savings that they had managed to accumulate in the previous six months of struggle and hardship. "Yes, I will sell," said Hugo. "But who knows what I will get."

Late in the evening, Hugo pulled me aside. "Come in the other room," he said. "We need to talk." I had been expecting him to approach me, and wondering why he had delayed. "Listen," he whispered, pushing his face close to mine. I smelled alcohol on his heavy breath. "I am going to give you a book. I don't want *them* to get it. It's very valuable, but it's worth nothing. I want you to keep it. You can't sell it."

The bars of our electric fire turned on for the first time in four months, glowed bright orange, and gave off a pungent scent of burned dust. Hugo raked his white hair back with his fingers. "You must," he said, taking me by the shoulders, "you, above all people, must forgive me." Despite the heat that was moving in waves up my back, I felt a chill go through me. He was weeping now, sobbing, his shoulders heaving as if he could never stop. Suddenly, Lotte and my father appeared in the doorway. They rushed to Hugo, put their arms around him, and led him back into the kitchen.

That night, my parents sent my brother and me to bed early. But, as was our custom when this happened, we crept halfway down the stairs to eavesdrop on the grown-up conversation. We sat in our pajamas, hugging the banister. In the brightly lit kitchen Hugo began to speak, in low tones and with a halting voice. At first we only caught words and phrases: "wife," "son," "arrangements," "waited and waited," "betrayed," "not even Lotte." Huddled on the stairs, we heard, clear as train whistles in the night, sharp intakes of breath around the kitchen table. Soon we grew used to Hugo's broken, hoarse whisper.

If, at any point in Hugo's story, my brother and I could have returned to our beds, we would probably have done so. But curiosity had called us to listen, and now we were trapped.

After ten or fifteen minutes, Hugo paused for a moment. My father got up and switched the lights off in the kitchen. It was a strange thing to do. Perhaps he wanted to take the harsh light of self-interrogation off Hugo. Now, Hugo's voice came up to us out of darkness. "The collection," he said, "the collection came to

Shanghai, but not my family." There was a long silence. "Soon after the war, I received a confirmation. My wife. Someone from the women's camp who was there. I received a letter. But my son, of course, unlikely — all right, impossible, but even so. Two weeks ago, a letter comes. You know. Sixteen years. An official letter: the place, the date." Hugo began a muffled sob. "My Hans, Hans Wasserman, Hans Wasserman." He said the name again and again.

It was thirty years before I opened the edition of *The Collected Tales* that Hugo had given me. My nine-year-old son's teacher had invited parents to come to school and share their favorite children's story with the Nintendo-obsessed throng. I thought for a while before settling (of course!) on Andersen's "The Tinder Box." My old, illustrated copy of the tales had long since been lost in some chaotic transfer from home to home. But I had managed to hold on to Hugo's gift. It was an ordinary-looking book, with a slightly torn blue binding and faded gold lettering on the cover. The early pages were spotted with brown stains. The frontispiece proudly announced "A New Translation, by Mrs. H. B. Paull." I flicked through the pages; they appeared unmarked. I turned to the Contents: a faint circle had been inscribed around "The Brave Tin Soldier." I found the story, and read it through. In the last sentence, two phrases had been thinly underlined in pencil: "instantly in flames," "burnt to a cinder."

Contributors' Notes

SHERMAN ALEXIE is a Spokane–Coeur d'Alene Indian from Wellpinit, Washington, on the Spokane Indian Reservation. He currently lives in Spokane, Washington. He is the author of five books, including *First Indian on the Moon* (Hanging Loose Press) and *The Lone Ranger and Tonto Fistfight in Heaven* (Grove/Atlantic). Recipient of a National Endowment for the Arts poetry fellowship in 1992, he has had his fiction, poetry, and essays published in *Esquire, The Kenyon Review, New York Times Book Review, New York Times Magazine, Ploughshares, Story, ZYZZYVA,* and others. Two limited-edition collections of poetry, *Water Flowing Home* (Limberlost Press) and *Seven Mourning Songs for the Cedar Flute I Have Yet to Learn to Play* (Whitman College Press), will be published in late 1994, and his first novel, *Coyote Springs,* will be published by Grove/Atlantic in 1995.

▪ A few years back, Thomas, one of my best friends from high school, killed himself on the day that I returned from a writers' conference in Oklahoma. In fact, he shot himself on an access road directly under the flight path of planes landing at the Spokane airport. I still wonder if I could've seen his little red car if I had happened to look down from the window of my plane.

I found out about the suicide from my childhood friend Steve, who received the news that his father had died of a heart attack in Phoenix, Arizona, a few seconds after he told me about Thomas's death. We were still on the telephone when Steve's mother came running into his house with the announcement.

Steve and I flew to Phoenix to take care of his father's affairs just a few hours after Thomas's funeral. Steve and I talked about death on the flight down, in Phoenix, and on the long drive back home. We haven't talked about death since. I needed to write about it, however, so I dropped two of my cast of characters into the story line and blurred the distinction between fiction and nonfiction.

As Simon Ortiz, the Acoma writer, says, "If it's fiction, it better be true."

CAROL ANSHAW is the author of the novel *Aquamarine,* which won the 1992 Carl Sandburg Award for fiction and a Society of Midland Authors Award. Her short stories have been anthologized, and published in various periodicals including the *Voice Literary Supplement* and *Story.* Anshaw also reviews books for publications nationwide, and for her critical essays in the *Voice Literary Supplement* won the 1989–90 National Book Critics Circle Citation for Excellence in Reviewing. She is currently on the faculty of the M.F.A. in Writing program at Vermont College, and at work on a new novel, *Seven Moves.*

▪ My partner Barbara and I found a listing in an offbeat Paris guidebook for these old Turkish-style steam baths. Once there, we both felt like total outsiders amid all the impenetrable ritual, and at the same time casually accepted into what was really a kind of clubhouse in the universal society of women. We hadn't really planned ahead, and so had no proper hammam gear with us — no towels or soap or sandals. We had to throw ourselves on the mercy and hospitality of the women who ran the bath, and just give ourselves over to the experience, which was mesmerizing. I have to confess we were too timid to sign up for the "NETTOYAGE À PEAU–55 FR" — a great regret now.

I knew by the time we were out on the street again that I wanted to set a story there. I then had to come up with characters I could walk in through those Moorish arches, two other unlikely visitors, and that took a while. I was looking for modern women with a modern dilemma that would contrast with this ancient setting.

I took the story through at least six or seven drafts. Almost everything good that happens in my writing happens in revision and so I've become patient with the process, giving it its own time.

I've had the opportunity to read this story aloud a few times now, and really enjoy bringing people into the steam along with the characters. It's a little like being a hypnotist.

ROBERT OLEN BUTLER won the 1993 Pulitzer Prize for his book of short fiction, *A Good Scent from a Strange Mountain,* stories from which appeared in *The Best American Short Stories* of 1991 and 1992. He is the author of seven novels, *The Alleys of Eden, Sun Dogs, Countrymen of Bones, On Distant Ground, Wabash, The Deuce,* and, earlier this year, *They Whisper.* His work has appeared in such magazines as *Harper's, The Sewanee Review, The Hudson Review, The Southern Review, New England Review,* and *The Vir-*

ginia Quarterly Review, where he won the Emily Clark Balch Award. He has also been anthologized in each of the past three years in *New Stories from the South.* In addition to the Pulitzer in 1993, Butler won the Richard and Hinda Rosenthal Award from the American Academy of Arts and Letters and a Guggenheim fellowship, and he is a 1994 recipient of a National Endowment for the Arts fellowship. He served with the U.S. Army in Vietnam as a Vietnamese linguist and is a charter recipient of the Tu Do Chinh Kien Award for outstanding contributions to American culture by a Vietnam veteran. He teaches creative writing at McNeese State University in Lake Charles, Louisiana.

▪ The narrator of "Salem" began to murmur to me with the spate of MIA articles that were appearing in newspapers in 1992. He was challenged to answer his government's call to bring forth any artifacts of dead Americans, and I knew at once this was difficult for him, for reasons he did not understand. When Rick Barthelme asked me to contribute something to an upcoming special fiction issue of *The Mississippi Review,* I decided it was time to let this former Viet Cong soldier ponder his reluctance out loud. His voice is the first of what someday will be a suite of voices in a companion volume to *A Good Scent from a Strange Mountain:* it's not just the Vietnamese in America who are our spiritual kin.

LAN SAMANTHA CHANG was born and raised in Appleton, Wisconsin. She attended Yale and Harvard and earned an M.F.A. from the University of Iowa, where she was a teaching-writing fellow. She has received support from the James Michener–Copernicus Society and is currently a fellow in the creative writing program at Stanford University. Her fiction has appeared in *The Beloit Fiction Journal* and *The Atlantic Monthly.*

▪ This story was inspired by a coincidence. During my second year in Iowa City, I had a part-time clerical job in the cancer unit of the university hospital (a benevolent employer, over the years, of many struggling writers). At the hospital I became acquainted with a charming eighty-year-old laryngectomy post-op, a former captain in the Marines who, like many laryngectomy patients, was unable to talk and communicated with pen and notepad. During his stay, which stretched into months, we had many "conversations."

He was especially interested to learn that my parents had been born in China. He explained he had been on the last U.S. ship to leave Shanghai during the Communist takeover of the city in 1949. As a former student of Chinese history and politics, I was intrigued by his story. One day I happened to mention it to my parents over the phone.

Here is the coincidence: It turned out that both my father and mother had been in Shanghai during those last weeks (although they hadn't met each other yet). My parents don't often talk about their experiences in the tumultuous years when China was changing from republic to Communist state, so this new bit of knowledge fascinated me. "Pipa's Story" was born, in part, of this fascination. Like much of my writing, it has its roots in an attempt to picture something about my parents' lives. All of the people and scenes in the story are invented, except for the final act, the decapitation, which my friend at the hospital described to me in his quavering handwriting.

ANN CUMMINS's fiction has appeared in *The New Yorker, Antioch Review, Sonora Review,* and other magazines, and has been reprinted in *The Best of the West* anthology. She lives in Flagstaff, Arizona, and teaches at Northern Arizona University.

▪ I took a job in a jeans factory when I was nineteen, and held it for three days. I was an abysmal seamstress, couldn't sew a straight line. Several years later, I took a job teaching fiction at Northern Arizona University, and during my initial semester I wrote the first draft of "Where I Work." I wrote it in an hour. It came as an emotional outpouring, the way stories do when emotion and words are in sync. Though I hadn't thought of the jeans factory in years, barely remembered it, really, it was a perfect metaphor for my emotional present: that first semester, teaching creative writing within the institution seemed every bit as baffling as sewing pockets on jeans. There were the committees to be sorted through, committee behavior to be figured out, the tenure track thing to be faced. And, there were swarms of students — seventy-five psyches per semester — each looking for guidance in putting order to chaos. I have always been a sucker for other people's chaos. I get absorbed by stories and forget to be critical. My natural tendency is to say, "And then what happened?" rather than, "Have you considered changing the point of view?"

Though the first draft came easily, I tinkered with the story for a couple of years before I let it go. John Wideman, an early influence on my writing, used to say, "All you need is enough plot to hang a character on." It took some experimenting before I found that little bit of plot for this character. The interior monologue is a problematic form when it comes to introducing action, and it was especially problematic in this story, since my character is so random in her thinking. She's also capable of anything, the type of character who could burn the house down (and in one version did). Though I like the macabre in fiction, I didn't want her to come off as psychotic (hers, I think, is a fairly healthy response to the factory), nor did I want the story to turn melodramatic or comic. So, I fooled with plot until I found the right hook on which to hang this character.

ALICE ELLIOTT DARK grew up in Bryn Mawr, Pennsylvania, where she attended Shipley School from kindergarten through twelfth grade. She received a B.A. in Oriental studies from the University of Pennsylvania and an M.F.A. in creative writing from Antioch University. Her collection of stories and novellas, *Naked to the Waist,* was published in 1991. She teaches writing at The Writer's Voice in New York City. She has recently finished a novel.

▪ After "In the Gloaming" was published, I got a lot of letters asking if it was really fiction; apparently it seemed autobiographical. I suppose it is, in the sense that I see it as a story about a woman trying to be a decent mother, a subject that was very much on my mind at the time I wrote it. I had recently become a mother, and was having bouts of vertigo whenever I thought of the scope of this new relationship. There were so many powerful, contradictory feelings to cope with: I wanted to encourage my son to have his own life, yet I hoped he would like me; I wanted to help him feel brave about going out into the world, yet when I imagined it, I instantly feared the harm that could come to him. Janet, the mother in the story, took on all this ambivalence and managed to behave with grace and honor toward her family under the worst of circumstances. I only wish I could do as well.

I was also overwhelmed by the impending death of my grandfather. I'd never really been able to make sense of death, and my grandfather's would be particularly hard to fathom. One day the first line of the story came to me. Originally, it was: "He wanted to talk again, suddenly." I wrote it down and just kept writing. He became Laird. I based his humor and handsomeness on a friend who died a few years ago, but in writing about him I found a new way to think about all the people I've lost, as well as to thaw the parts of myself that had been numb with grief. I'd never believed in an afterlife, but here one was.

The title came from my grandfather, the son of a Scotsman, who passed his love for the gloaming on to his family. There was some discussion about changing the title because the term was unfamiliar, but I asked to keep it and was glad at the pleasure my grandfather got from seeing one of his passions in the elegant *New Yorker* typeface before he died. I heard from several people that there is an old song of the same title. My mother-in-law gave me a copy of the words, which turned out to be surprisingly appropriate. The story was not conceived as being about any disease in particular. AIDS came in when Laird made a remark about his immune system, and I left it at that. I never thought of it as an AIDS story; from what I've seen of AIDS, the end of the disease is not as gentle as this, nor do most victims have situations as idyllic as Laird's. I wish everyone could have as much love, comfort, and understanding. The story is a fantasy and a wish. During the writing, I felt the way I've heard actors describe their involvement with their parts; I took on the responsibility of speaking for these people and could not shake my awareness of them when I put my pen down for the day. Janet and Laird were completely real and absorbing to me. I missed them very much when I finished.

STUART DYBEK's most recent collection of stories is *The Coast of Chicago*. He teaches writing at Western Michigan University and has been the recipient of two NEA fellowships, a Guggenheim, a Whiting Writer's Award, and, most recently, an award in fiction from the American Academy of Arts and Letters.

▪ I'm always wary of epigraphs. Short as they are, they too often seem like extra weight for a story to carry around. But in this instance, I felt obligated to include three lines from Yehuda Amichai's poem "We Did It." Had I not read that poem, I doubt that I would have ever written "We Didn't." In fact, "We Didn't" began as a poem I was writing as a comic — at least, hopefully comic — response to Amichai's poem. But as image begot anecdote, and as anecdote begot characters, I decided to let the characters take over and tell their story. They would have anyway, whether I'd let them or not. I'd like to think, however, that some of the impulse to write a poem still echoes through the story.

TONY EARLEY is a native of Rutherfordton, North Carolina, and a graduate of Warren Wilson College and the University of Alabama. His work has appeared in *Harper's Magazine, TriQuarterly, The Best American Short Stories 1993*, and *New Stories from the South*. His first book, *Here We Are in Paradise*, a collection of short stories, was published by Little, Brown earlier this year. He is at work on his first novel and lives, until his wife finishes seminary, in suburban Pittsburgh.

▪ I suppose "The Prophet from Jupiter" most closely resembles soup, made in a big pot from leftovers that did not prove to be very tasty or nutritious on their own. For years I had wanted to write a story about a man whose lethargic sperm was symbolic of the spiritual malaise in his marriage; I wanted to write a story about a great flood in the mountains of North Carolina. A giant fish (in that instance, a hammerhead shark) suddenly appeared at the end of a story in which it did not belong. Everyone who read that earlier story looked puzzled. "Why is this giant fish here?" they said. In an aborted novel, for two pages and no apparent reason, the ghost of a farmer stalked the flooded fields underneath Lake Norman, outside Charlotte. All of these abandoned ideas and snatches of stories lived heaped together, literally and figuratively, in a bottom drawer, and none of them, examined separately, was very attractive.

The lucky day for me as a writer came when a friend, a profoundly religious man and a great lover of fresh vegetables, said, "You know, in the last days Christians won't be able to get corn." For him this was a matter of some concern. For me it was a gift. Those words, I knew, belonged in the mouth of the Prophet from Jupiter. Suddenly I had a story idea capable of holding giant fish, great floods, lethargic sperm, and underwater ghosts, all at the same time. Not only did the story hold them, but it held everything else I could think of — bullwhips, bomber pilots, baseball, dead mules, the Rapture, a Labrador retriever named Shithead, a whole flooded town peopled by any number of ghosts. For a month I made up things and threw them into the story, and the story — with varying degrees of success, depending on whom you listen to — accepted them all. When I finished it, several anxiety-filled months passed before I wrote anything else.

"My God," I thought, "I put absolutely everything I know into one story." The style (I am particularly fond of the review in which it was called "cheerfully digressive") suggested itself. The story resisted all attempts at making it a more traditional narrative. That I studiously tried to make it something it obviously is not doesn't say much about my judgment. I finally just gave up. When I first showed it to friends, I said, "Here. Read this. I don't have any idea what it is." Later, I thought it marked a turning point in my work, that I had discovered a new way to write stories, but it didn't. I haven't written anything like it since. When I read it today, it still strikes me as strange, and I'm still glad I wrote it. I somehow think it's smarter than I am, and knows more than I do. I'm proud of it. I bristle slightly whenever I hear anyone call it "gothic," because anytime a contemporary southern writer hears someone call their work gothic, they know they are only moments away from being compared unfavorably to Faulkner and O'Connor, and then being asked to please get on with their lives. As a latter-day southerner who writes about the South, a South that still contains, and I hope will always contain, its gothic elements, my sincere hope is that anyone who comes to "The Prophet from Jupiter" through this anthology will consider it a new thing. It seemed like that when I wrote it.

CAROLYN FERRELL has lived, worked, and studied in Manhattan, the South Bronx, and West Berlin. Her stories have appeared in *Callaloo, The Literary Review, Fiction,* and *Ploughshares,* and in anthologies. Before beginning graduate work in English at the CUNY Graduate Center in 1993, she was a literacy professional for five years. She is at work on a collection of short stories.

▪ For four years, I worked at a literacy organization in the South Bronx teaching adults to read and write; in particular, I led a family literacy project, the focus of which included increasing communication between parent and child. Among other things, I was very interested in the dreams the parents (mostly mothers) had of their children's movement into the "literate" world, and the subsequent liberation the mothers knew they and their kids would experience. My story begins with a mother who has an impossible desire to do for her son, but who wants to graduate him into a good, safe world of possibilities.

"Proper Library" was born one afternoon as I stood on the platform of the elevated train at Prospect Avenue. I was on the Manhattan side with the people going back to *safe* New York, looking at several teenage children on the Bronx-bound platform do their usual thing: laugh, joke, stand still, curse, throw bottles between the tracks (which naturally landed on busy Westchester Avenue below), kiss, scream, laugh some more. I started thinking about the teenage rites of passage I had been subjected to when I was that age. They had happened ten years earlier, in a middle-class community on Long Island, and there were no subways. There were other things, other experiences, but life with the subway, in the city, seemed like something else.

The things that immediately interested me about the children were the questions: Who is being left out? How does one survive that? What about when you do go through with some rite of passage? Where does that leave you? Questions like these will always be in my work, in some form.

The experience of being marginalized at a time when it is so essential to be included is incredible. For one, it can take up a lot of energy, and devastate. But it can also build a new kind of strength. I saw Lorrie standing on the platform that afternoon, in the disguise of survival. His story wanted to be told.

JOHN ROLFE GARDINER is the author of the novels *Great Dream from Heaven, Unknown Soldiers,* and *In the Heart of the Whole World;* a story collection, *Going On Like This;* and a novella with stories, *The Incubator Ballroom.* A fiction contributor to numerous magazines, he lives in Unison, Virginia, with his wife, Joan, and daughter, Nicola.

▪ I began "The Voyage Out" after hearing the anecdote of a small child asking his mother for an explanation of the Trinity. An earlier seed was planted by two English schoolboys who crossed the Atlantic to live with my family in rural Virginia during World War II. Like the black-backed window shades we drew down in our hilltop home during air raid drills, the boys were proximate curiosities of very distant events. The two of them, with their precise diction and stubborn rectitude, became one as the story's lonely protagonist who's forced to relive a grueling ocean crossing and tormented toward maturity in a Canadian boarding school.

To pretend to an orderly, controlled process here would only produce a second fiction. The story did not manifest itself full blown. Nor did it arrive in a straight line of discovery. There was backing and filling informed, I suppose, by a couple of shopworn truths — that mystery and suggestion may be more compelling than revelation, and that plot may be advanced by narrators who appear to be busy with other matters.

DAVID GATES was born in 1947 and grew up in Clinton, Connecticut. He writes about books and popular music for *Newsweek*. His stories have appeared in *Esquire, Gentlemen's Quarterly, Grand Street, Ploughshares,* and *TriQuarterly*. His first novel, *Jernigan* (Knopf), was published in 1991; he's now working on a second.

▪ I wrote a version of "The Mail Lady" around 1984, sent it out to magazines, had it rejected, and put it away. The story was both sketchy *and* digressive, but I always believed it really was a story. The beginning and the end were right, I had liked impersonating Lewis Coley, and I was irrationally fond of the line "Can it have been 'The Dipsy Doodle'?" A couple of years ago, stuck for anything new to write, I took the story out and went back into it.

My mother had a paralytic stroke like Lewis Coley's, and my father cared for her at home. That long driveway with the mailbox down by the road is their driveway, but it's not their road, not their house, and not their story. Some of Lewis Coley comes from Samuel Johnson, particularly from Johnson's note summoning help after *his* stroke: "It has pleased God, this morning, to deprive me of the powers of speech; and as I do not know but that it may be his further good pleasure to deprive me soon of my senses, I request you will on the receipt of this note, come to me, and act for me, as the exigencies of my case may require." The dissonance between such written language and a stroke victim's speech must have suggested to me the story's diciest device: the aphasic Lewis Coley's fussily articulate inner voice. While rewriting, I checked the plausibility of a few details in a publication called — no kidding — *The Stroke Book*. But I didn't look hard enough to ruin anything I wanted to keep.

BARRY HANNAH is married to a blond ex-model condemned to be the first reader of his work. Between them they have five children. Hannah grew up in Clinton, Mississippi, and was educated in his trade at the University of Arkansas. He is a musician (trumpet) who was once good enough to play half as well as Miles Davis on his worst night ever. After teaching at several schools, including Middlebury, Montana, and Iowa, he returned to his home state as writer-in-residence at the university. He has lived and worked in Oxford for twelve years, just outside the shadow of one of his masters, William Faulkner. He has great affection for Harley and Triumph motorcycles, fishing, and tennis. Author of ten books, he has been nominated for the National Book Award twice (*Geronimo Rex,* '73; *Ray,* '80). Lately he has taught summer workshops at Bennington College.

▪ I approach my work with humility and supplication, begging for that without which nothing budges, nothing moves: voice. You might have a swell tale that might bring in and hold folks of some intelligence around a campfire for thirty minutes or upwards of two hours, but you will have only junk if you don't find the voice — inevitable, urgent, necessary, without false pride or hectoring. So I listen and when lucky I hear the first words in my mind, as I did for the boy/man of "Nicodemus Bluff." Of all qualities, voice is the most unteachable and the closest to magic, and it may be akin to a sort of natural music in the head that is God-given and has nothing much to do with common intelligence. I know dolts who can tell fine stories and Harvard snobs who piss away a good thing within three phrases of beginning one, for instance. I heard the boy/man who's been stoned, essentially, for thirty years and I knew I wanted to say something about a kind of man lately more evident in the South, the womanish man — a result perhaps of weak or absentee fathers. I have also observed athletes endure psychosis in the heat of competition. Witness the ravings of John McEnroe, for instance. Bobby Fischer, in chess itself. The advantage of living in a small but cosmopolitan town like Oxford, Mississippi, is that simply walking the streets and hanging out, you see and hear clearly a cast of rich personalities, as if God had animated some passionate mural for you. I have never had any interest in form, structure, or technique. There's no sense in wearing an Armani suit if you're only a monkey. I do see my audience as good intelligent folks yearning for the truth and music of new precincts. It is the duty of writers, I think, not to jabber on about conventional wisdoms that make for warm "bonding" between author and reader. Personally, around the campfire, I was always looking to be scared, outraged, and bothered, so that I would not sleep well for weeks.

THOM JONES's story collection, *The Pugilist at Rest,* was a finalist for the 1993 National Book Award. He is currently at work on a novel and a second short story collection.

▪ "Cold Snap" was written after a phone conversation with a very good friend who ordinarily calls me to complain about how hot it is. "Are you hot? Isn't it hot? I can't *take* this hot; I'm moving to Greenland! It's just hot beyond belief! Why is the weatherman always so cheerful when it's 80? Don't you just want to go into the TV and strangle him? Doesn't he realize that you just got back from the supermarket and your car has been parked on hot asphalt and is like 250 degrees inside? Doesn't he realize that I have to work like a slave in a hot building all day? Why can't it get cloudy and rain for a change? I just wish it would rain forever. I don't want to ever go outside again!"

The only time my friend ever called me to complain about the cold was the day I wrote this story. I had a bandage on my thumb after laying it open on the lid of a tin can and he had just cut his own thumb with an antifreeze tester. So we both had sliced-thumb tales, and as soon as we finished our conversation I sat down and wrote the story.

"Cold Snap" was the fourth short story I had published in *The New Yorker* in about two years, and the rapport I shared with Deborah Garrison, my editor there, was very good. We did the usual back and forth, but the whole process was a delight, everything went quickly, and there were no snags until we had to settle on a title. I love titles and went through the story line-by-line several times, looking for something to pull out. I couldn't come up with a thing. Finally, at the eleventh hour, D.G. said, "What about 'Cold Snap'?" I told her that was wonderful and that she deserved at least half of the money.

JOHN KEEBLE was born in Winnipeg, Canada, and raised in Saskatchewan and California. He and his family have lived in eastern Washington for twenty years, where they operate a farm. He is the author of five books: the novels *Crab Canon* (Grossman, 1971), *Mine* (with Ransom Jeffery; Grossman, 1974), *Yellowfish* (Harper and Row, 1980), and *Broken Ground* (Harper and Row, 1987), and a work of nonfiction, *Out of the Channel: The Exxon Valdez Oil Spill in Prince William Sound* (HarperCollins, 1991).

Keeble was the writer and literary consultant for a prize-winning documentary on the life and work of Raymond Carver, *To Write and Keep Kind*, aired on PBS in 1993. He has published essays on petroleum, ecology, community, and literature in various periodicals and is completing a short story collection and a novel, researching a book of nonfiction on culture and the petroleum trade of North America and the North Pacific, and developing a film project related to the *Exxon Valdez* oil spill.

▪ "The Chasm" was a long time in the making, as sometimes happens. Indeed, several other stories, articles, and a book were written between its drafts. Consequently, it's hard to remember exactly what all went into its writing. I know that it is among the more personal pieces I have written, although the incidents it recounts are less true as autobiographical facts than they are as imaginative approaches intended to lever open the meaning of family: the travails of a family, its occasional ruin and its pleasure, but most important the corrective effect a mutually held love can have upon individual confusion. The confusion in this case is expressed through the character Jim.

I also know that the accident that befalls another character in the story, Lem Holister, is told approximately as it happened to one of our neighbors. The neighbor was not a person we knew well, but rather someone we had hoped to know. The desire to have known someone who then became irretrievable, the deep melancholy this caused, and the astringent effect of being reminded of the chanciness of existence provided a path into the material of the story. The story is about a relationship between husband and wife and their efforts to carve out a home common to themselves and their children. It's also, incidentally, a story about a great, divisive war. A persistent irony of life, I think, is that loss often clarifies how to live the difficulty that remains before us, just as our true, lost neighbor clarified for me how the story could be told. He became the bones over which the flesh of all the remaining characters could be stretched.

NANCY KRUSOE lives in Santa Monica, California, and is a graduate student in the creative writing program at California State University, Northridge (CSUN). She was born and raised in Georgia. Her work has appeared in *Magazine, The Santa Monica Review, American Writing,* and *The Georgia Review.* She is currently working on a collaborative novel about Death Valley and the 1994 Northridge earthquake.

▪ I wrote this story while I was a student in Katharine Haake's Theory of Fiction class at CSUN. The exercise she designed is called the "burrowing exercise." The idea is to take a word or sentence and burrow into it — to supplement it — following wherever it takes you until it stops or you lose the desire to continue. Then add another piece of language and repeat the process. I began with "A barn is a beautiful place . . ." and worked from one word to the next, each set of words calling for another set, and I discovered that words in stories, like poems, could touch in pleasurable ways that would bring up new material, a new situation, and more words. This process became compelling and exciting, each word charged by its own necessity and surplus, and the distance was reduced between me and the sound of the sentence. At the same time, we were reading French feminist theory, specifically Julia Kristeva's notion of the *chora,* the semiotic rhythms of language primarily associated with women's writing, writing in which you work more closely with sound than narrative, although Kate Haake says this story is loaded with narrative and I guess it is.

LAURA GLEN LOUIS received a *Nimrod*/Hardman Katherine Anne Porter Prize for her story "Verge." She is currently working on a story collection.

▪ "Fur" was inspired by encounters my father had with a young woman of questionable ambition. From a jogging friend of his came Fei Lo's name and girth, his subsequent wealth, and finally the slowness with which he moved. Except for his generosity, the character in no manner resembled my father — a compact, spry man of modest fortune whose passion was not food but the grafting of trees. The young woman I never met, and what I had learned about her did not make for a sympathetic character.

Insight into Fur's character came, then, from a young girl I met at a reunion several years earlier, the niece of an old childhood friend and younger cousin to the friend's two vivacious and graceful daughters. The niece had not quite blossomed. Hers was the colorless face, the slightly turned-in toes, the overly loud voice. She seemed to always enter a room as someone else was departing. She refused to join us for the reunion photo, and only appeared after the camera was put away. And for good reason: her assault on her cousins' and aunt's closets was comprehensive. Bold lipstick had been applied in crooked, confrontive strokes; anything of value was on her skinny frame — halter tops, harem pants, and hand-made earrings. On her feet were her aunt's twice-worn velveteen shoes. The family lived in a rural area where the road had to be periodically redefined by Caterpillars. The shoes were near ruin. No one said a word. There was the usual flurry of hugs and kisses when it came time for me to leave. The niece hung back behind her father's pant legs. I don't think I had said more than two words to her the entire visit. I managed a wave. Her father tried to gentle her forward but she maintained her reluctance. I confess that I felt more than relieved to have been able to get into my car without having to touch her. Yet even as I turned away I felt compelled to look back, and knew in that instant which one of us needed to be generous. I crossed the distance, bent down on one knee, and she came into my fold. She let me hold her for what felt like minutes. Because she did not let go, I understood that my offer was incomplete. As I find it difficult to say anything I don't believe, I was very surprised to hear myself tell her that she was going to be all right. Because, how could I know? (She turned out great.) She may not remember this day as vividly as I, if at all, but hers were the eyes I saw when trying to reimagine Fur.

CHRIS OFFUTT grew up in the Appalachian Mountains of eastern Kentucky and now lives in the Rocky Mountains of western Montana. He is the author of the story collection *Kentucky Straight* and a memoir, *The Same River Twice*. He is a recent recipient of an NEA fellowship. The American Academy of Arts and Letters has honored his fiction with the Jean Stein Award.

▪ During the early stages of this story, I learned that my best friend from childhood had committed suicide in Kentucky. For the next week I worked on the story several hours a day, changing it drastically at each sitting. It became so tied to my friend's death that I had to set it aside. I did not write another short story for two years. Eventually I revised it eighteen times. Eleven magazines rejected the story before it got into print.

Where I'm from, it is not uncommon for people to avenge themselves or their family. This transforms the function of the lawmen as well as the jail itself. People will sometimes arrange to be locked up for their own protection, or a lawman may incarcerate people to prevent them from seeking vengeance. Spending time in jail doesn't have the same stigma that it does elsewhere.

I must stress that Melungeon people are no more or less violent than anyone, including me.

ROXANA BARRY ROBINSON lives in New York. She is the author of the novel *Summer Light,* the biography *Georgia O'Keeffe: A Life,* and the collection of short stories *A Glimpse of Scarlet.* Her fiction has appeared in *The Atlantic Monthly, The New Yorker, The Southern Review, Glimmer Train,* and other magazines. She is the recipient of a creative writing fellowship from the National Endowment for the Arts.

▪ When I was young my mother and her friends became involved in some UN scheme in which diplomats would come out to the country on weekends. These events took up enormous amounts of energy, and we all became very solemn and mannerly, and tried very hard to make the diplomats feel happy and at home. Years later, a friend of my mother's looked at me and shook her head, amused, amazed. She asked, "Why did we do it? Why did we do it? No one liked it." It was the first time it had occurred to me that the weekends had been funny, that they had been nightmares for everyone, they had been travesties of hospitality. It was liberating to think of them in that way.

JIM SHEPARD is the author of four novels: *Flights, Paper Doll, Lights Out in the Reptile House,* and *Kiss of the Wolf.* His stories have appeared in various magazines, including *The New Yorker, Harper's Magazine, The Atlantic Monthly, Esquire, TriQuarterly,* and *The Paris Review.* He teaches at Williams College.

▪ "Batting Against Castro" began the way most of my writing begins, with me staring into space, my mouth slightly ajar. It owes a pretty big debt to a piece by the old Pittsburgh Pirate star Don Hoak (with Myron Cope) about facing Castro in the Cuban Leagues. It was there I learned that Castro actually came out onto the field and inserted himself as a relief pitcher to face Hoak in the winter of 1950–51. It was also there that I found various details for my story: the names of the contending clubs, the yellowtails and eels on the coral reefs, the fact that Batista himself witnessed the demonstrations at the games, and finally Castro's dress shirt and slacks. The image, the premise of Castro on the mound, seemed both irresistibly silly and filled with implication. The narrator's invincibly ignorant and vaguely hapless voice probably started to come together halfway through that long third sentence, somewhere around ". . . and about nine of us in a row had just been tied in knots by Maglie and it looked like we weren't going to get anyone on base in the next five weeks except for those hit by pitches." After that, it was a matter of getting out of the way.

It occurs to me that I'm always writing about people who don't want to face things — about how passivity shades over into individual responsibility so that small inadequacies become large inadequacies, in terms of ethical consequences, especially during those times when, as they say in eastern Europe, history is let off the leash. Looking back over "Batting Against Castro" is by no means a string of uninterrupted pleasures for me now. But I'm happiest with the story when the thematic preoccupation described above yields what are, for me, its most resonant images: the baby cradled in the overturned fender, that young fan's face as a flash of spite, poor scared Castro blocking the plate.

CHRISTOPHER TILGHMAN is the author of *In a Father's Place,* a collection of stories, and *Ah, Sinful Nation,* a novel scheduled to appear in late 1995. He lives in Massachusetts with his wife and three sons.

▪ This story came out of the hardest couple of days in my life, when our oldest son — two years old at the time — was all but diagnosed with cystic fibrosis. When we got the news that it was a mistake, that the test was negative, that he and we were spared, my wife and I both burst into tears. But even in our outpouring of relief, I thought of the parents who would be sitting in this same room in a few minutes or hours, crying because the test was positive. I have rejoiced for them, in the past few years, reading of the progress in treating this disease.

Once having stared into the awful well of a child's grave illness, one can never be the same. I guess I wrote "Things Left Undone" to investigate that change and to cement my bond of empathy with all parents of sick children. The story was there to be written but I avoided it for several years, out of superstition and fear and the reluctance to traffic in other people's anguish. Finally it began to feel like a roadblock; I felt as if I couldn't go forward in my career until I had faced this material head-on. In part, the title, which some may recognize as the language of confession in *The Book of Common Prayer,* has a private meaning, referring to the story that had been left unwritten for those years.

JONATHAN WILSON was born in London in 1950 and educated at the University of Essex, Oxford, and the Hebrew University of Jerusalem. His recently completed first novel will be published next year by Viking, along with *Schoom,* a book of short stories. His articles and essays appear frequently in *The New Yorker* and the *Forward.* He is an associate professor in the English Department at Tufts University.

▪ Five years ago in June I went back to England to attend the funeral of my uncle Harold Shrier. Although we had spent most of our lives in different parts of the globe, and he was thirty years my senior, I always felt an affinity with Harold, who read widely and liked to argue and philosophize. Whenever we met, our conversations were spicy and pleasingly contentious.

Uncle Harold was a veteran of the terrible battles at Monte Cassino, and his experiences during the Second World War changed his life. No matter how successful he later became in the business world, he remained bitter on the subject of the war. He reserved a special anger for those among his peers who had profited by avoiding service and staying in England while he was in Italy under the German guns.

I think that for some time I had been mulling a way to tell his story in a story. There were all kinds of elements from his life that I wanted to borrow — including his musical laugh — in order to explore the anguish and confusions of a Jewish soldier in the British army.

In the ruthless way that writers have, I think I was already gathering material at the funeral, talking to relatives whom I hadn't seen for years and, surreptitiously, plugging them for information.

I began a conversation with another of my uncles, my mother's brother-in-law, Hans Klein. The far past and the recent and not so recent dead were our topics. We found ourselves reminiscing about the Saturday afternoon teas that took place in his northwest London flat in the late 1950s, when he and my father and *his* father, Richard Klein, sat, ate cheesecake, and analyzed the world. My uncle said, "I have never had such good conversations again."

My mind swirled with a great rush of memory. I used to sit under the table during the great discussions, tying together the shoelaces of the speakers, or simply listening to the amiable, high-flown talk that passed, with symbolic perfection, right over my head.

"From Shanghai," to my surprise, is a story about listening in on my uncle Hans's and not my uncle Harold's life: a reminder that the stories we set out to write are rarely those we end up telling. It contains so many autobiographical elements that to recognize them is an embarrassing confrontation with the poverty of my imagination. Perhaps all I should say is that my great-uncle Richard did indeed own one of the world's largest collections of Hans Andersen books, and that happily, his son, my uncle Hans (named after the great Danish writer), while hounded out of Vienna, did not perish in the Holocaust.

A note on "*lamed vav.*" In "From Shanghai" the narrator's father, Leslie Visser, signs his paintings with the Hebrew letters *lamed vav,* equivalents of *LV* or *LW,* a flourish I borrowed from the practice of my own father, Lewis Wilson. In Hebrew, *lamed vav* can also represent the number thirty-six. This particular number also functions as a descriptive noun: a person can be a *Lamed Vav.* In every generation, according to Jewish tradition, thirty-six Just Men (the *Lamed Vav*) are born to take the world's suffering upon themselves. These men are indistinguishable from simple mortals and, often, fail to recognize themselves for what they are. While my father was undoubtedly familiar with the source of the tradition, its legends, and

André Schwarz-Bart's contemporary reworking of the theme in his great novel *The Last of the Just*, I do not think that he was trying to nominate himself as a *Lamed Vav* when he signed his Hebrew initials: it would have been totally out of character for him to have done so. I, however, did want to make the connection, both for the character Leslie Visser, who, like the other English Jews in the story, has to confront the "world's suffering" when it is brought to his doorstep, and for the person on whom the character is based, Lewis Wilson, who, beyond the soft contours of my idealization, made blurrier still by the passage of thirty years, has a historic presence among those who knew him as very much the kind of person the Talmudists had in mind when they limned the character of the *Lamed Vav.*

100 Other Distinguished Stories of 1993

SELECTED BY KATRINA KENISON

Editorial Addresses of American and Canadian Magazines Publishing Short Stories

When available, the annual subscription rate, the average number of stories published per year, and the name of the editor follow the address.

African American Review
Stalkes Hall 212
Indiana State University
Terre Haute, IN 47809
$20, 25, Joe Weixlmann

Agni Review
Creative Writing Department
Boston University
236 Bay State Road
Boston, MA 02115
$12, 13, Askold Melnyczuk

Alabama Literary Review
Smith 253
Troy State University
Troy, AL 36082
$10, 21, Theron E. Montgomery

Alaska Quarterly Review
Department of English
University of Alaska
3221 Providence Drive
Anchorage, AK 99508
$8, 28, Ronald Spatz

Alfred Hitchcock's Mystery Magazine
1540 Broadway
New York, NY 10036
$34.97, 130, Cathleen Jordan

Amelia
329 East Street
Bakersfield, CA 93304
$25, 12, Frederick A. Raborg, Jr.

American Literary Review
University of North Texas
P.O. Box 13615
Denton, TX 76203
$10, 14, Scott Cairns, Barbara Rodman

American Short Fiction
Parlin 108
Department of English
University of Texas at Austin
Austin, TX 78712-1164
$24, 32, Joseph Krupa

American Voice
332 West Broadway
Louisville, KY 40202
$15, 20, Sallie Bingham, Frederick Smock

American Way
P.O. Box 619640
DFW Airport
Texas 75261-9640
$72, 50, Jeff Posey

Analog Science Fiction/Science Fact
380 Lexington Avenue
New York, NY 10017
$34.95, 70, Stanley Schmidt

Another Chicago Magazine
Left Field Press
3709 North Kenmore
Chicago, IL 60613
$8, 16, Sharon Solwitz

Antaeus
100 West Broad Street
Hopewell, NJ 08525
$30, 12, Daniel Halpern

Antietam Review
82 West Washington Street
Hagerstown, MD 21740
$5, 8, Suzanne Kass

Antioch Review
P.O. Box 148
Yellow Springs, OH 45387
$25, 11, Robert S. Fogarty

Appalachian Heritage
Besea College
Besea, KY 40404
$18, 6, Sidney Saylor Farr

Ascent
P.O. Box 967
Urbana, IL 61801
$6, 8, group editorship

Asimov's Science Fiction Magazine
Davis Publications, Inc.
380 Lexington Avenue
New York, NY 10017
$25, 27, Gardner Dozois

Atlantic Monthly
745 Boylston Street
Boston, MA 02116
$15.94, 12, C. Michael Curtis

Baffles
P.O. Box 378293
Chicago, IL 60637
$16, Thomas Frank, Keith White

Belles Lettres
11151 Captain's Walk Court
North Potomac, MD 20878
$20, 2, Janet Mullaney

Bellowing Ark
P.O. Box 45637
Seattle, WA 98145
$15, 7, Robert R. Ward

Beloit Fiction Journal
P.O. Box 11, Beloit College
Beloit, WI 53511
$9, 14, Clint McCown

Black Warrior Review
P.O. Box 2936
Tuscaloosa, AL 35487-2936
$11, 13, Leigh Ann Sackrider

Blood & Aphorisms
Suite 711
456 College Street
Toronto, Ontario
MGG 4A3 Canada
$18, 20, Hilary Clark

BOMB
New Art Publications
594 Broadway, 10th floor
New York, NY 10012
$18, 6, Betsy Sussler

Border Crossings
Y300-393 Portage Avenue

Winnipeg, Manitoba
R3B 3H6 Canada
$18, 12, Meeka Walsh

Boston Review
33 Harrison Avenue
Boston, MA 02111
$15, 6, editorial board

Boulevard
P.O. Box 30386
Philadelphia, PA 19103
$12, 17, Richard Burgin

Briar Cliff Review
3303 Rebecca Street
P.O. Box 2100
Sioux City, IA 51104-2100
$4, 4, Tricia Currans-Sheehan

Bridge
14050 Vernon Street
Oak Park, Ml 48237
$8, 10, Helen Zucker

Buffalo Spree
4511 Harlem Road, P.O. Box 38
Buffalo, NY 14226
$8, 16, Johanna Hall Van De Mark

BUZZ
11835 West Olympic Blvd.
Suite 450
Los Angeles, CA 90064
$14.95, 12, Renee Vogel

Callaloo
Johns Hopkins University Press
701 West 40th Street, Suite 275
Baltimore, MD 21211
$25, 6, Charles H. Rowell

Calyx
P.O. Box B
Corvallis, OR 97339
$18, 11, Margarita Donnelly

Canadian Fiction
Box 946, Station F
Toronto, Ontario

M4Y 2N9 Canada
$32.10, 23, Geoffrey Hancock

Capilano Review
Capilano College
2055 Purcell Way
North Vancouver,
British Columbia
V7J 3H5 Canada
$25, 12, Robert Sherrin

Carolina Quarterly
Greenlaw Hall 066A
University of North Carolina
Chapel Hill, NC 27514
*$10, 13, Bettina Entzminger, Brenda
  Thissen*

Catalyst
236 Forsyth Street
Suite 400
Atlanta, GA 30303
$10, Pearl Cleage

Changing Men
306 North Brooks Street
Madison, WI 53715
$24, 2, Jeff Kirsch

Chariton Review
Division of Language & Literature
Northeast Missouri State University
Kirksville, MO 63501
$9, 6, Jim Barnes

Chattahoochee Review
DeKalb Community College
2101 Womack Road
Dunwoody, GA 30338-4497
$15, 21, Lamar York

Chelsea
P.O. Box 773
Cooper Station
New York, NY 10276
$11, 6

Chicago Review
5801 South Kenwood
University of Chicago

Chicago, IL 60637
$15, 20, *Andy Winston*

Christopher Street
P.O. Box 1475
Church Street Station
New York, NY 10008
$27, 50, *Tom Steele*

Cimarron Review
205 Morrill Hall
Oklahoma State University
Stillwater, OK 74078-0135
$12, 15, *Gordon Weaver*

Clockwatch Review
Department of English
Illinois Wesleyan University
Bloomington, IL 61702
$8, 6, *James Plath*

Colorado Review
Department of English
Colorado State University
Fort Collins, CO 80523
$15, 8, *David Milofsky*

Commentary
165 East 56th Street
New York, NY 10022
$39, 5, *Norman Podhoretz*

Concho River Review
English Department
Angelo State University
San Angelo, TX 76909
$12, 7, *Terence A. Dalrymple*

Confrontation
English Department
C. W. Post College of Long Island
   University
Greenvale, NY 11548
$8, 25, *Martin Tucker*

Crab Creek Review
4462 Whitman Avenue North
Seattle, WA 98103
$8, 3, *Linda Clifton*

Crazyhorse
Department of English
University of Arkansas
Little Rock, AR 72204
$10, 13, *Judy Troy*

Cream City Review
University of Wisconsin, Milwaukee
P.O. Box 413
Milwaukee, WI 53201
$10, 30, *Cathleen Lester, Patricia*
   Montalbano

Crescent Review
P.O. Box 15065
Winston-Salem, NC 27113
$10, 23, *Guy Nancekeville*

Critic
205 West Monroe Street, 6th floor
Chicago, IL 60606-5097
$17, 4, *John Sprague*

Crucible
Barton College
College Station
Wilson, NC 27893
Terence L. Grimes

Cut Bank
Department of English
University of Montana
Missoula, MT 59812
$12, 20, *David Belman*

Daughters of Nyx
Rose's Fairy Tale Emporium
P.O. Box 1187
White Salmon, WA 98672
Kim Antieu

Denver Quarterly
University of Denver
Denver, CO 80208
$15, 5, *Donald Revell*

Descant
P.O. Box 314, Station P
Toronto, Ontario
M5S 2S8 Canada
$28.47, 20, *Karen Mulhallen*

Descant
Department of English
Texas Christian University
Box 32872
Fort Worth, TX 76129
*$12, 16, Stanley Trachtenberg, Betsy
  Colquitt, Harry Opperman*

Eagle's Flight
P.O. Box 832
Granite, OK 73547
$5, 10, Rekha Kulkarni

Elle
1633 Broadway
New York, NY 10019
$24, 2, John Howell

Epoch
251 Goldwin Smith Hall
Cornell University
Ithaca, NY 14853-3201
$11, 23, Michael Koch

Esquire
250 West 55th Street
New York, NY 10019
$17.94, 12, Rust Hills

Essence
1500 Broadway
New York, NY 10036
$12.96, 6, Stephanie Stokes Oliver

event
c/o Douglas College
P.O. Box 2503
New Westminster, British Columbia
V3L 5B2 Canada
$15, 18, Maurice Hodgson

Fantasy & Science Fiction
143 Cream Hill Road
West Cornwall, CT 06796
$21, 75, Edward L. Ferman

Farmer's Market
P.O. Box 1272
Galesburg, IL 61402
$8, 18, Jean C. Lee

(feed.)
P.O. Box 1567
Madison Square Station
New York, NY 10159
$16, 8, P. J. Mark

Fiction
Fiction, Inc.
Department of English
The City College of New York
New York, NY
$7, 15, Mark Mirsky

Fiction International
Department of English and
   Comparative Literature
San Diego State University
San Diego, CA 92182
$14, Harold Jaffe, Larry McCaffery

Fiddlehead
UNB Box 4400
University of New Brunswick
Fredericton, New Brunswick
E3B 5A3 Canada
$16, 20, Don McKay

Florida Review
Department of English
University of Central Florida
P.O. Box 25000
Orlando, FL 32816
$7, 14, Russell Kesler

Folio
Department of Literature
The American University
Washington, D.C. 20016
$10, 12, Elisabeth Poliner

Four Quarters
LaSalle University
20th and Olney Avenues
Philadelphia, PA 19141
$8, 10, John J. Keenan

Free Press
P.O. Box 581
Bronx, NY 10463
$25, 10, Rafael Martinez Alequin

Geist
1062 Homer Street #100
Vancouver, Canada
V6B 2W9
$20, 5, Stephen Osborne

Georgetown Review
G & R Publishing
P.O. Box 227
400 East College Street
Georgetown, KY 40324
$10, 12, Amy M. Luscher

Georgia Review
University of Georgia
Athens, GA 30602
$18, 10, Stanley W. Lindberg

Gettysburg Review
Gettysburg College
Gettysburg, PA 17325
$18, 22, Peter Stitt

Glamour
350 Madison Avenue
New York, NY 10017
$20.50, 3, Laura Mathews

Glimmer Train Stories
812 SW Washington Street
Suite 1205
Portland, OR 97205
*$29, 40, Susan Burmeister, Linda
  Davies*

Good Housekeeping
959 Eighth Avenue
New York, NY 10019
$17.97, 7, Arleen L. Quarfoot

GQ
350 Madison Avenue
New York, NY 10017
$19.97, 12, Thomas Mallon

Grain
Box 1154
Regina, Saskatchewan
S4P 3B4 Canada
$15, 21, Geoffrey Ursell

Grand Street
131 Varick Street
New York, NY 10013
$30, 20, Jean Stein

Granta
250 West 57th Street, Suite 1316
New York, NY 10107
$29.95, Anne Kinard

Gray's Sporting Journal
205 Willow Street
South Hamilton, MA 01982
$34.95, 4, Edward E. Gray

Great River Review
211 West 7th
Winona, MN 55987
$10, 6, Ruth Forsythe et al.

Green Mountain Review
Box A 58
Johnson State College
Johnson, VT 05656
$12, 23, Tony Whedon

Greensboro Review
Department of English
University of North Carolina
Greensboro, NC 27412
$8, 16, Jim Clark

Gulf Coast
Department of English
University of Houston
4800 Calhoun Road
Houston, TX 77204-3012
$22, 10, Susan Davis, Amy Storrow

Gulf Stream
English Department
Florida International University
North Miami Campus
North Miami, FL 33181
$4, 6, Lynne Barrett

Habersham Review
Piedmont College
Demorest, GA 30535-0010
*$12, David L. Greene, Lisa Hodgens
  Lumkin*

Hadassah
50 West 58th Street
New York, NY 10019
$4, 2, Zelda Shluker

Harper's Magazine
666 Broadway
New York, NY 10012
$18, 9, Lewis H. Lapham

Hawaii Review
University of Hawaii
Department of English
1733 Donaghho Road
Honolulu, HI 96822
*$15, 40, Carrie Hoshino, Michael
   McGinnis*

Hayden's Ferry Review
Matthews Center
Arizona State University
Tempe, AZ 85287-1502
*$10, 10, Theresa Delgadillo, Nick
   Norwood*

High Plains Literary Review
180 Adams Street, Suite 250
Denver, CO 80206
$20, 7, Robert O. Greer, Jr.

Hudson Review
684 Park Avenue
New York, NY 10021
$24, 8, Paula Deitz, Frederick Morgan

Hyphen
3458 W. Devon Ave., No. 6
Lincolnwood, IL 60659
$12, 8, Margaret Lewis, Dave Mead

Idler
255 Davenport Road
Toronto, Ontario
M5R 1J9 Canada
$28.50, 3, David Warren

Indiana Review
316 North Jordan Avenue
Bloomington, IN 47405
$12, 13, rotating editorship

Innisfree
P.O. Box 277
Manhattan Beach, CA 90266
$20, 100, Rex Winn

Interim
Department of English
University of Nevada
4505 Maryland Parkway
Las Vegas, NV 89154
$8, A. Wilber Stevens

Iowa Review
Department of English
University of Iowa
308 EPB
Iowa City, IA 52242
$18, 20, David Hamilton

Iowa Woman
P.O. Box 680
Iowa City, IA 52244
$18, 15, Marianne Abel

Italian Americana
University of Rhode Island
College of Continuing Education
199 Promenade Street
Providence, RI 02908
$15, 6, Carol Bono/Mo Albright

Jewish Currents
22 East 17th Street, Suite 601
New York, NY 10003-3272
$20, 8, editorial board

Journal
Department of English
Ohio State University
164 West 17th Avenue
Columbus, OH 43210
$8, 5, Kathy Fagan, Michelle Herman

Kalliope
Florida Community College
3939 Roosevelt Blvd.
Jacksonville, FL 32205
$10.50, 12, Mary Sue Koeppel

Karamu
English Department

Eastern Illinois University
Charleston, IL 61920
$6.50, 8, Peggy L. Brayfield

Kenyon Review
Kenyon College
Gambier, OH 43022
$22, 18, Marilyn Hacker

Kinesis
P.O. Box 4007
Whitefish, MT 59937-4007
$18, 6, David Hipschman

Kiosk
English Department
306 Clemens Hall
SUNY
Buffalo, NY 14260
9, Robert Rebein

Laurel Review
Department of English
Northwest Missouri State University
Maryville, MO 64468
$8, 20, Craig Goad, David Slater,
   William Trowbridge

Left Bank
Blue Heron Publishing, Inc.
24450 N.W. Hansen Road
Hillsboro, OR 97124
$14, 6, Linny Stoval

Lilith
The Jewish Women's Magazine
250 West 57th Street
New York, NY 10107
$16, 5, Susan Weidman

Literary Review
Fairleigh Dickinson University
285 Madison Avenue
Madison, NJ 07940
$18, 10, Walter Cummins

The Little Magazine
English Department
SUNY
Albany, NY 12222
$7, 25, David Bookbinder, Claudie Ricci

Lost Creek Letters
Box 373A
Rushville, MO 64484
$15, 10, Pamela Montgomery

Louisiana Literature
Box 792
Southeastern Louisiana University
Hammond, LA 70402
$10, 8, David Hanson

Louisville Review
Bingham Humanities 315
University of Louisville
Louisville, KY 40292
$10, 8, Sena Jeter Naslund

McCall's
110 Fifth Avenue
New York, NY 10011
$15.94, 6, Laura Manske

Mademoiselle
350 Madison Avenue
New York, NY 10017
$28, 10, Ellen Welty

Madison Review
University of Wisconsin
Department of English
H. C. White Hall
600 North Park Street
Madison, WI 53706
$14, 8, Andrew Hipp, Richard Gilman

Magic Realism
Pyx Press
P.O. Box 620
Orem, UT 84059
$12, 30, Julie Thomas, C. Darren

Malahat Review
University of Victoria
P.O. Box 1700
Victoria, British Columbia
V8W 2Y2 Canada
$15, 20, Derk Wynand

Manoa
English Department
University of Hawaii

Honolulu, HI 96822
$18, 12, Robert Shapard, Frank Stewart

Massachusetts Review
Memorial Hall
University of Massachusetts
Amherst, MA 01003
$15, 6, Mary Heath, Jules Chametzky, Paul Jenkins

Matrix
c.p. 100 Ste.-Anne-de-Bellevue
Quebec
H9X 3L4 Canada
$15, 8, Linda Leith, Kenneth Radu

Metropolitan
6307 North 31st Street
Arlington, VA 22207
$7, 13, Jacqueline Bergsohn

Michigan Quarterly Review
3032 Rackham Building
University of Michigan
Ann Arbor, MI 48109
$18, 10, Laurence Goldstein

Mid-American Review
106 Hanna Hall
Department of English
Bowling Green State University
Bowling Green, OH 43403
$12, 11, Ellen Behrens

Minnesota Review
Department of English
State University of New York
Stony Brook, NY 11794-5350
$10, 10, Fred Pfeil

Mirabella
200 Madison Avenue
New York, NY 10016
$17.98, 6, Kathy Medwick

Mississippi Review
University of Southern Mississippi
Southern Station, P.O. Box 5144
Hattiesburg, MS 39406-5144
$15, 25, Frederick Barthelme

Missouri Review
1507 Hillcrest Hall
University of Missouri
Columbia, MO 65211
$15, 23, Speer Morgan

Mother Jones
1663 Mission Street
2nd floor
San Francisco, CA 94103
$18, 3, Jeffrey Klein

Ms.
230 Park Avenue
New York, NY 10169
$45, 7, Marcia Ann Gillespie

Nassau Review
English Department
Nassau Community College
One Education Drive
Garden City, NY 11530-6793
Paul A. Doyle

Nebraska Review
Writers' Workshop
ASH 212
University of Nebraska
Omaha, NE 68182-0324
$10, 10, Art Homer, Richard Duggin

Negative Capability
62 Ridgelawn Drive East
Mobile, AL 36605
$12, 15, Sue Walker

New Delta Review
Creative Writing Program
English Department
Louisiana State University
Baton Rouge, LA 70803
$7, 9, Joshua Russell

New England Review
Middlebury College
Middlebury, VT 05753
$18, 16, T. R. Hummer

New Letters
University of Missouri
4216 Rockhill Road

Kansas City, MO 64110
$17, 21, James McKinley

New Orleans Review
P.O. Box 195
Loyola University
New Orleans, LA 70118
$25, 4, John Biguenet, John Mosier

New Quarterly
English Language Proficiency
 Programme
University of Waterloo
Waterloo, Ontario
N2L 3G1 Canada
*$14, 26, Peter Hinchcliffe, Kim Jernigan,
 Mary Merikle*

New Renaissance
9 Heath Road
Arlington, MA 02174
$11.50, 5, Louise T. Reynolds

New Yorker
25 West 43rd Street
New York, NY 10036
$32, 50, Tina Brown

Nimrod
Arts and Humanities Council of Tulsa
2210 South Main Street
Tulsa, OK 74114
$10, 10, Francine Ringold

North American Review
University of Northern Iowa
1222 West 27th Street
Cedar Falls, IA 50614
$18, 13, Robley Wilson, Jr.

North Atlantic Review
15 Arbutus Lane
Stony Brook, NY 11790-1408
$10, 9, John Gill

North Dakota Quarterly
University of North Dakota
P.O. Box 8237
Grand Forks, ND 58202
$15, 13, William Borden

North Stone Review
Box 14098, D Station
Minneapolis, MN 55414
$15, 4, James Naiden

Northwest Review
369 PLC
University of Oregon
Eugene, OR 97403
$14, 10, Hannah Wilson

Oasis
P.O. Box 626
Largo, FL 34649-0626
$22, 14, Neal Storrs

Obsidian II
Department of English
Box 8105
North Carolina State University
Raleigh, NC 27695-8105
$12, 8, Susie R. Powell

Ohio Review
Ellis Hall
Ohio University
Athens, OH 45701-2979
$16, 10, Wayne Dodd

Old Hickory Review
P.O. Box 1178
Jackson, TN 38301
$4, 6, Dorothy Starfill

Omni
1965 Broadway
New York, NY 10023-5965
$24, 20, Ellen Datlow

Ontario Review
9 Honey Brook Drive
Princeton, NJ 08540
$12, 8, Raymond J. Smith

Onthebus
Bombshelter Press
642½ Orange Street
Los Angeles, CA 90048
$28, 16, Jack Grapes

Open City
118 Riverside Drive, Suite 14A
New York, NY 10024
$20, 12, Thomas Beller, Daniel Pinchbeck

Other Voices
University of Illinois at Chicago
Department of English
(M/C 162) Box 4348
Chicago, IL 60680
$20, 30, Sharon Fiffer, Lois Hauselman

Oxalis
Stone Ridge Poetry Society
P.O. Box 3993
Kingston, NY 12401
$18, 12, Shirley Powell

Oxford American
115½ South Lamar
Oxford, MS 38655
$16, 12, Marc Smirnoff

Paris Review
541 East 72nd Street
New York, NY 10021
$24, 14, George Plimpton

Parting Gifts
3006 Stonecutter Terrace
Greensboro, NC 27405
Robert Bixby

Partisan Review
236 Bay State Road
Boston, MA 02215
$22, 4, William Phillips

Passages North
Kalamazoo College
1200 Academy Street
Kalamazoo, Ml 49007
$10, 8, Michael Barrett

Pikeville Review
Humanities Division
Pikeville College
Pikeville KY 41501
$4, 6, Jim Wayne Miller, James Alan Riley

Playboy
Playboy Building
919 North Michigan Avenue
Chicago, IL 60611
$24, 23, Alice K. Turner

Ploughshares
Emerson College
100 Beacon Street
Boston, MA 02116
$19, 15, Don Lee

Potpourri
P.O. Box 8278
Prairie Village, KS 66208
$12, 48, Polly W. Swafford

Prairie Fire
423-100 Arthur Street
Winnipeg, Manitoba
R3B 1H3 Canada
$24, 8, Andris Taskans

Prairie Schooner
201 Andrews Hall
University of Nebraska
Lincoln, NE 68588-0334
$20, 20, Hilda Raz

Primavera
P.O. Box 37-7547
Chicago, IL 60637
$9, 12, group

Prism International
Department of Creative Writing
University of British Columbia
Vancouver, British Columbia
V6T 1W5 Canada
$16, 20, Eden Robinson

Provincetown Arts
650 Commercial Street
Provincetown MA 02657
$9, 4, Christopher Busa

Puerto del Sol
P.O. Box 3E
Department of English
New Mexico State University

Las Cruces, NM 88003
$10, 12, Kevin McIlvoy, Antonya Nelson

Quarry Magazine
P.O. Box 1061
Kingston, Ontario
K7L 4Y5 Canada
$22, 20, Steven Heighton

Quarterly
650 Madison Avenue, Suite 2600
New York, NY 10022
*$30, 210, Gordon Lish, Jodi Davis,
Dana Spiotta*

Quarterly West
317 Olpin Union
University of Utah
Salt Lake City, UT 84112
$11, 10, Darin Cain, Jeffrey Vasseur

Rajah
411 Mason Hall
University of Michigan
Ann Arbor, MI 48109
Thomas Mussio

RE:AL
School of Liberal Arts
Stephen F. Austin State University
P.O. Box 13007, SFA Station
Nacogdoches, TX 75962
$8, 10, Lee Schultz

Redbook
959 Eighth Avenue
New York, NY 10017
$11.97, 10, Dawn Raffel

River Oak Review
River Oak Arts
P.O. Box 3127
Oak Park, IL 60303
$10, 4, Barbara Croft

River Styx
Big River Association
14 South Euclid
St. Louis, MO 63108
$20, 30, Lee Schreiner

Room of One's Own
P.O. Box 46160, Station G
Vancouver, British Columbia
V6R 4G5 Canada
$20, 12, collective editorship

Salmagundi
Skidmore College
Saratoga Springs, NY 12866
$15, 4, Robert Boyers

San Jose Studies
c/o English Department
San Jose State University
One Washington Square
San Jose, CA 95192
$12, 5, Fauneil J. Rinn

Santa Monica Review
Center for the Humanities
Santa Monica College
1900 Pico Boulevard
Santa Monica, CA 90405
$12, 16, Jim Krusoe

Saturday Night
184 Front Street E, Suite 400
Toronto, Ontario
M5V 2Z4 Canada
*$26.45, 7, Anne Collins, Dianna
Simmons*

Seattle Review
Padelford Hall, GN-30
University of Washington
Seattle, WA 98195
$8, 12, Charles Johnson

Seventeen
850 Third Avenue
New York, NY 10022
$13.95, 8, Sarah Patton Duncan

Sewanee Review
University of the South
Sewanee, TN 37375-4009
$16, 10, George Core

Shenandoah
Washington and Lee University
P.O. Box 722

Lexington, VA 24450
$11, 17, Dabney Stuart

Short Fiction by Women
Box 1276 Stuyvesant Station
New York, NY 10009
$18, 20, Rachel Whalen

Sinister Wisdom
P.O. Box 3252
Berkeley, CA 94703
$17, 15, Elana Dykewoman

Snake Nation Review
110 #2 West Force Street
Valdosta, GA 31602
$12, 16, Roberta George, Nancy Phillips

Soma
285 9th Street
San Francisco, CA 94103
$14.95, 6, Rebecca Paoletti

Sonora Review
Department of English
University of Arizona
Tucson, AZ 85721
$10, 12, John Payne

So to Speak
4400 University Drive
George Mason University
Fairfax, VA 22030-444
$7, 10, Colleen Kearney

South Carolina Review
Department of English
Clemson University
Clemson, SC 29634-1503
$7, 8, Richard C. Calhoun

South Dakota Review
University of South Dakota
P.O. Box 111 University Exchange
Vermillion, SD 57069
$15, 15, John R. Milton

Southern California Anthology
Master of Professional Writing
   Program WPH 404
University of Southern California

Los Angeles, CA 90089-4034
$7.95, 10, Richard P. Aloia, Jr.

Southern Exposure
P.O. Box 531
Durham, NC 27702
$24, 12, Eric Bates

Southern Humanities Review
9088 Haley Center
Auburn University
Auburn, AL 36849
$15, 5, Dan R. Latimer, Thomas L.
   Wright

Southern Review
43 Allen Hall
Louisiana State University
Baton Rouge, LA 70803
$18, 17, James Olney, Dave Smith

Southwest Review
Southern Methodist University
P.O. Box 4374
Dallas, TX 75275
$20, 15, Willard Spiegelman

Sou'wester
School of Humanities
Department of English
Southern Illinois University
Edwardsville, IL 62026-1438
$10, 10, Roger Ridenour

Stories
14 Beacon Street
Boston, MA 02108
$18, 12, Amy R. Kaufman

Story
1507 Dana Avenue
Cincinnati, OH 45207
$17, 52, Lois Rosenthal

Story Quarterly
P.O. Box 1416
Northbrook, IL 60065
$12, 20, Margaret Barrett, Anne
   Brashler, Diane Williams

Strange Plasma
Edgewood Press

P.O. Box 264
Cambridge, MA 02238
$10, Steve Pasechnick

Sun
107 North Roberson Street
Chapel Hill, NC 27516
$30, 30, Sy Safransky

Sycamore Review
Department of English
Heavilon Hall
Purdue University
West Lafayette, IN 47907
$9, 5, Michael Manley

Tampa Review
P.O. Box 13F
University of Tampa
401 West Kennedy Boulevard
Tampa, FL 33606-1490
$10, 2, Andy Solomon

Thema
Box 74109
Metairie, LA 70053-4109
$16, Virginia Howard

Threepenny Review
P.O. Box 9131
Berkeley, CA 94709
$12, 10, Wendy Lesser

Tikkun
5100 Leona Street
Oakland, CA 94619
$36, 10, Michael Lerner

Touchstone
Tennessee Humanities Council
P.O. Box 24767
Nashville, TN 37202
Robert Cheatham

Trafika
Columbia Post Office
Box 250413
New York, NY 10025-1536
*$35, 27, Michael Lee, Alfredo Sanchez,
  Jeffrey Young*

TriQuarterly
2020 Ridge Avenue
Northwestern University
Evanston, IL 60208
$20, 15, Reginald Gibbons

Turnstile
175 Fifth Avenue, Suite 2348
New York, NY 10010
$12, 24, group editorship

University of Windsor Review
Department of English
University of Windsor
Windsor, Ontario
N9B 3P4 Canada
$19.95, 12, Alistair MacLeod

Urbanus
P.O. Box 192561
San Francisco, CA 94119
$8, 4, Peter Drizhal

Venue
512-9 St. Nicholas Street
Toronto, Ontario
M4Y 1W5 Canada
$26, 4, Jane Francisco

Virginia Quarterly Review
One West Range
Charlottesville, VA 22903
$15, 14, Staige D. Blackford

Voice Literary Supplement
842 Broadway
New York, NY 10003
$17, 12, M. Mark

Wascana Review
English Department
University of Regina
Regina, Saskatchewan
S4S 0A2 Canada
$7, 8, J. Shami

Weber Studies
Weber State College
Ogden, UT 84408
$10, 2, Neila Seshachari

Webster Review
Webster University
470 East Lockwood
Webster Groves, MO 63119
$5, 2, Nancy Schapiro

Wellspring
770 Tonkawa Road
Long Lake, MN 55356
$8, 10, Maureen LaJoy

West Branch
Department of English
Bucknell University
Lewisburg, PA 17837
$7, 10, Robert Love Taylor, Karl Patten

Western Humanities Review
University of Utah
Salt Lake City, UT 84112
$20, 10, Barry Weller

Whetstone
Barrington Area Arts Council
P.O. Box 1266
Barrington, IL 60011
$6.25, 11, Sandra Berris

Whiskey Island
University Center
Cleveland State University
2121 Euclid Avenue
Cleveland, OH 44115
$6, 10, Kathy Smith

William and Mary Review
College of William and Mary
P.O. Box 8795
Williamsburg, VA 23187
$5, 4, Emily Chang, Allan Mitchell

Willow Springs
MS-1
Eastern Washington University
Cheney, WA 99004
$8, 8, Heather Keast

Wind
RFD Route 1
P.O. Box 809K
Pikeville, KY 41501
$7, 20, Quentin R. Howard

Witness
31000 Northwestern Highway,
   Suite 200
Farmington Hills, Ml 48018
$12, 24, Peter Stine

Worcester Review
6 Chatham Street
Worcester, MA 01690
$10, 8, Rodger Martin

Writ
Innis College
University of Toronto
2 Sussex Avenue
Toronto, Ontario
M5S 1J5 Canada
$15, 7, Roger Greenwald

Writers Forum
University of Colorado
P.O. Box 7150
Colorado Springs, CO 80933-7150
$8.95, 15, Alexander Blackburn

Xavier Review
Xavier University
Box 110C
New Orleans, LA 70125
6, Thomas Bonner, Jr.

Yale Review
1902A Yale Station
New Haven, CT 06520
$20, 12, J. D. McClatchy

Yankee
Yankee Publishing, Inc.
Dublin, NH 03444
$22, 4, Judson D. Hale, Sr.

Yellow Silk
P.O. Box 6374
Albany, CA 94706
$30, 10, Lily Pond

ZYZZYVA
41 Sutter Street, Suite 1400
San Francisco, CA 94104
$28, 12, Howard Junker